OR SO IT SEEMS

(Being Mr. Peterson's First-Ever Do-It-Yourself Workshop)

MY MOM SAYS YOU WON'T BUY THIS BOOK

"Who needs a book about a man who can't keep his pants on, for heaven sakes!"

"But Ma...!" I answered, "Paul Peterson is *fighting* to keep his pants on when the book starts. And the book isn't about that anyway."

"Oh yeah, Mr. Smarty, what's it about then?"

"It's about being on a spiritual journey, for one thing. And about putting your life back together after divorce separates you from your kids, your paycheck and a good part of your sanity. It's about trying to understand why life sometimes sends you cold fish when you ordered hot pizza. It's about reincarnation, schools of self development, soul mates and a fully-realized holy man with an exasperating sense of humor and an incurable case of the giggles."

"And while we're talking about it," Mom pursued, "why can't that *meshuggenah* Peterson stay in one place long enough to have a good meal or a decent night's sleep? He drives me nuts with all his jumping around from the past into the future and back again..."

"But that's how the story is told, Ma, through a Do-It-Yourself Workshop. He's not traveling in time, but traveling within himself—in the Sacred Present Moment, if you really want to know—only it seems like he's traveling in time."

"Hah!" she trumpeted. "And you think people are going to buy a book with all that silly crap in it?"

"I think a few of them will," I countered. "If only for the free movie passes I'm giving away."

(I lied. There are no free movie passes. You'll have to find another reason to buy this book.)

OR SO IT SEEMS

(Being Mr. Peterson's First-Ever Do-It-Yourself Workshop)

A novel by

Paul Steven Stone

Blind Elephant Press
Cambridge, Massachusetts

OR SO IT SEEMS

"Or So It Seems" may be ordered through selected booksellers,
Amazon.com, or OrSoItSeems.info
Paul Steven Stone can be contacted at:
OrSoItSeems.stone@gmail.com

Because of the dynamic nature of the internet, any web address or links contained in this book may have changed since publication and may no longer be valid.

This is a work of fiction. All of the characters, names, incidents, organizations, and dialogue in this novel are either products of the author's imagination or are used fictitiously.

ISBN: 978-1438207698

Printed in the United States of America

Jumbo thanks to the following for:
Blind Elephant Illustration: Gary Torrisi
Cover and Interior Design: Bill Dahlgren
Author and Mom Photo: Morris Trichon
(a/k/a Moish)

Dedicated with abiding love and gratitude to
Katie, Kristin, Jesse, Mom and Amy

And to the fond memory of Seth Mattson

So much we are given,
So much we have to lose.

Workshop Contents

Workshop Introduction

In Which We Present Our Credentials And Welcome New Visitors

This is my life's story in miniature, spread before your eyes like a schoolboy melodrama.

Paul Peterson is my name. Father of three, husband to none and advertising copywriter by trade. But more importantly at this precise moment, I am a witless victim who with surprising emotional distance observes himself being dragged across the long expanse of an upstairs apartment in a two-family home in Plymouth, Massachusetts.

You need to understand this drama is taking place in slow-motion—painfully slow, slow-motion—as if the universe has shifted into a lower set of gears without warning or asking for permission. So at the same time I am being pulled bodily across the room I find myself with surprising amounts of time to do whatever one is supposed to do in a crisis like this.

I can watch my life flash before my eyes, I suppose. Or curse my fate. Or create a list of all the whimsical things I meant to do with my life. Certainly I can choose from the usual items on the menu. But for now, as one who generally accepts the meager portions sent his way, I do nothing but look around.

Not much to see, is there? The room is poorly lit and barely kept up, the furniture old and mismatched like crude leftovers from an unloved college apartment. As dismal as the surroundings may appear, however, my protests remain quite spirited, as you can judge for yourself.

But I do not expect to fool you for long.

How transparent my protests will seem when you realize that all the while I am pleading for release I am also playing the role of mute accomplice. Sooner or later you will notice how unconvincingly I resist, how pitifully I bemoan my fate, but not so loudly that I wake the neighbors or with enough force as to actually free myself.

As you no doubt observe, the villain of the piece is not some big brute of a bully but a thin—make that *scrawny!*—bleached-dry blonde in her mid-40s named Allison who in a moment of hollow intimacy said I should call her 'Allie'. As you can see for yourself, Allison's former incandescent beauty, eerily highlighted in framed photographs throughout the drab apartment, has all but disappeared, leaving vague impressions on her pale features but little of its charm. Still between her jaded air of sexuality and surprisingly round breasts there remains something attractive about Allison in the driest sort of way. Like a magnet that has lost most but not all of its habitual pull.

As you may have also noticed, Allison possesses incredible strength of purpose. And appears to have little difficulty or unresolved emotion about dragging me toward that wide expanse of plushness which in less dramatic moments might pass for a couch but tonight clearly represents our marriage bed in Allison's plans.

To me of course it remains a couch. A couch whose brown velvety material has grown shiny and threadbare. A couch covered in random gray streaks which on closer inspection reveal themselves as patchy accumulations of dog's hair, the strands so thick and dry I imagine them to have fallen from the same breed of German Shepherd that Nazi soldiers once employed to intimidate my Jewish ancestors.

I know; I exaggerate.

I must remind myself that I am approaching a worn velveteen couch and not the gates of Auschwitz. And though I call myself a victim I cannot honestly resolve whether being this ambivalent about the situation I can rightly be considered the target of the attack or one of its instigators?

The fact that I am highly aroused—near total erection, in all honesty—only contributes to my confusion and lends more irony to my protests than urgency to my resistance.

What am I doing here if not to have sex with this overexcited woman? What did I think would happen if I let her bring me to her apartment to "check on Sucky" as she repeatedly insisted with wine-coated breath? 'Sucky' being short for her cat Succotash and only incidentally a description of my current emotional state.

Still I was hoping to accomplish something coming here tonight. There was a mission. And sex could have helped in that mission, I freely admit that. But whatever intentions I might have held, despite the obvious arousal of my sexual apparatus, in spite of the rough climax I appear headed toward on that couch across the room—despite all that!—there is no way I could ever maintain sufficient sexual ardor while trapped in this woman's cloying embrace. Not with her shopworn appearance so painfully poignant as she pulls on my arm and coaxes in slurred diction, "Relax, honey, relax."

And no less poignant when she adds, "Y'know how cute you are!" in a burst of wide-eyed appreciation.

"Cute?" I shout, exasperated. "Are you crazy?"

As I mentioned earlier, this is all taking place in slow motion, Allison and I moving through a vast syrupy world where if we moved any slower we would be captured in time like flies in amber.

And since it feels as though I have all the time in the world I might as well take advantage of that abundance to revisit the sequence of events that brought me here tonight.

But just so we have it on record, my mission was never about having sex with Allison.

As for what my mission was...?

Does one ever know the reasons one commits stupid and indelible deeds? As much as I can attribute a cause to my madness I came here tonight, allowed myself to be caught in Allison's web-like clutches, fell prey to this painfully loud throbbing in my forehead—all because I was trying to be a good father. Attempting in my own ill-conceived fashion to protect my nine-year-old son from colliding with one of life's numerous and inevitably sharp corners.

Before we go any further—since I seem to have so much time at my disposal—let me share something with you, an understanding I was given about the purpose of life. It was drummed into me over the span of fifteen years as a member of a 'school of self development'. Others might have called it a cult, I suppose, because it certainly looked cultish from the outside. But it was a school not a cult, perhaps even a spiritual community. At the very least, it was a fellowship of like-minded people searching for some sort of meaning to their existence, all of us trying to live by higher principles while living and working and enjoying 'normal' lives in the regular world.

I guess we were searching for something to believe in besides money, power and pedophile priests. We came from different backgrounds, had traveled by many roads, but found ourselves, like debris in a catch basin, all drawn to a worldwide organization immodestly named The Seekers For Truth and led by a holy man in India known as The Bapucharya. 'Bapu' being the Hindi term for 'Papa'.

And what to make of The Bapucharya!

Seen only in videotaped lectures, His Holiness The Bapucharya always struck me as surprisingly irreverent given the solemn weight of his guru status. Sometimes he acted more like a misplaced Jewish comedian than a fully conscious spiritual leader. A comedian, I should add, who never failed to giggle with almost childlike glee at his own jokes or at The Seekers' silly metaphors.

"Remember to *Drink Your RC Cola,"* The Bapucharya often advised in his high-pitched Indian accent, his laughter bubbling free at the edges. *'RC'* in typical Seekers parlance stands for 'Rest in Consciousness'. So *'Drink Your RC Cola'* was merely his way of reminding you to pay conscious attention to all that happens in your life. To live in the present moment rather than letting your mind get whisked away by thoughts or imaginings, which is far more difficult than it sounds given how one's attention generally flits about like a drunken mosquito.

Look at what is happening right now, right this very moment, as this lustful, adrenaline-pumped lady drags me across her living room floor! Rather than resting in consciousness my mind is flapping around frantically like a fresh caught fish. Thoughts, emotions and fantasies rush through my mind so quickly I cannot keep track of them. I am excited, annoyed, curious, sexually stimulated, amused, uncertain—all at the same time! Meanwhile, mental images continuously flash in a strobe-like effect, many of them featuring those fascinating round orbs that belie Allison's otherwise scrawny and underfed figure.

The idea of resting in consciousness at this singular moment—of trying to *Drink My RC Cola*—seems as ludicrous to me as trying to read a book while traveling down a landslide.

But what was I talking about...?

Oh yes, the purpose of life.

If you were to ask The Seekers For Truth about the purpose of life they would insist we are repeatedly put on this planet to learn a few important lessons. They would then explain that each of us is given a unique, one-of-a-kind coursebook to study during our time here on Earth, that coursebook being our Individual Life Experience or *ILE* as they like to call it.

With what purpose, you probably wonder? And under whose authority?

Good questions. I asked similar ones during my years in The Seekers' Boston school. Mostly I was told our purpose on Earth was to experience and study the lessons we receive 'on our *ILE*' (pronounced "isle" and talked about as though a lifetime were an island rather than a span of time). After years of studying the events, characters, recurring themes and major traumas that washed up on our *ILEs* we would be that much closer to understanding the whys and the wherefores of our particular soul's journeys.

Heady stuff all this talk about life's purpose and a soul's journey, but what would you expect from a school whose express *raison d'etre* is the search for truth?

To get to my point, however...under the purpose of life as The Seekers teach it, my main mission this evening would be to observe with *full consciousness* all that happens and only secondarily to attempt to free myself from Allison's hungry clutches. If I am meant to escape with my skin intact the escape will happen, seemingly without effort or difficulty as long as I remember to rest in consciousness. As long as I allow the mind to fall still (Hah!) and pay close attention to whatever happens here tonight—in other words, as long as I remember to *Drink My RC Cola.*

According to The Seekers For Truth this entire educational experience—studying the lessons of your *ILE* and endlessly consuming *RC Cola*—all comes down to a single goal: *learning to stay awake while the movie is playing.*

And whether I escape from Allison or not, The Seekers would soothingly advise me to sit back and enjoy the movie. Do not concern yourself if these concepts seem elusive. I was a Seeker for fifteen years and probably understood them only slightly better than my inebriated companion could comprehend them now.

But even if I failed to understand my specific life's lessons during my years of study with The Seekers For Truth I did learn that no one can live out those lessons for me. In that, my *ILE*—my Individual Life Experience—is the world's most complete and isolated course of study. And everything that happens on my *ILE* is a lesson meant specifically for me.

So on this *ILE* of mine, were I to bring full consciousness to bear, Allison would not be viewed as a faded flower blown my way on the winds of chance, but rather as a meaningful exercise sent expressly for my instruction. One of the periodic lessons in this lifelong course of study I could easily name 'Paul Peterson 101'.

There is no worry about failing any exams in this educational process because The Seekers teach there is no passing or failing, only learning or not learning. Whatever the outcome of any situation, all I am required to do is pay close attention to what happens—*while it is happening!* To live consciously in the moment. If it takes me 5000 lifetimes rather than 500 to learn whatever it is I am supposed to learn...well who is keeping count anyway?

Besides it probably took me 5000 lifetimes just to reach this evening's wretched turn of events.

But enough prattling. I waste precious moments in which I could be examining the sequence of events that brought me here tonight. Great insights are waiting to be gained, I know they are. All I have to do is search them out in a review process The Seekers term a 'Do-It-Yourself Workshop'. The Seekers claim you can achieve enlightenment or nirvana or whatever-you-want-to-call-it under the impetus of a Do-It-Yourself Workshop.

Of course you will far more likely achieve nothing. *Bupkas* as my Hungarian-born mother would probably say.

As if to underscore that rebellious thought my clinging companion issues a deep, devilish laugh that borders on the hysterical. To look at her you might think she is paying close attention to what is happening on her *ILE*. Truth is Allison's consciousness has slipped far beyond anyone's control and is now under the power of what The Seekers would term a *Frozen Idea*.

"Or so it seems," I mentally add, repeating one of His Holiness' favorite catch phrases.

But let us leave Allison for the moment, her consciousness frozen on the targeted velveteen couch, and move on with our course of study.

To review a sequence of events in your life through the prism of a Do-It-Yourself Workshop, The Seekers tell you to find a place of observation within yourself—*'within mind'* they actually say—that is so high and removed it seems as if you are looking down from the peak of a mountain. This is one of the most difficult practices in the entire Seekers training book and one that I never successfully completed in all my years at the Boston school. Supposedly when you move that deep within yourself, when you are that far removed from all thoughts and movements of the mind, you observe the movie of your life as though perched on a mountaintop. At the same time—and this is the difficult part to grasp—you apparently remain fully connected to whatever is happening in the present moment. From that high vantage point, according to The Seekers, you can look down and see all relevant events from your Do-It-Yourself Workshop circling the base of the mountain like beads on a necklace, each waiting in turn for your conscious attention. Simultaneously you continue to live out your mundane daily existence, working your job, feeding the cat, visiting the dry cleaners or whatever.

To connect with any single incident in this chain of linked events you merely aim the power of consciousness in its direction. When you are able to do that, according to The

Seekers, you are seated at the *Center Point of the Universe,* which in typical Seekers fashion is called the *CPU.*

And the *CPU,* unless I am suffering under some temporary delusion, seems to be where my consciousness is resting this very moment. You should understand that reaching the *Center Point of the Universe* is no minor accomplishment. As far as I know, and I have never heard otherwise, it generally signifies that one has reached the highest levels of consciousness. This is rarified territory, the state of angels and gurus and not one generally attained by wrestling with lust-laden maidens.

But nevertheless it is true...*I am at the center!*

As incredible as it seems—and I am still not certain this is really happening—a lens has shifted on some internal organ of awareness, dramatically altering my perception...*all* my perceptions! Allison is still dragging me in slow motion across the length of her living room toward the velveteen couch yet somehow she seems more like a character in a movie than a participant in an unsettled situation. I continue to hear sounds and receive impressions but they are muted and distant as if robbed of both impact and importance. After countless years of habitual failure I have apparently without great effort or directed purpose managed to attain the *Center Point of the Universe*—the *CPU!*

No that is not right. Some subtle instinct tells me I am not seated exactly at the center point but very close. Just the slightest bit off. And though everything is strangely different, seemingly shifted to some altered sense of reality, nothing in my outer world appears to have changed at all.

Do you see what I mean?

On the outside, for anyone who cares to look, I appear to be upstairs in a two-family home in Plymouth, Massachusetts being dragged in slow-motion by a rapacious woman across her living room floor. But on the inside—from where I look out—I am actually resting in a mild state of bliss, seated in a stillness that is poised *almost* at the *Center Point of the Universe.*

At one and the same time I am watching a movie unfold while acting out its principal role. Both a spectator and a participant, removed yet connected, distant but involved.

Do not ask me how this can be. I only know it is happening and it feels right. Actually it feels more than right. It seems as if this is the way I was meant to see the world and all those years of being caught up in the movie were merely unconscious attempts to find my way back to this removed point of observation.

I do not claim to understand it. There is no logic to this split perspective except the logic of its reality. It exists because I experience it, simple as that.

And look...! Can you see them? Those are all the events that led to my being here tonight. They whirl around the base of the mountain, strung together like pearls, as if each were not a memory from my life but a moment in time captured like a scene from a movie. Each fragment of my life trapped in a transparent bubble that emits a strange radiance.

And if that does not seem weird enough, watch what happens when I aim the power of consciousness down from the mountaintop toward the nearest of those faintly glowing, pearl-like moments-in-time...

The First Karmic
Gravitational Slide:

Down Among The Savages And Scouts

In Which We
Begin Examining
A Sequence Of Events
And Learn How
To Conduct Ourselves
At A Pinewood Derby

Lesson 1

How To Recognize A Disaster While It Is Still In The Development Stage

This is where it all begins.

And it feels strange to be here; physically strange I mean.

The Seekers For Truth would tell you I am having an acute reaction of my Physical Center brought on by over stimulation of my Emotional Center, both centers being so close in proximity they naturally affect one another.

I cannot judge if that is true or not but I can tell you it feels as if a number of my bodily sensations have switched on simultaneously, all of them beyond my control.

Perhaps you recognize the symptoms.

My stomach is upset, my shirt damp with sweat, my vision occasionally blurs, and my hands tremble when held up for observation. Also, far above the tumult of noise surrounding me is a persistent rattling-type sound as if an object were being shaken in a container. The rattle echoes in my head, clamoring for attention.

All of this relates, no doubt, to concerns I have about my companion who is nowhere in sight as I look around.

I am not so much worried about where he is right now as I am about where the movement of this morning's events may eventually take him. If you look around this riotous, over-crowded church basement you will eventually run across him I am sure. He has brown hair and wears a blue cub scout shirt topped by a neatly rolled, banana-yellow bandana. Only nine years old he is of average height for his age and thin. As a young child he possessed wispy golden curls but now in their place lies a thick field of brown matting with a cowlick rising from the top like a perpetual waterspout.

The boy looks much like I did at his age even down to a part in his hair which runs barely longer than the thought that created it.

I am talking about my son of course, my nine-year-old cub scout Mickey whose given name is Michael and who is somewhere in this large basement hall contributing I am certain to the deafening volume of noise and chaos that surrounds me.

Yes I believe chaos is the right word.

How large would you say this crowd is? I estimate more than two hundred cub scouts fill the room, their screams and animal-like cries rebounding off the linoleum floor and green painted walls of St. Christina's basement hall without noticeable rhythm or pause.

Mickey and his fellow scouts maintain this constant roar as background to the long awaited Pinewood Derby taking place in the center of this large windowless room.

If you are a parent you have been in countless halls like this. They are easy to remember, these anonymous rooms dedicated to civic ritual, because they are so similarly forgettable you only need remember one to remember them all. These are the rooms where parents organize book fairs and bake sales, where Brownies cross over "The Bridge" to become Girl Scouts, where little leagues hold their spring sign-ups and, yes, where cub scouts gather in early February dragging their fathers out of post-NFL depression for the Cub Scout Pinewood Derby.

If you look in the approximate center of this swirling mass of blue shirts you will notice an imposing structure that looks like the downhill segment of a miniaturized roller coaster. This is the official Pinewood Derby racetrack. About four feet at its highest, it descends on a steep plane for twenty feet or more then bottoms out gradually for another ten feet. Three parallel wooden tracks run down its length, each with an elevated guide rail in the center. It is upon these tracks, their tires straddling the guide rail, that the Pinewood Derby racecars compete for all of five furious seconds.

I marvel at how something that happens so quickly can be exciting and satisfying for nine- and ten-year-old boys but then I realize we are dealing with new age children whose attention spans blink on and off in nano-seconds.

Have you ever been to a Pinewood Derby?

This is my first Pinewood Derby and already it has become a landmark lesson on my *ILE.*

At times it can be almost hypnotic to watch the individual races or heats as they are called. Once the three racecars are placed in position by their cub scout owners the thunderous buzz of noise and energy subsides as if a muting switch has been thrown. Then the individual gates, little more than metal pins that retract into the guide rails, are simultaneously withdrawn by Mr. Matthews, the Scoutmaster, who stands behind the structure myopically observing each race through thick wire-frame glasses.

"An-n-n-nd they're off!" he announces through a scratchy hand-held megaphone, mimicking I am sure some hambone racetrack announcer he once heard in his younger days.

Instantly the noise level shoots back up.

Then under the rising storm of screams and cheers the three racecars abandon themselves to the pull of gravity and streak down their individual rails for all of four or five seconds. The winner in most heats is usually decided in the split second after the restraining pins retract, but a few contests remain seesaw battles to the end.

If you are not feeling the desire to personally visit a Pinewood Derby do not be alarmed. Observing it from a distance it is not an experience whose pleasures are easily discerned. Without being here in person surrounded by the harsh uproar of two hundred boys in play, entranced by the surprisingly stylish look of the home-made racecars, beguiled by the titillating presence of a table filled with Pinewood Derby trophies, each with its gold-leafed racecar pitched upwards in a strutting pose, you are left with little more to consider than a child's painfully protracted game of mindless amusement.

There it is again! That strange rattling noise...I believe I can hear it in my head.

Can you hear it?

And look, my hand still trembles...

The thing to do of course is to ignore these minor annoyances, giving them no more power than they already possess. In The Seekers For Truth we were taught that the power of consciousness channels tremendous energy into anything you focus upon. The choice we have in life is to "...bestow consciousness with attention; to control it for our own purposes," Mr. Samuelson, the British-born Head of the Boston School, once lectured, "or to squander it with the same measure of thought a drunkard gives to—excuse the unpleasant reference—urinating in an alleyway."

To control consciousness or to give up control.

That is the choice we have every waking moment of our lives, The Seekers would have you believe. Choose one you become master of the mind, choose the other you become its monkey.

"Or so it seems," The Bapucharya would likely interject, giggling as if he were the only one to understand some painfully obvious joke.

But forget all that for a moment and take a closer look at this object in my unsteady hand.

Allow me to raise it up for your inspection.

This—in case you cannot identify what you see—is one of those rare Pinewood Derby racecars destined for glory. So far this morning this humble creation has powered itself to victory in five different heats, two of which were decided in runoffs.

Look closely at this leading contender for one of those fifteen dollar gilded trophies and you will understand why my Emotional and Physical Centers are in such a state of fulminating distress.

Now tell me—if I had not already identified the function of this unsightly creation, what would you think it was?

It would not be easy, would it?

At first glance you would probably be shocked to observe this elongated, six-inch block of wood has foolishly been painted fuchsia. I say 'foolishly' for the simple reason this shade of fuchsia is so bright and garish it is patently inappropriate for an object this small. I also say 'foolishly' because there is the distinct possibility some observers might look at this hastily painted wood block and imagine its color to be pink instead of fuchsia and nothing would be more foolish or self-destructive than to bring a pink model racecar to a Cub Scout Pinewood Derby.

You begin to see my difficulty.

But continue to rest your eyes upon this object in my hand and observe what happens.

Gradually its shape starts to grow familiar, am I right? You begin to detect car-like qualities in the way its various aspects come together and occupy space. Yes its shape definitely bears rough resemblance to some primordial vision of a car.

In the middle section of the racecar, which sits lower than the front and rear segments, a protuberance sticks up like the topmost nub of a child's finger. This protrusion, painted the same fuchsia as the rest of the car but topped with a white dot, could easily be viewed as the head of a driver, or at least the top third of his head. And the boxlike segments to the front and rear appear to be the engine and trunk of a model racecar. And there, black, shiny and upright on both sides, are four plastic tires, the only elements that actually resemble their real life counterparts.

We are gazing upon the final product of a weekend's futile efforts. A weekend where too few hours were stolen from too many activities to allow anything more than this gaudy imposter of a model racecar to emerge from the block of wood my little boy had been given.

I hasten to add that if the black plastic tires seem true to life it has little to do with our modeling skills and everything to do with the fact that tires and axles come fully manufactured and included in the kit, as if a minimum amount of realism was needed to keep cub scouts and their fathers on solid ground.

And if keeping our feet on solid ground was an object of the exercise this handiwork proves how far short of the goal Mickey and I have fallen.

Take for instance our laughable attempt at applying racecar graphics. Look on both sides of our model's bright fuchsia exterior. There where another father and son team might have sensibly applied adhesive racecar decals you will notice instead crude, hand-painted white symbols, one on each side. At first glance these symbols appear undecipherable, like primitive caveman drawings. Their legibility is not helped by the fact that the whiteness of the paint is barely maintained against the bleed-through of the fuchsia, which creates of course the false impression that the blurry white symbol has transformed itself into a pink graphic, which it has not.

Now if you squint your eyes and look squarely at either side of the racecar you start to see the number 2 surrounded by a poorly drawn circle. That number of course seemed like an obvious choice at the time.

"We will make it number two," I innocently suggested a short week ago, both of us at my kitchen table hovering like inattentive gods over our model racecar.

"Two?" Mickey queried.

"Just like there are two of us working on it," I explained. What do you think?"

"That's cool," Mickey decided with a thoughtless shrug.

Looking at it now there is nothing 'cool' to be seen. We should have omitted the '2' entirely and left the surrounding circle as testament to the number of people on our team who actually knew what they were doing.

Had I been working on Mickey's Pinewood Derby racer under the guidance of The Seekers For Truth, my lack of experience would not have been a problem, merely another opportunity to put consciousness to work.

"Let the mind rest on the working surface, Mr. Peterson," one of The Seekers would have gently instructed. "Now, allow consciousness to focus on the precise point at which the work is taking place. Knowledge of what is needed—and what *you* need to do—will automatically arise."

I know it sounds ridiculous.

But it works.

My years with The Seekers gave me dozens of instances that proved how well the exercise works. Many times I witnessed much-needed knowledge arising from the working surface of one project or another. By 'working surface' The Seekers mean wherever the work is being done. A desktop, nail head, mixing bowl, pencil point or window pane are few of the more obvious working surfaces.

What is most amazing, however, is not that the practice

works but that I unerringly forget to use it when I need it most. As if the memory of all those years of Seeker instruction had been accidentally erased. The countless times I could have benefited from this and other Seeker exercises I either forgot what I had been taught or only remembered after it was too late to put it to use.

Now it appears something has shifted; that a door has opened and I have been allowed to step back inside the world of The Seekers For Truth, closer to the *CPU*—the *Center Point of the Universe*—than I have ever come before.

Having been cut off from Seeker knowledge all these years I am not quite used to having it back. Most likely it would feel the same to get behind the wheel of a car after years of not driving.

In one of his videotaped tutorials His Holiness The Bapucharya explained why my fellow students and I had been chosen to join The School and receive its frequently forgettable teachings.

"You were all selected as Seekers because your essences are almost fully cooked," he announced with bubbly delight. "Being almost fully cooked gives you responsibilities as well as entitlements, and so you will not be allowed to merrily climb out of my frying pan whenever you lose your appetite for the truth." Giggling like a grade-schooler he concluded, "No, my children, you can no longer leave our pleasant little school..." and here is the relevant threat, "unless you are prepared to accept the consequences."

His Holiness was laughing at his cooking metaphors, smiling at us from the rectangular framework of the TV screen, but his 'consequences' seemed no less a threat for all his comic good cheer.

Perhaps this forgetting of Seeker practices, especially when they are most needed, is one of the consequences The Bapucharya was speaking about. Clearly consciousness was not resting anywhere in the vicinity of Cambridge last Saturday when Mickey and I did most of the damage to our racing car which I have now come to think of with mock affection as Old Number Two.

Surprisingly Mickey does not notice my discomfort. Nor has he seen or heard anything to make him realize how unsightly a model racecar we have brought with us to the Pinewood Derby.

That is the real surprise of the morning. Not our winning five consecutive elimination heats nor remaining undefeated while legions of meticulously designed racecars have fallen by the wayside, but our making it through all this complex, unfolding activity without being spotted or called out for the poorly dressed clowns and imposters that we are.

For me it is a wonder that resembles a penny balloon floating up into the heavens. You watch it climb, awed by the grandeur of its flight, all the while knowing it will burst once it reaches an altitude where the pressure is too great.

I cannot do anything at the moment but watch the balloon as it continues to rise.

Mickey on the other hand seems delighted. Rather than measure himself against other scouts in terms of racecar aesthetics he is proud to be the owner of a competitor-blasting, killer racecar...

There he is! I see him now...

Over there on the other side of the room running back and forth with Billy Montcreif, Louie Serino and two other boys. They are playing some sort of tag that requires minimum adherence to any set of rules.

Involuntarily I feel a smile arising on my face; feel my facial muscles shifting into positions I would have thought were lost to memory. If I smile upon sighting my little boy, however, it does not mean I have been released from the bondage of my concerns, only furloughed for a few fleeting moments.

What a joy it is to see him at play. A rare sight too since he usually expresses his emotions more discreetly and mostly by himself. It is no less a window into his present state of mind to watch him running after an elusive Louie Serino than it would be to hear him relate his deepest feelings to Dr. Rivers, my gloomy, gray-bearded psychologist.

Five times Mickey has carried our clunky, tropical-colored creation up to the starting block and five times he has survived elimination runs where all the other cub scouts competing against him have not. And each time he scampered up to the racing area, retrieved Old Number Two and proudly carried it back to his seated father who, if the truth were known, sits quietly waiting for our luck to catch up with us. Waiting for my son and two hundred other blue-shirted scouts to discover what a shamefully ugly piece of work we have brought with us to this year's Pinewood Derby.

That we have not yet been discovered—*that* is the real miracle of the morning!

Lesson 2

Removing Mr. Ping And Mr. Pong With A Little Help From Mrs. Costadazzi

You know of course we are living on borrowed time.

Sooner or later we will be discovered and denounced. Sooner or later these buzzing, elbow-high children of the damned will descend upon us in a pitiless swarm.

I know this as well as I know who is to blame for our coming here with a model racecar that looks like an arts and crafts project from The School for the Blind.

The Seekers view this headlong rush toward an inevitable destiny as a Karmic Gravitational Slide. If I am correct and Mickey and I are in the grip of a Karmic Gravitational Slide that would mean there are higher forces at play than can be readily understood with our ordinary faculties and limited, human-being point of view. Which also means it would be foolish and unfair to blame anyone for any of this.

How can I blame an individual for what is clearly an inevitable outcome of the dance of the universe?

How can I indeed!

Contrary to obvious reality, however, I know exactly whose fault it is that Mickey and I have come here this morning with a racecar that looks like it was crafted under the influence of some perception-distorting substance. And there is only one suspect in this particular crime. You may scoff if you wish but at some level this is definitely all Marilyn's fault.

Marilyn's fault...Marilyn's fault...

For the last hour that phrase has been repeating inside my mind like a runaway mantra.

But how can I blame my ex-wife, you ask? How can anything in our complex universe be so simply reduced to a single cause? Can I blame Marilyn for the choice of colors, the childish carpentry, the amateurish look of our racing graphics? Can I reasonably suggest Marilyn, who never so much as lifted a tool or made a suggestion, played any role, much less a decisive one, in the creation of this pathetic parrot-colored racecar?

Can I indeed!

Divorce is a surreal adventure where nothing makes sense and logic holds little counterweight to emotion. Most of what I went through—the breakup of my marriage, the unraveling of my family, my whole life being turned upside down—seemed like a badly scripted movie whose subplots were invariably beyond the realm of anyone's logic or my control.

Why not blame Marilyn since she will never be judged for one-tenth the harm she has done to me?

There it goes again.

That rattling sound. It seems to be echoing in the hollow regions of my skull if that makes any sense.

Can you hear it?

Earlier I suggested we ignore it, deny it the consciousness it needs to enliven itself. But my years with The Seekers now lead me toward a different response. To no longer reject the sound but to acknowledge it and hear what it has to say. For all I know it could relate to something important, something the universe is trying to tell me. Something I will never uncover unless I move beyond the limited range of my physical perceptions.

The Seekers insist the workings of the universe are entirely logical, quickly adding that its logic lies beyond the grasp of most scientific minds.

I myself have little regard for logic. Most of what I deal with in life seems more irrational than logical. My divorce, my struggles as a single father, the questionable value of a career devoted to creating advertising (also known as 'cultural crap' to anyone with half a brain). And then of course my penchant for getting trapped in unfortunate situations...

How many people you know would let themselves get trapped in a Pinewood Derby waiting for the sky to fall? O become prisoners of lust in a second-floor apartment in Plymouth, Massachusetts?

But am I really trapped, you ask?

The Seekers would have you remember that no matter how much I appear to be ensnared in a series of unfolding events I am also watching those same events from a quiet—call it *serene*—perch within myself. High atop an inner mountain, you recall, looking out from close proximity to the *CPU.*

The *Center Point of the Universe!*

Where is the logic in *that?*

No I do not need logic. It is not necessary for this persistent rattling noise to have an obvious cause as if it were belched up from the rusty coils of St. Christina's heating system. Nor does it need to be an easily explained delusion, perhaps arising from the troubled coils of my own internal systems which are seriously stressed from the mounting uproar and lack of air in this overheated coffin of a basement hall.

The truth is I do not need to understand the sound, I only need to stop resisting it, thereby breaking down the polarity that exists between a persistent noise and a resistant listener.

According to The Seekers For Truth, dismantling this mechanism of resistance—and it is a mechanism since it operates under principles far removed from conscious direction—is called *Removing Mr. Ping and Mr. Pong.*

These conflicting points of view—Mr. Ping and Mr. Pong—create an energy field in which the subject is pushed in opposite directions by opposing forces and inevitably gets stuck in between. When you remove Mr. Ping and Mr. Pong you remove the polarity from a situation and free whatever has been trapped within its energy field.

"This indeed was the awesome power behind Mr. Gandhi and his movement of non-violence," The Bapucharya once told us on video. "Mr. Gandhi's *Satyagraha* was not the opposition of one force to another, but the withdrawal of direct opposition to a force that was already in place and oh-so-very powerful. Mr. Gandhi's capacity to deflate a swaggering imperialist empire lay in his removal of opposing force, did it not? And the replacement of that resistance with love, honor and, most important, civility!

"What a devilish idea," His Holiness exclaimed, giggling as usual, *"We will not play in your game but look how much fun we are having, playing so nicely in our game!"*

The Bapucharya was right of course.

Take this unidentified rattling noise. No matter how persistently it fights for my attention I persist in denying it its right to any consideration. The more it pushes, the more I push back. Which means of course the seesaw stalemate could go on indefinitely unless the underlying dynamic of the situation is somehow altered.

Unless someone *Removes Mr. Ping and Mr. Pong!*

Easy to say, not so easy to do.

Anyone who has tried to stop smoking knows how difficult it can be to *Remove Mr. Ping and Mr. Pong.* Resisting one's desire for a cigarette more often reinforces the habit than puts out the fire.

The Seekers For Truth developed a number of techniques for disarming resistance. Of the two that spring to mind *Embracement* seems the most appropriate in these circumstances. *Embracement* relies on the resister—myself in this case—embracing the very experience I have been resisting.

But let me show you...

The first thing one does is come to rest.

Drink your RC Cola!

Watch how I sit in a comfortable position and let my body find its natural balance, at the same time letting all thoughts and ideas gradually fall away. There is no need to push my thoughts away; I merely allow them to leave by freeing them from my attention.

Next I close my eyes, shutting out this landscape of agitated cub scouts and under-caffeinated fathers, and picture in my mind an object that is large and overwhelming. My fellow Seekers used to imagine redwood trees, buses, skyscrapers—something suitably gigantic. With me it was always an image of my fifth grade teacher Mrs. Costadazzi.

As I begin to internally recite my mantra—a secret mystical sound given to each Seeker student—letting my mind rest on the individual sounds as they repeat in sync with each breath, my inner eye scans a sea of darkness and waits.

And here she comes now...

If you could see inside my mind you would observe Mrs. Costadazzi, all 300 pounds of her, slowly materializing and as huge and good natured as she was when I was 11 years old and sitting in her class.

Involuntarily my chest fills with a sigh as she bathes me in her warm, maternal smile. Exactly as I remember her she peers at me over her squared bifocals with pleasured interest. I can even smell the scent of her perfume with that orchid-like, almost medicinal air I always associate with the smell of chalk.

If you could see into my imaginings you would observe her massive form looming over me as it did so often in the fifth grade. You would also notice she is not dressed in one of her usual floral dresses but instead, through the power of my imagination, is draped in a fabric made entirely from the very sound I have been trying to ignore.

Yes Mrs. Costadazzi is totally cloaked, almost hidden, within layers of that insistent rattling noise. The material is dingy white like used dishwater and covered in splotches of black that vibrate in sync with the clattering of that mysterious sound.

At this point where logic might suggest I let go of my resistance by releasing Mrs. Costadazzi's image from my mind I actually reach out to embrace it and be embraced by it. Letting the dull, rattling sound and Mrs. Costadazzi herself come as close and as deep within me as my own breath.

For a moment I am back at PS 45 in Brooklyn being crushed upon that oceanic bosom, clutched lovingly against the brittle buttons and the little silver watch fob hanging upside down on the vast plateau of her mountainous bust.

And so as I cling tightly with great fondness, almost suffocating within this massive enfoldment, I no longer reject that strange rattling sound.

I embrace it.

In this moment of silent, crushing acceptance, I break through the mystery and come to understand the true nature of the sound itself.

And now I have to laugh!

Without thinking I open my eyes and look around for someone with whom I can share my sudden and amusing insight only to realize I may be sitting amongst hundreds of cub scouts and their parents but I am nevertheless pursuing this Do-It-Yourself Workshop on my own.

I resist saying *alone* because there is a typical Seeker wordplay that translates 'alone' as 'all-one' and that is not what I mean to say.

Of course Bill McAndrews is sitting in the chair next to mine but Bill would not be a person with whom to share anything of value, much less a sudden insight.

"A rattling sound, Peterson?" he would exclaim in his booming voice. "What the hell are you talking about? Who cares about some silly sound when there's so much in life you can see and reach out for!"

No I will keep my insights to myself. At least while I attempt to track the now-explained sound back to its original place and time. If there is something to be learned, that is where I will learn it.

To go there I need only find that inner mountaintop again which, as you no doubt recall, lies excruciatingly close to the *CPU*. Then resting in consciousness I will focus on the next stop in our Do-It-Yourself Workshop, the next closest of those luminescent beads running around the base of the mountain.

So here I go again, slipping effortlessly into heightened consciousness as if it were a comfortable slipper.

Trust me I was never that gifted a Seeker student that I could so easily come to rest in consciousness. Never in all my Seeker days was I able to come this close to the *CPU* much less find myself looking down from its inner heights.

If it seems strange to you imagine how it seems to me!

Now I can seemingly fall into a conscious state at will and jump from one event in my life to another without restraint or significant effort. Clearly something is different. Something has changed.

I have changed.

No I have evolved!

Or so it seems.

In any case my *Embracement* is leading me to the next

memory bubble running around the mountain. Now it is simply a matter of directing consciousness toward that singular moment from my generally unexciting and mundane existence...

Which is why after a few seconds of deep-seated rest I find myself standing in the kitchen of a familiar home in St. Bart's Bay, a charming little coastal community about 45 minutes south of Boston.

I say *familiar*, but only to me, not to you.

You see I have traveled back through time to the Saturday a week before the Pinewood Derby. I have come here as I do every second Saturday to pick up my children and bring them to my apartment in Cambridge for the weekend.

And here is my son Mickey standing in the kitchen that used to be mine but now wholly and solely belongs to his mother. See him nervously shaking that white cardboard box, causing some unseen object to rattle around with no great significance?

Yes exactly!

You recognized it right away, did you not?

Our mysterious rattling sound!

The irony is I already know the contents of that small rectangular box.

And I would not be lying if I told you it contains the raw elements of a time bomb.

Lesson 3

How To Make Stupid Decisions About Important Matters

As you can see for yourself, it is an ordinary kitchen, nothing special except for the fact it was once partly mine but now fully belongs to my ex-wife.

Speaking of possession, see how tightly Mickey holds the white cardboard box with both hands as if it represents something of great value and irreplaceable significance?

As I have already pointed out, that box is the source of the clatter resonating in my mind so mysteriously at the Pinewood Derby. I cannot claim to understand why a sound created in this kitchen would be echoing a week later at St. Christina's but it tells me to pay careful attention to what happens here this morning.

Though no longer a member of The Seekers For Truth I still harbor hopes of discovering whatever secrets lie buried across the landscape of my *ILE*. In that regard I doubt that any longtime student of The Seekers school ever fully leaves its influence or its lessons behind.

One thing I have left behind, at least for now, is my self-assurance. Standing around in my former home makes me feel awkward, like a tradesman waiting for payment on an overdue invoice. I silently urge my habitually slowpoke daughters Suzie and Cathy to hurry up as they gather whatever clothing, books and playthings they need to survive another weekend at their father's apartment in Cambridge.

"Do you have your stuff?" I ask Mickey, the question more a formality than a concern since his customarily lumpy backpack is resting on the floor near his feet.

"Got it!" he answers, lightly shaking the box in his hands

for proof. Whatever is inside rattles with the weight and certainty of a single large item but I give it little attention.

To be honest Mickey could be setting fire to the house and I would probably not notice. My mind is lost in a swirl of confused thoughts and highly charged emotions. If there is a focus to my thinking it concerns where in the house my ex-wife might be and whether she is likely to make an appearance before we leave. Her presence is something I simultaneously dread and desire, like a reformed alcoholic who both fears and longs for his next drink.

Once I loved the woman and felt affection at the simplest thought of her. Today more than four years after moving out of this house those feelings still cast lingering shadows.

Perhaps because Marilyn sought the divorce against my wishes, perhaps because I never fully accepted its reality, or perhaps for no other motive than habit…for whatever reason some deep-seated attraction to my ex-wife still remains, refusing to release me from its grip, only from its charm.

"What is that?" I finally ask Mickey, more to distract myself from my thoughts than to learn about the box. "A school project?"

"My Pinewood Derby kit," he replies as if I have forgotten something told to me in a previous discussion.

The memory comes back fuzzily.

"We were going to work on that weeks ago…" I casually note. "Some cub scout project or something?"

"Yep," he answers, trying not to show his feelings about the matter.

"…and things kept getting in the way," I vaguely recall.

"Yep."

"Well, I have not forgotten my promise, Mick, but we have a real busy weekend planned…"

"Da-a-ad," he interrupts anxiously, "the Pinewood Derby is next weekend! I entered 'cause you said we'd go; that you'd help me make a model racecar. And now there's no time left to do it."

The rising anxiety in his voice surprises me and makes me turn to face him for a closer look. Something in what he said or the way he said it sharply reminds me of disappointments I felt as a child over my own father's failings.

In less than a second I let go of my discomfort to deal with his.

"Who said we have no time left?" I ask with mock indignation. I tap the cardboard box with a finger. "Is this it? The racing thing...the kit?"

"Yep!"

"Well, what are we supposed to do with it?"

"Fix it up so it looks like a racecar," he answers as if struggling to conceal how dim-witted a question I had just asked.

"Well, that sounds easy enough," I reply, unaware of how inaccurate a statement that will prove to be. Releasing a soft exclamation of mounting interest I take the box from his hands and shake it near my ear.

"Sounds like a full kit," I comment with the knowing air of a professional. Lifting off the white cardboard lid I discover a squared block of blond piney wood whose dimensions are mill-sawed to accommodate the shape of a model racing car. I take out the block for closer inspection, surprised by the smoothness of its fine sanded surface. Turning it over I find two slits running the width of the underside, probably meant to anchor the tire axles which came bundled along with four black tires in a clear plastic bag. The bag and the block of wood make up the entire kit.

I put the wooden block back in the box.

"Where are...?" I start to ask.

I raise my head to look at my little boy.

"What...?" he asks, reflecting back my obvious concern.

"There are no instructions..." I remark with a troubled lift of my eyebrows.

"I guess we don't need instructions," he suggests.

His obvious lack of assurance is hardly encouraging.

"Did anyone else get them?" I ask. "Will I be the only father who worked on this without instructions?"

"Dad," Mickey says, holding back his exasperation, "none of the kits came with instructions. You're supposed to know what a racecar looks like. You don't have to do anything that needs instructions."

"You sure?" I ask, still uncomfortable. "Absolutely sure?"

"Mrs. Mitchell went over the contents with us when we

got the kit. Nobody had instructions." He looks at me with an air of paper-thin tolerance. "Don't you remember we talked about this? And you promised?"

Yes I remember; some of it at least. Enough to know I am running out of options. Other memories come back as well.

In most of them I see myself when I was Mickey's age, waiting for *my* father. Waiting for him to come home nights before I went to sleep, waiting for him to wake up on Sundays so we could go for our family outing. Mostly I was waiting for Dad to notice me, to give me attention; perhaps to accidentally discover there was a whole world I inhabited apart from his.

When I think of all the times I swore to be a better father than my father and here my son is waiting for me to remember my own lightly made and easily forgotten promises...!

Dr. Rivers, my grumpy gray-bearded therapist, says adults usually take on the very attributes they despised in their parents. According to him it is our way of compensating for behavior we could not control when we were young.

The Seekers on the other hand would characterize Dr. Rivers' theory as a low-level analysis of a high-level phenomenon; what they invariably call a *Blind Elephant's Opinion.* Which if you have not heard the story relates to five blind men who each grab a different part of an elephant's anatomy and end up with five totally different perceptions of what an elephant looks like. Why they call it a *Blind Elephant's Opinion* rather than a *Blind Man's Opinion* goes back, I suppose, to The Seekers incessant need to be clever and memorable.

In any case, if you were to ask The Seekers about this "waiting for papa" business that one generation of Peterson males inflicts upon the next, they would tell you we are trapped in a *Karmic Echo,* which is nothing more than a particular movement of energy repeating itself over and over.

I do not know what causes a Karmic Echo but I was told it could go on indefinitely, generation after generation, until the universe gets bored with the game or one of the Peterson men finally learns to break the chain.

But anyway, who writes the rules to this game? And where do they keep the instructions that tell you how to become the better father you always wanted to be?

It occurs to me that I often have difficulty finding the right instructions.

"Da-a-ad?" my little boy pursues with growing impatience.

"Yes, I remember, I remember," I assure him.

"You know, Dad," he says accusingly, "We did talk about it. You did say you'd help me."

"I remember," I assure him, handing back the open kit. "I did not forget."

Not surprisingly Mickey's mother (and my former wife) Marilyn enters the kitchen at the precise moment my failure as a father has become the unstated subject of our discussion.

"Forget what?" Mickey's mother inquires walking wearily across the room, her familiar housecoat unbuttoned over a blue nightdress. She has the unmistakable air of a woman who has just risen from bed.

Seeing me hand Mickey the kit she asks directly with a look of concern that might warm the heart of the unsuspecting casual observer, "Well, can you help him? He has been waiting weeks for you to do it…to help him build a model car. Just like the other kids and their dads."

She pauses a moment, for effect I guess.

I feel as though I have been caught committing some reprehensible act, having her walk in as I was handing back Mickey's Pinewood Derby kit. Not quite as despicable as shooting a puppy, but almost.

"Put it away," I tell my little boy, handing him the lid to the box.

"There is really no time left," Marilyn continues, walking over to the counter where half a pot of coffee is sitting in the Braun coffeemaker my Aunt Ruthie gave us as a wedding present, "so if you cannot help him this weekend, just say so."

Marilyn pours a cup of coffee and puts it in the microwave. She sets the timer, hits the start button and turns back, asking with awakening impatience, "What is it going to be? Your son needs to know?"

Here she is for your perusal, the woman who can set off all my emotional alarms whenever she comes within shouting distance. No longer the beautiful girl I first met with her ever-ready smile, long dark hair, and firm but modest figure. Nor has she remained the beautiful woman I eventually married. She is older now, more mature and substantially heavier. Her once-long dark tresses are cut painfully short, an indication of how little attention she craves from men like me who prefer their women with long hair.

No there is nothing particularly attractive about Marilyn these days. But if you could see the vibrant young woman she was fifteen years ago you might understand why all these years later this puffy, middle-aged woman in a worn housecoat still maintains a lingering hold on my emotional well being.

"Well, can you do it?" my ex-wife pursues. "Can you help your son with his cub scout project? Or…" and you can see how helpful this next question is, "will I have to do it?"

Standing in the presence of someone I once loved who offers me spoonfuls of scorn beneath the shadow of her smile, my discomfort grows so large that all three of us must feel surrounded by it in the confines of this modest kitchen.

But how does it feel for her, I wonder? Does it feel hurtful? Does she have any regrets? Or are these exchanges merely additional fruits of her hard won victory? My emotional discomfort simply one more trophy she takes away from our marriage along with the house, the kids and Aunt Ruthie's coffeemaker?

"What?" I answer awkwardly.

She continues to push, reminding me, "He has been waiting weeks, three weeks at least, because you kept telling him you would do it…" but I am only half listening to the flow of her words. I have stopped drinking my *RC Cola* and have begun to catalog this event for future purposes.

I often record commentaries to events as they happen; a misguided attempt perhaps to help myself comprehend them.

Dr. Rivers would say it was my way of distancing myself to avoid pain. The Seekers would probably agree. The only difference is Dr. Rivers would argue that my mind has the right to protect itself from discomfort while The Seekers would insist we were given minds expressly so we could fully experience life head on. In The Boston School we were taught that everything has a purpose, even pain, and if you experience your suffering consciously you have a chance to move through it and eventually beyond it.

The kicker is if you ignore the pain—if you resist rather than embrace it—it will keep coming back. Just like the rattling sound from Mickey's Pinewood Derby kit would have never let up without Mrs. Costadazzi coming back from the dead to give me a hug.

If Mickey were a young man now instead of a child and I could use this interaction between his mother and me as a point of study for his own development there would be much to highlight.

Pay close attention, I would instruct, for here is a perfect example of how an ex-wife quickly gains the upper hand in a conversation. First I would point out his mother's strategic decision to discuss my failings as a father in front of him; far more destructive—and guaranteed to put me on the defensive—than opening up a two-way dialogue in another room, comfortably removed from Mickey's silent, watchful presence.

And did you notice the way she spoke to me? Every single statement rose to an accusation at the end. With all those *'will you's?'* finishing up her sentences the casual listener would think I was a chronic disappointment to my children instead of a single father struggling to do his honest best.

But enough commentary...

"Stop!" I interrupt Marilyn with a cry that is just short of a shout. "Just back off. I know what I have to do, and I know what I promised. So just back off."

"Hey, Dad," Mickey says in a nervous whisper, pulling on my sleeve, "we can work in the basement. You can use your old tools and things. I've got my trains on the workbench but I can clean them off real quick."

I look down at my son and allow myself a moment to cool down. Maybe two moments.

"That is an idea, Mick," I finally answer, nodding thoughtfully.

I take back the cardboard box and heft it as if weighing its possibilities as well as its contents. Suddenly a dim realization breaks through the gray clouds of my swirling emotions and I find myself dealing with a new set of practical considerations.

There is a problem you face when leaving the family home at the age of 41; actually there are many problems but the one that comes to mind right now concerns the loss of all my tools—everything down to my last jar of nuts and bolts.

Nuts and bolts: the perfect example!

To see all the nuts, bolts, screws, washers and nails I collected during the years of my marriage you only have to go downstairs to my ex-wife's basement. There, neatly organized on six-inch shelves exactly as I left them when I moved out three and a half years ago, are all my jars and cans. Most of them are a quarter full or less. Unreplenished in my years of absence, victims of the divorce. And if you want to see my tools you only have to look into the drawers of the workbench or on the pegboard mounted on the wall.

I say '*my* tools' but my divorce agreement stipulates otherwise.

Staring blankly into space I wonder where I might find the tools or the workspace to convert this block of virgin white pine into a model racecar.

"We better do it downstairs, Dad!" Mickey suggests with mounting enthusiasm. "Your saw and stuff are still there."

I look to his mother who does not appear to be registering any complaints and awkwardly ask, "Would that be all right?"

"That would be okay with me," my ex-wife says with little emotion or visible interest.

Then she looks up, catching my eye before I can turn away, and in seven words takes back everything she just gave me.

"Just clean up when you are finished."

Here is the conclusion to my son's future lesson...

Now pay close attention, I would instruct, for this was the turning point, the critical moment when fate—aided by your hard, unforgiving mother—pulled sharply on the rudder and turned our ship toward the rocks that lay waiting for us in the shallow waters of the Pinewood Derby.

In that moment, the instant she said those words, my

decision was made and our fate deftly sealed.

One more link in the chain of events had been forged, one step closer had been taken. Though I could not see it in all its imperfect glory our Karmic Gravitational Slide had moved too far down the track to call back.

From this point on, I would instruct my son, there was no way I could allow myself to use the tools I once owned. Or the workbench I once built. Or the basement I once set up as a workspace. They belonged to your mother and neither the tortures of hell nor the promises of paradise could convince me that a semblance of my self-respect would remain if I exchanged my pride for the use of her tools.

But that is a lesson meant for the future. For now I will merely turn to his mother and softly say, “Thank you,” with an excess of politeness, “but we will not need your tools.”

I listen to the words come out of my mouth one by one and think how amazing it is that something said so swiftly has the potential to resonate for years in a person’s life.

“Excuse me,” I mutter softly, stepping around Mickey and moving toward the door that leads to the living room. “Su-Su!” I call even before I am fully out of the kitchen.

From upstairs my 14-year-old daughter Suzie calls back, “Just a minute, Dad. We’re almost ready.”

“Wait,” I shout back, walking toward the stairs. “I am coming up. I need you to find something for me.”

As I reach the stairs I am wondering against all likelihood whether Suzie might still have the toy tool set we gave her years ago for Christmas. She would have been five or six at the time.

“Su-Su,” I call, walking up, “remember your toy carpentry kit…?”

“My what?” Suzie calls down.

“Those toy tools we gave you,” I shout back as if they should be on her mind if not her dresser. “Remember, they came in a yellow plastic case…?”

If you could see into my mind you would find it fixed on an image of a six-inch toy carpenter’s saw. You would quickly notice that its teeth are not very long or finely pointed yet the saw looks sharp enough to cut wood.

At least I tell myself it does as I climb the stairs. After

all, how sharp does a toy saw need to be to cut wood?

Yes that is right.

This too is what The Seekers would term a *Frozen Idea.*

Lesson 4

How To Identify Your Prophetic Navigational Device Then Learn To Ignore It

But what have we here?

Apparently Do-It-Yourself Workshops have their own automatic pilot function, or so it seems, because I am suddenly back in St. Christina's basement hall and my son Mickey is standing in front of me catching his breath. Unburdened by the fear that hovers like a rain cloud above his father, he has come running up in a flurry of excitement and barely concealed motivation. I know he wants something. I only need wait a few seconds to learn what it is.

But why wait?

"Something I can do for you?" I ask, tilting my head in a questioning gesture.

"I need a dollar," he answers, leaning against my leg, still breathing hard. "For an orange soda!"

"You do not *need* a dollar," I answer in my customary instructive manner. "You cannot *need* a dollar if you do not *need* an orange soda. What you really mean is you *want* a dollar, is that right?"

"Yeah," he says, flicking away my train of logic with a quick grimace and a blink of his eyes, his usual defense against unpleasant ideas.

"But I love orange soda," he pursues with a whining air of self-justification as if his desire can easily overshadow my logic. "Can I have a dollar, Dad? Can I?"

"And...?" I say, expectantly.

"And what...?" he asks.

"And what little word am I waiting to hear...?"

"Please!" he growls with a facial gesture that indicates how close he is to running out of patience.

"Well, since you are so polite..." I say, pushing him back so I can place our foolishly festive racecar safely beneath my seat. Upright again, I take out my wallet and hand over a dollar bill.

"Do not spend it all in one place," I advise him.

"I won't," he responds with an impish smile.

"Bring me any change."

As I bend down to retrieve Old Number Two, he impishly repeats, "I won't,"—the wise guy!—and hurries off.

He certainly loves orange soda; he was right about that.

And I was right to give him the dollar of course, since a can of orange soda is not that big a deal. Which may be obvious to anyone witnessing our brief interchange but not to someone like myself whose father was often difficult about 'unnecessary' expenditures.

When you wanted something from my father it was hardly worth working up the courage to ask for it. In the right sort of mood my father would dole out the money and perhaps even enjoy doing so. But most of the time he was not in the right sort of mood. Which meant he would more likely offer my siblings or me a menacing scowl along with whatever small change was involved or shrug off the request with four words I grew to hate as they echoed throughout the course of my childhood.

"You don't need it," he would say time and again. Simple, indisputable, powerfully conclusive: "You don't need it."

My father was right of course if you wish to get technical about such things. Why would we need anything other than a roof over our heads, clothes on our backs and food in our stomachs? Most everything else, according to Dad, was strictly an optional add-on.

You could argue about it of course if you cared to risk a smack in the mouth or a slap on the behind—two of my father's more persuasive debating techniques.

Suddenly a voice pulls me from my childhood memories.

"Got a story to tell you, Peterson," the voice says, sounding like a pronouncement from a radio announcer. But it is not a radio announcer, merely Bill McAndrews, a plastic bag salesman of all things.

McAndrews is sitting next to me, as you can see. He is

the large sized fellow on my left who like myself is somewhat bald—balder than me as you can easily see. He has a deep resonant voice that could have easily led to a career in broadcasting had the lure of plastic bags proved less compelling.

You would be shocked to learn how much money one can make selling plastic bags!

McAndrews is one of the few cub scout fathers here today whom I actually know. I have met others of course, but not often enough to fix their names in my memory.

"What kind of story?" I ask, gathering my senses.

"It'll just show you the madness I have to contend with," he pronounces grandly as he loves to do.

"I was up in Manchester last week...", he continues, not waiting for me or anyone else to express interest in his story. "I told you I'd been given southern New Hampshire, didn't I?"

"I wish someone would give me a state," I respond dryly.

"That's good!" he booms appreciatively in his richly modulated voice. "Very good! But to get back to Manchester...I was visiting a company that distributes to hardware stores, the kind of business that lives and breathes plastic bags. There was a fellow behind the counter, office manager type, must have been the original trusted retainer, know what I mean? Protecting the silver candlesticks, keeping fires lit to frighten off wolves—not too large in mental capacity but loyal as a rock. You get the picture?"

"Uh-huh."

"Actually, I was there with one of my salesmen, Sal Landers, a young guy I've been breaking in," he continues, unaware that my mind and attention are drifting off into other realms.

I have no interest in his story and little fear that McAndrews will think me rude or unkind for my abstraction.

This act of cutting myself free from Bill McAndrews is very different from allowing consciousness to slip away unintentionally. In purposefully removing myself from Bill McAndrews' influence I am obeying one of the basic tenets of The Seekers For Truth which, typically, they phrased in an easily remembered rhyme:

Place consciousness where you choose, not where you lose.

According to The Seekers it is no minor matter to give

your attention to negative or false influences. Whatever you attend to, they warn, is essentially what you become. Of course this is not some child's game where the devil catches you watching dirty movies, shouts *"You're it!"* and you immediately become a syphilitic idiot. The transformation, whether for good or bad, takes place over a period of time.

But make no mistake, your individual consciousness absorbs and enlivens whatever you give it to. And if you continually feed it negativity, selfish values, manipulative relationships and bad companions you are likely to end up far less evolved than Mother Teresa in your next go-around.

By the way, The Seekers For Truth place no judgment on that. There is no right or wrong in their book, only the question of whether your actions put you further ahead or further behind on your personal *Path Of Seeking Truth* as they like to call it. A path which inevitably leads, I have often been told, to the *Center Point of the Universe.*

Yes all roads on The Journey lead to the *CPU*. The same *Center Point of The Universe* to which I presently find myself in such close proximity.

Are you listening to any of this?

ILE, CPU, Path Of Seeking Truth!

Sounds like I am speaking in a foreign tongue.

At times I marvel at The Seekers use of language. As an advertising copywriter I have always appreciated the way they employ marketing techniques not only to sell their ideas but to make those ideas more memorable. It would not surprise me to learn that a few Madison Avenue advertising-types were sprinkled among The School's original founders.

Take the way they use acronyms to create metaphors! Like *ILE,* one's Individual Life Experience. It not only sounds like an island but The Seekers speak about it *as if it were an island!*

How better to underscore the loneliness of our solitary existence, the essential reality of being marooned in an individual body for a lifetime, than by referring to that lifetime as an island?

According to The Seekers' view of the cosmos, each of us is in fact an island. An island cut off from the unity of creation. And just as an island cannot exist without a surrounding body of water, we are surrounded and kept separate by a sea of forgetfulness. This, they would tell you, is the essence of the journey: to wake up, realize you are on an island then swim across those fathomless waters back to the mainland.

"There is no great mystery other than this," The Bapucharya once said. "Wake up, children, and realize it is *you* the Bible speaks about. *You* are the prodigal son. *You* are the lost sheep for which the shepherd leaves the other 99 behind. *You* are the treasure buried on Treasure Island; though I realize that it is not so much a biblical story…" Here again His Holiness' words dissolved into a non-guru-like spate of giggles.

Other Seeker metaphors are just as unique.

Take *PuNDit* for example, which stands for an individual's Prophetic Navigational Device.

Essentially the *PuNDit* is a warning mechanism buried so deep within the Spiritual Center that only those whose essences are "almost fully cooked", as The Bapucharya likes to say, can realize and benefit from its presence.

At lower levels, for those who have not yet traveled too far on their Paths Of Seeking Truth, the *PuNDit* expresses itself anonymously in other centers, helping them discriminate right from wrong, good from bad, helpful from harmful.

My 12-year-old daughter Cathy has a particularly well-developed *PuNDit,* which helps explain her decisions to become a vegetarian and to use her weekly allowance to sponsor a five-year-old Guatemalan orphan named Conchita.

If you are not aware of your own Prophetic Navigational Device think back to instances where something alerted you to hidden dangers or made you follow your duty instead of your desires—good impulses rather than bad. The signal could have been as subtle as a vague unease or as obvious as the voice of your conscience. Most often, when it is not whispering in one's ear, the *PuNDit* makes its presence felt as a pulse that throbs lightly in the center of the forehead in the exact position of the third eye.

For a senior level Seeker Of Truth, however, when a particular individual or circumstance presents a negative spiritual influence the *PuNDit's* alarm immediately goes off.

Usually dispensing its warning in proportion to the perceived danger. Again there is no judgment implied, only a concern with a student's progress on his or her Path Of Seeking Truth.

Most members of The Seekers For Truth become senior level students by their seventh or eighth year, so my *PuNDit* was highly developed by the time I resigned after 15 years in the school. Unfortunately for me, my *PuNDit* appears to be the one Self Actuation Device *(SAD)* that did not diminish in power or intensity after I left the school.

But more about that in a moment...

In my present circumstances owing to the proximity of certain--let us call them 'non-spiritual'—influences, my *PuNDit* is sounding a mild warning; what I term a Code Yellow Alert: apprehensive but not alarmed. You can probably hear it yourself if you listen closely. It sounds like a rhythmic 'click', as if someone were playing with a retractable ballpoint pen.

I remember when they first introduced the concept of a Prophetic Navigational Device.

"Each of has an internal pundit," Miss Barber, co-director of the Boston school, told our senior men's class. Wearing the school's regulation ankle-length skirt she walked over to the whiteboard at the front of the classroom and asked, "Who knows what a pundit is?"

Well-accustomed to this Socratic dialogue we called out answers one after another, a few of which Miss Barber chose to transcribe onto the board in neatly written block letters.

"A wise man," "A guru," "A teacher," the senior men in my class called out. When Martin Simons hesitatingly offered, "A prophet?" Miss Barber shouted, "Yes, precisely!" and added the word with brisk resounding strokes of her marker.

"We are talking about a *Pundit,*" she reminded us, vigorously erasing all the other words on the board before writing out *PuNDit* with half the letters capitalized. Then below the word she wrote the individual letters *P, N* and *D* in a vertical row leaving ample space for the additional letters that would eventually make up *Prophetic Navigational Device.*

As Miss Barber went on to explain, "The Prophetic Navigational Device was implanted by the Absolute Entity to provide you some assistance in staying on your Path Of Seeking Truth. It is an organ of Spirit. As you already know, just as you have organs of the body you also have organs of Spirit. The purpose of this organ is to sound the alarm whenever something is about to tempt you off your Path Of Seeking Truth—away from your true self, and away from your own best interests.

"Like the prophets of ancient Israel," Miss Barber concluded with what she undoubtedly regarded as her punch line, "your *PuNDit* will only come down from the mountain when you stray off the path of righteousness."

Pretty clunky stuff, huh?

Sometimes The Seekers For Truth could get a little heavy-handed with their biblical analogies. When you listen to some of their verbal acrobatics outside the context of the school it sounds as if someone is up in the attic stomping around in heavy rubber boots.

Speaking of which, I doubt my next-chair neighbor Bill McAndrews hears much of anything except the resonant sound of his own voice.

McAndrews is actually a pretty good storyteller. It is just that his stories tend to repeat themselves...here, this is a good example! Once again he is proclaiming his passion for making sales calls on total strangers.

"You know, Peterson," he confides, lowering his volume for effect, "most salesmen despise cold calls, but I love them. They're marrow to my bones."

"Really?"

"Absolutely!" he booms. "A cold call is all about power—who has the most, who uses it best? It's a power struggle in its purest form—you alone against the almighty prospective customer—and I'm the type that generally rises to the top in power struggles. I always thought I should have been born in a Communist state."

I am not certain why someone who enjoys power struggles should be born in a Communist state but my minor interest is not strong enough to transcend my galloping indifference. Some other time I might choose to listen to his story—surprisingly it is not one I have heard before—but I am not in a mood to be steamrolled by an incontinent storyteller. Not while Mickey stands so close to the edge of disaster. And certainly not while other attractions in this church basement seem infinitely more worthy of my attention.

I say that because my eyes have once again fallen upon the attractive, full-bodied, female form sitting directly behind McAndrews. A cub scout mother no doubt, she is wearing a bulky, oatmeal-brown turtleneck sweater and appears by all the usual indicators to reciprocate some of my casual interest.

I have not had a chance to speak with her yet. Having McAndrews for a neighbor does not allow for long unbroken silences. Our eyes have met once or twice and we briefly exchanged polite, cautious smiles, but otherwise I have done little except luxuriate in the proximity of her fulsome attractions.

I do not know if you can hear it but my sparked interest in the cub scout mother, as casual as it might appear, has turned up the dial on my *PuNDit's* alarm. The pulse in the middle of my forehead throbs louder and steadier now with a deeper resonance than a clicking pen yet still within the limits of a Code Yellow Alert.

Do not ask me why my *PuNDit* has remained active all these years I have been out of The Seekers' school, sounding its alarm whenever I am drawn to certain influences and most annoyingly whenever I find myself amorously engaged. I suppose it is still diligently working to prevent the dissipation of any sexual energy which could otherwise be transformed into spiritual energy. Spiritual energy, as The Seekers proclaim, providing the best and purest fuel for one's journey along the Path Of Seeking Truth.

But why me? And why after all these years?

Seven years ago I resigned from The Seekers For Truth but I still cannot find a way to resign from my *PuNDit!*

When I was with The Seekers I was told the *PuNDit* was programmed to inflict itself only on *senior* students, those who had been in the school long enough to forge a solid spiritual commitment. Nobody ever said a word about senior students who left the school! Nobody ever said the commitment was unbreakable. Nobody ever told us we would be married to our *PuNDits* for life.

And speaking of marriage, as far as I can recall the *PuNDit* never sounded the alarm on *married* students no matter how much sexual energy we dissipated. So it was not until two years after leaving The Seekers, right after my marriage fell apart, that I discovered two previously unknown facts about my *PuNDit.* First, now that I was single again it clearly regarded any sexual activities with what I would call prudish, overactive concern. And second, there was no apparent way to shut the damn thing off!

Which means that when my interest is drawn to a desirable woman like the one behind McAndrews I only have two real choices concerning my *PuNDit's* predictable show of concern. I can either turn my attention to safer, more spiritually rewarding items of interest such as reading the Bible or watching a Disney movie. Or I can say 'to hell with it!' and do my damnedest to ignore the *PuNDit's* censorious throbbing.

Having no interest in living my life as an asexual biology specimen I decided I would not relinquish healthy sexual pursuits for a life of chaste, unfettered progress on my Path Of Seeking Truth.

Taking a page from The Seekers' book I created my own rhyming aphorism which declared: *Better to let my* PuNDit *thump away than to give up humping and other play!*

And speaking of humping did you notice the lady to my left is not wearing a wedding band?

For a single man like myself the ring finger is the second place you look when you notice an attractive woman.

Never mind about the first place.

Lesson 5

Presenting A Brief Study Of A Difficult Species

You would not notice of course but they are trying something different with this year's Pinewood Derby.

Instead of completing first round heats before going onto the following rounds they are alternating first round trials with second and third round elimination heats. Which explains why a repeat winner like Old Number Two, which started racing in the earliest rounds, can win half a dozen heats before some of the other entries have raced even once.

You can see for yourself the growing danger that represents for a racecar whose physical embarrassments become more evident as the competition thins out.

Suddenly I feel two small hands pulling on my shoulders from behind.

"Uh-oh," I cry, raising my hands in quick surrender. "We are under attack. Who could that be?"

"It's your worst nightmare," Mickey whispers into my ear, mimicking any number of movies we have seen together.

He squeezes through the chairs to stand in front of me as I predictably ask, "Did you say hello to Mr. McAndrews?"

"Hello," he dutifully responds.

"Hello, Michael," Bill answers broadly. "You've been burning up the field with that racer of yours!"

"I guess," Mickey answers back.

"Well, good luck with the rest of the Derby."

"Dad..." Mickey says, starting to reach for my hand.

"Sweetheart, Mr. McAndrews just wished you good luck. What do you say in response?"

He turns to Bill, dutifully offers, "Thank you!" then turns back to ask, more demanding than dutiful, "Can I have the racecar, Dad?"

"Another heat? So soon?" I ask, bending down to retrieve Old Number Two.

"I want to show it to Ernie's Dad," he explains. "They got 'liminated in their first race."

"EE-liminated," I correct him. "Unless you are saying they were made into lemonade."

"Yeah, right!" he responds, lifting our homely, forlorn enterprise out of my hands. "Gotta go," he says then turns and runs off.

Now this is interesting.

A little girl, most likely the sister of a cub scout, is standing a few feet away watching Mickey retreat into the distance. A blonde, blue-eyed wisp of a thing, no older than five or six, she wears a flowered print dress draped over brown corduroys and puffy pink snow boots.

I observe her as she watches Mickey vanish into the crowd, her face frozen in silent adoration. Somehow I know she has been following my little boy from pillar to post, drawn by an impulse too strong to resist though her shyness does not let her approach beyond a safe distance.

"Hello," I offer smiling, but the little girl, highly focused idol worshipper that she is, merely wrinkles her nose at me before running off in the general direction of my son.

It is a funny thing about Mickey, this attraction he holds for women; not just for young girls his age but for women of all sizes and denominations. His female teachers have always suffered a portion of their hearts to be melted into gooey distraction by his air of sweet innocence. It has become such a consistent feminine reaction that I take it for granted.

For his part, women only confuse my little boy. He lives among them, shares their bread and sleeps under the same roof but still he cannot understand them; cannot translate or comprehend the subtle software of their operating systems.

Time and again I have seen him observing his older sisters and their friends, watching for clues that would help explain or predict their behavior.

"Dad," he once asked in studied confusion, "girls are funny, aren't they?"

"Yes," I answered. "They are different from us...but very nice," I hastened to add.

Still puzzling it out he pursued, “Were they like that when you were my age?”

“Yes, they were” I replied. “Exactly like that. It is the way they are made. They act funny when they are young, and they act funny when they are older; just in a different way.”

“I don’t think I understand.”

“I think this is one of those things you have to learn for yourself when you are a grownup.”

After pausing to contemplate the idea he answered, “That’s cool”, his way of affirming the rightness of things, even those too difficult for a nine-year-old to comprehend.

It is not easy to be a small boy in a world of big sisters. You are never smart enough, fast enough or cool enough to satisfy anyone. Your jokes are never funny. Your opinions are never worth listening to. And your feelings...well all bets are off when your sisters see you crying.

Cathy and Suzie are two of the hardest, tough-minded, rough-talking sisters in creation...until the first droplets begin to roll from their brother’s large brown eyes.

Well they are, after all, his big sisters and deep down they do love him and how can they help but break down and show their true feelings when they see giant tears running down his apple red cheeks?

But most of the time Mickey is not crying, which means most of the time his sisters have little solace or good-hearted attention to share with him. And the few instances where his tears have warmed their hearts I marvel at how someone who has been made to suffer so frequently by these young women can allow himself to be drawn so easily to their embraces in the clutch of a moment?

For his part, my little boy does not concern himself with such discrepancies. He is pleased to suck up their affection when it falls his way, thirsty desert flower that he is.

Funny to think that my little boy and his sisters are the happy results of an otherwise ambivalent marriage with a woman who vowed her love but proved to have more affection for our house and garden.

Difficult to remember now but I used to laugh at Marilyn’s compulsion to be so demanding. Back when I thought we were happily married she would often say things that underscored how much higher her expectations were than mine. Invariably I would tell myself, "That is just Marilyn," usually with a laugh and an air of grudging approval.

Now I see what I never let myself acknowledge back then; that she was a woman intent on getting what she wanted no matter what price I was forced to pay.

Another lesson learned. A lesson I will not share with my children, at least not until they are grown up. They love their mother and rightly so. She has been a good mother to them all the time she has been a torment to me. It would only cause them pain to witness my anger and frustration. Truth be told it would only take them farther away from me and they are far enough away as it is.

Still my relationship with Marilyn would be an excellent case study to highlight the underlying differences between men and women.

Let me show you what I mean.

I am beginning to get the hang of piloting this Do-It-Yourself Workshop and it seems almost effortless now to return to specific events from my past, to the time even when Marilyn and I were still married. There is one special conversation I have in mind...

Yes I know. It is dark.

That is because I am sitting in a darkened room. Sitting alone—'all-one' as The Seekers might say—in the darkness of our living room at St. Bart's Bay struggling to undo the knots and pressures of a long, seemingly endless day of work. That beautiful music you hear echoing through the darkness is the sound of a George Winston piano solo, "Thanksgiving", a piece of music that possesses almost magical healing properties.

As your eyes adjust to the lack of light you will notice I am sitting in a heavily stuffed chair, my feet on a matching ottoman, my eyes closed as I drift in reverie.

I can feel the tension oozing from my pores. It has been a long day's journey to arrive at this moment but now the day is done, my work is finished, my dinner consumed and the children are asleep in their beds.

Oh yes and Marilyn is reading in the kitchen.

Well sort of reading...

"Paul, did you look at the toilet yet?" she calls through the closed kitchen door, the words barely penetrating the darkness or the soothing mood.

"What?" I answer, vaguely aware that someone has said something.

"The toilet?" she repeats, this time louder. "Have you fixed it yet?"

"Was I using it?" I call back, slightly distracted.

"You said you were going to fix it," she reminds me in her raised voice.

I can almost see her turning the page in her book, almost visualize her eyes following the words as she begins to manipulate my mood with mechanical ease.

"I will do it this weekend," I finally answer, hoping to end the discussion.

"Paul!" she responds with mounting impatience. "The gurgling keeps me up all night. Would you please take care of it *tonight*...like you said you would."

It would offer little instruction to Mickey or to anyone else to stay here and continue this conversation. After lodging an obligatory protest I submit to my fate and head upstairs. Five minutes later I once again face the concept of failure on my *ILE*. Toilets being the disagreeable appliances they are, ours will not allow itself to be fixed, at least not this evening—at least not by me!

This experience as mundane as it appears might one day prove highly instructive for my little boy. What better way to prepare him for his own imperfect relationships than to identify the subtle nuances buried near the surface in this brief interchange between husband and wife?

What did you notice about the conversation, I would ask? Did you observe your mother's use of language? Did you pay particular attention to the simple devices she employed to achieve a gentle sort of domination?

It was almost artful.

"...did you look at the toilet yet?" she asked, the use of the word "yet" indicating the patience she had already exhausted in dealing with this situation. *"You said you were*

going to fix it" highlighted how tightly stretched were the seams of my credibility. *"The gurgling keeps me up all night"* showed how insensitive I have been in previously avoiding this simple task. And of course, *"...like you said you would"* spoke volumes about my lack of commitment, not to mention my inability to keep my word.

Where is one supposed to keep his word anyway?

Mickey keeps miniature figurines on his dresser; tiny animal figures made from all kinds of materials and substances. Perhaps one day when he outgrows such novelties he will replace them with a collection of all the words he intends to keep.

But I am wandering...

Going back to the instructive value of Marilyn's seemingly casual assault on my reverie I would then ask my little boy if he had noticed the timing of his mother's intrusion? Because up until the moment she broke the silence we had basically achieved an equality of circumstance.

I would point out that neither of us was engaged in an activity that took precedence over the other's. We were not dealing with the demands of our children or doing anything for the communal good. We were merely following our own personal pursuits, each tending to his or her own needs. I do not claim my activity had more intrinsic value than hers. Reading her book was certainly equal in importance to my meditating in the darkness with George Winston.

There lay the problem, I would tell my little boy! Equality was of little or no interest to his mother. Somewhere in the house a toilet was gurgling and through its noise and persistent bubbling it was determined to undermine the foundations of a marriage.

But I will not tell such stories to my little boy. Not until he is much older and maybe not even then. Rather than teach him about the differences between men and women the story would only frighten him about the impact those differences might one day have on his life.

Besides, my little boy loves his mother.

If I know him at all he will probably in all fairness point out that I, his procrastinating father, never got around to fixing the toilet.

Lesson 6

Keeping An Eye Out For Janitors And Other Guest Lecturers

But what is this?

This is not where I intended to go.

Nor the moment in time I meant to visit next.

And I was feeling so cocky about my burgeoning navigational skills!

For some reason whoever is in charge of the cosmic gearworks has made an independent decision about the next destination—or subject matter—for my Do-It-Yourself Workshop.

Which is why I suppose I have been drawn back to this second floor apartment in Plymouth with its inebriated strongwoman and dog-haired furniture. Only this time you will notice I am watching events unfold from an entirely different perspective.

Do you see where I am?

No, no, up here, higher up!

I know you can see Paul Peterson down there still being dragged in slow motion by Allison across her living room floor, but can you also discern that simultaneously I am up here hovering close to the ceiling...?

Ironically it makes me feel light-headed even though I no longer occupy a body or a head.

Yes for some reason I have been momentarily set free from the restrictions of the physical world and I am floating above everything—myself included—in this shabbily appointed room. My consciousness hovers somewhere near the ceiling, I would judge, totally free of my body and tucked into a corner of the room. Yet something nags at me; something off-balance or unexpected.

Perhaps it is that strange odor?

What is that?

Some sort of scent I suppose. It is sweet and flowery, almost like incense. Nothing I noticed Allison wearing, or even smelled in her apartment earlier. Of course maybe it was there and I was too caught up in the swirl of events or the swell of her breasts to notice.

But look at us down there...!

Suddenly I am surprised by the sound of laughter and quickly realize it is coming from me.

I cannot help it. I have to laugh. Have you ever seen anything that looked half so funny?

Look how comical we appear, Allison and I, arms entangled, voices dueling, as we move in our slow motion dance across the length of the living room toward that silent jumbo couch? You could not choreograph a funnier scene for a movie; but the fact that it is not being staged—is actually happening on its own—is probably why our awkward tango seems so side-splittingly funny.

I hear the two of us arguing down there, hear Allison shushing me repeatedly as she tries to overcome my half-hearted protests. But for some reason the sound of my breath rushing through my nostrils feels closer to me in this instant—and louder—than the sound of the voices below. Which is funny if you think about it because up here I do not have a body, much less nostrils for my breath to pass through.

"That is still your body down there," a familiar voice declares in a highly nasal Indian accent. "You are both up *here* and down *there* at the same time, my young friend. And it shall be much more worrisome," he giggles, " if you do *not* hear yourself breathing!"

That voice? The accent? The gleeful, childlike laughter...?

"Oh dear, what a mess, what a mess!" the voice continues in a bubbly, amused manner I not only recognize but am bewildered to hear.

What is going on?

"Do not start with the questions, please!" the voice of His Holiness The Bapucharya instructs. Like me—or at least the 'me' that floats near the ceiling—he is without a body. But trust me he has a presence so strong I can almost see him in my mind's eye.

"But I am...confused?" I explain weakly.

"Of course you are confused. That is why I have traveled across the universe to speak with you."

"To speak with me?"

"Why else? Certainly not for the rewards! Bapucharyas do not earn frequent flyer miles." A joke he finds highly amusing, judging by the burst of giggles that follow.

"Speak to me about what, Holiness?"

"About what?" he says incredulously. "Look at yourself down there—and you ask *about what?* That is quite a stew you are cooking, Mr. Peterson! I turn my back on you for less time than it takes the universe to breathe one tiny little breath and what do I find? What a grand screw-up you have made of things! Your clothes are about to be torn from your body by a crazy lady of the highest insanity, your son is about to be—ohmigosh!—so painfully embarrassed before the entire assembly of the Boy Scouts of America..."

"Cub scouts!" I weakly protest. "And it is just a *pack*— a cub scout *pack."*

"Yes, of course, such a big difference to have yourself exposed fully naked before cub scouts rather than boy scouts," he quips, peppering the words with cheery amusement.

"But Your Holiness..."

"Please allow me to finish."

"Excuse me."

"...and here you are, allowed by divine grace and The Bapucharya to come closer to the *CPU* than a Harvard Divinity student. Here where childish complaints and petty grievances are like dust particles in the wind. And what is it you are doing? You are clinging to each particle of dust as if it were gold!"

"I do not..."

"Again you interrupt?"

"No, no, continue! I am sorry."

"You are making yourself into such a victim, Mr. Peterson, it is all I can do to keep watching your movie! *This crazy lady* does that to you, *that cruel ex-wife* does this to you; and where is the part where *you* do anything other than complain, I am wondering?

"Look at yourself down there: a lamb being drawn to its slaughter! It is not what is happening in your fate that keeps you in that wild lady's grip, but what is happening in your pants. Do you not see that? This is not a Do-It-Yourself Workshop, I am thinking. This is a melodrama! A melodrama of questionable entertainment value, a grade B movie, nothing more!

"...and so I ask myself what should a Bapucharya do? You have been given a gift, young sir, and you are squandering it like popcorn falling from a box in the movies. Well, there is only so much popcorn that can fall before the box becomes empty!

"And so someone must have the kindness to shake you roughly and wake you up. Who shall that be? Is there someone else besides a Bapucharya?"

He sprinkles the air with a few self-amused giggles before answering, "I do not think so, Mr. I'm-so-confused-and-victimized."

I listen to The Bapucharya's words and wonder what in God's name he is talking about? None of this makes any sense to me!

And what is he doing here? Never once in my fifteen years with The Seekers did I hear of The Bapucharya personally visiting anyone. As far as I know, no one from the Boston School had *ever* seen him outside the confines of a video monitor.

Of course I am not exactly seeing him right now either.

An amusing question crosses my mind about etiquette of all things! The Seekers For Truth place great importance on the observance of proper protocol and rituals, but how is one disembodied person supposed to act as host to another? How do you welcome a voice hovering near a ceiling? I cannot offer him anything to eat or drink. Not even a place to sit down.

"You can stop asking yourself such silly questions," The Bapucharya directs, breaking into my thoughts. "That would most definitely be a good way for a host to act. But we have had enough chit-chat, I am thinking. Now we have work to do."

"Work?"

"Would you call it, 'play?' I am here, Mr. Peterson, because it is no longer possible to sit quietly and watch your movie. Oh yes, there is no shortage of drama and tragedy in your movie, but where is the comedy? Something to make me laugh and feel good. Except for the part where the crazy lady tries to rescue the hero's sexual organs from his pants there is nothing to laugh about..."

Again I have to wait while The Bapucharya gets carried away by his own childish humor.

"Excuse me," he apologizes as the laughter subsides.

"All that aside, young sir, I am here! Certainly here in spirit, if not body. And I am sure you would like to know why! After all, did you not remove your partially-cooked essence from my frying pan? Did you not retire from the Seekers For Truth many years ago? Yet here I am interrupting your regularly scheduled programming once again...?

"Well, Mr. Peterson, there is no removing yourself from Bapu's frying pan; there is only *thinking* you have removed yourself. If I allowed every lamb to wander away, what kind of a shepherd would I be? A sheepless shepherd, I am thinking...

"That is good: a sheepless shepherd!" he repeats, his merriment again bubbling up. "I must remember that for my next embodiment."

"I do not understand, Holiness."

"Of course, you do not understand. If you were capable of understanding, you would not be down there with Ms. Allison Pratt, stubbornly stuck between Mr. Ping and Mr. Pong, fighting to preserve the very celibacy you are so anxious to relinquish. And what foolishness is that, we may wish to ask?

"No, young sir, if you understood half of what is happening to you, *you* would be The Bapucharya and I would be out of a job."

"But what are you doing here, Holiness?" I cautiously probe. "What do you want from me?"

"I want nothing *from* you, my young friend. But what do I wish *for* you?—that is the question! And why am I here? That is another question."

I see my chance.

"Yes, Holiness, why are you here?"

"Why am I here, you ask? Excellent question, Mr. Peterson! I am here because of a promise I have made to guide The Seekers For Truth through periods of darkness, whatever that may signify. And you, my young friend, are surrounded by darkness...in your present period." He laughs, pleased at himself for his clever wordplay with 'period' and 'darkness'.

"But when a Bapucharya makes such a promise," he continues, "it does not mean he can sit back and write fancy letters to the managers of the universe. There are times when personal intervention is the only remedy that will do the job.

"You, my young friend, are no less a concern of mine because you walked away from our school. One does not abandon one's children because they challenge your authority. And now, it is clear to me, that you require totally my premium personal guidance service, and so I have inserted myself into your Do-It-Yourself Workshop at the first reasonable opportunity. You will not object, I hope, if I interrupt your movie for a brief commercial message?" he asks, the question obviously worthy of a few more giggles.

"But your voice, your presence..." I question, "they seem so close, Holiness...?"

"That is because *I am so close!* There is no one closer to you than me. I am like that sticky paper you accidentally step on which stays stuck on your shoe wherever you go. You cannot get rid of me by walking faster. Nor can you turn into dark corners and strange alleys to shake me lose. And if you wiggle your foot in the air to shake me free," he adds, his voice sparkling with merriment," I am sorry, but you will merely look like a monkey passing gas!

"Think about it! If you are near the *CPU* and I am seated exactly at the center of the *CPU,* what does that make us if not neighbors?"

"But what do you want of me?" I challenge, frustrated by my inability to make any sense of this. "I left The Seekers seven years ago...?"

"No, my young friend, that is not quite true. You fool yourself into believing you can say *'bye-bye!'* to The Seekers

For Truth. But you can no sooner quit being a Seeker For Truth than you can wake up in the morning, look into the mirror and say 'Today I stop being bald,' or 'Mirror, I think I have had enough of this being Jewish,' or 'Starting tomorrow I will no longer be a six footer'.

"I would probably understand all of this if I were further advanced," I suggest. "Is that right, Holiness?"

"If you like. But I am not coming here to create new mysteries or celebrate old ones. I am here to help you understand the boatload of lessons that are being shipped to your *ILE*—with no rush charges, thank you—by your current predicaments."

"Which predicaments are those...exactly?"

"Oh my! So many predicaments to choose from, which ones shall I choose? We shall see, young sir, but before we go on—please to get off your chest what has been sitting there since my unkind reference to your baldness... "

I pause to consider my next words.

"Well, if we are being truthful, Holiness, I must mention that I am not really bald!" I reply respectfully. "A bald person has no hair on the top of his head. I have hair; it is just thin on top."

"Thank you, thank you," he replies enthusiastically. "Now we can get on with far less important matters like the fate of your son's wellbeing, the welfare of your soul and bridging any gaps we may find on your *PATH OF SEEKING TRUTH!"*

He speaks these last words so loudly I instinctively reach to cover my ears. Only, as I sharply discover, I have no ears nor hands with which to cover them.

"Thank goodness," The Bapucharya says with almost imperious sarcasm, "we have determined for the first-ever time that your lack of baldness results from the presence of thin hair on the top of your head."

Having nothing to add I remain silent while he falls into yet another fit of giggles.

"Laugh, young sir!" he suddenly commands. "Or at least have the wisdom to smile! As you have heard me say many times, a smile can be the mouse's tail by which the happy mood is snagged.

"But anyway," he continues, pretending to become serious, "for some time I have been listening to your complaints and I have been wanting like the dickens to change the channel or turn off the telly.

"Do you listen to yourself speak about this poor man who is so abused by his former wife? All melodrama and poorly written, if you are asking me!

"I listen to you and I wonder who is this woman you are talking about? When did Marilyn become this devilishly evil and controlling lady of the suburbs? Was she not greatly in love with you all the years you were together? Did she not love you without question even after you abandoned her…?"

"Abandoned her?" I react, sharply stung by the thought. "I…I do not know what you are talking about. What do you mean I abandoned her, Holiness?"

"But you remember that you removed yourself from the Seekers school; you remember that, do you not? And that you left Marilyn to be a Seeker For Truth all by herself? You are remembering that, too, are you not?"

"Yes. But she and I…we talked about it together. I did not just leave. I knew it was something that could bring problems to the marriage. We had seen it happen to Charles and Lucy Brigg's marriage. And to—what was their names, the couple from South Africa…?"

"Are you meaning Payton and Jane?"

"Yes, Payton and Jane Salazar! Marilyn and I were pretty close to them for a while. So we knew that other marriages had fallen apart when one member of a couple left the school and the other stayed. But what else could I do? It would have been dishonest to stay when I was feeling the way I felt. And it would have been wrong to ask Marilyn to leave. So what choice did I have?"

"Oh, what a tragic person you can become! *"What choice did I have? What else could I do? Tell me, Bapucharya, what was a poor boy to do?"*

"Well it seemed that way to me!"

"I am curious to hear what Marilyn said when you told her you were having to leave?"

"I cannot remember."

"That is why there are Bapucharyas. We remember *eve-*

rything! Marilyn told you she was afraid. She asked if you were afraid, and...oh, I see—*now* you are remembering!"

"Yes, it is coming back. I remember we agreed to give it a try—my leaving, I mean—and if it seemed like a threat to our marriage I would come back to the school."

"Well, I am guessing it has still not proven a threat to your marriage because you have not yet returned to The Seekers For Truth," he says, pausing briefly before adding with a hint of impish amusement, "Or so it seems."

"Our marriage fell apart almost three years later," I continue, choosing to ignore the implications of that last remark. "And not because I left the school but because of Marilyn's feelings. Simply put, she fell out of love with me. She as much as said so half a dozen times while we were in counseling."

"Oh yes, how could I forget? You are such a fine analyzer of why things happen! It is good to have people like you in the neighborhood to help The Bapucharya understand the workings of the universe.

"What else do you understand? Not the workings of a toilet! And certainly not a toilet that would be so inconsiderate as to break into your relaxation after a long day of exhausting work! I can hear the quiet tinkling of George Winston's piano now and the gentle gurgling of your toilet. It is a symphony of disharmony, is it not? But you! You only remember Marilyn mentioning the toilet after you had come to rest in the darkness of the living room."

"And, yes...so?"

"So, it is a very convenient memory you are having, Mr. Peterson. I remember things not so conveniently. In my memory Marilyn is trying to speak with you about the gurgling of the toilet earlier that evening, during dinner, and it is you who are barking like an angry dog, *"Do we have to talk about this now, while I am eating? I will take care of it after dinner."*

Those words—*my words!*—come back to me the instant I hear them. And the voice sounds like mine, the way it sounded all those years ago...

I forgot that I had said that...that we...I had forgotten.

"But that is enough for now," The Bapucharya abruptly

declares. “My contract stipulates I will only do so much heavy lifting in one sitting.” His words are once again truncated by high-pitched, nasal giggles.

Finding nothing to say I offer no response.

A moment later The Bapucharya sighs theatrically and says, “I am starting to wonder about you, Mr. Peterson. Perhaps it would be better to have a sense of humor implanted in your Spiritual Center before we perform our janitorial duties.”

“Our what…?”

“Janitorial duties. What else would I be calling them? Why else are we here, hovering close to the ceiling without clothes or bodies, if not to clean up your act?”

“Clean up my act?” I repeat, incredulous.

“Yes, clean up your act,” he repeats with solemn assurance. “What else is a Bapucharya for?

“And, please—while I am thinking of it—remember to *drink your RC Cola!*”

Lesson 7

Some Tips For Retaining Consciousness In The Middle Of A Busy Intersection

I hear a voice.

A voice that is not floating near the ceiling.

My eyes are closed and the voice breaks through the darkness of my shuttered eyes like the dawn racing in after a long night, instantly erasing any lingering presence of The Bapucharya.

I open my eyes and...wait!

Before I turn to respond to the owner of the voice let me take a moment to gather my senses. It is no easy transition from conversing in a disembodied state with a Hindu holy man to being flung back almost without warning into a Pinewood Derby cruising along in high gear.

I pull out my cell phone to check the time, almost stunned to discover I have been sitting here with my eyes closed for—could that be right?—for mere seconds. *Maybe less!*

The Bapucharya's visit, the entire confusing conversation—it all happened in the time it takes to blink an eye; all of it compressed into the tiniest sliver of physical time.

I would continue to ponder the incredible nature of time but the voice has other plans.

"That was a close one," the voice says with a deep-throated, sultry resonance that sets trumpets blaring and pennants waving across the unsettled landscape my mind. It is referencing, I assume, the last derby heat which has just ended though cheers from the crowd still echo through the reaches of this crowded church basement.

Make no mistake, this is no ordinary voice.

Deep and throaty, worn rough by years of smoking, imbued with a sexy sort of wariness that seems to suggest it could unexpectedly dive headlong into a sea of bawdy laughter, this voice has the power to stir a man's thoughts. Its sandpaper texture and soft intimate inflection cast off a surprising familiarity that makes the hair on the back of my neck, if not exactly stand up, at least start to tingle.

Not surprisingly my *PuNDit* has also been stirred. I feel it pulsing aggressively now in the center of my forehead. As always it has the curious effect of making me pay closer attention to whatever is happening in the moment. In effect forcing me to *drink my RC Cola.*

Have you begun to see what this business of *drinking your RC Cola* is all about?

Resting In Consciousness?

Paying close attention to whatever is happening in the present moment?

Sounds simple yet there is nothing more difficult.

It requires you to fix on something so strongly in the present moment that you cannot be lured away by the movements of the mind as they are called—the thousand and one sensations, impressions, ideas and whimsies that pass through the mind like traffic moving through a busy intersection. It is almost impossible to keep your undivided attention on the intersection itself rather than have it swept away by the fast-moving vehicles passing through.

The Bapucharya once told us, "If you can *Drink Your RC Cola* for ten full seconds you will no longer need a guru. You will *be* a guru!"

Of course he could not leave it at that.

"But I must warn you," he continued in his self-amused manner, "the pay and working conditions for gurus are not *'happy days are here again!'* We gurus are so neglected that I am thinking of starting a Guru's Betterment Society. Hah! How would that be?" he pressed his unseen audience, "A Guru's Betterment Society? I like that."

The Seekers' practices are so entwined with The Bapucharya's Hindu background that it should come as no surprise they rely on mantras to help stay connected to the present moment. To help them *drink their RC Cola.*

Remember what I said about the ultimate goal of our repeated visits to the planet?

To stay awake while the movie is playing.

Which is almost impossible without having some form of mantra to cling to.

"Consider the world around you," Mr. Samuelson, the Boston School leader, once explained in his proper British accent. "It is practically a storm, is it not? With winds blowing every which way at incredible velocities. So whether you are on land or sea, when the winds begin to pick up, you need to be anchored to something that will not be blown around with all the other debris. That is the purpose of your mantra. To which, if you wish to survive the storm, you had best fasten yourself with great purpose."

Most likely you already know this, but a mantra is a word or a group of words whose essence is as much vibration as it is a meaning or definition. When you begin your meditation you sound your mantra over and over at the beginning as though you were trying to start a reluctant engine. Then supposedly, once the engine catches, the mantra repeats on its own for the next 20 to 30 minutes during which time you attempt to give it your fullest attention. When you are going about your daily business, however, the mantra allows you to stay consciously focused on whatever activity or experience is foremost on your agenda.

To stay awake while the movie is playing.

That of course is what you are told—the party line—but my mantra never seems to understand its role nor give any indication of what alternate role it might prefer instead.

Though I was told to keep it an absolute secret, as if revealing its name to non-Seekers would diminish its power, I will risk disclosing that my mantra is *Higher Will* and that I am supposed to mentally intone "Higher" as I take in a breath and "Will" as I release that same breath.

Breathe in *Higher,* breathe out *Will*—as simple as that.

I do not know if there is anything particularly self-willed about the mantra or just my use of it, but generally my *Higher Will* seems to have a will of its own, repeating itself when—and only when—it wants, which is not very often. When I try to fire it up it at the beginning of a meditation it usually turns out to be what The Bapucharya laughingly reers to as the "...dead battery of a stalled-out meditation."

But still there are many for whom the mantra works as advertised, like a beacon lighting the way across the dark waters of the mind. I am certain they must be further up their Paths Of Seeking Truth and sure to reach the exact *Center Point of the Universe* far ahead of me.

For now I am quite content—and really it is quite an unexpected accomplishment—just to be *almost* at the *CPU, the Center Point of the Universe.* And if that turns out to be all I accomplish I will not complain.

The voice apparently growing impatient interrupts my thoughts to comment, "They're really something, these races, don't you think?"

Oh my goodness, the voice!

How could I have forgotten, you wonder? Or allow myself to be whisked away from the present moment by thoughts ironically about how difficult it can be to stay in the present moment? Idle thoughts that might on first blush seem relevant but were merely distractions passing through the busy intersection of my mind.

You see how the mind works?

But did I mention that the voice—that interruptive, persistent voice—belongs to a woman? A tall attractive, broad-figured woman at that?

You remember the large, decorous lady sitting behind McAndrews?

And did you hear what she just said?

"They're really something, these races, don't you think?"

With such an air of casual curiosity as if we were chummy single parents and not at all separated by anonymity or Bill McAndrews's empty chair whose back she now leans against.

"Excuse me?" I respond, pretending not to have understood. "Did you say something?"

In this particular mating ritual one is supposed to fabricate a certain lack of interest on first contact even if you have been directly staring at one another for six hours.

"I said that was a damned close race," she repeats. "I couldn't tell who won or lost. And those tiny tot racecars practically cross the finish line in front of us."

She is speaking, as I said, from behind the empty chair on my left which belongs to Bill McAndrews who has gone off to dispute, with thunderous articulation I am sure, an earlier racing decision that eliminated his son from the day's competition. Thus McAndrews has generously left the chair empty and the passage clear for any suburban mating rituals I care to pursue.

"Oh, I bet you can tell a winner when you see one," I declare with my most charming smile.

You can see how quickly the players move on from their opening expressions of casual disinterest.

She laughs lightly then leans toward me to ask, "Don't you think it's hot in here?" pulling at the rolled collar of her oatmeal-colored sweater.

Before I can answer, and not too sure I am supposed to, she continues with a series of comments strung together in the form of questions: "You ever have so much fun in one place? You're sure you're not hot? How long you think this is supposed to go on?" And lastly in response to my shrug of ignorance she stands up and looks around, her eyes eagerly scanning the outer perimeter of the room as she asks, "Isn't there some kind of food served at these kids functions; something to eat?" with her hands describing small circles in the air.

I resist the impulse to point across the room to where Mickey purchased his orange soda, choosing instead to silently observe her imposing figure from my vantage here below.

As you can probably tell, her standing up serves two immediate purposes. First of course it allows her to search the premises for any sign of a kitchen or snack counter. But more important it allows me from beneath the benevolent shadow of her breastworks to fantasize climbing up the long slopes of her alluring, almost beckoning womanhood.

Notice that my *PuNDit's* throbbing has accelerated dramatically, climbing out of Code Yellow into Code Orange and clearly signaling my rising interest.

As I indicated earlier she is tall for a woman, probably close to six feet, broadly built but still highly attractive. At a minimum she is two inches taller than my own modest height and if the truth were told carries a little too much heft for my customary taste in women. But I love her look, her casual style, the way her dark brown hair cascades over her forehead in bangs and lifts up gingerly towards the rear in a makeshift pony tail.

If she fails to reflect my usual standards for a desirable woman it may be time to have those standards re-calibrated. Or to make an exception for someone who appeals to me as much as she does.

Aside from guessing her to be in her mid-thirties and a cub scout Mom I know nothing about her. I do not know her name, who her son might be or what religion or moon sign she falls under. But I do know I am attracted by her apparent openness and the way her winter clothes snuggle up to her fulsome but still shapely body.

How would you describe her? Not so much her looks as her style?

For me there is an ever-present incongruity to the impression she gives off. I do not think she could have spent more than five minutes dressing this morning. Probably drew on those thick-ribbed, chocolate corduroy slacks and oatmeal sweater in the same general movement then ran a brush once or twice through her shoulder length hair before gathering it up in the elastic. No more thought than one might give to putting dishes in the sink or straightening the breakfast chairs.

Towering above me now, a symbol of my rising ardor, this amiable lady was one of two women in the room who quickly became points of interest for me when Mickey and I first arrived this morning. And between the two there was little contest. Almost from the start, my tall, husky neighbor with the waterfall bangs and cable-knit sweater became the favored entry, so much so that I quickly grabbed this front row seat using my acquaintance with Bill McAndrews as a convenient shield.

I smile to think how easily she caused me to adjust my standards. With most other women her size I would have quickly decided we would not make a good match. But something about her—the frank, open personality perhaps—keeps me hungry and seated at the dinner table. Rather than turning me off by its size or making me feel somehow insufficient, her body opens doors in my mind I would ordinarily leave shut.

Hers is a body I can easily imagine myself wrestling with. I can almost picture her without that sweater; and without...but what am I thinking?

This is not the place and especially not the time for such flights of fancy!

I can almost hear The Bapucharya laughing, "See how quickly your penis takes over from your mind!"

I actually shake my head and blink my eyes—something Mickey would do—to dispel the persisting image in my mind of this highly attractive, half-undressed woman. Before I can bring my attention back to the present moment, however, I begin to brood again about Mickey's sad misfortune in having a father who cannot keep himself focused on his son's delicate situation.

Realizing I was not only distracted but sexually aroused sends waves of guilt coursing through the deepest reaches of my being. Once before I had abandoned my watchdog responsibilities for Mickey at a time of extreme need. And when the crisis struck, where was I? Swimming around in a sea of sexual imaginings and fantasies!

And now history threatens to repeat itself as this highly exotic and desirable woman travels through the intersection of the present moment and easily drives off with my attention in tow. Fortunately this time my consciousness was captured only momentarily.

Now I am back again in the present moment—the *Sacred Present Moment* as The Seekers call it—conscious of myself participating in this riotous event and very aware that somewhere in this room is a nine-year-old boy whose future has been placed, perhaps foolishly, in my hands.

In *his* hands, you will remember, is a pathetic piece of home-crafted handiwork whose creation I suspect he and I will regret for years to come.

How could I let myself forget even for a moment that riot of fuchsia now in Mickey's possession?

Funny, is it not, how we not only make mistakes on our *ILEs* but the same mistakes over and over?

No it is not funny.

See how my hand shakes when I lift it up?

That is not funny.

"What are you doing?" my neighbor asks with a catch of surprise in her voice.

"Testing vibrations," I explain dryly, my mind still on Mickey.

"Good vibrations, I hope," she replies, laughing warmly and touching my raised arm.

Her touch instantly reconnects me with my earlier sexual fantasies, raising both the level and frequency of my *PuNDit's* alarm.

See how quickly you can be drawn from one set of imaginings to another?

"Absolutely," I respond, looking up with mounting enthusiasm. "Great vibrations!"

Without another word my hand drops quietly to rest on my lap. Old Number Two is not sitting there at the moment but I can sense something else beginning to stir.

"No, but really," she continues, "how long do you think this kiddie race will go on? We've been here for hours already, and it's not even time for me to wake up yet." She pulls her hand away to consult the time on a cell phone she wrests from a tightly clinging pants pocket.

"Really, I should still be sleeping," she says seriously as though she had violated some secondary clause in a contract.

Yawning, she adds, "If I were home I'd probably be slamming the snooze alarm just about now."

With a floppy hand she mimics a groggy search for a phantom alarm clock.

I lean toward her and suddenly discern, to my profound regret, the stale smell of cigarettes.

There goes another of my baseline standards!

Up till now I have refused to date women who smoke. I detest the odor that invariably clings to them, the dingy grayness of their smoke-stained smiles, the thick yellow film inside their car windshields. Long ago I decided that smoking assaults too many of my sensibilities to allow it into my world through an intimate relationship.

Apparently that was then and this is now.

Because *now*, after an instantaneous internal debate, I have voted for a change of official policy, having decided there are any number of things worse than the foul effects of tobacco.

See what I mean about altering my standards? This woman may help me write an entirely new codebook.

"To answer your question..." I say.

"What question was that?"

"About how long this thing goes on?"

"Oh," she cries in mock surprise, playfully reaching out to touch my shoulder, "I'll have to watch what I say. You actually *listen!*"

"I try to," I reply. "But in any case, to answer your question, we should be here for some time. They are not even at the quarter finals."

My eyes drop to search under her seat but there is no model racecar to be seen. "I do not see..." I start to say. "Is your boy...?"

"His name is Ricky," she offers.

"Is Ricky still in the running?"

"Running for what?"

"For a trophy, I guess."

"Trophy?" she asks in studied bewilderment, her fingers still resting on my shoulder. "Look, I told you this was too early for me."

"Has his Pinewood Derby racecar been eliminated," I ask slowly as if repeating a difficult word in a spelling bee, "or is he still in the running for a trophy?"

"Oh, for heaven's sake!" she says with a sudden explosion of laughter, "I guess he's still in the running since he hasn't raced yet. Not once!" Suddenly her hand takes a tighter grip on my arm as she leans over to whisper, "I haven't seen this much foreplay in years."

As I watch her start to laugh I begin laughing along with her. She is really something, this striking and seemingly unguarded woman—two characteristics not generally combined in most single women. But why is she seemingly so interested in me, I candidly wonder? Am I the only single father here this morning or just the one close enough to easily haul in?

It is a sad fact but women this attractive—especially ones her size—do not generally fall so quickly under the spell of my 5'10" brooding presence.

"Hey," she suddenly asks, sitting down sideways on her chair and still facing me, "tell me how you go about following these races? In about half of them I can't even tell who the winner is. Of course, my *intended-ex* always tells me I need glasses..." She pushes against my arm, laughing, "even when I'm wearing them! That's how much attention he pays to anything that isn't related to his business."

"They're called 'heats'," I point out.

"What?"

"'Heats,' I repeat. "The individual races are called 'heats'.'"

"Whatever. I still can't tell who wins."

"So, what is an *intended-ex*?" I abruptly ask.

"A husband you intend to make an ex-husband," she explains simply. "Have you got one?"

"An ex-husband?"

"Yeah, right."

"Yes, I do," I say, noticing the weariness in my voice. "I guess you would call her a *former* intended-ex."

"Which means?"

"She 'exed-out' two years ago when we finally got our divorce." I offer my hand. "My name is Paul...Paul Peterson."

"Ellie Eichorn," she replies, taking my hand and holding on to it. "Paul Peterson? Why does that name sound familiar?"

Conscious of her cool, smooth touch and the unstated communication that seems to travel like a million sparks across the invisible, sub-atomic space that now separates our hands, I explain for maybe the thousandth time in my life, "Paul Peterson was an actor who played the son on the Donna Reed Show, a TV sitcom from the 1960s. You see it sometimes in reruns."

I have lived most of my life acknowledging and explaining that fellow and most times when I remind people who he was, they do not even remember him.

"I never watch TV," she says closing the subject with an impatient glance at her watch.

Suddenly I spot a quickly moving figure from the corner of my eye.

"There...look!" I point. *"That* is my son!" I assert as if confessing to the commission of a minor crime. "That bundle of energy just jumping off the chair!"

"Cute!" She says drawing out the word with an appreciative facial gesture. "Just as nice looking as his father!"

I lean across the narrow space separating us and laughingly confide, "I once married a woman for saying less than that."

After a long moment in which my comment seems to echo in the space between us she asks, "Ever notice that marriage is like a snooze alarm?"

"How is that?"

"Well...a fool like me..." she says, reaching out her hand to repeat her groggy-eyed pantomime with the snooze alarm. "I'll keep taking shots at it till it lets me rest in peace."

That strikes me funny and I begin to laugh.

"I like that!" I admit.

"Well, I'm glad you do," she responds, also laughing.

And as we both laugh in concert I find myself breathing in her rich perfumed scent, doing my best to ignore the stale odor of cigarette smoke clinging to her clothes. All the while I cannot help but wonder what is going on here? What unstated intentions are hiding behind that full and gorgeous smile?

I can tell she likes me. I can almost feel the heat radiating off her rising interest.

But still it makes me wonder.

What does this woman want from me?

Lesson 8

Traveling By Chutes And Ladders Into A Mansion Of Unnecessary Magnitude

"What does this woman want from me?"

The question sets off a vibration inside my mind that pulls at me with an urgency I do not understand. An urgency that draws me inside myself, away from the noise and the cub scouts and the increasingly fascinating Ellie Eichorn.

The Bapucharya would say I am having a *Chute And Ladder Experience,* which is an involuntary process that sometime occurs during a Do-It-Yourself Workshop. Its name refers of course to the children's board game. Only instead of two squares on a game board connecting via a chute or a ladder two moments in time are connected by the same thought resonating at the same vibratory pitch.

"What does this woman want from me?"

Do not worry about why it happens or how it works. Just think of time as a straight line then imagine some universal timekeeper folding the line in on itself so that two points in time are suddenly placed next to each other and easily traversed.

Or so it seems.

But whatever is happening, the simple act of my questioning, "What does this woman want from me?" echoes with such force that without explanation or warning I am whisked away to an entirely different moment in time. To a moment when the same questioning of Ellie's motives occupies my thoughts. Only this particular moment takes place some three weeks *after* we met at the Pinewood Derby.

This is what The Seekers term a *flashforward* and it happens so suddenly it appears unintentional, without conscious purpose or intent, as if I accidentally hit the wrong function key on a computer keyboard. It does not feel as if my body has been dramatically yanked from one experience and dropped into the next but rather as if some movie I am watching has inexplicably morphed from one scene into another.

But I do suddenly feel cold and vulnerable.

You will notice I am lying on a bed...no, that is not quite right! More accurate to say I am lying in a state of exhaustion, basking in the soft afterglow of what has been a most energetic session of lovemaking. As healthy a specimen as I am, the lovemaking went on for so long and at such high intensity you now find me lying here exhausted, a man wholly depleted of intent or energy.

My *PuNDit* which earlier had been sounding off like a full brass orchestra is now ticking along with mannerly ease, still mildly aroused but apparently willing to regulate its complaints according to my energy level.

"That was exhausting, almost death defying," I feebly decry. "You are an animal. A total animal."

"Thanks, honey," a scratchy, deep-throated voice replies, adding with a purr-like softness, "You're not so bad yourself."

You will notice of course we are in a warm, spacious and highly feminine bedroom—far more preferable, I would suggest, than a cold and crowded church basement.

When I find the strength to turn my head I will happily find a striking female figure, somewhat warm and spacious herself, lying naked on top of the covers next to me.

Next to my own less-than-striking naked figure.

Though the bedclothes are rumpled and sweaty they have maintained the crinkly feel of expensive new linens and are so redolent of Ellie's scent I suspect she must periodically spray them.

You have no way of knowing this as you look around this grandiose bedroom but we are in a mansion-sized home in the Olde Harbor section of St. Bart's Bay. When I first discovered this imitation Rajah's palace was in fact Ellie's humble abode I had to overcome my innate prejudice against wealth and ostentation just to drive up the circular driveway.

It is true.

Silly as it sounds, on some level I was afraid that merely

by visiting this house I was abandoning my moral and ecological values and going over to the enemy. I felt so out of place heading up the driveway, and so ready to bolt, I would not let myself utter even one of my usual caustic remarks concerning palatial, ostentatious homes of the rich and not-so-famous. I guess that makes me a reverse snob, but I never...

Suddenly my thoughts are interrupted by an unexpected question from an unexpected source. Without warning I am instantly pulled from my body and drawn to a location near the ceiling from which I find myself looking down and once again *watching myself!*

"And so, Mr. Smarty-Pants-Without-His-Pants-On, what should you be doing here?" The Bapucharya asks impishly. "Is this a demonstration of your 'ecological values' to be lying next to such a large and lovely lady? Though I very much enjoy the way she dresses when she is entertaining company," he adds with the usual giggles.

Not allowing myself to register surprise or complaint, knowing that neither will do me any good in this conversation, I simply reply, "It is...just what you see, Holiness."

"And what shall that be, Mr. Peterson?"

"Two adults lying in bed."

"And nothing else?" he pursues.

"I do not know yet," I answer in all honesty. "I am attempting to find out."

"My mistake," he replies, bubbling with laughter. "I thought you were attempting to mount the young lady's skeletal structure."

I would say something to let The Bapucharya know how little I appreciate his humor but the next moment, as you can see, I am whisked back into my body as I turn to ask my naked companion, "And how long have you lived here?"

"Not quite two years," she answers. "Mark wanted to come back to St. Bart's Bay to show his parents how successful an unpleasant offspring could be. You like it? I hate it. It's too big—huge! *Monstrous!* Don't go wandering off without a map. I've already lost two dogs, an electrician and one of Ricky's friends."

I laugh breezily.

"So buying this house was his idea? Mark's?"

"You didn't think it was *mine?*" she rasps incredulously. "I wanted to buy an eighteenth century colonial that one of the Kennedy kids was selling, but Mark had to be close to the ocean in a house that was bigger than everyone else's. I suppose it made up for the size of his dick."

"Well, it is a big house." I respond.

"And it isn't such a big dick, if you want to know the truth. It's a monstrosity, actually—the house, I mean! You need any more evidence that the bourgeoisie can't be trusted with money? How about you, honey? You have any?"

"Money?"

"Yes, the green stuff—money!"

"I do all right," I answer noncommittally.

"Good," she says, turning her head to smile.

I may be paranoid but perhaps you saw it too—a slightly hungry look in her eyes?

Affectionately she rubs the back of her hand against my cheek, whispering softly, "You're too nice a guy to be scratching around for a living."

"Thanks," I respond, covering her hand with mine but offering no incentive to continue this discussion of my finances.

Does it seem chilly in here? It does to me though the room being large enough to have its own weather pattern does not help.

Exaggerating a groan from the sudden exertion I lift up my rear end, pull out the bedclothes from under me, then pull them up to cover my growing colony of goose bumps.

"Cold?" Ellie asks, looking over with mild curiosity.

"Just a little."

"Well, pass me the ashtray before you go to sleep," she instructs, adjusting her pillows. Clearly she does not feel chilled or over-exposed—or self-conscious for that matter!

I let my eyes run appreciatively over her amply-sized body, the monuments to womanhood that are her breasts, the rounded slopes and darkening inclines of her curves, all of which seem vast and imposing without covers or clothing to distract the eye.

And once again I find myself surprised to be here. *Here*

in this house lying in *this* bed next to *this* body. It feels as if I am in a movie that keeps taking sudden surprise turns in its plotline, startling me—the main character—as much as any moviegoer who might be in the audience.

But as I said before Ellie's body is of such large proportions it would ordinarily not attract my interest. Same with this outsized lifestyle of hers. Living in overcooked luxury yet kept cash-poor by a vengeful husband. The end result being she cannot afford to pay for much of anything on her own.

There is a segment of the universe where women still expect a man to pay for everything. But it is not a part of the universe where I choose to spend much time.

Or so it once seemed.

So what is going on here? Why have I allowed myself to become such a chivalrous suitor? Not only paying for drinks and meals when Ellie and I go out but for a steady flow of flowers and Hallmark greeting cards as well. Do you think I have lost my sense of myself? Am I so infatuated with Ellie that I will let myself be drawn into a costly and inappropriate relationship? A relationship I cannot actually afford?

"These are all good questions, I am thinking," The Bapucharya declares.

For the second time his voice pulls me back to the upper reaches of this high-ceilinged room so that I am floating once again without benefit of a warning or a body. The Bapucharya's flowery scent softly envelops me.

"Believe me," I candidly confess, "I do not pretend to understand what is happening here. None of it—you nor she."

Just think about it. I have been back on the street single for almost four years and rarely do I ever pay for a woman's share of a date. Certainly never two dates in a row. How could I afford to? With child support for three children and the expense of maintaining a separate household for the four of us there is never any extra money left over.

Never!

Which means when I go out on a date and pay for Ellie—sometimes even paying for her son Ricky—the money has to come from somewhere. The universe may be bounteous according to The Seekers For Truth but in the regions I inhabit there is only a finite amount of wealth to go round. So the choice is quite simple. I can either go into debt to support this relationship or take from the pitiful sum of money I would otherwise spend on my own children.

After three weeks of going out with Ellie—and we have dined in some pretty nice restaurants—I have yet to see her pull out a credit card or a change purse when the bill is brought to the table.

"And you are too easily distracted by the heavenly movements of oversized bodies and boobs to mention it, are you not?"

"I have tried, Holiness. But she does not seem to hear me when I bring it up."

"And why is that, I am wondering?"

"What would you have me say to her?"

"You could ask how much she is charging for the complete merry-go-round ride?" he replies gleefully. "That is a question you could ask."

No, in ordinary circumstances hers is not a body, a lifestyle or a set of values I would be attracted to. Nor would I be drawn to her time-warped ideas about a man's economic responsibility toward a woman.

But all that changed somehow or got turned around once we connected.

Once we *really* connected.

That first time we made love at the end of our first date we started out from the same place, I think. If we shared an interest it was in the pursuit of some pleasurable sexual experiences. Nothing more. So we were equally surprised then to find ourselves experiencing some profound and deeply felt emotions as well. It happened suddenly without warning while we were making love. And it felt as if we had each discovered an old friend seemingly brought to us from across the vast emptiness of the Universe which was represented in some dream-state blurring of reality by Ellie's king size bed.

The Seekers would probably say we were *Karmic Companions*, friends or lovers from previous existences slated to meet in this lifetime but not consciously aware of it. Apparently these things are all arranged long before bodies and lifetimes are selected if you can believe it.

Maybe that is true, I do not know. What I do know is

that once we connected there was a part of me that felt I had always known Ellie. And that our connection was something I had been hungering for, unknowingly perhaps, since the breakup of my marriage.

Possibly for my entire life.

And in that singular instant when both our souls opened to create a bridge between two previously disconnected and isolated *ILEs* my standards for women's sizes and shapes and smoking habits changed irrevocably.

So both of us must have 'seen' something in each other besides the obvious when we met at the Pinewood Derby. And whatever that *something* is it has a strength and a power impossible to ignore much less understand.

I would go on but The Bapucharya's distinctive, nasal giggling makes it difficult to hold onto my thoughts.

"What is so hard to comprehend here?" His Holiness asks. "You are not only addicted to this large lady but to her large house, her large bed and her large appetites. Now that I think of it, you have not become addicted, you have become *ENLARGED!*"

Once his giggling subsides, I reply, "Very funny, Your Holiness."

"It is funny but also true, Mr. Peterson. Is it not?"

"Well, something has a hold on me; I admit that freely. Something that makes me tingle and start to harden at the thought of Ellie waiting for me to come over after work."

"Is that what it is?" he asks, clearly amused. "That she is waiting for her winner-of-bread to come home, his paycheck fetched between his teeth, his tail hanging between his legs?"

"Go ahead and laugh," I protest. "But this is not all fun and games."

As captivated as I am by the lady's charms and our unexpected bond of intimacy, Ellie's air of entitlement still annoys and nags at me. Almost constantly in fact. Which is why I suppose The Bapucharya has joined the chorus of voices in my head, all of them urging me to confront my lusty companion.

But what were we talking about? What was I saying...?

"Money," The Bapucharya reminds me with an edge of ironic amusement. "You were telling her that you do not need to scratch around for money."

With The Bapucharya's taunting giggles still echoing—I cannot tell if his screechy laughter rings in my head or the upper reaches of the room—I find myself back under the covers and turning toward my companion.

"So what does Mark do?" I ask nonchalantly. "To afford a house like this?"

"He owns things," she replies enigmatically. "Factories, fast food restaurants, billboards, power plants ..."

"Billboards?" I interrupt. "Ahh!" I cry in sudden comprehension. "Now I know why I dislike Mark so much; and all along I thought it was this house!"

"What are you talking about?"

"Billboards!" I exclaim. "Do you realize what a pestilence billboards are? They are perhaps the most insidious and evil form of advertising there is. In the entire creation."

"Evil? But honey, you're *in* advertising. You *do* billboards."

"Well, yes, that is true," I admit. "Yes, I do billboards, so I know what I am talking about. Tell me, what is the name of Mark's billboard company? Is it one that I know?"

"I'd tell you if I knew but I never pay attention to details. Not as long as the money keeps flowing."

"The money," I repeat, thinly disguising my disdain.

"Don't knock it unless you've tried living without it. Nothing does half as good a job at paying my bills. I've lived too much of my life without money, honey. These days I listen very carefully when money talks."

She looks over to me with serious intent, her words running across the gravel in her throat: "You know what I mean, darling? You hear what I'm saying?"

"I think I do," I answer quietly.

In the silence of my thoughts I deride myself for being such a coward.

"Idiot!" I silently shout. "There was your opportunity and you blew it."

Was it only a three weeks ago that we met?

Could my tastes and standards have changed so much in that short span of time—perhaps *adjusted* would be a better word? How could I be interested in a woman so enthralled with the power of money? A woman who could live in a house like this even while she proclaims her disgust!

You only have to look around to see there is nothing—absolutely nothing—in her life or in this house to enrich the mind or nourish the spirit.

Spirit, there is a laugh. My spirit would shrivel and die if I were living in a home like this.

I hear The Bacpucharya exclaim, "Hah!" derisively, pulling me out of my body and back to my overhead vantage in the highest reaches of the high-ceilinged room.

"But your sexual organ," The Bapucharya continues, "Ohmigoodness, there is no shriveling and dying in that part of your physical being. Am I right? Or is your *PuNDit* also lying in bed, very depleted of energy and—ohmigosh!—practically drained of life itself? My young friend, do you not listen to yourself? You are starting to live your life like a used-up car battery instead of a Seeker For Truth."

"I am no longer a Seeker For Truth, Holiness."

"Oh yes, I forget. You are now a seeker of six-foot behemoth women and not at all interested in discovering the truth anymore."

"I did not say that. I just meant I no longer belong to The Seekers, that is all."

"But still there are some truths you seek, are there not?"

"Such as?"

"Such as what this large, pretty-faced-lady is wanting from you? And whether you can afford to give it to her without taking second employment as a robber of convenience stores.

"Oh my, yes!" he exclaims, pushing through a few errant giggles. "There is a thought. You can become a robber of convenience stores. And when you have accumulated enough additional income you can buy a house of even more unnecessary magnitude than this one."

"Hey, did you forget...?" Ellie interrupts, unknowingly whisking me back to bed where my nakedness is still half hidden beneath the covers.

"What?" I reply, slightly startled.

"The ashtray."

"Oh," I exclaim. My eyebrows arch in surprise. "I guess I

did."

Picking up a red crystal ashtray from the nightstand I make a face at the army of dead cigarette butts scattered amidst gray ashes in the bottom of the small bowl, commenting, "This not pretty."

"I don't want to eat out of it," she answers dismissively, taking the cut glass bowl from my hands.

As she rearranges her pillows to sit up straight my eyes rest on the oceanic movement—the back and forth sway—of her full pendulous breasts.

"Did you see my cigarettes?" she asks, turning back around to test the pillows.

"I am not observing your cigarettes," I answer dryly.

She looks over to me for a moment then laughs in her throat. A very sensual sound, you agree?

"Okay, score one for my tits," she smiles. "But did you see my Camels?"

"I believe they were under your pillow."

A little more movement from the other side of the bed, a cry of success, then seconds later a flash of fire breaks through the darkness of the room. I hear the paper and tobacco crackle as they ignite and smell the vaguely tempting scent of burning tobacco. Once upon a time I was a smoker and still longingly recall the flavor and soothing presence of tobacco.

Especially at moments like this.

"Nothing better after a good lay," she says as if reading my mind.

"Careful you do not set the bed on fire."

"I will be careful, I will not set us on fire, I am a good smoker, do not worry," she rattles off, mimicking the way I speak without using contractions, one of the more noticeable side effects of my fifteen years with The Seekers.

She looks over to me and laughs.

"Honey, I don't know what to make of you," she declares affectionately, still adjusting her position on the pillow. "The one question remaining is which planet you originally came from?"

The smell of Camel Lights mixes with the perfumed scent of lilacs and roses. It is a mixture I have come to identify as the scent of my desire.

"I have the same problem," I softly respond.

"But tell me again," she continues, not hearing or maybe just ignoring my last comment. "Explain it so I understand; why do you hate billboards?"

"Do you really want to go into this?"

"No," she says teasingly, "but tell me anyway."

Adjusting my pillows to match hers I begin with a shrug, "What can I say? I am a little strange when it comes to these things."

Sitting back at her level I continue, "But let me ask you—what gives anyone the right to insert advertising messages into your mind whenever they want to? On a billboard or anywhere else? The problem is you are so used to them doing it you cannot see anything wrong with it. Well it is wrong! The fact that someone spends money to get inside your head does not give them the right to go there."

Ellie breathes out a few thin laughs along with a stream of smoke.

"Better than letting them get into my pants," she counters sexily.

"There is more than one way to fuck with you," I point out. "But think about it: no one chooses a road the way they select a TV channel or a magazine. Living in the real world we have no choice but to drive on whatever roads they build; even roads with billboards. Remember, these are not private roads, they are public...*conveniences,* for want of a better word."

"But, honey, a restroom is a public convenience."

"Yes, that is true, but of no particular relevance to this discussion."

"Don't get smart!" she warns, blowing out a plume of light gray smoke.

"I was just pointing out that placing a commercial message on a public thoroughfare raises invasion of privacy issues. Just because somebody owns a small piece of real estate and sticks up a billboard does not give them the right to intrude into your thoughts."

"But, honey, that's called *property rights."*

"No, honey, that is called living in the twenty-first-fucking-century! Where advertising is such a major part of our lives you even find it in schools. Think about *that*. Advertisers pay school systems for the right to prey on their captive schoolchildren. How fucked up is that?"

"But honey, the schools need the money. That's just good fiscal—I don't know?—management?"

"Enough of this twaddle!" a peevish voice interrupts, pulling me back to the ceiling. "This is what I shall call a waste of time. When do we see the part of the movie where the actors say what they really mean?"

"I am getting there, Holiness," I assert. "Just give me a little time."

"I know where you are getting, young sir, and it is not any closer to the answers you want."

"I am sure she will understand things, once we talk about it," I counter. "There is no great mystery in what I have to say. I need her to help carry her share of the load, that is all. Not so hard to understand. Nor unreasonable for me to ask..."

"Not unreasonable at all," The Bapucharya concurs. "But my agreeing with you does not lessen the difficulty. Your problem," he continues as bubbles of mirth begin to rise, "will be getting *her* to agree with you. And that, I am thinking, will not be such child's play."

I hear Ellie asking me something but I miss the question.

"What was that?" I respond, trying not to breathe in the smokier air from her side of the bed.

"I said tell me which billboard of yours is your favorite?"

"My favorite?" I repeat.

"Yeah, the one that makes you proud, the one you will never forget."

The one I will never forget?

"Actually, there is one," I suddenly remember. "...a billboard I will never forget. Not that it makes me proud."

How can I forget it? One day I hope to burn it down.

"I have had enough!" The Bapucharya says in disgust. "All this avoidance of the issue is giving me the fidgets. I am going off to get lost in this house of unnecessary magnitude. You do not need to come with me, Mr. Peterson, since you are already hopelessly lost."

I would wish him goodbye except I believe he has already left.

Lesson 9

We Visit A Jungle Where The Natives Have No Mercy, Do Little Work, And Submit Killer Bills

My most memorable billboard?

The one I will never forget?

It was an advertisement for fish sticks. Not just any brand of fish sticks of course but Crunch Ahoy! brand fish sticks. Fat-laden, totally non-nutritious, undeniably greasy but oh-so-very crunchy. So crunchy in fact they inspired one of my most famous taglines: "Have You Been Cr-r-r-runched Today?" Which happens to be the headline on that same 'most memorable billboard' I am thinking about.

Rather than think about it, however, let me show it to you.

We only have to go to my workplace.

Just take your eyes off my statuesque neighbor, which I understand is not an easy thing to do. Ellie is far too much a distraction—far too busy an intersection—all her own.

If you have any difficulty letting go of Ellie apply a little *HW-40.*

Did I forget to mention *HW-40?*

It is The Seekers mantra—you remember *Higher Will?*—used in situations where the movement of energy appears to be bogged down and needs a little push. In addition to being a closely guarded mantra *Higher Will* is also a powerful force in its own right. The Seekers For Truth have a thousand names for consciousness and *Higher Will* is primarily used when speaking about the application of consciousness. *Higher Will* is consciousness put to work, so to speak, and The Seekers constantly remind their struggling students when energy or renewed effort is needed, "Give it a squirt of

Higher Will."

Only they usually say, "...a squirt of *HW-40!*"

Yet another of those silly mnemonic devices The Seekers love so much. It makes *Higher Will* seem like a spray dissolvent you apply when anything gets stuck. Which is exactly what The Seekers want you to recall when you need some heavy-duty assistance.

Difficulty sleeping? Apply a little *HW-40* before bedtime.

Sluggishness on the job? Spray some *HW-40* around your office with an extra concentration near your desk.

For The Seekers *HW-40* is a universal lubricant!

To apply *HW-40* you need only add one slightly embarrassing ingredient to your normal meditation technique. In addition to reciting the mantra (breathing-in *Higher*, breathing-out *Will),* you are instructed to tightly grip or clench the body's Root Chakra. Without going into it too deeply, the chakras are seven energy zones in the body that run from the base of the spine to the crown of the head. To tap into the universe's inexhaustible supply of *HW-40* The Seekers advise you to practice your meditation while firmly clenching your Root Chakra, the body's lowest chakra, which serves to stabilize and balance you as you journey along your Path Of Seeking Truth. For the purposes of squirting *HW-40,* I should explain, the Root Chakra is most easily clenched by squeezing one's sphincter as if it were the bottom of a toothpaste tube.

Excuse my indelicacy but now you know.

So join me as I take a sip of my *RC Cola,* silently recite my mantra while rhythmically clenching my Root Chakra. As I do all this unbeknownst to my naked neighbor I also hold lightly to the idea of visiting Mercer, Dumont and Killen, my place of employment in Boston's Back Bay. Strangely enough I can see it in one of those luminous time bubbles at the foot of the mountain...

By now you are an old hand at *flashbacking* and *flashforwarding,* Seeker terms for sending consciousness backward or forward in time. Notice I said *consciousness* rather than *bodies* because we are not speaking about a time machine with any of this, merely a shift in perspectives for The Internal Observer.

Yes The Internal Observer.

The One who always watches.

And even though it appears we are moving backward and forward through time, the truth is we remain rooted in the present moment resting deeply within consciousness, observing everything from an inner mountaintop.

Almost at the Center Point of the Universe.

You will notice the lovely Ellie Eichorn and her panoramic bedroom are slowly fading-out like one of those longer movie transitions that denote the passage of time. And in their place begin to materialize the sights, sounds and textures of an advertising agency.

And yes...

Welcome to the offices of Mercer, Dumont and Killen, purveyors of occasionally effective and always expensive advertising. If you cannot tell, we are on the eighth floor of the John Hancock Tower in Boston. The agency actually occupies the seventh, eighth and ninth floors and like a healthy virus has spread beyond anyone's control to satellite offices in New York City, Washington D.C., Los Angeles and Atlanta.

This is where I have been gradually eroding my life and spirit for the last eight years, unprecedented stability in a field where copywriters typically change jobs every two to three years just to get their salaries adjusted. But do not mistake my constancy for devotion. I have always feared that no matter how much I dislike No Mercy, Do Nothing and Killer Bills—the employees' pet name for the agency—conditions would most likely only be worse at the next agency down the line.

The devil you know is always less of a threat than the devil around the corner.

Anyway this is where I do most of my damage as an advertising copywriter for which I will eventually, I am sure, reap serious Karmic repercussions.

Now follow me down this hallway and I will show you the actual scene of the crime...

Do not be distracted by the constant drone of our busy office or the hustle and bustle of all these people running around looking productive but basically doing nothing of positive import for the universe or its citizens.

Yes once you get me inside an advertising agency it becomes as obvious as a pizza-burned upper palate that I am burdened with an excess of cynicism. Standard operating equipment, I fear, for all creative-types like myself who toil in the fields of advertising…

Ah here is someone I actually know and like.

"Hi Jean!"

Works in our Research Department. A nice-looking girl but happily married or so I have been told.

Now this fellow approaching is not married except to his digital camera system.

"Renaldo!" I wave with a smile. "How is it going?"

"It goes," he replies with a wan smile.

Neither of us slow down as we pass each other.

Renaldo is a freelance photographer. Not very good but priced just right for a few of our cheaper clients. Marks Brothers uses him and for the most part they deserve each other.

Marks Brothers Shoes.

You never heard of them?

One of my larger accounts, they have thirty-five shoe stores in malls throughout Massachusetts, Rhode Island and Connecticut. Everybody knows them.

"Marks Brothers Shoes—For The Sake Of Your Sole!"

No I did not author that vaguely heretical tagline but my fingerprints are on most of their TV commercials. The ones with the dancing shoes…?

Well you would remember them if you saw them.

Now tell me what you think of these colorful arrangements of geometric shapes mounted on the wall? Reminds me of the crayon drawings I did when I was a mere kindergarten artist. These are Hauschengaards, genuine originals or so I have been told. Have you heard of him, Hauschengaard? Big name in Confusion Art?

Around here we generally have difficulty pronouncing his name so we call him 'Who-should-care!' The general consensus being that road kill mounted on the walls would be highly preferable to these original and highly eruptive Hauschengaards. But most of us are biased, you must realize, since we cannot help but associate the unwitting artist with the tasteless agency owners responsible for plastering his work all over our office walls.

Art collectors?

Who do they think they are kidding?

They purchase art as an investment whose tax liability magically disappears when it gets listed as office decor rather than partner enrichment.

We are nothing here at Mercer, Dumont and Killen if not ahead of the curve on sheltering investments.

And here comes one of my creative teammates...

"Hey Max, you showing me that layout today or what?"

Max Dibbons is one of the art directors I work with on Boston's Museum of Modern Art account, not exactly a pro bono account but as close as you can come without getting pregnant if you know what I mean.

"Soon as I finish it!" he replies with a decisive nod and a thin smile.

"Almost funny," I smile back. "Take any longer they will start selling off the artwork for lack of visitors."

"Soon as I finish it!" he repeats to annoy me.

We turn here.

These are the bathrooms in case you have the need. And this is the employee lounge where once according to local history they used to allow smoking before workday people were forced to go outside and puff their cigarettes on the street, which explains why so many of us in the creative department end up with bad colds and lousy moods for most of the Boston winter.

Shhh! We have to walk quietly now because everyone is usually asleep in this area.

This is 'VP Row' where a number of the agency's vice presidents are warehoused. Not the Top VP's, you understand, just the ones making low six-figure salaries.

My colleagues and I—those of us toiling in the Creative Department—refer to these vice presidents as the "Peasant VP's" in comparison to the "Landowner VP's" who possess rooms the size of small duchies on the ninth floor. When we formally address those elevated personages upstairs we bow low and say in a soft obsequious voice, "Yes, your VP-ness!" or "Very good, your VP-ness!" or something in that vein.

You will notice that each of the offices on the left side has its very own window looking out on Copley Plaza eight floors below. Having your own window indicates a person's importance at a much higher decibel level than a fancy title or a company car. My boss Wizzner Peabody—one of the last of the olde Brahmin Peabodys—is a vice president himself but his office is a small windowless affair that butts up against one of the building's stabilizing pillars. Which ranks Wizzner just above the mail clerk and the Salvadoran night cleaner.

What makes these account supervisors on the left—the ones with the windows—so special is that they are the ones capable of keeping our most fidgety clients from walking out the door and into the waiting arms of another overpriced agency with its own modern art displayed according to the IRS code.

But keeping a client's mood stabilized is far different from creating advertising to sell their products. And if these highly sociable VP's ever see a day of honest work it is only by turning away from their windows and observing the worker bees on the other side of the office, those toiling within the darker confines of the agency's inner recesses.

But enough of this travelogue!

As you can see, once we turn this corner we are suddenly approaching the honeycomb of cubicles in which my modest work cubicle is situated but invisible to the distant eye.

Before we plunge into the maze let us take a moment to observe this sea of interlocking cubicles spread out like a modern day Bedouin camp. Except for Wizzner's office built into the shadow of the stabilizing pillar there is not a single floor-to-ceiling wall in this entire, vast space. Just six-foot blue and gray panels connected to six-foot blue and gray panels connected to six-foot…you see what I mean.

This is the main campground for the agency's copywriters and art directors. We like to call it 'The Sweat Box', named I believe for the corrugated iron cell in which Alec Guinness was slow-cooked for days in "The Bridge On The River Kwai."

Forget everything you have seen up until now; this is where the actual advertising gets created at No Mercy, Do

Nothing and Killer Bills.

Now let us seek out my own humble cubicle.

The Sweat Box, as you begin to see, is a virtual rabbit warren with pathways zigging and zagging through a maze of six-foot-high divider panels. Most of the invisible worker bees hidden behind the blue and gray fabric-covered walls only get to see the outside world through the openings in their individual compartments.

"Paul...?" a high-pitched female voice calls out as I pass one of the openings. Quickly coming to a stop I make brake-screeching sounds then retrace my steps.

"Wendy, my sweet!" I answer glibly, offering a guilty smile and a limp wave. Wendy McNamara is my art director teammate on the Crunch Ahoy! Account.

"You know..." she starts to say in a scolding voice.

"I know, I know," I cut her off with an impish grin. "Johnny needs copy, you need copy, all God's children need copy."

"Preferably before the magazine deadline."

"I am rushing back to my desk to disgorge the copy from my iMac even as we speak."

"Sounds very appetizing," she says with a grimace.

"Watch your mailbox, kids. The copy is on its way!"

"I'll be watching for it."

"See you later, gator!" I exclaim moving on.

You could fire a cannon over this sea of dividers and not risk hitting anyone. The entire population of this walled city is hidden as if by the work of some magician's sleight of hand. But once you penetrate its exterior you discover a small army of individuals sitting at their desks and surrounded by furniture crammed with great efficiency into tight little cubicles.

"Gloria!" I call to a woman who looks up with surprise from her computer screen. Recognizing me, a friendly smile replaces her startled look.

"You again?" she replies before turning back to her computer screen and pushing her eyeglasses higher up on her nose. "People are looking for you," she adds with only half interest.

"People are always looking for me," I answer back, stealing one more glance at her attractive, slightly bohemian appearance before continuing on my way. Her name is Gloria as you might have guessed and a more glorious Gloria I have yet to see. She is not married but tediously faithful to a female partner whom she no longer pretends is just a roommate.

Uh oh! Trouble ahead.

"Hey, Johnny!" I wave with lighthearted abandon.

"You still owe me that copy for the fried flounder introduction," he heatedly fires, ignoring my friendly greeting.

"It is done," I lie.

"Done-da-done-done" I add, mimicking the classic four-note "Dun-da-dun-dun" music theme from Dragnet, a TV show from the early days of television. "All done; beautifully done—dun-da-dun-dun! Just need to review it for accuracy."

The fried flounder copy.

My kingdom for a taste of fried flounder copy!

I keep meaning to write it but I am feeling so uninspired by fried flounder these days…

"Accuracy?" he replies as if discovering the flaw in my argument. "You're full of shit!"

"That would probably be more digestible than Crunch Ahoy! fried flounder," I glibly retort.

"Just get it to me before the end of day, wouldya?"

"You will have it before the clock strikes midnight, Cinderella."

Johnny Robbins is one of two assistant account managers on the Crunch Ahoy! account. When he graduated from Yale and joined MDK he was told to lean on his copywriters and art directors like a feverish tax collector otherwise nothing would get done on time.

They were right of course but they did not instruct him on the proper way to motivate the slaves; they just gave him a whip which was supposed to make up for the absence of any guile or charm.

And here we are…arriving at and instantly filling up my cozy little office space. Pretty neat, huh?

Not that you will find any neatness within its three and a half, fabric-covered cubicle walls.

It may not be much but it is all mine! One desk, one

bookcase, a half-size file cabinet and two large pushpin boards adorned with multiple layers of overlapping ad reprints, rough layouts, notes to myself, a few Christmas cards and two ancient crayon drawings from Su-Su and Cathy. Half a dozen ad reprints are also pinned against the fabric of the cubicle walls.

Amid the cluttered landscape of my desk you will notice three photos of me and my kids at different stages in our development as a single-parent family. The eight-by-ten is the picture I had taken when we were just starting out; Suzie was nine then, Cathy seven and Mickey four. On the other side of the desk, a five-by-seven of us grouped the same way—Cathy to my right, Su-Su on my left and Mickey in front—but taken three years later. See how tightly all three kids are grouped like sardines around their father? We were at a Single Parents summer beach party and they were the only children present that day except for a retarded 12-year-old boy who had difficulty respecting boundaries.

And here, this last picture on the desk...! And the main reason for our office visit. Another 5 x 7 photo but the only one with a Crunch Ahoy! billboard in the background.

See it there? Blending into the cityscape behind us?

The little girl standing between Cathy and Su-Su is named Hava; her mother Illyana is taking the picture.

What do you think?

Of the billboard I mean, not the family group? Not one of my more creative billboards but not particularly offensive either.

It is hard to tell from the photo but if you look closely enough at the billboard you will see a young boy and girl, supposedly brother and sister, smiling at the world, each holding a fish stick in their mouth at the precise moment of the first bite. The headline reads, "CR-R-R-RUNCH!" with the letters merrily dancing about. I am not sure you can see it clearly but below the children is my world famous slogan, "Have You Been Cr-r-r-runched Today?"

I remember my kids proudly pointing out the billboard to Illyanna and Hava that day we were down in Boston's historic Quincy Market.

Illyanna who is Russian asked, "What does it mean, to

Cr-r-rrrrunch?"

"It is purposely misspelled," I explained. "More of that American advertising magic you Russians love so much. It is supposed to make the word sound *crunchier* I guess, adding the extra 'R's"

"Yes, yes," she answered in that very deliberate manner she has. "I understand what you are saying. But still I do not think it is such a good advertising message."

"Yes, yes," I replied smiling thinly, "but still I do not think you know what the hell you are talking about!"

She was right of course. Except for Wendy McNamara's little trick of making the capital 'C' in *Cr-r-r-r-unch!* look like a fish's mouth about to swallow the other letters there was nothing particularly ingenious or creative about the billboard.

As the lady said, not such a good advertising message.

But then again what do Russians know about American advertising?

Lesson 10

Fun Activities To Pursue With Children And Russian Immigrants

I see the billboard off in the distance, hear myself explaining my reasons for spelling "Crunch" with four 'R's, all the while sensing a vague discomfort in reaction to Illyana's flatly stated, "...but still I do not think it is such a good advertising message."

"Yes, yes," I reply, hiding my annoyance behind a thin smile, "but still I do not think you know what the hell you are talking about!"

I have no intention of revealing my feelings. Not to someone who could so thoughtlessly criticize my work without regard for those feelings. Besides it would only embarrass me further to reveal that my author's pride—my author's *ego,* more accurately—could be so easily wounded over something as inconsequential as a billboard.

Have you noticed that we have flashbacked to a hot Sunday afernoon in July? To the very same day that photo on my desk was taken?

Sometimes these flashbacks can happen very quickly, especially once you are firmly seated in the *CPU* or very near the center.

This is the furthest back in time we have flashed so far. About three and a half years before the Pinewood Derby when Mickey, as you can see, is only five years old.

See how tightly he clutches my hand as we wander amidst the hordes of tourists and ancient granite buildings in Boston's Quincy Market?

"Girls!" I call worriedly to Cathy and Su-Su who persist in running ahead, more to distance themselves from Illyana's daughter Hava, I am sure, than from any excess of energy.

"Stay near!" I caution. "I do not want you getting lost."

As I have already mentioned, Illyana is Russian. She is also a single mother whom I know from the Single Parents Group at the Jewish Community Center...but that is another story.

We have come to Quincy Market, one of Boston's oldest shopping districts and probably its most popular tourist attraction. Here you can see how easily history blends with modern commerce. Walks paved with cobblestones and illuminated by historic gas lamps surround massive granite buildings jammed to the rafters with dozens and dozens of high priced shops and restaurants. The wide, cobbled walkways separating the cluster of granite buildings, all originally built when John Hancock was a local citizen rather than an insurance company, become *al fresco* stages for street performers during the warm months of spring and summer.

As we enter the plaza that separates Faneuil Hall—Boston's oldest public auditorium—from the rest of Quincy Market, Hava, imperious four-year-old that she is, pulls her mother to a standstill and points to a colorfully costumed performer in a jester's hat.

"Mommy, a clown," she cries, all of us immediately understanding her agenda even before she adds, "I want to see the clown!"

"That is not a clown, Havi," Illyana answers in her thickly-coated accent. "He looks maybe a juggler or something."

"But I want to see him anyway," the girl insists. "Please!"

"What about you guys?" I ask my own children. "Want to see the show?"

"I'd rather get a drink," Cathy, a peevish eight-year-old herself, quickly responds.

Su-Su and Mickey just shrug. Any interest they might have in the show would be offset by their mounting irritation with Hava. They have been jerked back and forth by her bossy demands and indulgent mother for the last hour and a half.

"Doesn't matter," Su-Su finally shrugs.

"Sure, I guess," her brother says, always one to go along.

"Well, let us see..." I say noncommittally.

I turn to Cathy. "How about just for a little while?" I ask with a smile that pleads for indulgence.

"Then we'll get a drink?" she bargains.

"Agreed," I nod with a smile, affectionately rubbing her cheek with the back of my fingers.

"Stop that!" she protests, pretending to be annoyed as she wiggles away from my touch.

"Is it all right?" Illyana asks, half-embarrassed that Hava is once again making decisions for all of us.

Attempting to conceal my simmering impatience I reply casually, "Sure. Why not? At least for a little while."

There is a long story I could tell you about Illyana but I will merely relate that she suffers from an unusual form of epilepsy that does not allow her to drive a car or operate dangerous machinery. I invited her and Hava to join us in a mindless act of charity—one that my children immediately resented and I more leisurely came to regret. And so for most of the morning I have been struggling to draw a line between my obligations as a host and my responsibility to defend my children's reasonable interests against the incessant demands of a four-year-old tyrant.

Bending over I point out to Hava that the performer's sandwich sign indicates he is a magician rather than a clown.

"Well, he looks like a clown," she snootily replies.

It only took a few minutes this morning for me to develop empathy for Illyana's ex-husband who probably decided to leave the family as soon as Hava began speaking.

"When's he going to start?" Cathy asks impatiently.

"Soon," I predict. "He is just trying to build up his audience."

"Why?" Mickey asks in all innocence. "Aren't we here already?"

"Let's move to over here, Havi," Illyana says pushing her daughter up to the rope barrier. "Just don't lean on the rope."

Instantly envious Mickey shouts, "Me, too!" and fights his way through his sisters and up to the rope. Since his hand is attached to mine I naturally go along.

While we are adjusting our positions the magician struts around the roped off area that defines his stage. He is a tall, pleasant looking man in his twenties with a mustache that runs down both sides of his mouth. His patchwork silk clown's outfit is topped by a jester's hat with three droopy fingers that bounce about continuously, a jingle bell at each pointy end.

Swinging a large black-handled bell he cries out like a carnival pitchman, "This way, please, ladies and gentlemen, boys and girls! Plenty of room. Step up to the front—*please!* In just one moment you will witness the most extraordinary sights. Magic from the mystic wilds of the unknown Orient. Feats of derring-do too frightening to describe in front of the children. Sleights of hand, flights of imagination, the whites of their eyes—all brought to you by your humble servant, magician *and* juggler, Marco The Magnificent!" With a low courtier's bow he concludes, "At your service."

Marco continues to trumpet the show's many charms until enough of a crowd has gathered and then quickly moves into his act.

He is quite good, I realize, watching him skillfully juggle objects of disproportionate sizes, weights and shapes—balls, hats, knives, firesticks—occasionally dropping one of his mismatched objects but always making the most of his misfortune with a comical remark. He also interweaves a variety of magic tricks, most of them familiar, never ceasing his frantic comic banter.

At one point in the show he takes out long fingers of colored elastic and fills them with air one by one from a small cylinder hidden inside the many folds of his shirt. Prancing back and forth across the cordoned-off stage he creates in lightning-quick succession a menagerie of balloon sculptures. One moment his hands are filled with long, thin colored balloons, the next they contain poodles, giraffes and rabbits. Each animal quickly finding a home with a child in the audience.

"Me, me!" Hava pleads loudly, pushing into the rope with her arms outstretched. "I want one! Me, me, me!"

Mickey makes similar sounds and gestures but in the end neither of them ends up with a balloon animal.

"What do you think?" I ask, looking from child to child with the air of a beneficent father. "Pretty good, huh?"

"Oh yeah, he's great!" Suzie says enthusiastically.

"How long are we staying here?" Cathy wants to know. "I'm hot!"

"Oh, just a little longer, darling," Illyana says soothingly. "He is very good, no?"

Mickey pulls at my hand and pleads, "I want a giraffe! Can I get a giraffe? Dad? Can I?"

He is a five year old boy who has just witnessed other children getting balloon animals. Of course he wants a giraffe.

"I do not think he is doing giraffes anymore, Mick."

"Very observant," Cathy snips. "He stopped the balloon stuff five minutes ago!"

Quickly opening and shutting his eyes to blink away our replies Mickey clenches his hands and insists, "But I want one!" as if a simple statement of his need should be all that it takes to get it answered.

"Me too!" Hava joins in. "Me too!"

"Let's get something to drink," Cathy suggests.

"Later," I answer. "Let us just watch for a few more minutes. It would be rude to leave now."

Did you hear what I just said?

I said I did not want to be rude *to a magician!*

It would have been more truthful to say I did not want to go against the wishes of Illyana and Hava; that would have been more honest. I took the easy way out, pretending concern for the magician. After all, I knew my children would have little resentment built up for Marco The Magnificent while they already had tons accumulated for Hava and her mom.

In any case what Cathy heard from me her father was that I had more concern for a strange magician's feelings than I did for hers.

How sad. And how low on my list of priorities she must have felt, magicians and Russian immigrants clearly taking precedence over biological offspring.

But why should she think anything else?

How many hundreds of times had my children seen me

suit my actions to avoid offending total strangers? Waiters in restaurants, people in elevators, passersby on the street? I am always in an overwrought state that someone might think me discourteous or unkind. Yet how many times had I offended these three human beings standing next to me? And never noticed until their frigid silences provided clues even I could not ignore?

If I were in a therapy session right now, Doctor Rivers would challenge this obsessive concern I have over other people's opinions. "Does it seem familiar?" he would softly ask.

And I would have to answer, "Yes, it does." And go on to explain how it reminds me of my father, of the way he used to act. Especially of his obsessive need to be liked by almost everyone in the universe except his wife and three children.

Then if Old Man Rivers continued to probe he might ask, "Could there be some other motivation—some other fear, perhaps—behind this concern you have how others see you?"

Now I would be squirming in my seat but once again I would answer, "Yes," realizing that deep down, once you scraped off the veneer of my innate desire for social acceptability, I was scared to death of being embarrassed or brought to shame in front of total strangers. So painful is this fear and so compulsive its pull, it has evolved into an obsessive need to avoid attracting attention out in public.

To be suddenly yelled at in a fury or hit on the side of the head or turned around for a sudden spanking—things that happened frequently when I was out in the world with my father—were all part of the 'family game' as my father played it. That was not him being abusive to his son, those were just the fathering rules he played by; the rules by which he would teach me to become a man and someday even a father. Those were the rules his father played by. And they were rules I never questioned until I became a father myself and began adopting them for my own family game.

Not a good idea, I quickly discovered. I found it much easier to be Attila's son than Attila himself.

So my absurd expression of concern for the feelings of a street performer is not just protecting Illyana and Hava from criticism but myself as well. In some strange way the Karmic

Echo is working its compulsive magic, forcing me to attempt in even the most insignificant of situations to maintain my amiability.

Interesting, eh? I would stop to give it more consideration but there is too much else that requires my attention.

Like dealing with the needs of my children.

Returning to the present moment I am just in time to hear Cathy question my concern over the magician's feelings.

"Rude?" she asks as if the word offends her sense of logic. "Why is it *rude?* Are we at a party or something?"

"The show is almost over," I explain, not wishing to argue. "You can wait till then."

I hear her mutter something but do my best not to discern the words or guess their meaning. Better to concentrate on the show out in the center of the clearing.

"For my next trick," Marco The Magnificent calls out with great importance, his eyes sweeping the audience, "I will need a young assistant."

Suddenly the magician spots the perfect boy for the task.

At the same instant Mickey tightens his grip on my hand.

"There he is!" Marco shouts triumphantly and in four long strides manages to glide across the open performance area, only coming to a stop when he stands directly in front of us.

"Excuse me," he says leaning over to speak with Mickey. "Young man," Marco implores in a loud stage voice, "would you like to help me with a magic trick?"

"Me, me! Pick me!" Hava cries, virtually panicked to have the magician so near yet so disinterested. She jumps up and down waving her hand in his face, promising, "I'll help, I'll help!"

Aside from pushing away her hand Marco does not appear to notice Hava's frantic pleas, so intent is his focus on my little boy.

Mickey takes a small step backward looking for more of his father to hide behind.

"Dad?" his small voice squeaks uncertainly.

"It is okay, Mick, " I say reassuringly. "He just wants to talk to you."

Marco smiles benignly at my little boy then shakes his hat's jingle bell tendrils in Mickey's face.

"Tell me," he asks, still in his stage voice, "Would you help if I asked you nicely?"

Mickey silently shrugs.

"Extra nicely?"

"Uh-uh!" he shakes his head.

"How about if I promised you a present?"

I listen for another protest but instead hear a tiny voice squeak, "A present?"

"Yes, a present!"

"A giraffe?" Mickey suggests, his voice suddenly charged with interest.

"Absolutely!" the magician gleefully replies. "A giraffe! The biggest balloon giraffe you ever saw!"

No longer afraid but still tentative my little boy decides, "Okay, I guess...I can help."

"Hey, Mick..." I start to say as he comes around from behind me.

Suddenly I feel his hand drop from mine. The next moment he has taken Marco's extended hand and is walking under the rope.

"Good luck, sweetie!" I call as he moves toward the center of the circle.

"Hey, there goes Mickey!" Su-Su exclaims, starting to wave at her brother. "Good luck, Mick!" she calls out, loving older sister that she is.

"Oh great," Cathy sighs, stamping her feet. "Now we've got to stay for the whole goddamn show!"

"Maybe you will be next, Havi," Illyana says brightly, trying to console her envious daughter.

"Funny," I think to myself, surprised by the speed with which Mickey changed his mind.

I guess he is not so afraid.

More accurately, I guess he really wants that giraffe.

Lesson 11

Things To Keep In Mind While Experiencing A Karmic Gravitational Slide

You realize of course we are not merely standing in front of Faneuil Hall watching a street performer who is half magician and half juggler. Life on my *ILE* is far too rich and much too ironic for things to ever be that simple.

No at the same time we appear to be mere spectators at an outdoor street performance there is something else happening and it is not unlike the movement of forces behind the steady unraveling of our protective cloak of anonymity at the cub scout Pinewood Derby.

We are being pulled or more exactly *carried* along under the impetus of some tremendous force towards our destiny.

The Seekers For Truth would say we are operating under the influence of a "Karmic Gravitational Slide" and that Mickey and I are fully engaged in the act of *Sliding*.

Sliding in the parlance of The Seekers is what happens when you find yourself being drawn through an apparently haphazard chain of events towards an inevitable climax. As with a magnet, the pull of circumstances grows only stronger, the conclusion more inevitable, the closer you get to the climax's magnetic core, which is often some life-altering confluence of events.

Do not ask me how an apparently haphazard chain of events can lead toward an inevitable outcome; it is as confusing to me as the concept that we somehow enjoy *Free Will* in situations where the outcome is already predetermined under the influence of Karma.

Go figure that one. I dare you!

Of course you do not understand.

You would have to be a Bapucharya to comprehend such

an intricate network of paradoxical interconnections. Who but a saint could get beyond all the inconsistencies?

"Do not fret your heads, children," The Bapucharya has said when talking about these contradictions, "the universe was not designed so that snotty-nosed children could read the blueprints. To comprehend the higher laws of Spiritual Physics you have to work very hard, burn the midnight oil, attend special classes; it is very wearisome, I agree. Far better to be fed scraps like birds in a cage than to choke on chunks too big to swallow," he concluded, his words breaking up in the usual giggles.

Confusing? Very!

Is it meant to be? Without a doubt!

For some reason that seems to only make sense to Hindu holy men the universe was constructed with Automatic Universal Misunderstanding *(AUM)* as a core element in its composition. We are purposely led to believe that the physical world we see around us is the *real* world, the entire world, the only world in which we live and die. And if some entity called God exists He is probably hiding on another planet or at least in the clouds, only coming down for special occasions like the six days He spent creating the world.

We have been led to believe by our parents, teachers and scoutmasters, who have all been fooled before us, that what we see is what we can expect. Except perhaps for a late-inning visit to heaven for those fortunate enough to donate a lot of money to their churches.

But that is not how the universe works according to The Seekers For Truth. In their universe we are all witnesses to a gigantic shared illusion constructed out of vibrations and fancy dreams—and please do not ask me *whose* dreams.

In this universe, according to Seeker doctrine, we have each agreed to live in this illusory world and pretend it is real. Then to make the whole thing even more incredible we have agreed to forget that we ever agreed to play this game in the first place!

For The Seekers it is like we are all staring at the same movie screen believing it to be life in its entirety. As if we decided to disremember everything else in the world except for what we see up on the screen.

So having forgotten we are merely watching a movie we live out our lives paying off the obligations and debts we owe from previous lives which, by the rules of the game, we have also forgotten. At the same time other individuals are paying off debts and obligations to us from lives they do not remember either. While all of this is happening nobody seems to be consciously aware of any of it!

No wonder everyone looks at you as if you were crazy when you offer even the thinnest glimpse of the cosmos as seen through the eyes of The Seekers For Truth.

"Tell me that again? I have lived many lifetimes and you have lived many lifetimes but neither of us remembers any of them? And during some of those lifetimes I have done things to you that make you do things to me and neither of us remembers that either? And the main thing we are supposed to do while playing this game of pretend is to discover that we are playing the game?"

It is virtually impossible to comprehend the mechanics of the universe as seen through the eyes and spiritual teachings of The Seekers For Truth.

If you do not agree, then explain to me how an individual can have the freedom to respond to events whose outcomes are determined in advance? That is like being able to win a tennis match whose final score is already fixed against you.

"You must have faith," The Bapucharya has said over and over. "There would be no reason to keep traveling up your Path of Seeking Truth if you already possessed the truth you are seeking. You are on the Path Of Seeking Truth specifically because this grand prize of all grand prizes has not yet been given to you.

"Stick your nose out, children, take a big whiff—ohmigoodness! Can you smell it? Of course you can. It is the scent of fresh cut grass, is it not! You do not need to see with your eyes or hold with your hands the fallen blades of grass to know they are all around you. Just the same you do not need to have this oh-so-elusive thing we call the truth in your hungry little grasp to know that it, too, is real.

"Do not forget you are children and oh-so-naturally see things through a glass darkly, as the prophet says. So please stop being such colicky children. It is no one's fault—except for the Great Actuator himself— that you must work like a dog and have faith you will be given a bone in the end.

"Unless of course you would prefer dog biscuits," he added from his video monitor with a chorus of self-appreciative giggles.

I never fully understood how a Karmic Gravitational Slide is supposed to work but apparently the universe is under the influence of both determined outcomes and free will at the same time, so at key junctures in our lives we are seemingly presented by chance with obstacles and challenges that were in reality destined for us—fated to show up on our *ILEs*—from the moment we were born.

Perhaps even before.

'Sliding' is the act of moving down along a track within that predetermined set of circumstances. Ordinarily you do not realize you have been *Sliding* until you look back with the clarity of hindsight to see the inevitability of the chain of events that took place.

I look back now and see that my separation and divorce was one incredibly long, totally unavoidable *Slide.* I could not have stopped it from happening if I had marshaled all the powers of the universe in my cause.

Of lesser import perhaps but no less inevitable is this march toward some momentous climax or outcome under the impetus of a comic magician who is merely trying to make a living here in Quincy Market. And the same is true I fear of the Pinewood Derby, which is advancing inexorably toward a grand finale with the same kind of earth-shaking undercurrent and subtle drumbeat that exudes what The Seekers term the *Long Distance Call of Fate.*

Both events, you will notice, feature myself and Mickey caught up together—tied torque-tight together—in the pull of forces as if we were a Karmic Unit operating under the influence of predetermined influences. Just what those influences may be I have obviously agreed to let myself forget.

Or so it seems.

In any case here I am in this plaza in Boston under a warm July sun with no idea of what is to come, only a sense that events are moving beyond my capacity to control them. Were I not also firmly positioned inside myself, high on a peak from which I can see almost the entirety of my *ILE*—and beyond!—I would be as blind to the fact that Mickey and I are *Sliding* as I would be to the strange similarities that exist between Marco the Magnificent and another unwitting servant of my life's unwinding destiny.

You remember Allison?

The frantic, blonde manhandler with the firm, roundish boobs?

How could you forget her? She is the very reason we are flashing backward and forward across this seemingly random series of events which in reality are strung together on Karmic thread like Japanese lanterns.

Did you think we would never return to Allison's apartment?

Or do you comprehend that we never really left?

Lesson 12

Reviewing Our Progress To Date

"Careful," I object angrily.

For some reason my protest squeaks out in a lower voice as if I might be worried about disturbing the neighbors or Allison's previously mentioned roommate.

"You are ripping my sleeve!" I complain.

"I'll rip more than your sleeve if you don't stop being such a drag," Allison warns bitingly, also lowering her voice.

All this whispering makes us seem like shareholders in a conspiracy.

As I watch the brown velveteen couch loom ever closer in slow motion my thoughts about the events that brought me here and the lessons still waiting to be uncovered on my *ILE* continue to occupy my mind, playing in succession like movie trailers before the main feature.

And this is where my first-ever Do-It-Yourself Workshop becomes tricky.

Because one has to make assumptions in identifying lessons for one's *ILE* and those assumptions can just as easily prove erroneous and misdirecting if one is not careful.

If that happens you may go through many lifetimes before you actually realize and have a chance to correct your mistakes. In that, it is much like plotting a course in space where a small fractional mistake could send you drifting off course for millions of miles.

Or so it seems.

But here on this planet we are being drawn towards some obvious dramatic climax in a darkened room on the second floor of a two family house and, as I said earlier, clearly under the frantic impetus of a woman in the throes of a Frozen Idea.

For those unaccustomed to working with Seeker concepts the question might arise as to whether Allison's Frozen Idea is working in assistance or opposition to my Karmic Gravitational Slide? Could one set of objectives be opposed to the other? Or is the synchronistic lunacy of the universe such that one person's Frozen Idea becomes the lubricant for another person's Karmic Gravitational Slide?

As a former Seeker For Truth I would have to answer—all puffed up as if I knew what I was talking about—that the Frozen Idea in this instance is clearly in service to the Karmic Gravitational Slide. But then if I am honest I would also have to add 'maybe' or 'I guess' or 'so it seems' because I really do not know what the hell I am talking about.

In any case this particular Karmic Gravitational Slide seems to be continuing its progress in slow motion, leaving me free to persevere on my mission to examine the events that brought me here tonight to Allison's apartment.

To underscore how far we have come in our course of study I would count off three events taking place on my *ILE*, all seemingly penetrated and connected by the same force of Karmic gravitational magnetism. And though each takes place at a different time, in Earth time, there is a way in which they all occur simultaneously when they are viewed from the *Center Point of The Universe!*

And seen in the Sacred Present Moment as The Seekers sometimes call it.

But let us review.

First there is the cub scout Pinewood Derby where Mickey's and my fortune seems inextricably bound up with Old Number Two. That masterwork of woodcraft, ugly and near-pink as it appears, seems to have us sliding inevitably toward some form of social catastrophe.

Then there is Marco the Magnificent's outdoor magic and juggling show where five year old Mickey, in greedy pursuit of a balloon giraffe, is stepping into the center of a ring formed by sixty or seventy total strangers. Something is about to happen there, though whether it will be bad or good we have not yet seen enough to predict.

And lastly of course there is the pallid, undernourished and overly aggressive Allison whose apartment seems to be giving off a scent I noticed earlier; something from my long-ago past that reminds me of...?

Sen-Sen!

Could it be...Sen-Sen?

I wonder...do they still sell Sen-Sen? How many years has it been since I smelled its slightly medicinal and flowery aroma? If it is not Sen-Sen it is something very close and equally familiar from my adolescence. Something that has so penetrated the bones of my memory that at the slightest whiff it has the power to transport me across decades. Back to when my friends and I in our rebellious boyhoods used to suffer the unpleasant taste of those dark, powdery, square tablets to cover up our smokers' breath. Most likely fooling nobody except ourselves.

But is that what I smell?

Sen-Sen?

There is something here, I am certain of that. But then again this woman is so crazed and her boobs have me so distracted I could easily be suffering olfactory hallucinations.

So lastly then, in an aura of Sen-Sen laden lust with my Prophetic Navigational Device throbbing like a geiger counter hovering above a uranium lode, I find myself in this bosomy blonde's upstairs apartment in Plymouth, Massachusetts where she and I appear to be moving toward a date with destiny on a brown velveteen couch.

Under the spell of this uniquely engaging slow motion drama I look at Allison and notice her facial features set with such grit and determination that I cannot resist a smile before closing my eyes.

Before my incipient smile has a chance to establish itself, however, an angry male voice interrupts, resonating superb diction and great distaste as it declares, "He is so full of crap!"

I open my eyes to find Bill McAndrews dropping his massive frame onto the chair next to mine.

Giving me no time to marvel at how suddenly—instantaneously really—I have flashbacked to the Pinewood Derby, Bill turns his head in my direction, looks at me quizzically, then smiles as though his outburst was nothing more than an unexpected passage of air he can excuse away with a sheepish grin.

"Bad news?" I inquire sympathetically.

"Oh, Peterson!" he moans in grand theatrical style, "God must have loved idiots to have created so many of them." His eyes turn briefly to the high-mounted racetrack then back again. "Did I miss anything?" he asks with a visible lack of interest.

"Bill, you missed everything," I say to myself. Clearly my anxiety over our grotesque fuchsia racecar is still offset by the magical appearance this morning of Ellie Eichorn who you will recall has gone off to find something to eat.

"Nothing much," I answer out loud. "How did you do?"

He shakes his head, pretending to shiver, then scoffs, "Anybody his age who dresses up like a boy scout has to have his head up his ass."

He is speaking of course about Mr. Matthews, perennial scoutmaster of Troop 123, whom you will remember is standing just over there behind the three-railed racetrack.

In case you have forgotten, this is the same Bill McAndrews who went off to argue about his son's second place finish in a race that was nowhere close enough to dispute.

However, it is not my nature to confront people or challenge their point of view, so rather than question McAndrews' paranoid fantasy about being victimized by our scoutmaster I benignly ask instead, "You mean he would not listen to your argument?"

"Said he couldn't," McAndrews replies, slowly drawing out the words with a sneer. "Said he'd have to give everybody else a second chance if he did—what a crock...!"

"That is too bad," I lament softly with little real interest.

"Now we'll just have to wait here," McAndrews says with his arms crossed, "till Dennis has seen enough of this pre-adolescent stock car fantasy, when we can finally go home and tackle the dozen chores my *kommandant* wife," he snaps off a salute, "has lined up for me on this otherwise dismal day."

Bill raises both hands in a questioning gesture, looking up to the heavens in what must pass for him as supplication. Slowly turning his head with that same exquisite sense of timing that turns everything into high melodrama he points heavenward and decries in his loudest whisper, "No one's home!" dramatically mouthing each word for emphasis.

Then he places a questioning hand on my shoulder asking in a moment of shared comradeship, "Does your life ever seem like a chore list that never ends, Peterson?"

Finally something to which I can relate!

"It used to," I answer, the lift in my voice giving evidence of how things have improved. "All the time, actually. That was one of the few things about the divorce I never regretted—I got the boot but Marilyn got the house and the chores."

"HAH!" McAndrews explodes in a burst of appreciation. "Very good—that's very good, Peterson!"

Serious again he continues, "Yes, but the reason I ask is that my life has evolved into the mindless execution of unimportant tasks done to imperfect standards. Do you understand what I mean?

"This morning's excursion to the Pinewood Derby, a prime example! Dennis and I must have spent weeks in the garage working on that dysfunctional racer. And for what? For five seconds of glorious ignomy...?

"Ahhh...! he interrupts raising a cautionary hand to prevent some imagined protest on my part, "I know what you're going to say: a second place finish is better than third. But tell me, Peterson, *how* is it better? Are you suggesting that the father of the third place racecar feels any *worse* than I feel? Feels like a bigger schmuck perhaps? I'm sure he feels just as frustrated as I do. And now he goes home a loser just like me, Peterson. Home to his wife and the chores she has waiting for him—*just like me, Peterson!*

"So, why should I congratulate myself for coming in second? Racehorses may earn prize money for a second place finish but salesmen earn *bupkas!* As far as I'm concerned, anything less than first place and you're perfectly positioned to eat the other guy's excrement."

Ten minutes later he is still at it.

Can you hear him?

By now I am only listening absently to McAndrews heaping abuse against the fates, our scoutmaster and above all against the tides of life that have brought him "in extremis,

Peterson!" to the shores of this morning's Pinewood Derby.

"And what a desolate stretch of beach it is!" he declares, continuing with his tidal metaphors. "Look at the flotsam and driftwood that surrounds us; can you see one redeeming aspect to any of this, Peterson, other than keeping two hundred delinquents off the suburban macadam for a few hours?"

I register the increase in McAndrews' agitation, the shrill edge to his sonorous voice, but I do not find them worthy of my concern.

Right now, even though I am sitting next to him, my thin wedge of consciousness is clearly more interested in moving on to the next lesson in my Do-It-Yourself Workshop.

Unbidden, the memory of that day four years ago draws me back inside myself. Back to the *Center*...well *almost* to the *Center Point of the Universe.*

How quiet and calm things suddenly become. Notice? Even though my body is still surrounded by noise and chaos, none of those sounds nor the ceaseless activity in the room disturb the solidity of the stillness I feel while seated here. Within a hair's breadth, I am sure, of the *CPU.*

And now suddenly I can sense a growing connection with a different moment in time, and people and circumstances from that other moment begin to materialize like wraiths out of the fog to become real and alive in the present moment.

The Sacred Present Moment.

Instinctively my eyes begin to search for my nine year old son in the realms of St. Christina's basement hall but when I finally find him he is five years old again and walking away from me outdoors toward the center of Marco The Magnificent's roped-off performance area.

Looking off to my right through the crowd I can see a billboard raised about 20 feet above street level at the other end of the long cobbled thoroughfare that runs the length of Quincy Marketplace.

Do you recognize it?

"Cr-r-r-runch!" it proclaims loudly in giant-size letters, before asking the most critical question of all.

"Have You Been Cr-r-r-runched Today?"

"N-n-not yet," a voice answers in a weak attempt at being wry.

A voice that sounds very much like my own.

Lesson 13

Nine Reasons You Should Never Turn Your Back On A Magician

As Marco The Magnificent sweeps Mickey into the center of the roped off arena I hear a low moaning sound coming from Illyana's direction.

"Oh, this is wonderful!" I mutter, turning to confirm what I already know.

Illyana is having one of her seizures.

She is gone. I can see that. Her arms are hanging limp at her sides, her eyes have a faraway vacant look, and her body stands motionless in place as if someone has turned off the power and left her here like a discarded toy.

By now I know what to do.

Nothing.

Well not exactly nothing.

"Hava," I say trying to pump-up the interest level in my voice. "What do you think will happen next? Will Mickey do a trick?"

"No," she replies authoritatively. "The magician will do a trick and Mickey will just watch. They just pretend that kids help them, but they're just fooling."

"Really!" I reply, trying to sound impressed by such a strong and interesting opinion. "I would have thought just the opposite. That Mickey might..."

"I've been to lots of magic shows," she interrupts like an irritable supreme court justice, "and I should know!"

"What are you two talking about?" Illyana's voice, a little unsteady, breaks in.

She is back. From where not even she could say.

The seizure was like most of Illyana's attacks where she suddenly vacates her body as if someone had accidentally brushed against a light switch and turned it off. Then usually in a few incremental ticks of a secondhand she is totally animated again, the Russian peasant returning to full vigor.

I am certain that no one else—certainly not my kids or Hava—saw any of this. Illyana's well-developed body stayed pretty much where she left it. And she was not in the middle of a sentence or thought when the attack struck so there were no obvious signs unless you knew what to look for—to *listen* for, really!

Just the sound of air escaping in a steady stream accompanied by a deep whining sort of moan. That was all there was to give her away.

Next thing you know, here she is back with us and good as new.

"We were just talking about Mickey," I answer casually.

"Mickey...?" Illyana repeats, still struggling to find her bearings.

"Yes," I say tilting my head towards the center of the stage, "The new magician's assistant."

Her eyes follow my head movement and suddenly it all becomes clear.

"Oh, yes!" she realizes. Smiling appreciatively she nods, "Yes, yes, thank you. I see. This I think it should be very interesting!"

"Well, we will certainly see for ourselves," I say doubtingly, turning to watch the show.

Never before have I known anyone who suffered from periodic blackouts so Illyana's condition seems strange to me, almost exotic. From what she has told me it generally happens at the oddest moments with barely any warning. For some still-to-be-discovered reason she abruptly lapses into inner visions of exploding light where thousands of starbursts go off inside her head. Those fireworks presage an attack but never allow her enough time to prepare for it. Then as if the plug were pulled, she disappears, escapes her body entirely, leaving the outer shell behind like a discarded suitcase.

At first I found her seizures upsetting, do not ask me why. After awhile, like anything else that happens on a regular basis, one gets used to it.

Before leaving on our trek downtown this morning I specifically asked Illyana if she had taken her medicine and she told me she had. Which meant that her attacks—and she has probably suffered one or two already this morning—would be brief and hardly noticeable.

What worries me now is the thought that maybe she was lying and had not really taken her medication. She has lied to me before, a few times in fact. Always to allay my fears, never to cover up for a faulty memory. But as a result I no longer fully trust her.

Twice I have seen attacks when she has neglected to take her medication and they both lasted minutes instead of seconds. Each time they occurred in the midst of some energetic activity which perhaps because of its over-stimulation seemed to bring on the attack.

Like the first time...

Excuse me. This is not easy; but I was going to say...*like the first time we had sex together.*

Obviously it shows a lack of proper respect and manners to reveal your intimacies with a woman but I cannot think of another event in my life that created such an impression of being lost in a dream while still fully awake.

More like being lost in a nightmare.

The Seekers talk about parallel worlds that exist as glimpses of the way things might have been. They are called *Glimmers* and they exist because of the strange mechanics involved in running a universe where events are karmically determined but people still have free will.

Glimmers are like scenes that never make the final edit in a movie. Scenes in which the characters chose different lines or the story takes on a different twist. Ordinarily *Glimmers* rarely appear in your life and have no bearing on any of the other people or events that ultimately make the final cut. But there are times, The Seekers assure us, when we all experience *Glimmers.* Though we rarely see them for what they are.

Or for what they are *not.*

Looking back I cannot help but wonder if that first intimate evening with Illyana really happened on my *ILE* or was just a *Glimmer* of what might have happened. It certainly seemed real yet so cut off and apart from the rest of life as I live it on my *ILE*.

Before that night at Illyana's, (assuming it really happened and wasn't just a *Glimmer* of some alternate reality) I had never before experienced such a bizarre mixture of shock, dread and bewilderment...but listen to me prattling on about the strange attractions of a bachelor's life at the precise moment that my five year old son is stepping onto a new stage in his personal development.

Ah, the golden lure of a balloon giraffe!

Turning my attention back to the center of the open air stage I find Marco strutting in a wide arc around Mickey, introducing him to the crowd with grandiose gestures.

Well actually I have not yet turned *all* my attention back to Mickey and his show business debut. I must admit that images just recalled to memory, scenes from the first time Illyana and I made love, have caused a slight stiffening between my legs which is now competing for my attention. As is the more subtle but constant pulsing of my *PuNDit* which has begun to sound its prudish warning in the middle of my forehead.

So with part of my mental apparatus focused on Mickey and another part hugely and hungrily distracted by 'dirty pictures' of Illyana now running through my mind, my eyes acting under their own impulse travel back and forth from the center of the Magician's staging area to the much closer and more exotic realms of Illyana's fulsome and previously explored bosom. A bosom, you will notice, that is partially and alluringly revealed through the low cut of her summer dress.

And though I cannot see her nipples fully revealed, their outlines against the fabric of Illyana's blue and purple dress cause me to clearly imagine them as though I had Superman's vaunted X-ray vision. I would say it was a trick of the mind but actually it is more an offshoot of a skill I developed when I was with The Seekers For Truth.

You remember? I told you about it earlier. How imagination plays a big role during an activity when one needs to rest one's attention on a working surface?

"Mr. Peterson," says a generic Seekers voice arising from

memory, "just let consciousness rest on the working surface where the work is taking place."

Obviously in most situations I cannot see the working surface because it is usually obscured by my hand or a tool or some complex piece of equipment. But I can always *imagine* I see it and that is the key. If the working surface is hidden from my vision, I imagine it. Just as I am now resting my attention on Illyana's dark elongated nipples, clearly seeing and celebrating them through the power and benevolence of that same highly developed imagination.

And what beautifully dark and extended nipples they are!

I told you, did I not, that Hava still occasionally sucks on them?

As do I.

All of this sexually-focused mental activity is of course taking place at the same moment the father in me is also concerned with his son's embryonic career in show business.

Speaking of which, Mickey is now standing in the center of the magician's roped-off performance area being introduced with overstated importance by Marco The Magnificent who holds up my little boy's arm as if announcing the winner in a prize fight.

"Folks, give a big hand to my new assistant, a boy by the name of...?"

He stops, comically exaggerating his movements in a show of momentary confusion.

"Oh my Heavens!" he exclaims covering his mouth in embarrassment, "I forgot to ask his name!"

The magician turns to Mickey with an inquisitive dip of his head that shakes the jingly bells on his jester's hat.

"And your name is...?" he prods.

"Mickey," my little boy answers softly. Then louder, "My name is Mickey!" perhaps remembering the giraffe.

"Mickey," Marco calls out with exaggerated relief. He turns Mickey around in a slow circle for the crowd, raising both of my little boy's arms in a theatrical salute. "Folks, a big hand for my new assistant, Mickey!"

Before the applause fully subsides, the magician's eyes fall down to his pants pocket where for no apparent reason a finger of red silk magically appears.

"Why, what have we here?" he calls out in mock surprise. Then with a greatly exaggerated "Aha!" he declares, "Perfect timing! I will ask my new assistant to assist me by removing the colored handkerchief from my pocket."

He swishes his hip, pushing the red silk scarf in my little boy's direction.

"Go ahead, take it," he directs Mickey who once he understands the request reaches for the red silk only to have it pulled away from his little hand as Marco pivots his hip in a gesture that brings titters from the audience.

After shifting his hips back and forth a few times Marco finally allows Mickey to pull out the red scarf. At which point a blue scarf is suddenly sticking out from his other pocket.

Another swish of Marco's hips and Mickey pulls out the blue scarf. Next a green silk scarf pops up from a shirt pocket...

Before too long, brightly colored silk scarves are materializing everywhere one after another—from pockets, sleeves, even from the inside of the magician's shoe. With each silk kerchief Mickey pulls out, another magically appears.

Finally holding up all the scarves in his hand Marco calls to the crowd, "Now, we'll test your powers of observation. I'll give a prize to anyone who can tell me how many scarves I am holding up?"

"Nine!" a man calls out with conviction.

"No fair!" Marco cries woundedly. "You've seen an earlier show."

In three leaps he is back to the center of the clearing where my little boy stands quietly next to the prop table. The magician picks up an empty metal tube, holding it up so the audience can see that it is in fact empty, a mere hollow cylinder. He places a lid over one end, transforming it into a canister which he hands to Mickey open side up.

Then pulling out the red scarf that started it all, Marco The Magnificent shouts "One!" and stuffs it with two sure strokes into the depths of the canister. Then he and the crowd as if they had planned it in advance loudly count out each kerchief that follows.

Soon they are shouting "Six" and a pink scarf disappears

inside the canister. "Seven," a candy-striped piece of silk goes in. "Eight!" a maroon kerchief follows. And on "Nine!" the last kerchief, purple with yellow stripes, is tucked into the deepest recesses of the open can.

The magician places a lid over the canister and takes it from Mickey's hands, giving him instead a white-tipped magician's wand.

"Mickey," he calls out for the crowd's benefit. "I want you to take your magic wand and wave it over this magic container."

As Mickey starts to lift the wand Marco stops him, shouting "Wait!" and feigning cautious surprise. "You didn't say the magic word."

"I don't know the magic word," my little boy explains. The squeaky words from his underdeveloped vocal chords carry thinly, like the distant clinking of glass, across the open space.

Marco considers this new wrinkle, rubbing his chin.

"Aha!" he exclaims holding up a single finger. "Tell us what you had for breakfast this morning?"

Puzzled, Mickey answers, "Sugar Flakes...?"

"Well, 'Sugar Flakes' is a fabulous magic word," Marco enthuses. "All the best magicians say 'Sugar Flakes'. Go ahead, wave your wand and say 'Sugar Flakes'."

Mickey lifts the wand but Marco's hand again shoots out to restrain him.

Apologetically he explains, "Sorry, Mickey, but before we do the trick we need to know what magic we are performing.

"Do you remember how many scarves we had?" he asks as if struck by an idea.

"Nine," Mickey's tiny voice replies.

"What if we magically add a tenth scarf? Would that be a great trick?"

Mickey squirms, uncertain how to respond. Finally he answers, "Su-u-re" with anything but certainty in his voice.

"O-o-kay!," Marco says mimicking Mickey's uncertainty and drawing a laugh for the effort. "Well, let's try it, anyway. Go ahead, wave the wand."

Mickey lifts the wand but waits this time.

The magician smiles declaring, "You're a pretty smart

kid. You know I need to add one more element to hold the trick together. That's why you waited, right?"

He reaches into his pocket and pulls out the end of a string.

"Something to 'hold the trick together—get it?" he impishly declares pulling out vast lengths of string from his pocket and letting it gather on the ground until it has been transformed into a small mound at his feet. Gathering it up he rolls it into a tight ball then lifts off the canister lid and places the string inside.

"Now..." he says with an air of finality, replacing the lid. "Now, we are ready!

"Wave your magic wand," he shouts to Mickey who obediently waves the wand back and forth over the canister.

Next in a stage whisper Marco prods, "Mickey...the magic word—quick, quick—the magic word!"

"Sugar Flakes!" my little boy cries out with a surprising jolt of vitality. Perhaps at last he is enjoying this unexpected start to a show business career.

"Sugar Flakes it is!" the magician shouts, popping off the lid triumphantly. Holding up the can in his left hand he reaches in with his right and pulls out the end of the string which quickly reveals one, two, then three, colored silk kerchiefs hanging down separately, each secured by a large knot in its corner.

"Here Mickey, you have to hold up your end," he jokes handing my son the end of the string to hold.

"Hold it high," he instructs, lifting up Mickey's hand then drawing the canister further away to reveal the fourth silk scarf dancing on the line.

As the fourth scarf is revealed he stops to ask, "Four?"

"Four!" the crowd answers, quickly chanting "Five!" as further backward movement reveals an orange scarf. "Six!" is pink. "Seven!" candy-striped. "Eight!" maroon...

"Wait!" the magician cries suddenly.

He stops his backward movement just as we all catch a brief glimpse—just the tip, really—of a purple and yellow silk scarf which quickly disappears back into the can.

"How are you doing, Mickey?" Marco calls across to my little boy who is holding up his end of the line.

"Okay," Mickey answers, his discomfort registering in his voice.

"Excellent! Now pay attention to this..."

Turning to the crowd Marco explains, "Before we learn if we've succeeded with our little trick, I must warn you that with this particular magic trick it is not unusual for the spirit world—which always helps me with my magic—well, sometimes the spirits like to play tricks. Spirits are very funny helpers. They like to joke around, get silly, do wild things like change the colors of my scarves or tie funny things to the string. And they especially love to steal things."

He pauses for effect, looks skyward as if his attention is momentarily captured by a thought, then leans over and peers into the canister.

"Ahh! It's just as I suspected!" he declares. "It's those pesky spirits again..."

Then with his voice rising like a carnival barker he proclaims, *"...and this time they've stolen Mickey's underpants!"*

With that monumentally cruel declaration Marco The Magnificent pulls back sharply, revealing in a startling flash the last two items strung on the line: a purple silk scarf with yellow stripes and a small pair of boy's white jockey shorts.

Marco's cruel declaration instantly pulls me from my fascination with Illyana's breasts in a rush of energy that approaches panic.

Fear rising in my throat I search out Mickey as waves of laughter and startled exclamations fill the air. Their mingled, uneven, almost screeching ruckus chills me to my bones. All the while my little boy stands there in the center of the clearing, frozen stiff, uncertain what to do, his hand still holding up the chain of scarves. Even from this distance I can see he is scared to death that perhaps somehow those jockey shorts stretched wide on the line and bouncing free in all their wild incongruity are actually *his underpants!*

In a misguided effort at reconnaissance his eyes travel down the length of his body as if he might be able to actually see through his pants to determine if the magician was telling the truth. Failing to find either his underpants or some source of reassurance his eyes begin to move hauntedly from side to side like those of a laboratory test animal staring at the dead end of a maze.

My son seems like a trapped and very confused creature to say the least.

Dazed and confused myself I stand frozen to my spot staring in disbelief as a nearby child's voice calls excitedly, "Look, Mommy, look! Mickey's lost his underpants. *Mickey's lost his underpants!"*

"Havi, *shhh! No!"* Illyana says harshly. "You will harm his feelings. Look at how sad he is feeling."

Yes look at how sad he is feeling indeed!

So sad his face distorts into a grimace while his little boy's body seems to fall in on itself as if there is no other way to hide from 70 total strangers whose growing chorus of laughter must seem totally overwhelming. Not for all the world and all its treasures would I want to be a five year old boy whose underpants are hanging on a line for everyone to see.

Suddenly I hear The Bapucharya's voice inside my mind.

"You remember what I so wisely said before?" he laughingly reminds me, "...such a big difference to have yourself exposed fully naked before cub scouts rather than boy scouts?"

"Not now, Your Holiness," I intone softly.

"On the contrary," he replies, amused as ever. "No matter where you are, and what is happening, it is always *now!"* he laughs.

I leave this scrap of unwelcome wisdom unanswered, keeping my eyes and attention glued to the five-year-old boy in the center of the plaza.

If Mickey were not so frightened, I am sure he would drop the line of scarves and run off. But he is frozen in place like a rabbit caught in the headlights; too petrified to do anything but wait for whatever is coming. Unable to run yet so exposed he does not even have the option of crying. All he can do is drop his head and close his eyes to hide from these people who so cruelly surround him with their laughter.

The only thing he can really do of course is wait for his father to rescue him.

Finally after what seems like the passage of a lifetime I step free of my own paralysis and hurry into the center of the open arena.

I do not expect you to applaud but you should realize it is not easy for me to overcome my own fears of public embarrassment even to rescue my own child.

As soon as I reach Mickey I kneel down and stare straight into his eyes which happen to be scrunched tightly shut.

"Mick, Mick, it is okay," I assure him. "Would you like to stop?" I say the words slowly and gently so as not to further frighten him. "Should we stop now?"

His eyes now open and staring back into mine, a thin voice on the edge of tears squeaks out a weak and frightened, "Yes."

"Okay," I say with a reassuring smile, "it is over. Simple as that: it is all over!"

Gently with a sense of purpose, as if in removing Mickey from the show we are bringing some primal ceremony to a close, I take the string from my son's hand and let the scarves fall to the ground. I am proud to say there is not a single thought in my mind for the magician or for the crowd. Let them approve or disapprove, it does not matter.

In this rare moment on my *ILE* my only concern is for my child.

Standing up with Mickey in my arms I search out Marco The Magnificent and brusquely inform him, "Show is over."

He smiles back weakly, his face showing the discomfort he must feel over this unexpected conclusion to his grand finale.

"Wait," he calls, abruptly waving a raised hand to keep us from leaving. "My assistant has earned himself a prize."

I feel Mickey's head lift off my shoulder at the sound of the word 'prize'.

For a moment at least Mickey's pain is forgotten as he watches the magician blow up six elongated pink and blue balloons. As each balloon fills with air Marco twists it in a squeaky blur of effortless craftsmanship, joining each one to the whole till they all intertwine to form something resembling the shape of a French poodle.

Mickey wipes a moist eye, takes the balloon poodle from Marco's outstretched hand, then puts his head back on my shoulder without a word.

Moving off, I shout, "Come on, girls!" to my small flock. "Ladies, Illyana...!"

Moments later my little boy weakly mutters something into my neck, his words obscured by the sound of squeaking balloons.

"What," I ask pulling my head to the side. "What did you say?"

"I said I didn't get a giraffe," he repeats in a sad monotone.

"No, you did not," I agree. "There must be a lesson in that."

"What lesson?" he asks dispiritedly.

"A big lesson," his sister Cathy pipes in. "Never trust a magician!"

My little boy groans.

He is not ready to apply humor to his wound or to let his sister do it for him. Who can say when, if ever, he will be ready to let go of his pain?

Cathy is correct, astute as ever.

Never trust a magician.

"Yes," I say out loud in response to a billboard that looms ever larger and more ironic as we walk toward it through the mid-day crowd.

"Yes...now I have been C-r-r-runched today!"

Briefly an urge flashes across my consciousness.

But I am not the kind of person who sets fire to billboards.

Lesson 14

The Whys And Wherefores Of Random Cruelty And Mandatory Suffering

Except for Hava who acts as if nothing important has happened—and for her of course nothing important *has* happened—we all walk away from Quincy Market wrapped in a heavy blanket of silence, sharing Mickey's pain in quiet communion.

With Mickey clinging fiercely against my neck it is a pain I experience physically as well. Feeling responsible for the whole miserable experience and for the skyscraper Milestone I know we have just erected on Mickey's *ILE,* I say nothing about my discomfort, choosing instead to suffer stoically as part of my penitence.

Suzie and Cathy walk on either side of us, occasionally reaching up to stroke and soothe their quietly brooding brother. Mickey does not seem to notice their attentions; does not even turn to look when they reach out and touch him. He is both physically and emotionally frozen in place. He will not leave my arms, will not even agree to walk a step until we are back at our car. By then, not surprisingly, I have developed a painful crick in my neck.

But there is more to worry about than a little physical discomfort. Definite injury has been done to my little boy this hot July afternoon. How significant an injury we have yet to discover, but as I mentioned a moment ago the experience will have certainly erected a gigantic new Milestone on the still sparsely developed landscape of Mickey's *ILE.* Of that I am certain.

As The Seekers For Truth will tell you, a Milestone is not only significant in shaping the terrain of an *ILE,* it can be a dramatic force for accelerating the journey up one's Path Of Seeking Truth or for throwing one off the track altogether.

And this Milestone business is not to be taken lightly.

When an event is so singular and impactful it stands high above the ordinary run of life's experiences it becomes a marker on your *ILE*, a Milestone that by its very height serves as an obstacle on your Path Of Seeking Truth. Of course it does not always have to hinder your journey. Like a runner's hurdle it can also force you to increase your velocity, enabling you to vault over even the highest of Milestones.

Assuming you can land without hurting yourself.

Assuming you do not crash into the wall or stumble during your leap.

Assuming your psyche has not been crushed by a mindlessly cruel magician.

We all develop Milestones on our *ILEs* but the ones placed there by our parents are the ones that usually pose the highest obstacles.

This tragic episode with the magician—all fifteen minutes of it—will resonate perhaps for the rest of Mickey's life, possibly for a few lives after that. And because it happened while he was so young and vulnerable, supposedly under his father's care and protection, his humiliation is as much a gift from me as if I had purposely planned it.

If that sounds unfair to you, The Seekers would remind you that a father who was drinking his *RC Cola* and resting his attention on his child's unsettled situation rather than a companion's hauntingly extended nipples might actually observe dangers early enough to prevent them.

Failing Mickey as I did outside Fanieul Hall explains why four years later I am so mindful of the perils we face at the Pinewood Derby. And why I am so fixated on the need to make our escape from that fateful church basement.

Assuming there is still time to escape.

Assuming the pull of its Karmic gravity is not too powerful to resist.

I do not kid myself. With the Pinewood Derby, Mickey and I have been locked into a Karmic Gravitational Slide from the moment we entered St. Christina's. Sliding in a straight line on some spiritual navigational chart toward whatever Milestones lay in perilous wait.

The main difference being that by this time in my life I

am old enough to navigate around new bumps or Milestones on my path while Mickey is still so raw and vulnerable you cannot be certain what lifelong price a new Milestone might extract.

An experience like the one with the magician could turn a lesser child into a recluse; could serve as the pivotal point at which a weakling gets transformed into an emotional cripple. At the very least there is now an obstruction on Mickey's *ILE* that is placed squarely on his Path Of Seeking Truth. And if he is to continue the journey, as he must, he will be forced to confront over and over again the same Milestones, the same set of demons, in order to eventually move beyond their influence.

Driving slowly through downtown Boston all of us choose to be quiet if not solemn, even Hava. I steal a look at Mickey in my rear view mirror and although he is scrunched between his sisters he seems very much alone. So alone, I anxiously notice, he does not even realize that Hava has taken possession of his balloon poodle.

I say nothing about the balloon poodle. Nor do I offer any of the humor or corny wit I would normally use to lighten the heavy mood in the car.

What can I say?

What can I tell Mickey that would make him feel better? What can I say that would help him comprehend and absorb this unforgettable day's lesson? Is there anything I could offer that would help him to climb or vault over this newest Milestone? If not today then someday?

Do I know enough about the workings of the universe to hazard some attempt at a point of view? Enough at least to answer his number one favorite question: 'Why?'

Why?

As if life were a school where instructors explained the most difficult lessons.

Nobody explains anything in this lifetime, I would have to tell my little boy. It is a school perhaps, but you must do most of the coursework on your own. And the simple truth is I do not know why things happen the way they do.

Why for example did Marco The Magnificent select you out of all the other boys that were there? And why would he risk his audience's disapproval by humiliating you the way he did?

For a laugh? For a cheap laugh?

Of course some things are not so difficult to figure out.

Clearly the magician needed a boy your age, I would tell Mickey, if for no other reason than the size of the jockey shorts hanging on his line. The joke would not have been funny with the wrong-sized boy. Or with any-sized girl. That is why Hava could never have been selected. And why Marco passed over smaller and bigger boys.

But beyond that...why he selected you rather than another five-year-old boy or why the fates put you within his grasp? Those are questions too cosmic for me to answer.

If the universe meant for you to be given a Milestone this morning, the why of it is something you will have to figure out for yourself.

I look at your sad, five-year-old face in the rearview mirror and though your lips do not move I can still hear you asking with silent urgency, "Why?"

Why?

How many times a day do you ask me that?

Why this, Daddy, why that? Why yes, why no? Why is this black, why is that white?

All those whys and each one so important you search out my eyes to ask it.

"Why...?" I usually repeat just to give myself time to think up an answer.

Like when you recently asked, "Why do I have to go bed if I'm not sleepy?"

Why? I repeated, waiting for the right answer to present itself.

Looking into your questioning eyes I thought to myself, "Because I say so, that is why! Because parents have always said so since the dawn of time—or the dawn of bedtime to be more exact. But why you choose to obey me, *that* I do not understand. Most children do not listen so well to their parents, certainly not your sisters. Just look at your sisters! They argue with me or pretend to listen but then go ahead and do what they want anyway. While you my docile friend, you are so reasonable it causes me to smile and periodically gives rise to a dull ache in the center of my being."

That is the answer I heard in my head but not the answer I gave you.

"Because you are young and need your sleep," I finally replied out loud, "even if your body does not know it!"

No big deal as far as answers go but it was enough.

So many questions. So many 'Whys?'

So many in fact that sometimes I pretend not to hear them. And then you get annoyed; sometimes you even bristle.

Like the other day when you shouted, "Daddy!" making me half jump out of my skin, startled by the measure of your irritation as much as your shout.

"What?" I asked, surprised. "What is wrong?"

"I asked you a question."

"What question?"

"Why you and Mommy are not living together?"

"Oh, *that* question," I said jokingly, quickly deciding that discretion would be the better part of valor. "That is a question for your mother to answer, not me. Since the divorce was her idea she should be the one to explain it."

A reasonable answer to a difficult question and strangely enough it seemed to satisfy both your curiosity and your overactive sense of fairness.

And then there are questions whose answers will never make any sense...like when you asked, "Why is soup so good when it's hot and so yucky when it's cold?"

I loved that question. It appealed to the sense of awe in which I hold life and its most intriguing mysteries. We were eating lunch in my Cambridge apartment, a bowl of tomato rice soup on the table obviously the instigator of your question.

I gave you one of my adult, upside-down answers that you never came close to understanding.

Yes I sometimes forget you are only five years old.

"Think of it like a wish," I said fancifully. "A wish you had in the middle of a day when you were watching clouds move across a blue sky and suddenly you were struck by this powerful urge to fly. How real and wonderful that wish was—the desire to fly!—especially with that image you had of yourself up in the sky.

"There you were imagining yourself flying over fluffy white clouds, chasing birds from their branches, playing hide and seek with the sun..."

"Dad!" you tried to interrupt, but I would not stop.

"Just wait, okay?" I persisted. "Three or four hours later, that same wish to fly—exciting as it was before—seemed out-of-place and not very exciting when you remembered it while watching TV.

"If you can remember a time like that, you will realize it is not the soup that tastes yucky when it grows cold. It is the taste of a desire—or a wish—that has been left sitting too long."

I should have anticipated your reaction.

"Dad," you exploded in protest, "I can't understand you when you talk like that! I'm just a kid, you know!"

And so you are. And so I must learn to construct explanations that will make sense to someone other than an adult who has spent fifteen years with The Seekers For Truth.

But I stray from the real question...

What about Marco The Magnificent—that would be the question you would most want answered? Why did he choose you? Of all the boys there that afternoon why were *you* the one chosen to be humiliated?

Why?

My answer to you would not mention Milestones.

Instead it would assert, "Bad things happen, that is why!"

Then of course you would pipe up, "Why?" without a second's hesitation.

And I would wonder why bad things do happen to good people? Why some of us receive life's lessons without sufficient proof we need the instruction?

Why indeed!

What could I tell you that would make this lesson in life less painful?

That life is like that? That each of has to learn to take the cheese pizza when it comes even if we ordered pepperoni? That sometimes you do not get a choice about such things?

I could tell you about the Law of Karma generating events in this life to pay off debts and obligations from previous lives. But that would only strike you as unfair since you cannot recall a single thing you had done wrong in a previous life. And besides to suggest to you right now when your shame still burns at its brightest that there was some purpose or intention behind your public humiliation would only make you feel as if the universe were ganging up on you.

I could point out that life often seems unfair. That I never had a choice when your mother decided to divorce me and break up our family. And that nobody conducted a study to see if I deserved the trauma that would follow or the Milestone it would leave behind on my *ILE.*

A huge colossus of a Milestone!

But I cannot tell you that. It will not help you understand anything except perhaps my dislike for your mother. Which will not help at all.

And I will not tell you about Milestones, Karmic Gravitational Slides, Legacies, Glimmers or any other incomprehensible concept The Seekers revealed to me. Those are pieces of knowledge you unfortunately have to discover for yourself. Nobody can feed you information about the purpose of life and expect you to digest it. And certainly not at the tender age of five.

The Seekers tell us that when a person is ready for the truth, the truth will present itself.

Rarely in the form of a parent I would hasten to add.

The one thing I can tell you though, which I deeply believe, is that suffering can make you a better person. It can make you stronger, smarter, more understanding and more accepting of all the lessons and surprises you have to face on your own Path Of Seeking Truth.

Maybe if someone gave us instruction manuals when we first became human beings and told us that suffering was good for us—that it would help shape our characters and make us better people— perhaps then there would be fewer imperfect human beings like you and me complaining about the bumps in the road or the lumps we take traveling over them.

Yes suffering has a purpose, I would tell you. According to The Bapucharya, *everything* that exists in this Great Unrevealed Mystery we call the creation has a purpose. At the physical level suffering exists everywhere, almost like oxygen. Which means it definitely belongs in your life whether it comes in the form of a magician or a pitifully crafted Pinewood Derby model racecar.

You can take it as a gilt-edged guarantee that suffering will come into your life whether you invite it in or not. The trick is not to fight it when it comes but to face it head on. Not merely to jump over the next Milestone but to leap as high as you can when you do.

Oh yes I can just hear your response.

"There you go again, Dad! I can't understand you when you talk like that!"

And you would be right of course!

So I will not talk like that.

Instead while continuing to drive our solemn group back to Cambridge I will silently step back inside my mind, seat myself at the top of that inner mountain, far far away from this moment filled with hurt and confusion. In that still, silent space almost at the exact *Center Point of the Universe* all is peacefully devoid of wind or pain, struggle or thought. Nothing is wrong and everything is exactly what it is supposed to be.

What a perfect place to apply a little *HW-40.*

Let us see where it takes me.

Lesson 15

How To Stand Up Like A Man When All Else Seems To Be Falling Down

"Why're you smiling like that? What're you thinking? What's happening?" a voice intrudes, penetrating my thoughts with its rapid-fire questions and bringing my travels to rest.

I blink my eyes then rub them briskly as the Pinewood Derby comes sharply into focus.

"Oh, you are so bad!" she continues. "You look like that cat from Alice in Wonderland. What's his name? The one that keeps leaving his smile behind?"

Recognize the raspy voice? The endless stream of questions? The casual air of sexual innuendo?

Who could forget?

"The Cheshire Cat," I answer with a smile as I contemplate the lovely—and fully clothed—Ellie Eichorn who is standing in front of me holding two white Styrofoam cups and a brown paper bag.

"Give that man a cigar!"

Speaking of cigars...

"I was just thinking about you," I remark sitting up straight.

"Good thoughts, I hope."

"You said I was smiling."

"Great!" she responds eagerly. Handing me one of the coffee cups her smile drops into an exaggerated frown. "They didn't have hazelnut but I bought you a doughnut to compensate. Is that okay? You don't mind?"

"That is just what I need," I reply with mock severity, gently patting my expansive tummy.

Short on sympathy she waves away the idea. "You overweight? Give me a break! Just enjoy the doughnut!"

For no reason I will ever understand I apparently feel the need to include my neighbor in this discussion so I nod in his direction and declare, "Bill and I have been anxiously awaiting your return."

McAndrews who has been sitting quietly, brooding I suppose over the unvarnished cruelty of scoutmasters, turns as if surprised to discover there are other adults at the Pinewood Derby.

Having no choice but to follow through on the introductions, I fire off, "Bill this is Ellie, Ellie this is Bill."

"Hello," McAndrews says with a strangely piercing look. "Nice to meet you." At this moment he is no longer the self-assured salesman who devours entire states but rather a fellow human being as uncertain of the scheme of things as the next guy.

If I have to guess I would say Bill is in shock over the familiarity I have achieved with our attractive neighbor.

Hello," Ellie curtly nods in response.

Her cool manner surprises me but just about everything related to Ellie surprises me.

For instance those long fingernails of hers which, in an artistic frenzy, she painted a dark metallic red—those I find surprising! Just imagine what those nails could do to the skin on some lucky devil's back!

"Perfect timing," I smile taking a doughnut from the open bag she waves in my face. "I am ready for this."

I take a bite in subdued celebration.

Oh my!

This is a doughnut?

This is *horrible* whatever you call it! I cannot believe this is actually intended for human consumption. The texture is dry and crumbly, more like dried mortar than dough, and the taste more-than-slightly rank as if it had been fried in grease previously used for frying fish. It is all I can do to keep from gagging and spitting it out. But instead I point to my mouth, raise a brave smile and tell Ellie through a mouthful of unmasticated doughnut, "Great...just great! Thanks!"

"Don't mention it," she breezily smiles back.

Another thought crosses her mind.

"You're sure this was okay—you don't mind? I feel like such an idiot going out of the house with barely enough change for Ricky's snack..."

I try to respond but between the fetid doughnut crumbs in my mouth and the lack of a suitable opening into the conversation I have no choice but to wait for the entire train to pass by.

"...and, no big surprise, they don't take credit cards at cub scout events. Duh, smart me! You sure you don't mind? I mean, really, it's okay...? You're not going to hate me?"

Finally, my chance.

"Let it go." I smile quietly into her momentary pause. "I am just glad I could help. No big deal."

"As long as you're sure," she smiles gratefully. "You are a sweetheart," she adds for good measure, walking over to where there's a break between two front row chairs.

Returning to her seat behind McAndrews she notices, "Oh look, it's starting again."

Meaning of course the scoutmaster Mr. Mathews has begun a monosyllabic reading of the Derby standings, a sure sign that the next Derby heat is about to be called.

Which partially explains why McAndrews reaches out and taps his fingers heavily on Old Number Two which Mickey earlier returned to its customary parking spot on my lap.

"Time for Quasimodo to race again?" McAndrews asks, almost snorting out the question.

The word "What?" starts to form in my mouth but somehow cannot find audible expression.

"Time for that execrable piece of crap to win its next race," he continues as if I might actually share his nasty opinion.

"Heat," I correct him, the word rising like an involuntary reflex.

Other than that I have nothing to say. I am literally struck dumb. Turning to face him I feel myself being drawn into dangerous waters.

"What...?" I finally exclaim, grasping for comprehension. Then through a spray of flying doughnut crumbs, "*What* did you say?"

"No offense, Peterson," he retorts in a derisive whisper that can probably be heard across the room, "but who designed that appalling piece of shit? And when did he lose the use of both hands?"

Now I am not only startled but shocked.

"Bill, what the hell is your problem?" I ask, biting each word as it passes through my clenched lips.

"You wouldn't understand," he says dismissively, "but that's exactly what I hate most about these father and son tag-team events! I mean, how in the world does something that obnoxious..." he nods toward the humbly appointed model racecar on my lap, "something *that* irritating to the eye, manage to win six straight heats? You must have spent all of what...two hours on it?"

I look down to Old Number Two and receive no comfort from its silent presence. If anything the racecar looks even uglier and more ill-conceived than I remember.

"We have won only five heats," I correct him. Do not ask me why at this moment of rising tension I feel the need to address factual misstatements but apparently I do.

"Listen, Bill..." I start to say, shaking my head as if the gesture might help clear up the confusion that suddenly threatens to envelope me. "Was it something I said?" Struck by a sudden thought I conclude, "My God, you are taking your son's bad luck out on *me!* Is that it? Is that right?"

"I said *no offense,* Peterson," he responds curtly. "But why don't you stop your crybaby complaining and look at things squarely. Admit that it's not fair! Anyway you look at it, it's just not fucking fair!"

"What is not fair?" I ask, struggling to comprehend. "What in heaven's name are you talking about?"

"You know what I'm talking about."

I feel like a character in a play being fed lines from the wrong script.

"I have no idea what you are talking about," I snap back, suddenly aware my voice has an edge to match his. "Something is unfair, I get that. But what it is, I have no idea! Your son's derby loss? Are you *still* bitching about that?"

"Would you call *that* fair?" he asks, once again derisively tapping the fuchsia racecar on my lap.

"Bill, keep your *fucking* hands to yourself," I whisper in a harsh spray of doughnut crumbs and saliva. The moment I hear the 'f' word flying from my lips I realize things are beginning to spin out of control.

In fact the energy and tension of this dialogue has grown so dangerously high I can no longer take the risk of sitting here with my hands full. I lean over and place the cup of coffee and the fish-fry doughnut on the floor beneath my chair.

If Bill heard the threat in my voice he does not choose to give me the satisfaction of a response. Instead he continues his journey down the same dark path, returning my fierce look and instructing me, "Just look closely at what you have done, Peterson. I mean you did absolutely nothing to make that hideous thing race-worthy. Even the most oblivious of fathers used graphite or grease on the wheels of his son's racer. But you? Not you! It was an act of pride with you, I would venture, to totally ignore the laws of physics and aerodynamics. You didn't even condescend to add lead weights for traction or speed. Not one! And look at it. The damned thing's so hideous it should die on the track from embarrassment..."

I open my mouth but nothing comes out. I do not know what to say. I am literally shocked into silence.

"I don't mean to be harsh, Peterson," he continues, not at all conciliatory, "but you've got a damn nerve bringing something that shabby to a cub scout father and son event—and then *winning with it*, for god's sakes!"

"Bill..." I stammer, searching for something I can grab onto. "Bill, you had better...stop...!"

"So what happens...?" he asks, ignoring my half-completed threat. "I'll tell you what happens. Your son's criminally ugly racecar wins six—no *five* heats, thank you—and my boy's Pinewood Derby racer, which we literally worked on *for weeks,* goes down in flames after two. In a race so close I still can't see how they had the nerve to say we lost. You call that fair? I call that bullshit!"

Funny how after all these years of disengagement from my Seeker training it suddenly takes over in a situation where I feel so powerless and lost.

As McAndrews continues his tirade, notice how my lips

which are tightly drawn and pursed as if ready for battle suddenly begin to relax? And my arched eyebrows slowly fall back to rest as if a gentle calm is spreading itself over my features?

All that is happening because I have separated myself from the rising tide of my emotions and have let my attention rest on the sound of McAndrews' voice. Not on the words he is speaking but on the sound itself. The sound that shapes, carries and propels his harsh, angry words and gives expression to the workings of his churned up mind.

As a result, a realization has bubbled up to the surface of consciousness like a pocket of air in a bathtub. Were tensions not so high I might raise my finger and shout "Aha!" But this is not the time to shout anything even if I begin to understand the reasons behind McAndrews' nasty turn of behavior.

He is jealous!

He is jealous *of me!*

Once you listen to his voice—really listen—you cannot miss it. Strangely enough it is not Mickey's and my winning heats with Old Number Two he resents so much as my apparent success with Ellie Eichorn.

Yes that may sound strange but it is true nevertheless. I am certain of it.

Realizing there is little point in arguing with someone so hopelessly lost in a tempest of unreasonable emotions I grab onto Old Number Two and begin to stand up. I have no plan, no thought about where to go or what to do. I just know I cannot stay here next to this simmering volcano and wait for it to explode.

Before I am fully standing—only half-upright in fact—I feel a sudden immovable resistance at the point where my left hand is grasping the model racecar. Something is rigidly resisting the pull of my rising body, holding me in place and threatening to take the racecar out of my hands. I look down to see that McAndrews has shifted around on his seat to enable his left hand to grab hold of Old Number Two and keep it frozen in an unyielding, vice-like grip.

Part of me observing all this is quite surprised at how large McAndrews' hand is. I find myself commenting in my mind about what an enormous bone structure McAndrews appears to have. Which in the curious way my mind usually works starts me wondering about the size of his penis.

Well if nothing else, *that* instantly pulls me from my straying thoughts, yanking me back to the present moment.

"What the heck are you doing?" I demand, both defiant and incredulous but still managing to keep my voice down to a harsh whisper.

"My duty as a parent," he self-righteously answers.

If I am honest I will note—in case you missed it yourself—that my agitation in the form of pursed lips, furrowed brow and a general air of panic has returned.

Now begins a silent battle of wills that brings forth not only a surprising show of strength from the deepest wells of my being but also a little buzzing voice in my ear.

"Pull it in such a way," the voice mischievously suggests, "that your damn ugly racecar breaks apart."

Yes it suddenly dawns on me that this bizarre duel of wills between McAndrews and myself could easily present the very opportunity for escape I have been praying for. This could be fate intervening in the form of a slightly illogical, totally enraged and absurdly jealous cub scout father.

Just look at Old Number Two patiently waiting for me to make my decision. Poised in zen-like equanimity as two forces of temporarily equal strength push and pull fiercely in different directions.

But which of us is Mr. Ping and which is Mr. Pong?

My mind plays with this new idea: the thought of *accidentally* damaging Mickey's Pinewood Derby racer. An interesting possibility, I muse, while struggling to maintain the concentration I need to keep a competitive hold on Old Number Two. In one easily-explained, blameless moment I could end this melodrama, free Mickey from his Karmic Gravitational Slide, prevent the construction of a mammoth Milestone on his *ILE* and free myself from the aching paralysis that has gripped me ever since I first realized the scope of the tragedy I possibly helped shape with my mindless hurried crafting of Old Number Two.

All I have to do is shift my grip. Nothing more. Just hold onto the thin wedge of wood on the forward side of the front axle, grasping it tightly till something gives. If enough of the front section breaks free at the axle groove there will not be enough wood left to grip the axle.

Or I could just let go of the racecar entirely…?

There is an idea!

And it would be in keeping with my Seekers For Truth training! Mr. Ping frees both himself and Mr. Pong by letting go!

By practicing *Releasement* as The Seekers call it.

How is that for an officially sanctioned, Seekers For Truth higher-consciousness solution?

I can just let go! Let McAndrews have the racecar all to himself and see what he does. He is so infuriated, as you can see, he would probably throw it on the ground and break it into a dozen pieces.

Just let go.

Remove Mr. Ping and Mr. Pong.

Do it, Peterson! a voice whispers.

Just release your grip. Open your fingers. All it takes is a little *Releasement* and McAndrews will do the rest.

I tell myself to let go but as I stare into Bill McAndrews' face contorted with rage and exertion I see other faces hiding just below the surface. Faces also distorted but more from the strain of trying to grab hold of my life rather than a model racecar. Faces bent to the effort of gaining control over me even for the briefest moment so they can twist my life to their own selfish purposes, creating something entirely unrecognizable to myself.

I see Marilyn's face for one. Contorted in the effort of trying to wrest from me my children's love and respect as well as the few remaining possessions I still own.

And of course the face of that sex-crazed madwoman in Plymouth whose round boobs and aura of faded beauty are holding me in place just as tightly as the steel tension of McAndrews' muscular grip.

Warren Goldsmith's face is there too. Warren is the account supervisor on the Wayco Mattress account—*"Wayco Is The Way To Go!"*—and you could never hope to meet a more devious human being outside the boundaries of an advertising agency. Most of the time Warren is so adept at manipulation I cannot figure out how he gets me to do things

I would normally refuse to do.

And then there is the face of The Bapucharya. A face I have never ever seen except on a video screen or inside my mind. A face long ago left behind, I thought, but which has suddenly returned as a presence that refuses to go away. A presence that refuses to release me from The Seekers For Truth. Refuses to stop making bad jokes…

Refuses, I guess, to stop trying to save my soul.

No surprise I can hear him even now, amused as ever, goading me on as if I were still an upside-down first year student: "Oh my, you have caught a tiger by the tail! If you let him go, just be careful not to wait around for his show of appreciation." As usual, even in my mind, a series of strangled, high-pitched laughs punctuate his words.

I do not understand how such a peace-loving man as myself gets caught up in so many melodramatic battles! Each battle pitched to such ridiculous heights of importance and drama that it wearies me just to think about them.

And now poised halfway between sitting down and standing upright, my knees bent in a highly uncomfortable position, my hands clutching Old Number Two in a painful and desperate grip, I am lost as to what to do next.

Something inside of me—and it is an aspect of myself I do not hold in high regard—wants to release my resistance and allow McAndrews to take control of this out-of-control situation.

But I cannot let go. This is one time that Mr. Ping must stand up for himself and not let go. But what are my other choices?

The only option I can see is to fight this goliath of a plastic bag salesman for possession of my son's model racecar. It is an option that appears more inevitable and less attractive the longer I am stuck in this position.

I am truly at a loss.

I have no ideas, no impulses, no next step to take. I feel totally alone in the universe without any resources to draw on. This is exactly how I felt when I first separated from Marilyn, leaving our family home with three dollars and sixty-six cents in my pocket.

Back then I was able to move in with my sister Gail.

Right now all I can think to do is to give up. To surrender. If I could just...

A familiar voice inside my head interrupts to admonish me, "Would you please stop talking to yourself and tell me why you are standing there like a cripple? Are you an elevator stuck between floors or are you a man?"

"A man, Your Holiness."

"Then find a place inside yourself that will allow you to stand up like a man," he instructs sounding unusually stern and forceful. "And remember, when all else fails it may be appropriate for Mr. Ping to outmuscle Mr. Pong!"

Suddenly something is shifting inside of me so that everything appears different. I do not know if it was The Bapucharya's words or merely an act of grace but I no longer feel myself without options or resources.

Drawing on the full power of Higher Will in the form of *HW-40,* I allow consciousness to rest "where the work is taking place," precisely where McAndrews's downward thrust and my upward response meet and resist each other—at the energy field surrounding Old Number Two. Clenching my Root Chakra, which you and rest of the world would probably call my sphincter muscle, I begin taking short, shallow breaths as I mentally intone "Higher" on the in-breath and "Will" on the out-breath. At the same time I envision the force of consciousness being drawn into my body through my Crown Chakra at the top of my head from where it travels down to my tightly sealed Root Chakra then back up again and out through my nose. While this happens I allow my conscious self to retreat from the jumbled emotions of the situation, pulling myself back from the intersection crowded with wildly scattered thoughts and uncontrolled movements of the mind, back to that observer's post high atop a mountain just a hairbreadth away, if you recall, from the *Center Point of the Universe.*

Suddenly McAndrews and the Pinewood Derby are but distant elements in an infinite landscape. Highly visible for sure but no longer the emotionally charged elements that mere moments ago seemed to threaten the very peace and well-being of my *ILE.*

"Yes! Yes indeed!" the Bapucharya's voice says, instantly

approving and giving weight to my dramatic shift in perspectives. "This is a much better place to stand up like a man!"

From my new vantage point high above the dark clouds of emotion that swirl about the Pinewood Derby McAndrews appears more like an overgrown child than an out-of-control, upside-down adult. More to be pitied than feared or hated.

Of course I am only in close proximity to the *CPU,* not exactly in the center, so it is not surprising that I still feel remnants of my emotions; still detest the man, actually. The difference is I no longer feel prey to the force of those emotions.

Guided by a power I cannot explain, my right hand reaches out with all its fingers fully extended, comes to rest on McAndrews' bald pate and firmly pushes down. In the same moment that he cries out "Whaaa ... ?" in startled confusion, I focus my conscious energy—now surprisingly robust and available—onto my left hand which is holding Old Number Two in tight embrace. That is the 'working surface', the precise point where The Seekers would say the work—*my work*—is taking place.

The next moment I lift my left arm as if nothing were holding it down and Old Number Two pulls free of McAndrews' grip as if his strength and animal ferocity have melted like butter under the fiery heat of concentrated, sharply focused consciousness.

I hear McAndrews releasing a cry of pained disbelief then witness myself telling him as if listening to someone else speak, "Be quiet, Bill. You have already caused too much trouble!"

It is not so much my words as their air of absolute authority that startles me.

As I hear those words spoken, my right hand continues to push down on McAndrews's head seemingly unbothered by his pitiful and weakening resistance.

It is only when he whimpers, "I'm sorry, Peterson, I'm sorry. Please stop!" .that my hand comes to a stop and releases the pressure. Almost automatically I release my Root Chakra and bring my rhythmically repeating *Higher Will* mantra to a stop.

Notice how the sounds of the room seem to flood over me

once again. "Good timing," I tell myself as the Scoutmaster Mr. Matthews lifts up his megaphone to call out three names for the next heat.

As you probably notice, "Michael Peterson" is the last name he calls.

"Coming," Mickey shouts from somewhere in the crowded room.

As for McAndrews, something in his manner has decidedly changed.

"I have to do something…I need to…go somewhere…" he says weakly, getting up to walk away. I do not think he and I will be fighting, or even discussing the weather, anytime soon.

I feel a friendly tug on my sleeve and hear Ellie excitedly whisper, "Don't mind him, honey. He's the type likes to pick pennies off a dead man's eyes. Good luck with this next drag or heat or whatever you wish to call it! I wish I had some money so I could bet on you."

Almost overwhelmed by her sudden torrent of words I turn and notice Ellie looking back at me with a reassuring smile. I smile and offer her a "Thanks." Turning back around I am just in time to ready myself for Mickey's catapult arrival.

"Hi Dad," he calls, grabbing hold of my leg to brake himself. A moment later he becomes the second individual in recent memory to try and pull Old Number Two from my grasp. In the absence of Mr. Ping's resistance, however, he becomes the first to succeed.

Before he can make good his getaway I grab hold of him by his yellow bandana.

"Just a moment," I explain. "I want to make sure you are ready?"

"Ready for what?"

"The race I guess."

"Yeah," he answers cockily, lifting up the racecar. "This'll be my sixth win."

"If you win," I remind him.

"No sweat, Dad," he grins widely. "How can I lose?"

"You can lose easily," I caution. "More easily than you realize."

"That's cool, Dad, but I've got to run."

"Well, good luck." I pull him closer for a kiss.

"Hey!" he calls, squirming away from my approaching lips.

Deferring to his manly pride I declare, "Sorry," with a suitably remorseful frown. Making a show of releasing my grip I offer my hand in a more appropriate display of fatherly affection.

"We can at least shake hands, can we not?"

As his little hand reaches mine I grab it and pull it close. "No matter what happens," I say softly, searching out his eyes, "you will always be my champion."

"I know what's going to happen, Dad. I'm going to win!"

"And I will be thrilled when you do!" I assure him. "Mine will be the loudest cheers you hear."

"Great!" he says starting to pull away.

Maintaining my grip I quickly add, "But if you do not win this heat..."

"Yeah...?" he says, waiting.

I pause a moment to consider my next remark.

"You will still be a winner to me!"

"Yeah, Dad, well...thanks," he grins, acting smart again. "Maybe I just better win."

A moment later, as you can see, he pulls himself free from his father's clutches and is running off. A blue and yellow form diminishing as it moves further away. In his hand a killer of a model racecar—winner of five previous Pinewood Derby heats.

My little boy and Old Number Two.

Off to the races one more time.

Lesson 16

In Which I Review My Performance As A Founding Member Of A Father And Son Team

I wish I could freeze this moment in time.

Stop it dead in its tracks.

If I could, I would go around to the back of the set and make some minor adjustments. Mostly I would tone things down: the noise of the crowd, the echoes in my mind, the constant antlike movement of blue-shirted boys, the underlying tension and especially my nine-year-old son's ridiculously high level of expectation.

As I watch Mickey run off to do battle with life in the form of a Pinewood Derby I feel nervous and frightened. He is so excited now, so hopeful, it makes me shiver to think how fragile and fleeting his exultation could prove to be.

Can you imagine how I feel?

Here we are in a crowded church basement where 200 cub scouts with 200 marvelous looking model racecars have come to race against my little boy and his outlandish, fuchsia-colored, woodblock on wheels. Now after an hour and a half of heats we are down to the final rounds, facing other winning finalists, all of them raging beauties compared to Old Number Two.

With so few racecars still in the running for a trophy, our aesthetic deficiencies have become more obvious to the world and more worrisome to me. I find it harder now, more painful, to let my eyes rest on Old Number Two—yes even the number itself, the Dali-esque '2' inside the palsied circle, offends me more each time I see it.

And the slightly raised nub in the driver's seat created by a flurry of imperfect sandpapering and highlighted with a bubble of white paint looks less like a representation of a driver and more like another visual joke Mickey and I were not able to pull off.

If one day I am forced to compose a resume of my accomplishments as a father I will neglect to mention anything about Pinewood Derby model racecars.

Or magicians for that matter.

I could use a magician now, I realize, almost amused by the thought. Up to this point in the Pinewood Derby we have been able to remain anonymous, lost in a crowded field of entries. But now I feel trapped and under threat like a beggar at a fancy dress ball who finds his presence increasingly exposed as the dance floor empties.

Perhaps for the thousandth time this morning, the thought races through my mind that all this luckless endeavor can be traced back to the cruel words and attitude of my darling ex-wife. But no sooner does the idea arise than I sharply recall The Bapucharya's earlier mockery of my self-victimization.

Besides what does it matter who is at fault? I am not even sure you can logically ascribe blame where a Karmic Gravitational Slide is concerned. The universe, I suppose, must bear the brunt of responsibility, or perhaps the individual whose Legacy has invoked the series of Karmic occurrences we are facing.

Yes *Legacy…*

Another Seeker concept of course, a Legacy is merely a way of talking about the Karma we create while we are here on our *ILE.* Put simply, each significant deed or action we commit (called an 'Action of Consequential Effect' or *ACE)* that affects the lives of others or ourselves also creates ripples in universal consciousness. Those ripples somehow lead to all the mischievous machinations that Karma is prone to.

There is a whole body of Seeker thought about karmic ripples and their many impacts but that is grist for discussion at another time. Perhaps a time when someone's Legacy—mine or Mickey's—is not about to blow up in our faces on a cold February morning.

Yes I know. This must sound strange to your ears, and I apologize for not taking the time to explain all these things in detail. But understand I am not here to explain the workings of the universe to you but to understand its workings for myself. This after all is my *ILE* we are traveling across, my Do-It-Yourself Workshop we are experiencing.

My *first-ever* Do-It-Yourself Workshop as The Bapucharya would most likely term it.

Anyway the cruelest irony of all, as McAndrews harshly pointed out, is that Mickey and I did nothing to justify our astonishing success on the racecourse. Where others strategically attached lead weights, sprayed silicon on the axles, rubbed graphite over the wheels and performed all sorts of wondrous tricks with their racecars, my little boy and I did nothing. Absolutely nothing.

Full credit must be given to fate or the perverse ironies of the universe for whatever magic has allowed Old Number Two to outlast dozens of slick competitors that were far more aerodynamic, far less foolish and certainly far less pink.

I sit here in awe of the effort and craftsmanship that went into creating such sleek and beautiful model racing cars, some with meticulously carved and painted drivers sitting upright in their cars like tireless sentries. Model racing cars whose painfully crafted bodies have curves instead of edges. Model racing cars that do not look like painted blocks of wood but like real model racing cars, their sleek painted bodies lacquered to a brilliant shine and covered with Pennzoil logos, multi-colored flames or hand-lettered inscriptions.

Ask yourself what kind of a father would go to the trouble of painstakingly hand-scripting 'Bobby's Dream' or 'The Speedster' on a Pinewood Derby model?

Clearly not my kind.

My kind of father specializes in the number 2 surrounded by what can only be described as a 'jagged circle'.

No I am not proud of the handiwork we have brought with us to this morning's Pinewood Derby. It may reflect the state of my woodworking skills but certainly not the measure of my concern for Mickey's feelings or wellbeing. Had I known when we were creating this monster, the patience and care other fathers and sons would lavish on their model racecars, I would have forced myself to do more. Or failing that I would have opted to do nothing.

Better to fail as a father in private than succeed as a fool in front of a whole troop of cub scouts.

Most likely I would have put in the extra hours to make Old Number Two appear less boxlike and less cartoonish. I would have sanded down the firm edges which so crudely recall the original form of the wood block. I would have cut away enough of the 'blockage' to give its form the sleek feel of a racing car. I would have borrowed whatever power tools I needed and rejected out-of-hand the idea of using Suzie's junior carpenter set.

That would have been a brainstorm by itself!

But finally and most importantly I would never have painted it red. Never! And even if I did decide to paint it red I would never have painted it that silly, girly shade of 'fuchsia'. Never!

Not even if my life were at stake.

You probably wonder why if I am so concerned with Mickey's well-being...why did I allow myself to come here this morning with the world's ugliest racecar?

You may not believe this but up until the moment we walked into this crowded basement hall I actually thought we had created something pretty nifty—a model racecar that almost looked like the real thing. *Almost* was the operative term. *Almost* was as close as one needed to come in this sort of affair or so I believed. You cannot imagine my shock when I saw through my own eyes how close the other fathers and their sons had come to imitating the real thing.

In an instant I saw what my little boy, even after almost two hours of racing, has failed to see—that our model racecar compares dismally in appearance to everyone else's. So dismally you might surmise we worked from a different set of instructions.

Ours were the 'almost' instructions

But what is that?

Can you hear it?

At first I thought it was someone coughing; someone in a distant part of the room. But now the sound is quickly multiplying into a chorus of sounds, no two of them following the same measure or rhythm; each detonating on its own, contributing to an erratic sequence of sounds resembling the rising chaos of a drunken boys choir.

I sense an animal energy has been let loose in the room and before it is brought under control someone will be scarred for life.

Now do you recognize it?

Ellie taps me on the shoulder.

"Well, good luck..." she starts to say but stops.

"What is that?" she asks instead. "Do you hear it?"

"Yes, I hear it," I answer softly, "and I know what it is."

How could I not recognize it?

It is as familiar to me as the sound of my children's tears. It is the sound of an engine dying, a plane crashing, a hope being extinguished. It is the cadence of a dangerously irregular heartbeat. It is the symphony of sounds that augur the construction of a giant Milestone on my son's *ILE.*

It is the one sound I most dreaded hearing this morning: inescapable proof of a Karmic Gravitational Slide reaching its final destination and locking in place.

You recognize it, do you not?

It is the sound of laughter.

Lesson 17

The Perils Of Ordering Fried Rice Without Eggs, Onions Or Bean Sprouts

Do not ask me why but we are no longer at the Pinewood Derby. No longer languishing in fear and self-pity in St. Christina's basement hall, no longer tortured by the rising laughter of a troop of sadistic, ego-destroying cub scouts.

For whatever reason, all sights and sounds have been switched off and replaced, as you can see, by the familiar scene of people dining out in a restaurant.

A Chinese restaurant.

A strange Chinese restaurant by the look of things.

Look around, you will see what I mean by 'strange'.

Notice how oversized everything appears, from the dimensions of the chairs and tables to the size of the people who are seated, not only throughout the vast dining room but around the perimeter of this large round table where I find myself perched on a shortened chair.

On second thought the chair is not short nor the people especially large, it is just that I have somehow been reduced in size! And now that I look more closely, these are not just any people sitting around this large circular table, they appear to be members of my family.

Really!

Those two are my mom and dad, sitting next to me is my sister Gail, the rest are cousins, uncles and aunts.

But everyone seems so young...?

Which leads me to the startling realization that I am not actually reduced in size, even though my face hovers surprisingly close to the blue and white dishes of my place setting, but that I have traveled backward many years in time to a day when I am much younger. No more than twelve years-old, maybe thirteen, I would have to guess.

You do not find that strange?

Well certainly in the context of all the other *strangeness* of my Do-It-Yourself Workshop, 'strange' is a hard concept to pin down. But still it seems strange to me to be here in this Chinese restaurant this far back in time. None of my other flashbacks went this distant into the past.

Would you agree?

"Of course, I am agreeing," a familiar voice responds, pulling me out of my small child's body and up near the ceiling once again. "But I am a most agreeable guru," the voice giggles, "so naturally I would agree to almost anything! Yes, this is your first-ever flashback to the days of your youth. But tell me, have you some special memory or knowledge of this restaurant? I am finding it most exotic."

This time The Bapucharya's surprise appearance does not surprise me. If anything it adds flavor to a mystery already in place since I am extremely mystified as to why I would journey this far back in time or why The Bapucharya would chose to come along as a tour guide.

Listening to my voice, however, you hear nothing but calm acceptance of all these odd happenings as if no external event could possibly disturb my inner tranquility.

Very Seeker-like, I must admit.

"Yes, Holiness, I know where we are," I reply softly in the quiet of my mind where our conversation is taking place. "It is a Chinese restaurant called The Shanghai Gardens."

"Ahh, The Shanghai Gardens!" he exclaims broadly as if recalling the many happy times he has eaten here. "Such a fine name for a Chinese restaurant! And have you no memory, my young maker of mysteries, what it was that once occurred here at the Shanghai Gardens?"

"I would find it hard to forget, your Holiness."

"Yes, I am sure that is true. This is the setting for one of the Milestones on your Path Of Seeking Truth, is it not? A rather large Milestone, perhaps the size of the moon," he suggests, chuckling once again at his own joke.

"Large enough," I answer dryly, finding little humor in his nonsensical comments.

I do find it interesting, however, to see myself at this age and to be watching from outside my skin, so to speak. I am a little chubbier than I remember and certainly less thoughtful and self-possessed than the adult I will later become.

"And look at all that hair!" I exclaim, more than a little excited if not transfixed by the size and sheen of the pomaded pompadour crowning my young adolescent head.

"Oh my," The Bapucharya exults, "Mr. Elvis Presley Jr., I am thinking!"

Looking down from up here the restaurant seems very different from my memories. I always remember it as a large dining room but I do not think I realized how much like an open function hall it was with all of its tables and fixtures freestanding and little else to break up the vastness and noisiness of the room.

If it were not for the Oriental-flavored decorations, the brass Chinese characters hung on its yellow walls, and the two oversized and colorful tropical fish tanks, you could turn this room into a bingo parlor or union hall in less than an hour's time.

"Oh, I am remembering now!" The Bapucharya exclaims broadly. "You do not enjoy laughing at the movie of your life. Such a disagreeable critic you are, Mr. Peterson! Is it that you cannot see the humor in your life's movie or do not enjoy appearing in such a comical production?"

"I do not understand, Holiness? Do you expect me to answer your questions?"

"No," he replies breezily, "but thank you for asking."

"Very funny," I reply.

That bit about "...thank you for asking" is a sarcasm offered for my exclusive benefit. Ever since I moved out of the family home and discovered life as an impecunious single father I have reacted to most of my children's requests for money or expensive activities with an instantaneous and usually heated "No!" Most times the weight of the response far exceeds the threat of the request, but what can you expect...? Going through a period of great emotional upheaval I feel so vulnerable I am literally unable to prevent myself from barking "No!" when my children suggest some expenditure that seems in the instant of its mention to threaten my very survival. Nevertheless, seconds later as my emotions settle down I invariably hasten to add in a much kinder and more fatherly voice, "...but thank you for asking."

All three of my children automatically groan when they hear those five words as if that has become their role in our scripted drama. As incongruous as it seems, this hastily appended coda provides some relief from the weight of my explosive "No!" A response by the way that is exactly like the "No!" I would hear all through my childhood, except my father would never think to add anything additional besides the flat of his hand or the threat of his belt.

Amazing how much The Bapucharya knows about my life!

As if to prove it he now asks, "You are perhaps wondering what we are doing here, wandering around in your not-so-watchable childhood like a couple of high-floating private detectives?

"I will tell you the bad news first, my young friend. At your son's Pinewood Derby from which we are taking a much-needed refreshment break, you are about to be kicked in the backside by the *TOE of God*. Like a good guru, Bapu is here to hold your hand as the blow strikes.

"Such a ferocious and painful kick it will be, Mr. Peterson, and it will be delivered as you are walking down the final stretch. By 'final stretch' I am not meaning the end of the race-that-is-called-a-heat. I am meaning the final chapter in your son's Karmic Gravitational Slide. And I would humbly advise anyone in the vicinity to hold onto their hats as we come in for a landing!"

"The *TOE of God?*" I repeat, vaguely recalling the term from my days with The Seekers For Truth. Superficially I remember it relates to 'The Oneness of Everything'—another way The Seekers have of describing The One Indivisible Unity or 'God'—but I am struggling to recall what it means to be kicked in the ass by the *TOE of God...*?

"Why must you always choose to struggle?" The Bapucharya asks, clearly both amused and frustrated by my struggle to recall Seeker terminology. "When you have been placed next to a dictionary, do not sit there until you crumble to dust wondering how to spell difficult words! What a booby you are, Mr. Peterson, and such an endless source of amusement!"

"I do not understand, Holiness. What are you trying to say?"

"Use what you are given!" he answers sharply. "If the bounteous universe gives you a dictionary, use it! If you have questions about the flavor of your *GUM* and you are sitting next to a Bapucharya, ask The Bapucharya for answers!"

"Yes," I reply softly, "I see what you mean."

"You see nothing!" he laughingly snorts. "You see the hind quarter of the jackass in front of you and very little else, I am thinking."

GUM, in case you do not know or remember, is yet another Seeker acronym. It stands for the 'Great Unrevealed Mystery,' which relates to the entire gearworks of the creation, the whole ball of wax—Karma, *ILEs,* reincarnation, Milestones, Legacies, *ACEs,* flashbacks, the *CPU* and so on—all wrapped up in one seemingly impenetrable package.

It is sometimes called The Truth or, if you ask The Bapucharya who describes himself as "a practicing, know-it-all Hindu," it is also referred to as *Brahman!*

When you talk about an individual's unique experience of The Truth—especially the way it manifests itself on that person's *ILE*—you are speaking about their particular flavor of *GUM.* Also referred to in Hindu jargon as *Atman.*

"I have many questions about the flavor of my *GUM,* Holiness. So many I am afraid to ask even one."

"That is good," he says appreciatively. "A wise man never asks questions to which he does not wish answers. But let me be your 'tour guide', as you so cleverly called me earlier, and we will see if some of your questions do not get answered during our tour."

"I notice my brother Henry is not with us at dinner," I remark, leaving the unstated question hanging in the air.

"Yes, we are without Henry this evening," The Bapucharya replies with a hollow sigh. "Such a loss! But he is seventeen, your brother—practically an upside-down grownup! And as a young man of seventeen, he no longer accompanies your family on these Sunday dinner outings.

"Something you will probably not recall," he continues, "is that Henry stopped going out with your family on Sundays a few months before this particular family excursion. It was soon after Henry made the second of two most important, Eureka-grade discoveries."

"Discoveries?" I ask obligingly.

"Yes!" he answers brightly, "Henry has discovered both the presence of girls on the planet and the fact that his penis was designed to do more than pass water! Such a wonderful combination of discoveries! And how dull one would be without the other, like an electrical appliance without an electrical outlet."

Breaking up into a thin series of laughs, he asks, "Was that not humorous? An electrical appliance...?"

Offering no encouragement I wait for him to continue, which he does a short moment later.

"No, your brother Henry is not sitting at this crowded table waiting to eat Chinese food. Being a Bapucharya I can tell you he is out walking the pavements of Brooklyn looking to share these very exciting, Eureka-grade discoveries with a young girl of suitable age and charms.

"And you?" he continues almost accusingly. "At twelve years of age you are still a tadpole! A baby Elvis! And though you have noticed highly attractive female tadpoles swimming in your pond you still believe they are the same creatures as you only they are blessed with prettier tails to wiggle around and make cushy in a boy's face."

"I remember I used to have crushes on the girls in school," I softly recall.

"Such a woeful tadpole, indeed," he comments. "You are remembering the third grade?"

"Renee Winters," I hazily recall. "She was short with dark blonde hair. Sat in the front seat of the middle row if I remember correctly. I used to write her love notes; pretty embarrassing stuff."

"Yes, yes," he says mournfully, "the first of many unrequited romances. It is still a surprise how unmoved Renee Winters was by your blandishments. I especially thought your puppy dog rhymes would have won her third grader's heart."

In singsong verse, he begins to recite, *"Paul and Renee sitting in a tree..."*

"Holinesss...?" I attempt to interrupt.

"K-I-S-S-I-N-G!"

"Is this necessary?"

"But your sister Gail is here," he abruptly announces. "She is one female tadpole whose adoration is never refused you. See her down there at the table? Sitting next to you?"

"How could I not see her, Holiness? She is only inches away."

"Of course, *inches away* and waiting to be noticed by her older, such-a-snob brother! Three years your junior and oh-so-devoted to you...when the two of you are not trying to kill each other.

"Yes, she is right there, sitting between you and your mother. And over there to your mother's left sits your father in all his penny-wise-foolishness. What a happy family portrait! I await with great enthusiasm to learn what it is you will be ordering for dinner!" he exclaims gleefully.

Suddenly I am back at the table where my father, uncle and aunt are going over items on the menu.

My father as usual has taken the lead. Hidden behind a large, baby blue menu he offers suggestions to my Uncle Saul and Aunt Babe about the dishes the three of them as the adults in the family might wish to order for the rest of us. All from the family style section of the menu which limits us to so many dishes from column A and so many from column B. I do not remember if there is a column C.

My mother is not involved in selecting or ordering the food, leaving that as she does with so many things in the hands of my father.

"Lobster cantonese? Pork fried rice? Egg foo young?" my father rattles off from behind the outsize menu. "I think we want spareribs, fried wontons and Peking dumplings for appetizers. That sound right? Maybe double spareribs...?"

The last question is directed at Uncle Saul, my father's younger brother who is pointing a threatening finger at his son Billy and warning him to stop teasing his younger sister—my bratty cousin Angela.

"Sure, whatever!" Saul answers my father. "And don't forget, a vegetarian dish on the side for Angela."

Inwardly I groan.

Angela's vegetarian dish.

Angela always has to have her special vegetarian entrée from column A which nobody else likes and which she never does more than pick at with a look of utter disgust on her face.

"What about *lo mein?"* my father starts to ask as I interrupt with great urgency, "Dad, don't forget to order fried rice without eggs, onions or bean sprouts!"

You will notice at the age of twelve I have not yet dropped the use of contractions or sloughed off the worst excesses of my Brooklyn accent.

"We'll see," my father responds in a light almost singing voice, the tone of voice he uses to silence me and my siblings in front of others. When our family is by itself he employs another much harsher tone.

It was my brother Henry who first started me on this fried-rice-without-the-slimy-textures obsession. I in turn passed it on to my sister Gail. So now whenever we go out for Chinese food either she or I will ask for, "fried rice without eggs, onions or bean sprouts," rattling it off like a family anthem.

Most times, when it is just the five of us dining out, my father does not mind ordering "fried rice without eggs, onions or bean sprouts" even if it presents difficulties in explaining such a request to a waiter who usually speaks very little English.

But when we are eating out with others my father bristles at our enthusiasm for "fried rice without eggs, onions or bean sprouts" because it directly goes against his intentions of ordering our dinner family style. Family style being a whole lot less expensive but not suited to special orders.

Have I mentioned my father's aversion to spending money?

"Yes, yes, you have done so," The Bapucharya answers in a surprisingly soft tone. "Many times."

Well I should know better than to push this fried rice thing with my father. I know the symptoms well enough to know that his temper will rear its ugly head if I continue to pursue 'fried rice without eggs, onions or bean sprouts'. Rather than frighten me off, however, you will notice the element of mounting risk seems to spur me on.

"You're going to order our rice, aren't you, Dad?" I pursue with incautious zeal. "It's not just me, Dad; Gail wants it too. Don't you, Gail?" I prod, turning to my sister.

"Yeah, me too!" she calls out. "I want it, too!"

"Would you just *wait!*" my father says sharply, the dramatically raised volume of the word 'wait' signaling the danger of an approaching storm. "I told you we'd see," he adds with a withering glance I can easily interpret from three chairs away. "Now, just keep quiet and wait."

I lean over with very little subtlety and, trying not to move my lips, whisper into my sister's ear, "Tell Dad you want our fried rice."

Like a dutiful sister and a girl who is safely seated behind the merit of being my father's favorite, Gail turns to Dad and demands, "I want my fried rice!"

"Quiet," he warns again, tilting his head to peer over the rims of his glasses, first at Gail then most meaningfully at me.

My sister looks to me and I, trying to appear innocent, whisper out of the side of my mouth, "Ask him again! Angela's gonna get hers and we're gonna get nothing."

"Daddy...!" Gail starts to whine.

"Enough!" my father shouts banging the menu on the empty plates in front of him with a shattering report. "You better shut your mouth, Paulie!"

"Me?" I protest. "What'd I say?"

"Don't get me started," he threatens.

"But why can't we have our fried rice?" I challenge, assuming my customary alter ego as an outraged defender of justice. "It's okay for Angela to get her vegetable stuff..."

"You'll eat what I tell you to eat," my father answers bitingly.

By now, you will notice, he is no longer conferring with my uncle about fried wontons or shrimp with lobster sauce. All his attention is focused on what appears to be a mounting insurrection from the one political group whose resistance he can never tolerate.

When his children resist his authority my father is never particularly interested in *Removing Mr. Ping And Mr. Pong.* He grew up in a simpler less complex world where dictators like Hitler and Stalin set a standard for establishing parental authority so he knows that a strong, self-righteous Mr. Ping can easily steamroll over a smaller, unprotected Mr. Pong.

Unfortunately at the age of twelve I have not yet learned the value of removing opposition before it leads to an excess of force. I seem to be far more interested in keeping my eye and my sharp-edged tongue focused on whatever prize has beguiled and taken over my good sense.

Which is why I pay no attention to my father's mounting anger, easily seen in the arching of his right eyebrow and the deepening color around his throat. Instead of paying close attention to these potentially lifesaving warning signals I plow forward blindly, resolutely insisting, "We want fried rice without eggs, onions or bean sprouts!" and repeating it in full, not only to emphasize our resolve but to assist his memory when it comes time to give the order. I have always been a practical child when it comes to small details.

"Well, this is all you're going to get," my father snaps, angrily rising from his chair and leaning across my mother and a flotilla of blue and white dragon-patterned dishes, the four fingers of his right hand reaching out in an effortless backstroke that lands across the length of my mouth with a slap so loud it has to be heard all the way to Coney Island.

For a moment that seems to last forever I sit here—just sit here—numb from the shock and not yet feeling pain, hearing in my head the echo of that slap which hangs like an unanswered gunshot in the chilled air above the table.

There is something about this moment that seems to cut like a knife through the layers of my very being until it reaches and sharply penetrates my inner, seemingly unprotected, essence. This, I can only guess, is what it feels like to be kicked in the backside by the *TOE of God;* probably not unlike what Mickey felt when Marco The Magnificent cheerfully asked the assembled throng at Quincy Market to admire his underpants.

Seconds later I jump up, kick back and knock over my chair then weave my way through the other tables to run out of the crowded restaurant.

Outside it is a cold Sunday in March on the streets of

Brooklyn; much colder, you will notice, since I have run outside neglecting to bring my winter coat which unfortunately has been left behind in the unfriendly reaches of the Chinese restaurant. I could go back and get my coat but somehow that would weaken my stance as an angry and outraged victim.

No I will show them. I will wait out here shivering in my striped knit shirt, choking on my sobs trying to hold back the tears, taking shelter from the biting wind in this recessed entrance to a dry cleaners which like every other retailer in the neighborhood is closed on Sundays.

Perhaps I will catch cold and die from pneumonia. That will show them!

My shivering and suffering of course is merely further proof of my father's cruelty which has left me here waiting with mounting anger and diminishing tears next to a large window sign that exhorts "Do Your Martinizing Here!" while the wind howls and frets at my heavily slicked pompadour and my family indulges itself three storefronts away consuming large platters of Chinese food.

And while Angela no doubt moodily picks at her vegetarian dish.

Briefly, giving it no great importance, I wonder what Gail ended up having for dinner? Ironically I know my martyrdom actually improved her chances of getting Dad to order fried rice without eggs, onions or bean sprouts. The way these family things usually work, one sacrifice proves more than sufficient for the occasion. Especially when I am the one playing the role of the sacrificee.

I stare at the cleaner's exhortation to "Do Your Martinizing Here!" and murmur back, "Do Your Martyring Here!" with great bitterness, totally unaware I may have taken my first step toward a future career as an advertising copywriter.

At the moment, however, I am more curious about martinizing than I am about my life in the far away future.

What *is* martinizing, I wonder, staring at the large blue and white sign? Was it invented by someone named Martin? Is it something they do to your shirts or slacks?

Would you happen to know?

More important would you happen to care?

It does not matter, I finally decide. What does matter is that I have to stay here and wait until my family finishes their dinner, unable to go home because it is too far away for me to make it back without getting lost.

And boy is it cold! So cold I can see my breath!

I could easily get caught up in thoughts of how cold I am but I force myself to brush aside concerns about the temperature just like I brush away my tears and console my battered self esteem with thoughts of how much I hate my father.

"It is never easy," The Bapucharya says comfortingly, "this getting kicked in the backside by the *TOE of God*."

After a moment's silence, unable to stop himself, his thoughts bubble over into laughter as he adds, ever-enthusiastic comedian that he is, "And sometimes, I am thinking, it makes for quite a good weight loss diet."

Lesson 18

How To Recognize A Karmic Gravitational Slide In Its Final Stages

We are back at the Pinewood Derby.

Any relief I feel in escaping the cold, distant streets of Brooklyn or my vanished childhood quickly dissipates as I confront the harsh cruelty of events unfolding in this all-too-familiar church basement.

In an instant my stomach grows queasy, my head dizzy and light. In total disbelief I find myself watching dozens of demonic, blue-shirted cub scouts channeling their spiteful energy in the direction of my little boy.

Can this really be happening?

Sweat breaks out on my forehead and upper lip. I can feel it, just as I feel a trembling sensation in my hands.

Once again you might recognize the symptoms of an acute reaction of my Physical Center brought on by over stimulation of my nearby Emotional Center.

I was a member of The Seekers For Truth long enough to know there will be no relief from these symptoms until I somehow lift my consciousness above the realm of my panicked emotions.

I should be able to do that soon.

As soon as my nine-year-old son escapes from hell.

"Get out of there!" I ache to shout. "Run for your life!" But that would only further embarrass Mickey who, as you sadly see, is frozen in place almost exactly the way he was four years ago in the plaza outside Faneuil Hall.

Look at him the poor sweetheart, standing stiff and awkward like a deer trapped in the hypnotic hold of oncoming headlights.

"Run!" my entire essence aches to scream.

"RUN!"

I open my mouth but nothing comes out. Instead without thinking I put my hand to my lips where the psychic impression of my father's slap feels as real and present as his angry fingers felt—what was it?—33 years ago.

This is what The Bapucharya means by getting kicked in the ass by the *TOE of God!*

Two moments in time have been joined together. Two moments so alike in some mysterious way that they instantly forge a connection that transcends time and space.

Can you see the connection? The way these two events, twin traumas that reach across time, the universe and the landscape of my *ILE,* seem to mirror and detonate each other at some deep viscerally explosive level?

Not since my father's bony fingers hit me on the mouth in that Chinese restaurant have I felt so suddenly removed from the interwoven texture of life. As though I have been yanked rudely from reality and perched all alone on a shaky pinnacle that has risen like a desert atoll from subterranean eruptions of shock, humiliation and pain.

Gone completely is that inner place where I can hide and feel safe, that point of view I normally use to shroud my emotions and protect the part of me that is too sensitive to defend itself.

It is as if someone has wholly lifted off a walnut shell under which I have been hiding. Leaving me naked and exposed with nothing left in place to conceal my unworthiness.

There has never been another moment in my life so humiliating or defeating—where I felt so stripped of my humanity—as that instant after my father smacked me on the mouth in plain view of my uncle, aunt, cousins, sister and mother.

Not another moment I can recall that laid me so low in the harsh estimation of my own eyes.

Until now.

Just look at me sitting here with my mouth open! Powerless to do anything but give in to the pull of the drama. Eyes drawn like everyone else's to the center of the clearing where a rising tide of rude catcalls and nasty-edged laughter is being directed at my little boy.

Thank God he has begun moving again! I just wish he

would move faster.

Faster!

He moves like he is trudging through snow instead of ridicule.

Mickey would you please *hurry up!*

Has anyone ever looked so alone in a crowded room?

In a totally futile gesture he attempts to conceal Old Number Two behind his back, not realizing that half the audience is sitting—and laughing—behind him.

"This is not really happening," I tell myself.

Images from that horrible day four years ago pass fleetingly through my mind. Mickey holding up Marco's line of brightly colored handkerchiefs as the hurtful underpants come flying out of the canister. My little boy's moment of unbridled panic when his eyes travel down the length of his body to ascertain whether his jockey shorts were still on his body, still hidden beneath his pants, or had they really through the power of magic been yanked off his body and hung on a line for everyone to laugh at.

And most of all, Mickey just standing there like a statue frozen in place holding up that line with its knotted scarves and single pair of jockey shorts, too frightened to move, too embarrassed to do anything but wait there and slowly die of humiliation.

And here we are four years later!

See how far we have come?

See how much better I am at protecting my son from the cruelties of the world? See how carefully I can now nurture and defend his sensibilities?

Maybe more than anything, Mickey needs protection from the care and guidance of his father! But I will not let myself think about that now. Right now there is no time for blame or self-gratifying soul-searching. If I cannot give my son my protection, at least I can offer him my attention.

Each of us has a role to play in the drama and mine I guess is to watch helplessly...and perhaps pray.

"Yes, yes," a voice in my mind says softly, "prayer can be of definite assistance!"

The next moment as I watch my little boy move in excruciatingly slow steps toward the elevated raceway in the center of the clearing I hear myself whisper in the sanctuary of my mind, "Dear God, please help him get through this. Please!"

My prayer seems like thin soup indeed, competing as it does against the rising volume of jeers, catcalls and laughter echoing throughout the broad landscape of St. Christina's basement hall. Words like "pink" and "ugly" and "sissy" are rudely shouted out in a continuous volley of amused and overexcited insult. Crude jokes one after another vie for the crowd's mercurial attention and cheaply purchased laughter.

"Please, God, let this end *soon!"*

"Yes, my young friend, prayer can be of definite help," The Bapucharya softly advises. We are up near the ceiling again just like old times, hovering together in our disembodied states while watching both Mickey and myself down below where we are cooking slowly in our own juices according to an old cub scout recipe.

"But why do you pray for small things when it is only the big things that matter?" The Bapucharya asks. "Much better I think to pray for your little boy's *Legacy."*

By 'Legacy' he means I should be praying for a journey-enhancing outcome from this entire adventure rather than for relief of any temporary danger or discomfort. He means I should be praying for the ultimate good of Mickey's soul, which The Seekers sometimes call *TAO* or "The Ancient One." He means I should be praying for understanding rather than escape, for painfully purchased knowledge rather than pain-obscuring oblivion.

Remember, The Seekers For Truth believe the purpose of life is to learn the meaning of life, not to merely pass through the experience of life with the least amount of damage to your paint job.

"I have no time now to think about that, Holiness!" I protest, feeling anger begin to rise at his inopportune suggestion.

"Time?" he scoffs. "Do you hang around up here like an invisible balloon and tell me you have no time?" he giggles. "Please to tell me what kind of reality—or time—it is that you are referring to?

"Time, Mr. Peterson, is the one thing you have in excess

supply! I see no cans of wisdom in your pantry, no gallon jars of common sense. Your flow of consciousness seems to be sputtering, perhaps from a leak. And as for knowledge, my wiseacre, upside-down parent, yours has been nibbled to crumbs by the mice who are living rent-free in your attic.

"But time ... !" he admonishes, cutting off his incipient burst of giggling. "We have warehouses of time, you and I. Time is piling up on our docks waiting to be shipped to third world nations. Are we not wallowing in time, Mr. Peterson? Are we not dying an excruciatingly slow death at a Pinewood Derby at the same *time* we are about to have our pants pulled down by a highly inebriated blonde lady in Plymouth, Massachusetts?" Shriekish laughter once again punctuates his words.

"A Bapucharya does not worry about having enough time, dear boy. Such a one as myself is not living a life restricted by time. When you are living within yourself, high on a mountain at the *Center Point Of The Universe*—even in close proximity to the Center Point like yourself—you are never having a shortage of time.

"You are the star in a different movie when you are living in the *CPU*. In this movie, you do not answer to time. No, my young friend, you have changed roles and it is *you* who becomes the master of time and time who becomes your slave!"

Abruptly he shifts gears, asking more gently, "But you were about to finish saying your prayer, I am recalling."

As his suggestion hangs in the air, I am surprised to hear myself repeat the same prayer I offered earlier, "Please, God, let this end *soon!*" But without thinking I add, "And, please, help Mickey come out of this crisis a better person."

"Not perfect," my invisible companion says, "But now you are adding the right ingredients! Perhaps it could be better said but only, I am guessing, by a saint or a Bapucharya."

As I start to feel a surge of annoyance in response to his constant joking I suddenly find myself back in my body, seated on my metal folding chair and taking notice that the commotion in St. Christina's basement hall has abruptly gained in pitch and volume. What sounded before like a sea of voices is now breaking up into individual components, each boy shouting out his own nasty thoughts and trying to outdo the others for the crowd's easily purchased approval. All of them competing for laughs just as moments ago they competed for those gilded, toy-topped trophies.

"Why don't you put a dress on it!" a harsh voice calls out. A voice I quickly trace back to an overweight scout with little blond curls, no more than eight or nine years old himself.

Who is he to shout out insults? And where the hell is his father?

"Pink stinks, pink stinks..." another boy sings as if delighted at discovering a new anthem.

"Take that pink thing home, you homo," another shouts, nasty and ill-mannered.

Other cub scouts having no concerns about their manners pick up the unfortunate play of words and begin to chant, "Homo, homo, time to go homo, homo..."

All the while there is a continuous backdrop of laughter and agitated shouting which rises and falls according to the response each catcall evokes in this unraveling skein of malicious child's sport.

"Homo, homo, time to go homo!" the chant continues.

Somewhere a cub scout with a musical bent sings out misremembered phrases from Aretha Franklin's "Pink Cadillac."

"...take me driving in your pink Cadillac..."

I feel a hand on my arm.

I turn to see Ellie smiling sympathetically.

"I do not...this is...do you think...?" I start to say then stop. Finally I offer a weak smile and nod as I tap her hand appreciatively then quickly turn back to the disastrous events in the middle of the room.

"...you and me driving in your pink sissy Cadillac..."

"...homo, go homo..."

I cannot take my eyes off my little boy.

If you did not understand why he is walking that way, you would think him a cripple, am I right? His body leaning to one side, his hands behind his back, his whole physical presence seeming to twist in on itself?

You have to give him credit though. Now that he has approached the racetrack he has actually succeeded in concealing his fuchsia racecar behind his back. Everyone's view is either obstructed by his twisted body or the elevated racetrack. What cannot be hidden, however, is the pain of Mickey's embarrassment which has spread across his face in a bright, non-fuchsia shade of red.

Can this be the same cocky child I spoke to only moments ago? That boy was supremely elated and confident, caught mid-flight in some exotic adventure. Now the adventure has soured and this shell of a child has been left behind to tumble in on himself. A sandcastle overtaken by the tide, a little boy overtaken—and overwhelmed—by ridicule.

It was too much to hope I suppose that Mickey might navigate these shark-infested waters without being attacked. How quickly it all happened! At most it took maybe five or ten seconds from the time he picked up Old Number Two till the moment the entire cub scout troop became aware of how outrageous and ridiculous his humble racecar actually looks. As if blinders had been lifted from everyone at the same exact instant.

"It's pink," a boy cries out, finally realizing, I guess, what everyone has been shouting about, "can you believe that?"

"What an ugly piece of crap!" another future art critic snidely comments.

Suddenly I feel like I am falling—falling out of life and reality. As if a trap door has opened up at the very foundation of my existence and now I am slowly falling through.

And falling...

This must be how Illyana feels during one of her attacks. This must be what it feels like to be totally defenseless yet free of any responsibility for taking charge or being in control. There is no control.

Just falling...

"So sorry, young sir," a familiar voice says, "but you are not allowed to leave the party so soon."

As those words penetrate to some deeper realm of my mind I feel my fall starting to brake. A moment later I am sitting upright once again on a hard metal folding chair in a crowded church basement and I hear a voice in my mind telling me, "Go back to the mountaintop, Mr. Peterson. Where the wind does not blow."

"The mountaintop?" I question.

"The *inner* mountaintop," the voice, vaguely reminiscent of The Bapucharya's, softly urges.

Finally understanding, I attempt to go within myself but find a steel door blocking the way.

"I cannot get in there," I tell him.

"Try!"

"I am trying. The door is locked."

"Are you certain you have tried your best?"

"I am certain I cannot get in."

I am not so certain, however, if I hear them or just imagine hearing them, but the words "Or so it seems" seem to rise up and hang suspended in the atmosphere around me.

I raise both hands as if to chase the words away, shouting, "Keep going, Mick!" as much to encourage myself as my little boy.

"Just keep going!"

Finally— at last!—Mickey reaches Mr. Matthews who looks around distractedly as if trying to comprehend the cause of all the commotion in the room. He pushes his glasses back up to the ridge of his nose as he has done nearly a hundred times this morning.

"Thanks, Michael," he says watching Mickey hurriedly place Old Number Two in a starting position on the last open guide rail. As quickly as he puts it down Mickey spins around and runs back to his father, perhaps the only friend he has left in this hostile universe.

As soon as he reaches me he climbs onto my lap without saying a word, leaning his body into mine as if it were a cave into which he could disappear.

With Mickey gone from the public arena the catcalls and laughter fall away quickly, the noise in the room dropping to almost complete silence. It feels as if some instrument of torture has been momentarily turned off, bringing an instant measure of relief.

"An-n-n-nd they're off…!" Mr. Matthews calls as he pulls back the lever that drops the restraining pins and releases the three Pinewood Derby racecars.

The riot of noise abruptly returns, this time directed not at Mickey but at the three model racecars that speed down the parallel rails of the thirty-foot racetrack.

For a few seconds the heat seems closely contested, all three cars running nose to nose. I hold my little boy tightly as we watch the brightly colored racecars duel for first place.

This is it, I think to myself. No matter what happens we are done. Whatever the outcome Mickey will not want to continue racing.

But what if he wins, I worry?

The next moment the question becomes moot as the car on the farthest track, a bright metallic green racecar with an orange lightning bolt on either side, pulls out in front and handily beats the other two Pinewood Derby racecars to the finish line.

At last, finally! It is over.

We have lost.

"Too bad, Mick," I murmur weakly.

My little boy shrugs without comment then breaks free of my hold and jumps off my lap.

"Wait!" I call surprised, but he moves off before I can ask where he is going.

Following him with my eyes, he weaves through the crowd to where Old Number Two is being held by some boys. After a moment of angry negotiating he pulls it free from one of the boys' hands then, clutching it to his small, wiry body, runs off like a thief into the night.

I lose sight of Mickey as he disappears behind a wall of cub scouts and dads. Anticipating his intentions my eyes pick out the top of the swinging doors on the far side of the room just as they open briefly then shut again.

Now he is really gone.

I stand up taking both our winter jackets from a nearby seat. Suddenly—surprisingly, because I had totally forgotten her presence—Ellie leans against my shoulder with a striking air of casual intimacy and whispers in my ear.

At first my thoughts are so scrambled that her words do not penetrate or register.

"I am sorry," I say, overwhelmed by a growing sense of confusion. "What...what was that?"

She leans over and repeats in a louder whisper, "He's lucky to have a dad who cares. That's why God made fathers!"

I barely register the fact she is tucking a folded slip of notepaper into my shirt pocket.

"Don't lose that," she warns with a meaningful smile.

"Thanks for everything," I say, hurriedly putting down Mickey's jacket in order to put mine on. "I will call you," I add, searching for and unable to find one of my sleeves.

"Good luck," I say for no apparent reason.

"Good luck to you." She offers a consoling smile.

You will notice I am still struggling to put on my coat as I pass through this sea of noisy cub scouts. They pay me no attention whatsoever, continuing to buzz and vibrate on some sort of automatic program, waiting anxiously and impatiently for the next heat and ultimately for a single derby winner to emerge from the dwindling field of unbeaten racers.

In another moment I am through the swinging doors and outside the crowded room, standing on the bottom level of a darkened stairwell, the energetic buzz now muting as the doors swing shut.

It feels like I have been released from a pressure cooker!

The stuffy almost clammy feel of the packed and overheated basement hall is gone, instantly replaced by the cooler, drier climate of the dark, empty stairwell.

"Mickey?" I call softly, his name resonating like a stillborn echo in the hollow silence. I do not want to call too loudly, this being a church.

"Mickey, where are you?"

Silence.

I try again. "Mickey?"

The sound of my voice falls away once again into silence.

Idly looking around I notice a familiar wooden block lying on its side like a wounded soldier on the green linoleum tiles of the stairwell landing. It must have been dropped or thrown forcefully from the top of the stairs because three of its wheels have scattered and a triangular wedge of wood has partially separated from the car's body, the split starting where the right headlight would be and running two inches deep.

Something about the image of the damaged racecar

strikes me familiar. A moment later I utter a slight exclamation as I realize I am essentially looking at a physical replica of the damage I had mentally visualized for Old Number Two when Bill McAndrews and I were fighting for its possession. This was how our racecar looked to me when I fantasized the car breaking up in our hands.

Which makes me wonder if I am even more the author of today's tragedy than I realize.

Unable to decide if that is a lesson meant for discovery on my *ILE* or Mickey's—or both—I stoop to pick up the damaged racecar and, bending over, catch sight of one of the missing tires. The next few moments are spent searching for the remainder of the errant tires and missing axle.

Minutes later I walk up the stairs with Old Number Two safely ensconced, albeit in pieces, in the safety of my parka pocket.

Still missing of course is a badly bruised nine year old boy.

If I am any judge of nine-year-old boys, I suspect he will be easy to find but not so easy to pull together.

Still like the lady said, that is why God made fathers.

Assuming of course He did not make a mistake.

Lesson 19

Addressing The Question Of What Happens To Snow That Never Falls

My little boy is sleeping.

Lying next to him in our shared bed I hear him rhythmically drawing air through his open mouth.

A week has passed and we have not yet spoken of the Pinewood Derby. Truly spoken about it. We have of course mentioned small inconsequential matters relating to the event but only in the peripheral way one talks about the condition of a sick person when he is close enough to overhear.

"Bad break," I said to him later that day when we were seeking distraction from our sorrows at the South Shore Plaza Food Court. "We almost went all the way."

"No big deal," he answered, choosing to focus on the Johnny Rocket cheeseburger in his hand rather than the unstated issues in the air.

The fact that neither of us was ready to bring up the real cause for our discomfort is a good indicator of how tender the wound still seemed.

And what could I say? "I am sorry Old Number Two looked like such a fruit salad?"

I do not think so.

Which is why a week later I have still not made any effort to clarify and explore that traumatizing experience for my little boy.

Not that I would know what to say.

If the purpose of life is to reach some understanding about the meaning of life I will probably have to retake this Do-It-Yourself Workshop a few hundred times before I am ready to graduate from the program.

To me the meaning of life remains as unfathomable a mystery as it ever was. Perhaps even more so the closer I come to seeing how things work.

I may need to leave it to someone else—to a future Paul Peterson in a future embodiment—to figure things out. He will have to penetrate the false facade of Automatic Universal Misunderstanding *(AUM)* to discover why I was repeatedly forced to experience something as upsetting—and weirdly ironic, considering my history—as the public humiliation of my only son.

What could be the purpose of *that?*

And what meaning could it have?

Especially when I recall how often I was told that *AUM,* Automatic Universal Misunderstanding, is merely an illusion; an illusion shared by almost everyone on the planet. A very believable illusion for sure but an illusion nevertheless.

Maya, as the Hindus have termed it.

"The Great Pretender's greatest game of make-believe," The Bapucharya calls it, adding, "He has only to sound the precise vibration and—ohmigoodness!—the physical universe disappears and we are all becoming *(pause for giggles)* out-of-work actors!"

No I do not enjoy the flavor of my *GUM*—my particular view of this Great Unrevealed Mystery—and would rather chew on something else. Something less emotionally destructive.

Simply put, I have had enough of...

I feel a soft blow against my shoulder.

It is Mickey's arm flailing about as his body shifts under the covers, turning from one side to the other.

Without asking permission a smile spontaneously takes control of my facial muscles.

My little boy is facing me now!

Just look at him lying here next to me, his mouth half open, his eyes fully closed, his brow starting to crease in irritated response to the glare of the lamp. Look at the way the eyelid twitches as if a few errant light beams have already stolen their way in.

If the past provides any insight to the future he will soon grow irritated by the glare of my reading lamp and turn back onto his other side. But while he is facing in my direction I will take advantage of this fleeting opportunity to breathe in like a sweet breath of oxygen the spectacle of his unguarded innocence.

Have you ever seen anything more beautiful or with more power to pull at your heart? Lying here propped against my reading pillow, staring over bifocals that have once again dropped to the lower reaches of my nose, I realize how fortunate I am to be given moments like this. Moments where I can reach out and touch him as if it were the most natural thing in the world.

He would of course shake off my hand even in the midst of his slumbers. But he would shake it off automatically the same way he would shake off an annoying fly. He would not question my right as a bothersome, affectionate father to touch him, to reach out in the night to assure myself he is real and alive.

Why a father would need to do such things is another story, one he would not easily understand. But he would never challenge my right to claim that intimacy just as he would never question the right of the fly to land wherever it chooses.

For twenty three years I lived in the same apartment as my father until he died of a heart attack at the age of 49 and we never shared a bed together, much less one of life's major disasters like a Pinewood Derby.

And now every other weekend I live out the attenuated aftermath of my divorce, with two daughters sharing a sleeper couch in the living room of my tiny apartment and this vulnerable, trusting nine year old boy sharing my double bed in a bedroom that is barely larger than a closet.

This part of my divorce—having my children all to myself every other weekend—has been a gift. I may not always view it that way but occasionally on nights like this when I am far enough removed from my anger at Marilyn I can see it clearly for what it is.

Not as a sign of my loss but as evidence of my gain.

And then with nobody to hear my confession or smile ironically I can admit to myself that I probably became a better father for having had to work so hard at the job.

Without the divorce I might have put as little energy into raising my kids as my father did in raising my brother, sister and myself.

My mother was the one who raised us.

But you have already figured that out for yourself, I am sure.

Mom was the one who helped us shoulder our struggles in life. The one who took us to scout meetings, met with our teachers on open school nights, bandaged our cuts, brought us special presents when we were sick in bed and gave us all a reassuring sense that at least one person in the world was truly dedicated to our wellbeing.

And that that same one person loved us without reservation or regret.

I cannot remember my father saying he loved me—actually saying the words!—until I was sixteen. And then it was only in answer to an accusation.

We were arguing about a decision not to take me along on a trip to Florida. It was just a company sales convention but for some reason he and my mother had decided to take Gail and leave me behind in Brooklyn Heights at my Aunt Ruthie's.

After a few half-mumbled complaints I accused him angrily, "You don't care about me!" in my best James Dean quiver. "You don't care about anybody but yourself!"

Three years earlier I would have risked my life to say such a thing. But by the time I was sixteen my father had mellowed considerably. So instead of hitting me he merely responded, "That's not true," shaking his head at my accusation. "I love you, and care about you. But you're still not going to Florida, no matter what you say!"

And there you have the entire repertoire of my father's *I love you's* recorded during my lifetime.

Anyway I cannot imagine my father lying awake in bed, kept up by thoughts and worries about his children. I especially cannot imagine him disturbed by concerns about *me.* And just look at me 35 years later! Lying here unable to sleep, worrying about Mickey's emotional fallout from a disastrous Pinewood Derby and the Milestones that event will inevitably erect on his Path Of Seeking Truth! Milestones he will find himself facing time and time again as he moves through his life and journeys down his Path Of Seeking

Truth.

How Dad would have laughed at that. Parenting expert that he was he would have argued you only need worry about your children when they get sick, lost or beaten up. Anything else—well, that is their concern.

Of course Dad knew nothing about Legacies, Milestones or any such Seeker stuff. He would have called it all nonsense, I am sure, more likely 'a load of crap' and forbidden me to waste his time talking about it.

It is beyond my imagination to think what my father would have made of The Bapucharya. I have an image of a caveman staring with great confusion at the Mona Lisa but I cannot say exactly how that image serves as a metaphor.

And speaking of metaphors I have had this thought ...actually, it is more a fancy than a thought.

Yesterday here in Boston it was supposed to snow. The weather forecasters had predicted eight to ten inches with a foot more expected up north. What we actually experienced when everything was said and done was an unseasonably warm day in the upper fifties with the sun shining through high wispy clouds. A day as it turned out where thousands of snow shovels were sold in what was possibly the year's last frenzy of winter storm panic shopping.

Of course weather prediction is far from an exact science, especially in New England, but there is still something dramatic and momentous about a predicted snowstorm that never arrives.

When I was a child growing up in Brooklyn and would watch snow falling I can remember thinking that snow was some physical substance that collected in the clouds until there was so much accumulated it finally broke through. Almost like a mathematical formula describing the inevitable result of supply exceeding storage capacity.

One time when I was in elementary school we were told a major snowstorm was on the way but like yesterday's storm it never materialized. I recall wondering if someone might have made a mistake about the amount of snow that had accumulated in the clouds?

Maybe enough snow had not yet collected, I reasoned? Or maybe they were right about the amount of snow piled up but wrong about how much the clouds could hold...?

Well whatever the reason, I was certain that the snow which had been predicted—the snow that did not fall—was still up there, high in the clouds...waiting. Waiting for more snow to collect. Waiting until the clouds were so full and sodden with snow they had no choice but to burst open.

Then of course all the snow would fall down and cover the asphalt streets of Brooklyn in a numbingly soft and pure whiteness.

As a child such simple ideas were the foundation of my understanding about the way things worked. No different, I would guess, from the assumptions and beliefs of most children.

Today when I wander through memories of my father, my mind approaches the subject with that same childlike innocence. And somehow I believe that the love I never received from my father was like the snow that never fell from the clouds. It did not vaporize or cease to exist but was merely held over. Waiting for enough love to collect. Waiting until so much love accumulated it would break through all restraints and finally—freed at last—fall like a gentle snow upon my life and the lives of my children.

As childish as it sounds something in me wants to believe that love builds up in the course of human experience so that if it fails to shower down in one life it will inevitably find release in another.

That same inner part of me knows that the love I share with my children has been made large and overwhelming by the love that never fell from my father's heart.

That hunger for a father's love must have colored Dad's childhood as well, since his father—my grandfather Izzy—was notorious for being a stern and distant parent. Is it any wonder then that Dad, being so unfamiliar with love and how to get it, searched for it so relentlessly outside the boundaries of his family?

Searching for it in his work, his friends, even in the company of strange women.

My father's tragedy was that he never saw the abundance lying nearby for the treasure that was always beyond his reach.

I believe we are all waiting for snow that never fell. Some of us, the lucky ones, learn to create that snow for ourselves while others only learn to imitate the loveless behavior of their parents.

"Dad," Mickey mutters, squirming under the covers, "would you turn out the light!"

"In a few moments," I promise softly. "Turn over now and close your eyes."

He makes an angry noise and turns over as instructed.

"Thank you, sweetie," I whisper, tapping him softly on the shoulder.

"Grrr!" he answers.

"I love you," I tell him softly, almost singing the words.

"I love you, too," he grunts back with a testy shake of his body.

In scarcely a moment my little boy will be sound asleep again.

Most likely he will never remember waking up.

Most certainly he will never even know it snowed.

The Second Karmic
Gravitational Slide:

Dancing With The Universe

*In which
our workshop leader
braves exotic relationships
and dangerous deeds to
right wrongs and
secure his rights*

Lesson 20

The Noble Fourfold Legacy And How It Can Lead One To The Big Game

We have not yet talked about the concept of *Legacy*—really talked about it—and I begin to wonder why.

This Seeker doctrine of karmic inheritance, officially called the 'Noble Fourfold Legacy' or *NFL,* is the main reason I am here in this Plymouth apartment fighting with half-hearted vigor to keep this demonic blonde from pulling me bodily onto that coming-ever-closer, brown velveteen couch.

This is all happening in slow motion, remember, allowing me to spaciously pursue my Do-It-Yourself Workshop and review the series of loosely related events that have brought me here this evening.

Here to one of the most ignominious terrains yet discovered on my *ILE!*

Here to where heroic gestures get ground down by a cruelly ironic universe into comic relief for...?

For what, the journey across my Path Of Seeking Truth?

It is hard to keep such a vaunted purpose in mind while watching this vaudeville routine taking place in the dimness of Allison's apartment, listening to Allison's gleeful mutterings and enticements.

But at least I am starting to understand things. Starting to see the role played by Legacy in my fall from grace. Starting to realize that ambivalence—my own ambivalence—is the main reason I remain locked in this woman's wine-strengthened grip.

And speaking of ambivalence, can you believe how round and firm those breasts of Allison's seem to be? Even hidden beneath that plain white cotton blouse—which comes across as dingy and yellowed when seen in a better light—they reach out and clamor for your attention.

See?

They nod at you and wink—almost smiling—the little teases. And call to you like sirens who only recently learned to pronounce your name.

But how can there be such firm pineapples in the field, you may ask, when the rest of the plantation appears so tired and run down?

Can they be real, I begin to wonder? That is the question of the day. Could some cosmetic surgeon have poured new wine into old wineskins as we used to say in Biblical Studies back in college?

You are right of course. It is no business of mine.

And my *PuNDit* seems to think so too. Quite noisily in fact. Its self-righteous alarm throbs and drums in the center of my forehead as though I approach a danger point from which there will be no turning back.

But as anxious as its throbbing signal becomes, and as off-balance as I feel being dragged down the length of this living room toward that frayed velveteen couch, and as much as it appalls me to see myself so dominated, not merely by this voracious lady but by a cascade of irresistible forces—with all that motivation in place I still cannot seem to gain control over my overactive Sexual Principle.

Yes that is what The Seekers call it, 'The Sexual Principle', though it hardly seems principled to me. Cleverly hidden within the depths of my Physical Center it persists in painstakingly reviewing over and over the almost geometric puzzle of Ms. Allison Pratt's amazingly round and sensual breasts. Causing me to hang halfway suspended between the lift of her rising desires and the drag of my sinking apprehensions.

Say hello once again to Mr. Ping and Mr. Pong, erstwhile proponents of resistance, status quo and ambivalent behavior.

Mr. Ping and Mr. Pong!

Notice how one of them dedicates his energies to turning up my sexual thermostat while the other works feverishly to discourage my fascination with these alluring and hypnotic breasts, soberly reminding me that curiosity killed the cat.

To which his counterpart—Mr. Ping I guess—responding with a slippery smile reminds me that curiosity may have killed the cat but it probably also got him laid before he died.

But I was starting to talk about this concept of Legacy...

Even with all this energy in motion, sexual and otherwise, it still surprises me that we have not yet talked about the workings of Legacy which, if you study long enough with The Seekers For Truth, you will discover to be the primary engine that keeps the world spinning round.

The karmic world of course.

Somewhere around my fifth year in The Seekers I was introduced to the concept of the Noble Fourfold Legacy or the *NFL* as the non-athletic Seekers surprisingly call it. The *NFL* is perhaps the only measurement system by which any of us will ever be judged or graded for our life's work here on the planet.

To The Seekers, the behavior of ordinary, unenlightened individuals such as yourself is no more worthy or thoughtful than most animal species. It is only when consciousness enters our lives as an internal compass or guide that we gradually step up from our primal sludge to assume the mantle of something far more...well, *noble!*

Which is why, I suspect, they call it The Noble Fourfold Legacy.

As for my ignorance of the *NFL* during those first five years with The Seekers, I have come to see that as a period of grace, The Seekers For Truth obviously believing the universe is so benevolent it will not punish young children for behavior whose consequences they do not comprehend.

"It is like this," The Bapucharya explained on video. "Old Man Universe is a kindly old magistrate. This gray bearded officer of the court will not judge young children for their crimes as if they were full-grown, selfish-and-spiteful, upside-down adults. Indeed not! He will give them a slap on the side of the head and send them on their way—bad, bad children!

"But a full-grown, selfish-and-spiteful adult who commits the same crime—ohmigoodness!—Old Man Universe will hang him by the heels on the side of the road and attach electric lamps to make a new streetlight!"

That is not to say that living in ignorance protects you from the results of your actions. But it does reduce what appears to be the universe's response to those actions. Less karmic kickback. Fewer points taken off your grade so to speak.

Keep in mind this grade is nothing you will ever see posted on a bulletin board. But more a score added up on some cosmic calculator which somehow determines your individual standing in 'The Game'.

I know, I know: it sounds crazy!

I did not design the universe, I am merely reporting the way I was told it works.

As with anything I am told, however, I make my own decisions about what to believe and what to throw away. And I advise you to do the same.

Many times The Bapucharya has said that humankind is incapable of handling the Truth (capital T) without pouring *stupid sauce* all over it. *Stupid sauce* meaning dogma, ritual, holy mumbo jumbo and the like.

No matter how advanced a religion or a school such as The Seekers might become, it is still run by people, and no matter who or what they are—even a Bapucharya!— people always flavor the Truth with *stupid sauce.*

"The Truth will only come to you without *stupid sauce* when it comes from within," The Bapucharya has instructed. "So, children, when you are offered the Truth on a platter, make sure you understand that, yes, some of the fruit on the tray will bring you to Nirvana, but most of it, so sorry to say, will only give you a stomach ache."

Anyway this *NFL* score I mentioned which keeps accumulating over the course of our lifetimes supposedly has great significance for the four recipients of each individual's Legacy. Those recipients being cleverly named *The Home Team, The Fans, The Hometown Hero* and *The Game* itself.

You can pretty much figure out the principal players without benefit of a scorecard. But just in case...

The *Home Team* is made up of those individuals important to you during your lifetime, the ones in a sense who have lived with you on your *ILE.* Your parents, your children, your relatives and friends, even your enemies.

The most important members of your *Home Team*, however—the ones to whom you owe the most and for whom you take the most responsibility—are your children. And every Milestone you create as part of their Legacy becomes part of the Legacy you create for yourself. Which gives you some idea of the real trophies up for grabs at a cub scout Pinewood Derby.

The *Fans* now, those are the billions of individuals who exist beyond the boundaries of your *ILE—everyone* living in the outside world plus everyone for a generation or two that will follow after.

Yes I mean *everyone!* The whole planet is invited to this party.

As for your *Hometown Hero*, you are the one and only *Hometown Hero* in your Legacy. You have probably figured that out but most likely still do not realize that the Legacy you create for yourself as a *Hometown Hero* becomes your passport to your next and future lives.

Then lastly there is *The Game* itself.

This is *The Game!*

Everything you see and everything you cannot see. The wheels turning, the gears meshing, the clocks ticking. Everything The Seekers For Truth speak about; everything that relates to the hidden mechanisms that drive this universe of which we are both the smallest speck and the whole shebang.

The Game.

Also called Brahman, the Great Unrevealed Mystery (*GUM*) or the Automatic Universal Misunderstanding (*AUM*), depending upon which aspect of *The Game* you are speaking about.

But whatever you call it, someday when you are ready you will be given the biggest Milestone to jump over and that will be *The Big One.* The ultimate Legacy you create for yourself.

Your own personal Super Bowl.

If you think this sounds strange—and you would be weird to think otherwise—keep in mind you have been given the power of reason for a good reason.

To be used.

So make sure to use it, as often as necessary and more

often than you think necessary!

Use it to filter anything and everything you are told and especially to prevent *stupid sauce* from flavoring everything you take in.

Even from me.

And especially from The Bapucharya!

But enough idle chatter.

Stay with me now as I continue my quest to understand the curious strand of events that have brought me here to this second floor residence in Plymouth, Massachusetts. Our next station on the journey, I somehow sense, will find us at my apartment in Cambridge, though the word 'apartment' seems a bit grandiose for a three-room closet I once dusted end-to-end tethered to a five minute phone conversation with my mother.

But before we flashback to my apartment and a key link in this causal chain of karmic destiny we must first bid farewell to our blonde hostess.

Of course we are not really going anywhere so obviously we cannot be gone very long. No longer in fact than it takes to release an involuntary sigh. But if you wish, follow my example and allow yourself a quick glance, for a keepsake reminder, at those deliciously formed promontories jutting out from that white cotton blouse just below the lace fringe of my blonde companion's scalloped collar.

Hmm?

There is that odor again. Do you smell it?

Does it seem like Sen-Sen to you?

I wonder, do they still even make Sen-Sen...?

No matter. Better to shut my nose and keep my eyes open for signs that might explain how I ended up here—*here* in such a ridiculous position in this Plymouth apartment in the middle of my very own *ILE!*

In the firm and painful grip of Mr. Ping and Mr. Pong!

Valiantly struggling, as The Bapucharya would happily note, to remember to *drink my RC Cola.*

Lesson 21

Searching For God And Fairness In The Fourth Grade

And here we are!

In my Cambridge apartment as predicted.

It is early March, exactly three weeks after our momentous debacle with the cub scouts. Winter is still holding onto New England but with a grip that seems to grow more feeble every day. As does the trauma of our inglorious Pinewood Derby which, if not entirely out of our thoughts, is no longer the feature movie playing hourly that it once was.

Most likely—and Dr. Rivers has cautioned me about this— Mickey and I have taken our separate traumatic experiences of the Pinewood Derby and moved them like pieces on a Freudian chess board into the interior of our subconscious minds.

But today on this particular day in March I am occupying the more conscious regions of my mind, watching my little boy as he struggles to read a book. He, Cathy and I are sitting at the round wooden table in my Cambridge kitchen while Su-Su watches television in the adjoining living room.

The table, a dark hardwood of some indistinct variety, was given to me by my stepfather who was forced to shed an entire house full of furniture when he and my mother moved to Florida last year. Notice the table's thick skin of transparent urethane armor which I poured on in three chemically noxious coats. Depending on where you sit at the table you can search out in its glasslike sheen a reflection of anyone seated around the perimeter.

Having said that, however, you will notice that I am sitting too close to my little boy to see his reflection in the tabletop while Cathy's image clearly shines back at me, upside down on my left.

Both my young children appear to be reading but I can tell Mickey has not yet settled into the task. He is an excellent reader for his age group and has often been told so by his teachers. His problem now lies with the constancy of his attention.

Or the lack thereof.

It seems obvious to me by the way he repeatedly interrupts his reading to get up—sometimes for a drink, other times to go to the bathroom or visit with Suzie in the other room—that something is on his mind.

At one point earlier I asked him, “What are you reading, Mick?”

He had to read the title off the book’s cover to answer the question.

“Must be a good book,” I remarked to myself before going back to paying my bills and trying against all odds and expectations to balance a highly imbalanced checkbook.

But the answers to my questions—not to mention the secrets of the universe—are not waiting to be discovered on the pages of my checkbook register. They are waiting over there, hidden in the furrows that line my little boy’s forehead.

And of course in the unasked questions that echo in my mind.

Finally unable to hold off any longer I put down my pen and pull off my reading glasses, looking over to see Mickey fidgeting around on his chair.

“Either of you two want something?” I ask casually.

Cathy looks up from her book to think about my question, eventually deciding, “No thanks.”

“Nah,” Mickey mumbles, his face still half buried in his book.

“Something bothering you, Mick?” I ask.

“No,” he says in a voice that allows considerable room for doubt.

This of course is my opening.

“How are things at school?” I ask casually, playing with my pen.

“Okay,” he answers without conviction.

"That good?" I respond with lifted eyebrows.

“He’s been moping around for days,” Cathy comments with sisterly authority. “Haven’t you Mickey?”

“Have not!” he responds indignantly.

“Could have fooled me,” Cathy snaps back.

“Okay, okay,” I say making calming gestures with my hands. “Let us go back to what we were doing.”

“Can I go read in your bed?” Cathy asks.

“Sure,” I reply. “Just take off your shoes.”

As Cathy goes off to my bedroom which is directly off the kitchen, no farther than a few steps behind my chair, I mutter some inconsequential comments about the annoyance of paying bills and return to my unbalanced checkbook.

Over the next ten or fifteen minutes we sit in relative silence, Mickey displaying little energy in response to my occasional questions, none of them drawing more than a gruff, "I don't know" or "Who cares, Dad?" which prove enough of a rejection to keep me from probing too deeply.

At least until I begin paying the phone bill.

"I guess I must call you guys a lot," I jokingly groan, holding up the bill for him to see.

"Cool, Dad," he says as if bestowing some obligatory praise.

Clearly I have yet to gain his full attention.

A few minutes later I probe once again, “Mickey, it seems like something is bothering you. Is there something on your mind?”

“Huh?” he responds dully. “What?”

"Is something bothering you?"

He closes the book then declares, “Nothing’s bothering me,” with more energy than he has displayed during our entire conversation.

“Good!” I respond. “Just let me know when something *is* bothering you because that is why God invented fathers. We are supposed to be very good at helping young children with their problems.”

I smile and conclude, “You will let me know?”

“Sure,” he responds laconically.

And that is that!

Or so it seems.

Fifteen minutes later I am still sitting at the kitchen struggling with my finances when my little boy, who was watching TV with Su-Su, returns to the kitchen, walks up silently and stands next to me.

"Hello," I say softly without turning my head.

"Hi, Dad," he answers just as softly.

I say nothing, and wait…also softly.

"What are you doing?" he finally asks.

"Paying bills, just like before," I answer. "It is a pagan custom left over from the days of the Pilgrims. How is your movie?"

"Okay," he replies without interest. "I've seen it before."

"Oh," I respond.

He continues to stand there.

I continue to pay my bills.

"It's really a stupid movie," he finally declares.

"Is Su-Su enjoying it?"

"Sure," he says. "But she like those kinds of movies."

"Lots of kissing?" I ask.

"I guess so," he answers, not really interested in discussing the movie.

He continues to stand there watching me.

I continue to pay my bills.

"Is that a lot of bills to pay?" he questions idly.

"Oh, about the usual amount," I answer as I finish signing a check. "The trick is to stop paying bills before you run out of money."

"Did you ever run out of money?" he asks, for the first time expressing mild interest in the conversation. "Really?"

"Sometimes." I pause to lick the flap of an envelope. "But everyone does now and then. That is why God invented credit cards."

"Yeah," he smiles, getting the idea. "That's cool."

We are engaged in a process that to an outsider might appear casual and ill-focused. But I have been through this before and I know Mickey is giving me as much information as he can without violating a rule that most little boys live by. The rule has never been clearly enunciated to me but it seems to require a parent to accidentally stumble across important information rather than have it handed out on a serving platter.

"How are PJ and Mike doing?" I ask without apparent concern.

"Okay, I guess. PJ's going to Catholic school so I don't see him much."

"And the cub scouts? Are they going all right?"

"Sure."

"Good," I nod. "I thought maybe you were still having trouble with Mrs. Mitchell."

"She's okay. Mrs. Murphy helps her out now; comes to meetings."

"Oh."

Silence softly falls while I write another check.

"How are things in school?" I ask, repeating an earlier, unanswered question.

Mickey sighs.

I wait for more but a sigh turns out to be all the answer he is prepared to offer.

"What is the name of your teacher again?" I ask. "Mrs. Delaney?"

"Close, Dad. It's Mrs. Pratt. *Mr.* Delaney was Sue's teacher last year."

"I knew that," I reply playfully. "I was just testing you."

I continue to pay my bills.

He continues to watch me.

"Why do you think teachers have to yell so much?" he finally asks.

Now it is my turn to sigh, if only inwardly.

"Is that what Mrs. Pratt does?" I ask matter-of-factly. "She yells a lot?"

"I guess so."

"Does she yell at you?"

"Not really. Not as much as she does at some of the other kids. Like Beverly Keyes and Marty Sullivan. She really yells at John Tilden a lot, but he annoys everybody."

"And it bothers you?" I idly probe.

"Nahh!" he shrugs, shaking his head.

"Good."

"Well..." he wavers and I can almost see him pulling hard on the rudder.

"Yes...?" I say, waiting.

"Maybe a little."

"You mean it bothers you a little?"

"Maybe even more than a little."

So there it is!

Mrs. Pratt yells a lot.

I have the same feeling I get when one of my children has a thorn stuck in a finger and, after long minutes of painful searching and rubbing the finger roughly and looking through a magnifying glass, I actually find it. A little sliver causing a lot of pain.

Mrs. Pratt yells a lot.

You could easily miss it if you were searching for something massive standing out in the middle of a field. But as with most things that concern my little boy the smallest things burrow the deepest.

Mickey has never been able to tolerate injustice or the abuse of power when he finds it staring him in the face. He simply cannot accept it. That of course will eventually prove to be a big problem in his life because the world will rarely adjust its behavior to accommodate someone as sensitive as he is.

Sooner or later he will have to learn that life is not always fair, people in power are not always evenhanded, and stories most definitely do not always have happy endings.

I could tell him that now and he might understand, but he would never accept it. To Mickey it could never be acceptable for grownups in responsible positions to be unfair or cruel to young children or to get away with such 'sad' behavior.

Is it reasonable to demand fairness from life? Especially in a world that according to Automatic Universal Misunderstanding does not even exist?

Who can say?

Mickey would not know how to answer that question either. He would just know what he feels about things. And that he dislikes Mrs. Pratt's yelling at the kids in his class.

So what would he make of those singles dances I attend sometimes every week? What would he say about the callous indifference with which most people treat each other at those inelegant social experiments held mostly in the dark?

"Why did that lady refuse to dance with you?" he would ask were he to witness one of my numerous rejections.

"I guess she did not want to dance with me," I would simply reply.

"But why?"

"Because I was not handsome enough, maybe."

"That isn't nice," he would suggest.

"No it is not," I would agree.

"Does she know she could hurt your feelings?"

"Probably not," I would answer though in truth I doubt that she would care.

"She has every right to refuse me," I would explain, implying very subtly of course that it is okay for me to do the same with women I find unattractive.

But Mickey would not be impressed.

"Yeah," he would answer, "but it is not right to hurt someone's feelings. That is not a happy thing to do."

We still on occasion talk about 'happy' things that people do and 'sad' things as well, a throwback to Mickey's days at Montessori School.

At some point in our lives I will have to explain to him that in the adult world it is okay to do 'sad' things to people as long as you do them in an adult way.

But Mickey will not buy that explanation. He has an unshakeable faith in the goodness of things. If it were proven that God did not exist, then Mickey would probably believe that the qualities of God as seen through his nine-year-old eyes—love, charity, honesty, faithfulness—still exist as natural phenomena.

I myself have no difficulty believing in The Creative Principle or The Absolute Governing Entity or even The Great Prankster in The Sky as The Bapucharya sometimes calls Him. But I cannot believe in the kind of God Mickey believes in.

If there is a Creative Life Force or a Divine Energy, I believe it lies within each of us, not out in the world running around solving people's petty problems. And certainly not lounging around God's Heaven waiting for us to transgress His rules so badly he has to come down and punish us like bad children.

No God of mine would ever want to punish His children that way. But a God that lets those children punish and reward *themselves* as they make good and bad choices—there is a God who brings a little intelligence to the job!

All that aside, there is one aspect of my little boy's enduring faith that never ceases to amaze me. You see he not only believes in fairness and goodness and a benevolent deity, he also believes his father can still make his problems go away.

That is why Mickey is standing next to me in the kitchen watching me pay my bills and waiting patiently for my tender ministrations.

He does not believe I failed him at the Pinewood Derby three weeks earlier. That could not have been *his* father's fault. No I am still the cave he can crawl into, the warmth that can surround him, the shelter than can hold back the storm.

Talk about the power of denial!

"Shall I talk to Mrs. Pratt?" I ask him gently.

He grows visibly agitated, vehemently moaning "No!" as if the idea terrifies him.

"Okay," I say soothingly, reaching out to physically gather him in.

"Promise you won't!" he insists, knowing me only too well. "Promise you won't say anything to Mrs. Pratt."

"But if it might help…?"

"Dad!" he pleads.

"I promise," I say softly. "You have my word."

I put my hand on his shoulder as if sharing a confidence.

"But what shall we do?" I ask.

"Nothing, Dad. We don't do nothing."

"Anything," I correct him with a squeeze. "We do not do *anything."*

"Besides, it's no big deal."

"You are right," I agree lightly. "It is no big deal. It just seems like we might want to help Beverly Keyes and Marty Sullivan if we can."

"And John Tilden," he reminds me.

"The hell with John Tilden," I scoff. "He is nothing but a

troublemaker who deserves to be yelled at."

A smile breaks across my little boy's face. So small a thing yet it has the power to chase away clouds and lift my spirits.

"Yeah, John Tilden annoys me, too," Mickey agrees. "The hell with him."

"Hey, watch your language!"

"Well, *you* watch your language!"

I pull my son close and hug him. Then I pull back for a searching look into his face.

"I need a nuzzle," I announce with the seriousness such a declaration deserves.

Such a request is sacred at moments like this and there is only one way for Mickey to respond. He scrunches up his nose and extends it to meet mine. Then with familiar ease both our scrunched up noses rub against each other, back and forth three or four times before we pull them away.

"Good!" I exclaim. "I needed that."

"Me too," he says wiping his nose.

"Feel better?" I ask.

My little boy nods his head to say 'yes'. He is still smiling.

"Cool," I say crisply, stealing his customary line.

A few moments later he is back in the living room with his sister and I am back in my thoughts at the kitchen table surrounded by a scattering of envelopes, bills, assorted papers and my checkbook.

I sit here searching for some idea that will help me to effectively change Mrs. Pratt's behavior, given the fact I am not allowed to speak to her directly.

It is just like Mickey to present me with a problem then refuse me access to the most obvious solution. It is like asking me to clean a window without touching the glass.

I look around my kitchen for an answer. There is nothing to be seen.

"Just let it go," I tell myself, "Something will come to mind."

The way the universe works—not with some cloud-dwelling God playing out his role as our personal protector but in the ordinary twists and turnings of the Great Unrevealed Mystery—if you apply consciousness to a problem something will usually come to mind.

And something does come to mind.

Unfortunately in this case, it turns out to be something stupid—something very stupid indeed!

Lesson 22

A Few Thoughts Prior To Entering The Fray

Would you like to go to a dance?

Not just a dance but a 'singles dance'? Called so I suppose because married couples might otherwise make the mistake of traveling to a strange hotel to attend a dance filled with hundreds of mostly unattractive, unfamiliar, middle-aged single people.

The designation 'singles dance', like a 'Poison' sign nailed to a desert well, works diligently to protect the life and sanity of the non-single segment of the population.

All that being true, however, these singles dances are still a major part of my social life, an imperfect but ever available hunting ground for the ideal companion or mate, assuming such a creature exists.

How about it?

Besides it is time I took you to something a little more upside-down adult than a Pinewood Derby.

So follow me and stay close as we slip quietly through the crowd in this mirrored and marbled lobby. Up to where these middle-aged people are lined up at a short rectangular table that stands like a makeshift tollbooth outside the Plymouth Marriott's Mayflower Ballroom.

You can gauge the level of sophistication for the dance with one look at the glittering sign that takes up a third of the table's acreage.

All Singles We Invite
To Our Singles Dance Tonite!

Let us nonchalantly fall in behind these somber but fashionably dressed men and women who look more like they are queuing up for a painful vaccination than waiting to pay twenty dollars to have their hands rubber stamped to enter a singles dance.

Can you feel it? The sense of hope and exhilaration rising up inside yourself? It is always this way. There is no other moment in a single person's life where the possibilities seem as infinite as the moment before you enter a dance. Once inside you will very likely see the same crowd you see at most singles dances, which means the majority of the participants will turn out to be older, uglier and far more distant than the one man or woman—the ideal man or woman—you came here hoping to meet.

But right now standing here I can imagine a world filled with endless possibilities and limitless numbers of beautiful women, all of them waiting just for me on the other side of those slowly-approaching ballroom doors.

Just remember, anything is possible at a moment when everything is hoped for.

That is why I prefer singles dances to online dating though probably, like most people at the dance, I continue to dabble in both. It is just that computer dating takes more time than I can afford and too often the women I encounter online and later meet for coffee turn out to be five years older than their pictures and 30 pounds heavier.

At least with a singles dance you have a chance to actually see the goods on display even if the lights are kept low.

Have you noticed how quickly the line moves?

In no time at all with little effort on my part I am standing at the front of the line watching a young overweight lady take my money. See how she reaches towards me with her rubber stamp poised in the air?

Now watch!

Like a cobra weary of attacking strangers yet unable to resist the pull of habit she strikes with a flick of the wrist.

For some reason I have always enjoyed the sensation of a rubber stamp striking the back of my hand.

"What is that supposed to be?" I ask, holding up my left hand appraisingly and eyeing the indistinguishable purple smudge like a jeweler examining an exotic gem.

The effort proves unnecessary since half a second later

the lady of the rubber stamp reveals in an air of nasal disinterest, “That’s a star with a crescent moon.”

She is quite heavy-set for someone still in her early twenties and has little discernible interest in conversing with customers like myself or answering their questions. Her eyes, heavy-lidded to begin with, are almost closed shut under the weight of the mascara and eye shadow she has troweled in place.

If my little boy were here now and I were fulfilling my fatherly duty I would point out to him the cinematic nature of this woman standing guard outside the dance. No merry, bright-eyed hostess she, but more an omen meant to strike a jarring note in the mind of passersby which says ‘be warned, dear traveler, beyond these doors lies a land of strange and uninviting people’.

But I am not a character in a movie and this is not a Hollywood melodrama. This is my life and she in reality is more pathetic than prophetic, not an omen but a sorry reminder of all those souls who live on the fringes of social contact but never actually find their way in.

She wrinkles her nose in a quick, involuntary motion.

“You’ll need to show that,” she explains, indicating the stamp and offering the slightest of smiles, “if you leave the dance and want to get back in.”

I am surprised and even touched to find her reaching out to me, even with such a watery smile.

“Thanks,” I smile back, “I will remember that.”

In truth I do not need to remember anything since I already know the routine.

The inked symbol on my hand will be my passport back into the dance if at some point I decide to temporarily leave. It will glow and be recognized when I flash it under the black light lamp at the edge of the table by the door.

Even now a steady stream of returning dancegoers flow past me, one after the other, their hands raised under the glare of the lamp’s purplish glow in a gesture so mindless it appears somnambulant. They are returning to the dance after a brief hiatus buying cheaper drinks in the bar, ingesting questionable substances out in the privacy of their cars, or doing whatever else to themselves wherever they choose to do it.

Not my business. Not my concern.

The black light looks like an old-fashioned desk lamp. Probably something the dance promoter had in his room as a kid, the lamp buzzing interminably as he studied for math and Spanish quizzes.

Such trivialities aside, this passing parade barely occupies my thoughts long enough to give rise to a sensible sentence. My awareness is focused elsewhere, I must admit—on the open door ahead and the vaguely defined crowd in the darkened room beyond. Moving towards the door my attention rises briskly under the force of some inescapable impulse, focusing sharply on the present moment which seems intensely alive and brimming with promise as if someone has just given the wheel of fate an energetic spin.

And thus with all engines humming and all articles of faith in a benevolent universe held high above the waters of cynicism and doubt (for how else should we enter a battleground if not with songs of valor rising from our bagpipes?) I step boldly into the darkness and commotion that awaits me in the Mayflower Ballroom.

Come.

There is nothing to be afraid of.

Lesson 23

How To Distinguish Between Fear And Anxiety In A Therapeutic Relationship

"What are you thinking about?" Dr. Rivers asks, the question gently probing, devoid of any emotional texture. As always, his voice seems high-pitched for someone of his height and stature.

"Nothing, really," I answer with little emotion.

"Go on, tell me."

"There is nothing to tell."

"Are you sure?"

"Positive!"

"Well then, why do you seem so nervous, so afraid?" he questions gently, speaking over the fingertips of both hands which are touching in a prayerful pose.

"Afraid of what?" I snap back, not sure I want to hear his answer.

"I don't know exactly," he answers softly. "I was hoping you might tell me."

"Were you listening to me at all?" I ask with rising irritation. "I was imagining a world filled with possibilities and beautiful women, all waiting for me at a dance. Did you hear that?"

"How could I not hear you?" Dr. Rivers asks softly.

I cannot tell you how many times over the last two years he has answered a question of mine with a question of his. But I surely can tell you how irritating it has become!

And look at him sitting across from me on the only piece of comfortable furniture in the room! For two years I have squirmed and fidgeted for 50-minute intervals, sitting upright on this couch, my lower back propped with tightly-wedged cushions, while he has sat deeply ensconced in that black, hi-backed leather chair contemplating everything I say with an air of distant majesty and subtle distaste.

Rather stately looking, is he not? A tall figure of a man somewhere in his early 60's, I would guess, his entire demeanor lent an air of sagacious dignity by the gray-flecked beard he constantly strokes and picks at.

I like to watch him at times, totally absorbed in some thought or question, absent-mindedly twirling the dry gray ends of his beard around his fingers.

Sometime during this second year of therapy I began calling him 'Old Man Rivers'. In my mind, you understand, and not the part of my mind I generally open up for his inspection.

"We've talked about this before, " he says after a few moments of thoughtful silence, "your inability at times to admit to your feelings when they arise. The way you need to hold onto things long enough to let the event fade and the emotions die down before you're ready to deal with it."

He sits up in his chair then asks, "How many weeks has it been since the dance? Four, five?"

"Three," I answer defensively, "... and a couple of days."

"And you just bring it up now?"

Suddenly, of all things, I start to laugh.

"This therapy trip can be really strange," I say, still amused.

I look to the ceiling as if a remedy for my laughter might be hiding up there.

"Want to hear how strange?" I ask. "Hmm?"

Not waiting for an answer I push ahead, "I swear to you, right this moment I cannot think of a single other thing to talk about *except the fucking dance!* There is nothing else in my head. Nothing! It is a blank slate. I do not wish to talk about the dance now—or ever! But my mind is totally empty otherwise. Do you not find that funny? Certainly at least strange!"

"That's not for me to say," he replies. "But your aversion to bringing things up...I find that familiar. Don't you?"

"Yes, so...?" I respond, always happy to return a question for a question. Also somewhat relieved, if I am honest, that I will not have to face the implications of my mind drawing a complete blank. I have no idea what that means but it seems worrisome to think about.

"So, perhaps you were not facing up to your feelings when you entered the dance—or now, either—that's all I am saying," my gray-bearded therapist suggests. "You sit here and, to me, you seem anxious and upset as you start to describe yourself entering the dance."

"But I was just telling you how excited and expectant I felt! Did I not just say something about a world filled with endless possibilities and beautiful women? Does that sound like I was afraid? Or am I just crazy?"

I pause a moment waiting for a response.

A second or two later he grunts "Uh-huh! You're right!" and nods in a sort of grudging agreement.

I pounce on that slender thread of justification like a kitten going after string.

"Then how could you sift through everything I say and come to the conclusion I was *afraid?"*

"Well then, let's say *anxious,"* he suggests.

"Do you know anything about me? What really makes me afraid or anxious? When I was at the god-damn Pinewood Derby—*that* was frightening. I was scared shitless then..."

"Because of your son's pink racecar...?" he clumsily probes.

"It was not pink!"

"You're the one who keeps bringing up how inappropriate the color was."

"Yes, but it was not pink. It was fuchsia—probably just as dumb as pink but a different color entirely."

"Whatever..." he says, bringing his hands down and adjusting his position on the soft leather chair. "Are you avoiding my question or just in a combative mood?"

"What was the question?"

"Whether you realize why you seem afraid—or anxious—talking about the dance?"

Controlling my anger I answer slowly, "There you go again; stating a premise as if we both accepted it. Well, I do not agree that I am afraid to talk about the dance or was afraid at the time or that I am afraid now—or whatever it is you are saying. I might have been a little anxious that night but that is normal when you go to a singles dance."

"You were anxious but not afraid?"

"Yes."

"Is there a difference?" he asks.

"Yes."

Before he can ask the next question I point an accusing finger at him.

"I know you," I smile ruefully. "As soon as I insist there *is* a difference, you will shout 'Aha! There he goes again, denying the obvious.'

"Please allow me to shout for myself."

"...well, whatever! The fact is you will point out some avoidance of reality or intentional misunderstanding or...or something else sadly psychological. Am I right?"

"Not sadly psychological. Just normal," he says treading carefully, refusing to rise to my challenge.

"Okay, normal. But can we save a step here? Can you tell me why I was afraid? Not that I agree with your use of the word *afraid."*

"Do you mean to say there was nothing on your mind when you went to the dance? Nothing?"

I am about to voice a firm 'No' when a thought strolls slowly in large muddy boots across the front lobby of my Mental Center.

"We-e-ell..." I utter with some hesitation, the sound traveling through the congealed phlegm in my throat.

"Yes...?" he prods carefully.

After a moment of silence he adds, "You were saying...?"

"It was nothing," I reply softly, "really."

He drops his fingers from his beard, straightens his head and looks at me, focusing his sharply penetrating eyes on mine.

"Then tell me this...what were you doing all the way down in Plymouth? It probably takes an hour and a half to drive there from Cambridge..."

"A little over an hour!" I correct him. "If there is no traffic."

"Fine, a little over an hour! That's still twice as long as it would take you to drive to Burlington, or Newton. Was the Plymouth dance the only singles dance in the state?"

Still hesitant to get drawn into this discussion I respond "No-o-o...", drawing out the syllable as if it were a fence tall enough for me to hide behind.

Instead of continuing his attack Old Man Rivers stops himself in mid-flight as if struck by a sudden thought or an insight. Then as I watch in mild but appreciative surprise, his body seems to relax, adjusting its position in his chair as it falls into a more relaxed pose.

Uh-oh! Now he is smiling at me.

"Well, enough of that!" he says through that thin bearded smile, offering a sympathetic look that furrows his brow. "I'm sorry. This is not meant to be the Inquisition. You don't have to answer anything you don't want to answer."

He looks at me with a quiet air of acceptance.

"What would you like to talk about?" he asks, his head tilting expectantly.

This of course is Dr. Rivers' ultimate weapon. He knows my defenses will completely fall to pieces if he tosses me a rare display of fairness sprinkled with sympathy.

Rather than allow the pressure to keep building up I blurt out, "Okay, you are right, of course. I went to Plymouth for a reason. I was hoping to run into someone—someone in particular. I had reason to think she might show up at the dance. Maybe I was a little nervous about it, maybe not. I cannot honestly remember whether I was or not. "

He smiles then asks, "Well, who was she, this lady you were hoping to meet?" as though the question has little importance.

I smile back.

"I will get to that in time," I tell him, raising a hand to half-shield my embarrassed expression. "I need to give you a little background before I talk about that particular lady."

"So give me a little background."

"Well, where were we?" I ask, trying to recall where I had left off. It seems like hours have passed since he first interrupted my narrative.

"You were outside the ballroom..." he suggests, his lips hidden behind a prayerful brace of fingers.

"Oh, yes!" I recall with enthusiasm, "I was about to enter the dance..."

Lesson 24

The Perils Of Taking Stock Of Yourself At A Singles Dance

It feels as if we are entering a noisy, dimly lit cave filled with hundreds of shadowy figures.

Am I right?

This ever-dark ambience is a universal feature of singles dances, most likely because dim lights have the kindness to conceal the ravages of mounting years that bright lights so cruelly expose.

I remember like the fragment of some surreal dream a dance where the lights ran amuck. Someone with a warped sense of humor must have taken control of the master dimmer-switch because for most of the evening, at moments when you least expected it, the lights would suddenly shift from dim to bright, instantly revealing a room full of shockingly older single men and women, far less attractive than those that had been attending the dance just moments earlier.

It was as if monsters had been lurking in the shadows waiting to be cruelly exposed as soon as some frightmaster turned up the lights. What was even more unsettling was the way those ghastly apparitions melted from sight, back into hiding, once the lights were turned down again.

The experience was cautionary to say the least but also quite amusing for someone still under 50 and not yet relying on the discretion of darkness to help plead his cause.

I mention this so that you in all your innocence will not rely too heavily on what you *think* you see in the dark confines of this ballroom tonight. Nothing is as it appears. No one looks as they would look under the glare of less forgiving light. I have seen many of these same middle-aged men and women before, mostly at other dances, and I can guarantee they look very different under the solid beam of a lamp at full wattage.

Still I can see everything I need to see. *Dancegoers* being a species quite similar to *cave dwellers,* my eyes have adjusted quickly and without difficulty to the relative absence of light.

But let us keep moving.

We are lucky, we have come here on a good evening.

You can see for yourself the ballroom has already filled to the point where the dance no longer runs the risk of failure.

There is a strange phenomenon that occurs amongst middle-aged men and women that can easily cause the downfall of a singles dance. Surprisingly often, ample numbers of people show up at a dance but hold back from going in until they are certain of getting their money's worth. Ultimately, if enough of them hold back they create the very thing they are trying to avoid: a singles dance unworthy of its price of admission.

I have seen this kind of thing before. It is a curious working of the universe that people trying to control things often end up creating the exact situation they were hoping to avoid. Like policemen who overreact and excite the very riot they were sent to prevent.

It would all be humorous if it were only more... humorous.

As I said, there is already a good sized crowd in place which is why without hesitation or thought I have launched myself on a course that carries me towards a distant corner of the ballroom. My radar has been programmed to automatically scan for promising women as they fall within my tracking path.

I love this song.

"No Guarantee For Lovers."

It came out when Marilyn and I had just separated; I used to think there was a message meant for us in its lyrics.

I miss the ticking of the clock,
The sing-song way it rocks
And counts the hours

I could have spent with you.
See her? Moving up quickly on the right?
No, no, the brunette a little further back!
Quite attractive...in a mousy sort of way.

"Hi," I say with a broad smile, bringing myself to a sudden halt. "This is a pretty good tune; not too slow for a slow dance. Want to give it a try?"

She is nice looking. A little thin but actually rather classy for a singles dance in Plymouth. She looks at me strangely, no doubt puzzling over the meaning of my words which were half-spoken on the fly and probably only half understood.

I miss the morning of our days,
Watch seasons spin away
Into the years
I could have spent with you.

You are probably thinking she is a shade too young for me—and I would not argue the point. But then I am only asking her to dance, not to have my children.

"What did you say?" she asks as though she just realized I was speaking.

"I asked if you would like to dance."

Her trance mildly disturbed by my question she does not return my smile. Clearly her interest is not strong enough to warrant enthusiasm.

"Not now," she says, shaking her head and upsetting the thick wavy strands that fall so easily upon her shoulder. "Perhaps later. I'm waiting for someone."

Whether she is waiting for a girlfriend or a romantic interest she does not say. Nor does it matter. She is not waiting for me. That is all I need to know. Let someone else have this dance. Probably someone a little younger than me and slightly better looking.

You see, babe, there's no guarantee for lovers,
'Cause the promises dry up faster than the tears,
And the love we thought we bought to last a lifetime,
Should have never gone so long without repairs.

"I wonder if I look okay?" I fret as I continue on my way.

"Obviously, not good enough," a voice inside my head answers; a voice quite different from The Bapucharya's, I am happy to say. I wince at the incongruous thought of having The Bapucharya accompanying me to a singles dance!

I have enough difficulty dealing with the mood of cold disaffection one encounters at these dances, not to mention the repeated rejections. To have The Bapucharya giggling in my head or hovering next to me by the ceiling, both of us disembodied, would only turn me into a babbling idiot—probably within seconds.

No, this particular voice is concerned with my social failings, not my spiritual inadequacies—with particular emphasis on my questionable appearance.

Speaking of which...I look to the giant mirrors on the wall and see through the nether-light of the dimly-lit ballroom my reflection staring back.

"Hey, not so bad," a second internal voice decides, pleased that I still appear 'crisp' and that my hair is still in place.

"Maybe I was just too old for her," I muse, moving sideways to catch an off-angle view of myself, trying to see myself as others might see me.

"Not bad at all," the voice happily decides.

For most of us here tonight there is a single question that resonates in the mind above all others. It is a natural side effect of this almost compulsive quest to find an attractive companion who even in her middle life years is still available and halfway intelligent.

Like a hunter who constantly questions whether he has remembered his ammunition or brought enough shells or brought the right kind of shells, we each suffer doubts about whether our physical attributes have enough stopping power to bring down one of these semi-wild creatures in mid-flight?

Only we express those doubts in the form of a question.

For your benefit I will recite that question as I often hear it within the recesses of my doubting mind.

"How do I look?"

Yes "How do I look?" some inner voice questions, seeking reassurance that a mirror never quite manages to provide.

"How do I look?" that same voice repeats, riddled with doubt and insecurity.

"How do I look?" it asks again and again as if already

knowing the unhappy answer.

"How do I look—no, how do I *really* look?"

The question will arise spontaneously tonight whenever I pass my reflection in a mirror or approach an interesting woman or find myself rejected by one, or when for any other reason I begin to distrust my charms.

"How do I look?" that inner voice questions, seemingly under its own impetus. But if you search for that voice and dig a little more deeply below the surface you will observe that every single query is made up of a multitude of questions and answers in much the same way that atoms are made up of sub-atomic particles.

It is the sound of my ego of course seeking to defend and protect me. Attempting sometimes against heavy odds to shore up my courage and restore confidence. But ego is a schizophrenic son-of-a-bitch. It constantly argues with itself whenever it feels tense or nervous. Especially in situations where it fears people are sitting in judgment...like at a singles dance!

What a racket inside my head! All the bickering, the snide comments, the tired jokes—it is like a bad radio drama I cannot shut off.

Ego has many voices and each one has its own personality, its own point of view. A few of them, the ones I hear most often, I have even given names.

Perhaps an example might help you to understand.

Let us pretend I am again approaching that highly disinterested woman with the thick wavy hair. If you could tune into the noises in my head, aside from a low-level oscillation from my *PuNDit,* you would notice the question "How do I look?" start to resonate and repeat the moment I decide to intercept her elegant, slightly undernourished figure.

Now as I come closer, in a length of time that can be divided down to millionths of a second, I am able to question and monitor the state of my painstakingly arranged hair, my hastily-selected clothes, my vodka-laced breath, my cologne-scentet body, the white of my smile and a dozen other inconsequential details of my personal presentation. All of this questioning, monitoring and reacting being autonomous, happening without any effort on my part.

Take one of my major concerns—watch what happens when I bring up the subject of *my hair.*

Or more accurately *my lack of hair.*

Did you hear the voice? Immediately it sprang into action, protesting, "There is nothing wrong with my hair! I may be a little thin on top, but the same is true for just about every other guy in the room. It looks fine—really!"

I call that voice *The Defender.* As chief of my Social Insecurity Force, The Defender becomes panic-stricken and defensive whenever the subject of my hair comes up.

And then there is *The Nitpicker,* the resident voice of doom who will never let The Defender have the last word on anything.

"Face it brother, you are bald!" The Nitpicker declares outright, without any mercy. "Or damn close! And if this woman has half a brain she will not miss the fact you are almost entirely bald on the top of your head.

"Who do you think you are fooling, combing your hair over from the side like that? It would be laughable if you were not so pathetic in the belief it makes you look better."

"Are you going to start that again?" The Defender angrily retorts.

"I am not starting anything," The Nitpicker protests with an air of aggrieved innocence. "You asked how your hair looks and I told you. You should not ask a question if you do not want to hear an answer."

" ... with a useless commentary tagged on at the end!"

"No more useless than your childish attempt to camouflage your baldness."

"Gentlemen, gentlemen," a soothing voice joins in. "Why are we fighting when we have a simple job to do? Can we just tell Paul what he needs to know about his hair? Can we just do that?"

I call that voice *The Good Unitarian.* Notice how he immediately inserts an air of calm and purpose into the discussion.

Which disappears as soon as he finishes speaking.

"But I am not bald," The Defender asserts, deaf to The Good Unitarian's pleas. "I am *balding!"*

"The difference being what...?" The Nitpicker challenges.

"The degree of baldness that exists."

"On your head or in the hotel ballroom?"

"And that is supposed to be funny?"

"Gentlemen," The Good Unitarian interrupts, "I will only repeat myself once...can we just tell Paul that his hair looks okay? Can we just do that? Can we tell him it looks okay?"

"And it *does* look okay!" The Defender chimes in.

"To me, it looks ridiculous."

"Well, I think we should tell him it looks okay," The Good Unitarian pushes, "and that makes two of us. So, majority rules!"

Majority rules? More like chaos rules!

This on-again off-again battle between ego particles, though too subtle for casual observation, is no less energetic than a battle between young children in bumper cars. And the battleground is not limited to concerns about my hair.

They could just as easily be arguing about any personal grooming issue. Say my *five o'clock shadow.*

Watch as I rub my non-existent beard and think to myself, "Maybe I should have shaved before coming here...?"

As usual The Defender is first to arrive at the scene.

"For what? I look great!" he asserts.

"Pardon me, but I think you should have shaved," the loyal opposition responds, "...unless you enjoy looking like a rabbinical student."

"Is that such a bad thing?"

"At a singles dance? It sucks!"

No matter how I see myself there will always be a small part of me shouting in the quietest of angry voices, "Go home, fool. You are not handsome enough, charming enough, or even lucky enough to find the woman you are seeking. And even if you manage to stumble across someone of value, she will quickly see what Marilyn and all the rest have discovered—that you are just a bad penny looking to bum a ride in a warm pocket."

If I ever believed that—*truly* believed that—I could never show my face at a singles dance again.

So I ignore the voices and continue on the hunt.

And by the way I did shave before coming here tonight. I just said that so you could hear some of the outlandish self-doubt and criticism that goes on beneath the surface of this seemingly poised and handsome facade.

"And it is a handsome facade!"

"Handsome?" The Nitpicker questions. "By whose standards, handsome? On what planet?"

Do not listen to him.

I am sorry I pointed them out to you. But since it has already come up for discussion—how do you think I look? My general appearance, I mean?

No, no, forget I asked! It does not matter.

Tonight I am not caught up in the usual roundabouts of self-criticism and doubt, both of which usually have seductive powers over me. Nor have I been tossed here by the winds of fate. As you know, I have a slightly different purpose in being here this evening. I am not merely hoping to find a woman this time but a specific woman: one woman out of all the women on the planet—though who can say if she will show up at tonight's dance?

If I were a betting man I would say the odds against her showing up are a hundred—maybe even a thousand—to one. Except of course for the unexplainable fact that *I know* she will show up at the Plymouth Marriott tonight. I know it the same way I knew that we were caught up in a *Slide* at the Pinewood Derby. There is some place inside myself—probably quite close to the *CPU*—where I just know the way things are and the way things will be. Not specifically but in a general way.

And tonight, going against the odds and the improbability of predicting the behavior of a woman I never met, I am certain she will be here.

The romantics would call it Kismet or fate. The Seekers would say *I am centered in knowledge.* Either way I expect to see a certain lady showing up at the dance tonight.

But let us keep moving.

Stepping across the dance floor I troll the crowded waters of the ballroom watching for my prey but ready to haul in anything of interest that might be swimming nearby.

Moving at a controlled cruising speed I find myself easily able to *drink my RC Cola.* That is one of the peculiarities of a singles dance. The mix of stimuli is so unnatural and surreal and filled with so many subtle messages, one has to stay awake and reasonably attentive to gain any benefit. If an attractive woman suddenly walks onto the dance floor she will be scooped up so fast you will hardly have time to think about her much less mount an attack, and one tires very quickly of watching others skim off the cream from the ever-thinning flow of attractive women.

Notice how my vision remains sharply focused and my thoughts hold firmly to the business at hand. If someone interesting appears within sight I will not miss her. There is no casual drifting in and out of consciousness like there is with most activities. Which is why things appear so vivid, the shapes of bodies and forms so much more substantive, even those figures obscured by shadow or distance.

There is something in this world that is set so far apart from my daily life and its normal rhythms that I am reminded how, according to The Seekers, none of this world we see around us—this world we touch and feel and walk through—is real. None of it!

That is what The Seekers mean when they talk about *AUM,* Automatic Universal Misunderstanding.

That is the ultimate reality that lies behind what The Bapucharya calls, "The Chief Magician's most amazing trick."

As always, His Holiness told us about it on videotape. Smiling beatifically at the camera and sitting in his effortless lotus position he raised both hands, flipped them backward and frontward as if to show there was nothing up his sleeves then requested us to, "Watch me now. See, this is the universe all around us. We are surrounded in its glories and traffic jams of unconscious activities. We are ants on its ant-hill, bees in its hive. All of us rushing to catch the last train, so busy, busy, busy.

"Then Shiva, that great dance master of the Hindu Gods, after so many millennia of spinning in circles the poor chap finally says 'Enough. I am so tired and stiff from all this dancing. What I really want is a nap!' And what does this weary fellow do? He claps his hands and stops his dance. Just like that!" he said, clapping his hands sharply, "and the dance of the universe becomes a very effective work stoppage.

And just as suddenly, the movie of the universe is finished—whooosh...it is all quite unhurriedly gone.

"Bye, bye, children!" he suddenly called out, laughing and waving. Then of course the video monitor went blank, The Bapucharya's latest giggles still echoing in the air.

This illusion we all supposedly share—this Automatic Universal Misunderstanding—is like a dream of God, we were told, something He or She envisioned during a long uninterrupted nap. And within this dream lies the illusory formation of the entire physical universe.

According to The Seekers, the entire creation all boils down to a single momentary thought of the Creative Principle (yet another name for God) that occurs at a single point of time—which is occurring right now—but which plays itself out through our limited receptors as though it were taking place in linear time.

Confusing?

Absolutely!

But then of course we are merely illusory creatures inhabiting an illusory world. We are meant to struggle under the weight of our illusions (as The Seekers will happily explain) until we complete whatever journey is intended for us here on Earth—taking us through the illusion itself, across our *Iles,* up our Paths Of Seeking Truth, hopping over our Milestones till finally we reach our Grand Overriding Destination.

There it is. The ultimate acronym.

The Grand Overriding Destination.

And reaching that destination constitutes "The Big Game" as The Bapucharya likes to call it, deriving great enjoyment as always from The Seekers purloined Americanisms. "Yes, young children, the biggest game of them all. This is what the real Super Bowl shall be! If you play in this final game at the end of your season, you shall have had a very good season indeed!

"And if you score the winning touchdown, then you shall have the trophy to take home. No, that is not right," he paused, releasing a fit of high-pitched giggles. "You are not given the trophy, you *become* the trophy!

"And what is this trophy, you are wondering? Some call

it Nirvana or Enlightenment. Others know it as Cosmic Consciousness or Self-Realization. I call it, The Big Cheese!"

Call it what you will, but until we each win our own personal super bowl we will live in a world where time appears to unwind from a linear spool and we live out our chain of lives as if one moment follows another in endless succession.

That is *The* illusion, The Seekers tell us, *The Great Illusion* we all share. And because we all share it without having any choice in the matter, it is called *AUM,* the Automatic Universal Misunderstanding.

And speaking of misunderstandings, look who I see coming towards me, cutting through the crowded dance floor like a Coast Guard cutter on a life-or-death mission.

Yes you are right.

She is not the lady I came here to find.

Nor a lady I wish to have find me.

Lesson 25

Hell Hath No Fury Like A Woman Scorned Or Recently Impoverished

This is not good.

I spotted her over an hour ago but up until now she has been content to keep her distance, letting me run like a thief to different parts of the large ballroom without following me. Keeping far enough away to inspire hope that she might possibly choose not to confront me.

But recently she has begun tracing my footsteps, following in my wake, moving with certainty into the same territories I am traveling. And now when I stop to look around I invariably spot her nearby, her eyes resting on me as if I were a surprise finding from a government research project.

And her eyes are not smiling.

You may be wondering what I did to make her so angry and I believe that is a reasonable question. But the simple truth is I do not know. I cannot comprehend what movies are playing in her mind.

I know what angered her all right. That much I do know, being able to place events in their logical sequence. The problem is I do not understand the depth of her anger or the obvious rage she is fighting to contain.

Honestly what was so wrong or hurtful in the way I treated her? What did I do to make her feel that pissed off about me?

Do you recognize her?

It has been over two months since you first saw her at the Pinewood Derby but she has not changed all that much—certainly not to look at.

Yes of course it is Ellie.

And physically speaking she is just as attractive as she was back then only now I find myself recoiling at the thought of our shared moments of intimacy.

Well perhaps I overstate things. There are some moments I recall that still raise a warmth in certain parts of the body. But those feelings are easily overwhelmed by the fear I feel for this storm-tossed, angry woman who is following me hither and thither across the length of the Plymouth Marriott Ballroom.

See her?

Over there! Pretending not to notice me even as she begins a major move in my direction.

What do I do, keep running? Leave the dance? Maybe I should just wait for her to catch up and let her have her say?

I hate this...this whole confrontational aspect to the mating ritual. It almost makes me want to give up on women and find a hobby where people never yell at each other. I heard enough yelling as a kid. I do not need to find additional sources for that particular brand of pain.

Oh this is ridiculous!

Forty-five years old and I am letting myself be chased across a crowded dance floor like a kid in grade school!

For the last half hour I have been in constant motion trying to avoid Ellie. It would be funny to videotape my unbroken flight then replay it speeded up. I would see myself zig-zagging back and forth across the ballroom looking like a clown from a silent movie, turning sharply this way then that, looking over my shoulder in abrupt furtive gestures only to change my direction time and again.

What a wind-up toy! Erratically crossing the ballroom like a terrified soldier trying to outguess an enemy sniper. But still, you will notice, I manage to search out my reflection whenever I come within visual proximity of one of the ballroom's many mirrored wall panels.

But enough!

I have had my fill of this. No more running. I have made up my mind and will now stand here and wait for her to catch up to me. No longer will I be chased away like a frightened rabbit.

So now we will just wait.

An hour ago I had been waiting for a drink at one end of a small service bar blithely unaware of Ellie's presence at the dance. When I looked up to idly scout the talent, there she was standing on the other side barely four feet away. She smiled at me—broadly I would have to say—and I smiled back in a clipped effort before averting my eyes. Neither of us had anything to say right then; we just ordered our drinks and went our separate ways.

But Ellie's air of disinterest was only a trick, a ruse to lower my guard. About an hour after we separated she began turning up wherever I went, always nearby, always within sight. Sometimes she would pass in front of me, other times hang back a distance and make a show of watching me. And whenever our eyes met she would pull up that big bright, toothful smile of hers as if she were the keeper of some pirate's secret I was about to stumble across.

Look at her now. See how her face is half taken up in a smile? See how cold that smile is?

She is toying with me, leaving me standing here like a fool, waiting—for what I do not know.

Oh the hell with this! I could stand here waiting forever...

Before moving on again I give in to the impulse to look back at her statuesque form once more. After all she is quite attractive, probably the most striking woman in this ballroom tonight. And so I turn, hesitantly, and...hmm?...she is gone!

My lungs release a long-held breath and suddenly I can feel relief flooding through my body.

Ellie is nowhere to be seen.

"Could she really be gone?" I ask myself. I utter the words with measured hope, knowing quite well that life rarely lets you get away with things so easily.

Turning around to check out the crowd, I step back startled, a thin cry caught in my throat. Ellie now stands barely a dragon's breath away.

Where did she come from?

You will notice she is still smiling.

"Hello Paul," she says icily.

"Hi Ellie!" I smile back, experiencing the same kind of

nervous tension in my stomach that generally loosens my bowels.

"I missed your phone call."

Confused, I ask, "What phone call?"

"The one you didn't make."

I see now where this is headed.

"Ellie…!" I whisper plaintively.

"The one you were going to make after you let the fires of passion die down."

"You think that was easy?"

"What?"

"That phone call…?"

"The one you actually made?" she volleys caustically. "The one where you gave me some cock and bull story about things happening too fast? Well, we let things cool down all right, just like you wanted, you bastard. And by the time I figured out what was what, things had gotten so cold I was frozen out."

"Ellie, this is not the place!" I plead softly. "Not here."

"Was that 'cool' enough for you, you son of a bitch?" she pursues. Tall as she is, she has to lean over to push her face close to mine and the whimsical thought flies through my mind that a long-term relationship with me would probably put her excellent posture at risk.

"This is not the place for this," I repeat in all seriousness. I turn to walk away but something, most likely her hand, grabs the sleeve of my blazer, forcing me to swing around and again stand face to face with this soft, sexy woman whose anger could probably heat a small Russian village for most of the winter.

"What the hell is wrong with you?" she snaps angrily. "Are you so high and mighty you can't be polite or friendly?"

"Ellie," I answer back, "I do not wish to argue with you. Not here. Not anywhere."

Again I start to turn away but she will not release her grip.

Raising the volume of my voice I ask angrily, "Are you planning to hold onto me all evening?" Louder still, I insist, "Would you please let go of me!"

"Bastard," she hisses, looking around in embarrassment

and releasing her grip.

It strikes me as an ironic sidebar that Ellie's voice loses none of its gravelly texture or sexy allure even when it falls to its most bitchy register. Have you noticed?

"Good use of language," I say cuttingly. "Classy."

"Well, how classy are you, the way you've been acting?"

"Acting? What have I done?"

"Done? You've done nothing. Not a single thing. You haven't taken my calls or returned them. All in all, you've done exactly what I would expect from a self-centered asshole like you—less than nothing!"

"You know, it is easy to toss blame around."

"Meaning what?"

"That there is a lot more happening here than just my reticence."

"You bet your life there is," she shakes her head adamantly. "Like you getting your rocks off with me before disappearing."

"I would describe things a little differently."

"Well tell me, then. I want to hear."

"Ellie, we do not need to have this conversation." I raise my hands in a calming manner. "Especially not here."

"I don't give a shit where we are," she responds, pushing my hands away. "And keep your fucking hands to yourself!"

Something about her words strikes me as familiar.

Then I remember the sound of my own voice spitting out, "Bill, keep your *fucking* hands to yourself!" I also remember spitting out flecks of fried fish-flavored-doughnut along with my venom, both of which Bill McAndrews heartily deserved.

But I do not deserve this.

"Ellie!" I say, trying to shush her. "Will you please calm down!"

"Calm down? Why should I calm down? Tell me why?" Her voice suddenly drops to a whisper. "And tell me what I should think about a man who comes over to my house half a dozen times, shoots off his load, and then...nothing? It's like I don't exist.

"Tell me what I should think about a *fucking asshole* like that?" she finishes with a look that could nail a frog to a wall.

"Okay," I cut in, "you want to hear my side or are you

planning to spend the evening shouting profanities?"

"Tell me," she prods, "tell me something that will help me understand."

For the last few minutes I have been maneuvering us toward this less crowded section of the ballroom, toward the cheese and cracker table which we are now nearing and which had earlier been ransacked by hungry dancegoers, many of whom view singles dances in terms of their nutritional value as much as anything else.

Notice there are only a few broken crackers left along with some oddly shaped crumbs of cheese, a still life portrait oddly reminiscent of the relationship this woman and I once shared.

"Ellie, I hate to say this..." I begin.

Long pause.

I was going to tell her the truth whatever that was. The truth about my deeply held fears of being mistreated and undervalued by women. More particularly in this situation my fears of being exploited by a money-sucking vacuum machine disguised as an attractive, big-bodied woman.

That is what I would have said if I had the courage to say it. But apparently I do not possess that particular quality on this particular evening. So instead of admitting I dropped her like a hot brick because I was afraid she would financially suck me dry, I decide to once again take the easy way out.

"Ellie, I hate to say this... " I declare with great sincerity, "but you and I...we did not have...we just simply...it was the chemistry! ...we did not have the right chemistry!"

The look of shock on her face mirrors my own, I am sure.

Did you hear what I just said? Was that the most absurd thing you ever heard?

I cannot believe I said that.

We had the wrong *chemistry?*

Even as we stand here ready to gouge out each other's eyes I can feel my sexual sensibilities responding heartily to some inner, illogical trumpet's call.

And can you hear my *PuNDit* thumping away like a primitive tribal war dance? And I am only *talking* to the lady!

Chemistry? We had nothing but chemistry. I loved the way she looked, especially in those fuzzy sweaters she wore. I loved her soft touch and I especially loved listening to her rough kittenish voice as she purred in my ear.

Ever notice the devil never tempts you with ugly women or low paying jobs?

I may have been infatuated with her but I was never unconscious. Almost from the first I saw Ellie for what she was, saw what she wanted from me, and I knew no matter how attractive or sexy she was, she was not right for me.

How could I let myself get trapped in a relationship with a woman who on principal never carried her wallet on a date? A woman who expected a man to pay for everything, even her son's babysitter?

Now that really woke me up. Can you imagine me in my current financial state paying for her babysitter?

It was at the end of our first date.

"Paul," she said softly as we approached the front door to her oversized home—you do remember she lives in a mansion, do you not?

She took hold of my arm and was leaning into it, crushing her breasts against me as she asked, "Could you take the babysitter home? That'll give me time to freshen myself up. Would you mind, honey?"

"Sure. Glad to," I replied, already lost in images of her 'freshening herself up'.

"And do you have fifteen dollars; I'm a little short?"

"Sure," I replied, pulled back sharply from my fantasies.

"Do you want it now?" I asked, uncertain about what was she was really asking. I started to pull out my wallet.

"No, no!" she corrected me with an affectionate slap on the hand. "Just give it to the sitter, honey, when you let her off."

I looked at her. She smiled back at me. And in the warmth of that smile and the heat of my rising ardor any suspicions that were gathering quickly melted.

But only for the moment.

Give it to the sitter when I let her off?

She had a knack of asking for these costly favors as if each one were a key to unlocking her undying affection. So you were not just paying fifteen dollars for a babysitter, you were buying your way into her heart.

It all crystallized for me that night when we came back to her house after our third date. Ellie stopped at the front door and looked at me with an adorable kittenish expression on her lovely face then asked, "Would you be a wonderful guy—again—and take the babysitter home?"

I do not know why it is so difficult for me to say 'no' in such situations, but it is. Very difficult. So, instead of saying 'no' or opening up a discussion about my feelings I merely smiled, nodded my acquiescence, and took the fourteen year old babysitter home.

When I drove up to the sitter's house I reached into my wallet, pulled out three five dollar bills and thanked her. The usual routine, nothing more. Watching her run up the walkway to her door, however, I suddenly realized that this business of taking the sitter home and paying her evening's wages made me feel more like Rickey's father than Ellie's beau.

The most worrisome part was that the next date Ellie did not even have to ask. I paid for the sitter in mute acquiescence to some unstated expectation.

See how easily I can be trained!

Ellie, however, is another story.

Nobody ever told Ellie about Women's Liberation or Feminism, at least not the part about carrying your own share of the load. Six times we went out—six times!—and never once did she bring a wallet or her checkbook along for the ride.

I joke about it now but it mattered to me and bothered me like an infected wound. Ellie's air of entitlement gnawed at me incessantly, would not let me forget my ever-mounting resentment, not for any length of time except when we were making love. Then of course my *PuNDit* would throb so loudly I could not hear myself think about anything.

I tried to convince myself that Ellie would change; that one time, probably when I least expected it, I would hear her utter the magic words "Here, let me pay for it" and something wrong would be made right. That was my hope, at least at the beginning.

And speaking about the beginning—remember that? Now *that* really surprised me, asking me to pay for her coffee and doughnuts at the Pinewood Derby.

And for Ricky's snack, too!

Ever since then I have been watching her with a wary eye, hoping for better things but expecting them less and less.

I have seen this phenomenon before with other women who married rich and came up short when the marriage came apart. There was something about losing in both situations—in the marriage and in the divorce—that made these women feel they were entitled to receive love, protection and financial support from any man with the means to provide it.

It would have been easy to let myself be lulled into submission by Ellie's encircling air of sweetness and sensuality. There have been worse fates known to man. She could make it quite pleasant to be emotionally and financially enslaved, I could see that. More reason then to cut things off before they really got started, while Paul Peterson still had the opportunity and the willpower to run.

And how could I do otherwise? I do not earn enough money, given my child support obligations, to add Ellie and her son to my monthly budget. Not unless I jettison one or two children of my own.

The wrong chemistry!

You do not know how funny that is.

We had the right chemicals; I just did not have enough money to keep the laboratory running.

"Chemistry?" she repeats in an angry sort of laugh that forces her head back. "You're telling me we don't have the right *chemistry?"*

"Well, yes..." I answer tentatively. "Sort of."

It is hard not to laugh listening to myself talking about our lack of chemistry when in my mind I see nothing but images of us enjoying steamy, imaginative and chemically-rich sex.

I am in trouble if I have to blame our chemistry again. I will not be able to keep a straight face.

But how did things get so far off track? And so quickly? What happened?

What always happens?

Reality happened!

Just like reality is happening now with Ellie throwing up her hands in disgust, telling me, "Go fuck yourself!" and storming off in a steaming tempest of mute anger.

Reality is not always neat and very often embarrassing.

But we will talk about it some other time. Ellie has moved on for whatever reason and I prefer to let her totally disappear. Even from my thoughts.

You understand?

"There is much that I understand," a familiar high pitched voice answers, pulling me high above the crowded dance floor, "but not this lack of chemistry you are speaking about. If there was any more chemistry between you and the large lovely lady, you would need to carry around a fire extinguisher in your pants."

Waiting for his bubbly laughter to die down, I finally explain, one disembodied voice to another, "It was just an excuse. I did not want to confront her about being a gold-digging *schnorrer*. Why hurt her feelings now? What good would it accomplish?"

"Oh, yes, so clearly I can see that! So much better to lie and tell her she is no longer attractive to you. To let her believe that the chemical reaction between the two of you has been neutralized by some unexplainable phenomenon. So much better than telling the truth."

Hearing The Bapucharya say, "...the truth" pulls me abruptly from my sense of self-righteous justification, though I still do not see how I might have handled things better.

"What would you have me say?" I ask with honest curiosity.

"I cannot tell you the words, young sir, I can only wish the spirit that gives rise to the words be one of honesty and openness. What flows from that will be what it shall be."

"I am sorry," I tell him. "Maybe next time."

"Well, that is more hopeful!" he responds cheerily. "Let us see what happens," he giggles as if enjoying some big secret joke, "...the next time."

Well what do you know! For once The Bapucharya and I see eye to eye, so to speak. As for what happens with Ellie we will just have to wait and see.

For now, come back down to earth and follow me across the dance floor. It has gotten quite crowded—perhaps if we try to keep close to the stage...

The DJ doing his DJ-thing on stage is a hip black promoter of sorts named Bradley Winsome who once at another dance gave me a personal tour of the music library he keeps in those two large wooden boxes next to the turntable. Brad does dances, Bar Mitzvahs, funerals and kite festivals, among other things.

I wave at Brad and he waves back even though I am certain he does not remember me.

The tempo of the dance has picked up, have you noticed? There are at least a couple of hundred people in the ballroom now, men and women of all shapes and sizes, a good number of them out on the dance floor.

All around the darkened ballroom I see scatterings of men and women, drinks or plates in hand, most of them with friends or in a few cases with partners they just met. A few others are clearly by themselves and will most likely remain that way for the entire evening, maybe even their entire lives. They will not dance or make overt moves towards members of the opposite sex. Not unless pigs start to fly or the Messiah shows up before ten-thirty.

As for me, I am a 'hunter'.

Hunters understandably make up the majority of souls in this darkened ballroom. We are bodies in motion, male and female, moving through crowded ballrooms and bars with one singular object in mind: spotting our quarry and running them down. We are most of us divorced, most of us looking for a second or third chance to make it work, most of us resigned to the conditions in which we hunt.

And they are difficult conditions.

"Care to dance?" I suggest to a nice looking blonde who smiles back.

"Maybe later," she replies, not unfriendly but hardly inviting.

I doubt that she and I will dance together in this lifetime but, like her, I choose to maintain the pretense of possibility, no matter how remote.

And so I reply agreeably, “Maybe later. Let us hope so!” before moving on.

One rejection does not an evening ruin and within moments I am again traversing the dark waters of the ballroom searching for my next quarry.

Out of the corner of my eye I notice Ellie moving across the dance floor like a bowsprit cutting through the waves. I cannot tell if she is moving toward me again but as a cautionary maneuver I turn around and move off quickly toward the shadows that lurk in a distant part of the ballroom.

I have no desire to continue our discussion right now. Better to run than be forced to repeat my silly excuses about inert chemicals.

In the midst of my undignified retreat I am reminded of something similar that happened earlier today after my visit with Mrs. Bakewater, principal of the Myles Standish School.

You will remember that the Myles Standish School in St. Bart’s Bay is where Mickey attends fourth grade.

Yes, yes, I know.

I did not forget my promise to Mickey.

I promised I would not speak with his teacher.

But I never said a thing about speaking to his principal.

Lesson 26

The Proper Care And Feeding Of A 500 Pound Gorilla

"Can you wait a moment before you talk about your conversation with Mrs. Bakewater?" Dr. Rivers gently interrupts. "Would that be all right?"

I have no strong feelings either way.

"Fine," I shrug. "Whatever you want."

Old Man Rivers smiles.

"What I want right now is to check in and see if you still feel that tension—from talking about the dance?"

"Oh, *that* tension!" I reply ironically. Apparently we are calling it *tension* now instead of anger or anxiety.

"Yes, I am feeling tension." I say caustically. "Thanks for pointing it out."

"Pointing things out is my job. That's what you pay me to do."

"Yes, but I am starting to see that a lot of this is merely self-fulfilling prophecy. You tell me I seem tense, I buy into it, and from then on I feel tense."

He brushes my theory aside with a brisk, "No, no, no," then continues, "Remember what you told me the first time we met? When you came to interview me? You said you were looking for a therapist who wouldn't let you get away with things. You told me you'd gone for therapy two or three times in the past and each time the therapist was too easily charmed by your intellectual gifts. Do you remember that?"

"Yes, so...?"

"So when I take you at your word and develop a therapeutic relationship that allows me to challenge or test the things you believe—*resisting* your charms, intellectual or otherwise—you accuse me of being heartless, or biased in favor of your wife, or missing the essence of whatever it is you're telling me. While, in truth, I'm just giving you what you asked for!"

Sitting up he pointedly probes, "Can you hear me? Can you understand? *This* is the therapy *you* asked for. And if it offers any consolation, I think you were smart to ask for it."

"Yes, but what is it getting me?"

"Well, you're not in a position to judge that—I am, but you're not! And what I see makes me very hopeful. There's been tremendous improvement, especially in the last few months. I've seen you taking responsibility for your mistakes and errors of judgment. You no longer deny or defend the less helpful aspects of your personality, so there's a real possibility for change in those areas.

"And most meaningful of all," he says, pausing for emphasis, "is your growing impatience with therapy itself. That's a good sign. Very good. It usually means you've progressed enough to get a taste of being in a better state and you're hungry for more. That's excellent, really!"

With that the good doctor slides into his favorite at-rest position in the soft black leather embrace of his chair. Mission accomplished. The troops are all back safely.

"Speaking about survival," he suddenly adds without explaining about *who* was speaking about survival, "do you remember our session last week...what you said about Marilyn?"

"No," I answer.

"Really?" he exclaims, surprised.

"No," I repeat firmly, "I do not remember what I said."

"You mentioned that she had gotten engaged?"

"Are you kidding me? I did not say that!" I exclaim. "To whom, Lawrence Grafton? I would remember if she got engaged to that stuffed shirt. Trust me, it is not something I would easily forget."

"This is quite amazing," Dr. Rivers comments. "But you do remember her going out with Mr. Grafton...?"

"Well, of course I do. She has been going out with him for months, maybe longer, but they have not gotten engaged. At least not yet, as far as I know. Though I would not put it past Marilyn to eventually hook up with him. Grafton may be incredibly stiff but he is also financially secure. His family owned Grafton Mills in Lawrence, you may recall?"

"Yes, I remember. But to go back to last week, you also voiced some concerns—fears really—concerning Grafton's relationship with your children once he moved into the house."

"I said *that?"* I respond, startled.

"Yes, you were worried he might replace you in their lives; might become the father you can never be, living far away in Cambridge as you do."

"I *did?"* I ask, more shocked than surprised.

This is absolutely crazy. Not only did I never say any of these things, I would never think to say them!

"No, no," I tell him, laughing and shaking myself free from my doubts. "I did not say that last week or any week. I cannot see Lawrence Grafton replacing me with my kids. He is too quiet and stiff; my kids would hate living with him, that much I know. Where do you get this stuff?"

"From you," he responds, "sitting on that very same couch last week. Now, obviously you've changed your thinking since then, and that is fine. But I know what you said."

"And I know what I did *not* say!" I counter.

"You also told me you wanted to find some way to balance his influence in their lives. To remind them or reassure them, perhaps, of your own worthiness."

"Wait," I cry. "Stop! I do not remember any of this," I protest, my disbelief echoing in the air. "Honestly."

He reaches for his notepad which is wedged half down behind his seat cushion.

Flipping through the top few pages he stops at a page filled with a squiggly childish scrawl then looks up to ask, "You remember talking about a dream in which you cut off the legs of a tall stranger?"

"Well, sure...but that was months ago, not last week! And what does that have to do with Marilyn's boyfriend taking my place with the kids?"

"Yes, that was months ago, Paul, but last week we reexamined that dream together—given Marilyn and Lawrence's changing situation—and we agreed Marilyn's future husband was the man in the dream, the stranger whose legs you cut off."

I shake my head in disbelief.

"You may have analyzed it that way, but I certainly did not."

"It was your way of *cutting him down to size*, we figured, or..."

He pauses to refer to his pad.

"...*making the playing field even*. Your words, not mine."

I sit up in protest.

"I said no such thing!" I blurt out, shaking my head in disbelief. This conversation has grown so bizarre I do not know what to make of it. Is Dr. Rivers intentionally lying or is he actually imagining that we had this discussion?

"Sometimes I wonder if you get me mixed up with another patient. Have you ever checked to see if there was some screw-up like that? The way you keep bringing up stuff I never said, it makes me wonder...?"

I stop talking to search out his eyes.

"But in any case," I continue, "to play your game for a moment, did you ever think that maybe I was the stranger in that dream?" I ask pointedly. "The fellow who got his legs cut off?"

With the little I know about dreams that would be my interpretation; cutting off my legs being an obvious admission of my failure as a parent—of my falling *short* as a father.

Or so it seems.

"Agreed! Certainly!" he calls out, nodding his assent. "Of course *you* could have been the victim, that goes without saying. But before we go into that, let me draw a parallel between this 'victim' dream of yours and the experience you had with the Pinewood Derby. Is that okay?"

"Fine," I sigh. "Sure. Why not?"

"You're sure?"

"Yes."

"Okay. I wanted to ask if you still thought the Pinewood Derby fiasco was your ex-wife's fault?"

Do not blame me if you get whiplash following Dr. Rivers through a therapy session. He apparently suffers from Attention Deficit Disorder or some similar syndrome.

"What do you think?" he pursues. "Was it or was it not

Marilyn's fault?"

Something in me does not want to answer the question. But if I make a big deal and refuse to talk, he will fasten on my resistance as if it were buried treasure and I will then have to deal with it as a bigger thing.

This therapy game is wearying to say the least.

"I do not think it was *all* her fault," I answer, conceding half the distance to the goal. "But she was a key factor in my decision not to use my tools—do we really need to go into this again?" I ask testily.

"It would help me if we did," he answers, half-apologetically. "Now, which tools are we talking about?"

"*My* tools!" I repeat meaningfully. "Marilyn may have legal possession of them but they are still *my* tools, nevertheless."

"We're splitting hairs," he says lightly. "Tell me again why it was her fault you used your daughter's set of carpenter tools? You knew they were practically toys, right? No 'practically' about it— they *were* toys...!"

"Do you really not understand what I am saying?" I protest.

"I understand what you're saying, I just don't see the logic in what you're saying. Show me again the size of the blade on your daughter's toy saw. Was it this small?"

He holds up both index fingers and indicates a space that spans eight inches at the most.

He prods, "Is that accurate?"

I choose not to answer the question.

"A little smaller, perhaps?"

I watch him reducing the space between his fingers by a couple of inches and I get the weird sensation he is subtly indicating the size of my penis as well as Suzie's toy saw blade.

"Too small!" I say quickly. "You were closer the first time. But you still do not understand how I felt and why I acted the way I did."

"No less than I understand how it feels for someone to stub their toe or not be chosen in a pick-up basketball game. These are situations that have logical emotional reactions attached to them. They don't need to happen to me for me to understand how they make others feel."

"It is not that simple," I protest quietly.

"Of course it isn't," he agrees, trying to appear sympathetic. "And that's why I don't see Marilyn as responsible for the chain of events that led to your embarrassment at the Pinewood Derby. It's just not that simple."

"Well, then what *is* she responsible for?"

"In which case?"

"The one we are talking about? Do you give her responsibility for any of that mess? The crappy look of the model racecar? The anguish Mickey and I suffered? Any of it?"

"I'd rather ask why you prefer to give her *so much* responsibility?"

"Would you please stop playing with words!"

"Okay—if you wish to engage me—why do you choose to make Marilyn responsible for your procrastination? You had four weeks to work on the Pinewood racer, isn't that right?"

"That is what she would say."

"And what would you say?"

"That I had two weekends, given our alternating weekend schedule, and that I had three young children whose needs I had to take care of during those two short weekends."

"Okay, but why is she responsible for the fact that you only began working on the racer when there was no time left?"

"She is not responsible for that," I concede.

"But she is responsible for what…?"

"For being such a difficult bitch!" I conclude snappishly. "So bitchy that I would have to swallow my pride to use the goddamn tools. *My* goddamn tools!"

"Okay, I can understand that," he says reasonably. "She did make it difficult for you to use your tools. Given who you are and who she is, a delicate balance had to be achieved and she clearly wasn't going to help achieve that balance."

"Thank you."

"But why was it her fault you chose to use Suzie's toy tools and did such a hack job on the model racer?"

"I did not think it was such a hack job," I protest.

"Not until you saw all the other racecars," he reminds me.

"Well, how was I to know?"

"So, when does Marilyn become responsible, according to you? Before or after you realized what a mess you had created?"

"Boy," I say, shaking my head in disbelief, "you are being very disagreeable this morning. Was there something I said to annoy you?"

"I'm not annoyed. Are you?"

"Very."

"Why?"

"Because you seem to be taking Marilyn's side in everything I say."

"I'm not taking sides. I'm giving you my honest response and, hopefully, an objective interpretation, which apparently doesn't coincide with your view of things. There's nothing wrong with two people seeing things differently. It's healthy, actually.

His forehead furrows as he abruptly asks with a questioning smile, "But what makes you think I'm taking Marilyn's side?"

"You always do."

"Do I?"

"Sure you do," I insist, feeling the energy starting to build. "You can relate better to her than you can to me. You both work as counselors, even if she is only a high school guidance counselor and you a psychologist with a PhD. You have a lot in common and therefore a lot to protect. So she screwed up by letting her work spill over into her private life—by getting involved with one of her co-workers? Big deal, right? It happens all the time, right?

"And you, as a therapist who identifies with her, would prefer to see me act the way any therapist's spouse should act. With patience and understanding. Instead of which, I went ape shit, felt violated and would not tolerate Marilyn developing an intense emotional attachment to anyone other than me, even if there was no sex involved. In your eyes, I am the one who acted poorly, who was not understanding, the one who fell short of the mark. How many times have you pointed out I did not have to view Marilyn's relationship with that woman as a threat to our marriage? And how many times have I explained I could only judge things by what I saw or how they felt?"

Slowing down I continue, "You sometimes act as if I should have known better just because I was married to a guidance counselor. Well, the only thing I knew was that Marilyn seemed to have fallen in love with a female math teacher ten years her elder who collected pottery and vacationed on the Cape.

"It looked like love on the one side and felt like abandonment on the other. How the hell should I have known it was only a temporary outbreak of sisterhood or unrealized lesbian impulses or some such female-bonding syndrome?"

I pause a moment, giving him a chance to respond, but he continues to watch me, waiting for more I guess.

"This did not all happen at once," I continue, "I lived with it for two fucking years! And you sit here giving me a clinical analysis of mid-life crises and explain why the counselors who experience these disruptions need supportive and understanding spouses. Well, where the hell were you when I was going through all the torture and bullshit? It would have been helpful if you could have told me about platonic female relationships *then*...

I pause, waiting.

"Oh, the hell with it...!" I mutter to no one in particular.

For a long moment he sits there in silence, stroking his beard and staring off into space. When he speaks his voice is even softer than usual.

He shifts his large frame in the tall black chair. The squeaky protests of his thick leather cushions fill the room.

"Maybe we should talk about something else," he suggests softly.

My body does not shift.

"You are doing it again, you know...?" I lift my hand in the air grasping for words. "I...I cannot tell you the number of times you have stepped in to defend Marilyn or protect her honor. Hey, even if I am wrong, let me vent a little anger at the woman who rightly or wrongly I view as having ruined my life, broken up my family and taken away everything I ever wanted for myself."

"Yes, yes!" he interrupts, "but look how much power you

give her," clearly trying to explain and not provoke. "You have made her responsible for just about everything except the chaos in the Middle East."

I have nothing to say to that.

"You do give her a lot of power," he repeats.

"Whether I give it to her or she takes it, the fact remains she has it. A lot of power! And I need to attack that power any way I can."

"But why allow her to have so much?" he pursues.

"It is not something I choose," I explain coolly. "Sometimes things happen. Marilyn is a powerful woman. *You* try controlling her! She was the one who selected our home, decided how many children she wanted and, most definitely, she was the one who decided on the divorce. It was *her* divorce, not mine. I was a hapless observer reacting to things instead of making decisions. She had the questionable relationship with a colleague, she took offence at my disapproval and she was the one who sought out a divorce lawyer who did her legal best to reduce me to poverty. That was all Marilyn's doing. I never chose any of that."

"Yes, but you chose to hire me—to come for therapy; in a sense to strike back at your anger and confusion. Isn't that a step towards regaining power for yourself? And doesn't that start to take away some of Marilyn's power?"

At last, we are giving something back *to me!*

"Now, you are starting to make sense," I nod. "Right now, I cannot prevent Marilyn from having power in my life, I can only work to take some of it back."

"And you have," he insists. "Don't you see that?"

"The truth?" I ask.

"Yes, please."

"She is still the 500 pound gorilla in my life. I cannot stop her from doing anything she wants to do."

Old Man rivers smiles.

"What?" I ask.

"I like the image," he answers. "Reminds me of *my* exwife."

Just listen to that...

The sound of laughter.

The sound of *two* men laughing!

It is not often I hear myself laughing in this renovated den the good doctor calls his office.

Our eyes briefly meet as we exchange expressions that might someday grow up to become smiles. This is a rare moment indeed.

"That's one thing about life..." Old Man Rivers says softly.

"What?"

"There's never a shortage of 500 pound gorillas."

"Not in my neighborhood." I softly agree.

"Well, we'll keep working on it..." he mutters, adding, "next week!" when he notices the time on the clock on the floor.

Lesson 27

How A Janitor Describes Elephants To A Blind Man

As my eyes turn to look at the clock I hear a voice protest, "No, no, no! I am sorry, but never have I seen a room where so many blind elephants are walking around in circles on the carpet!"

You will recall that a *Blind Elephant* is a Seeker term for an opinion expressed by someone with a limited perspective. It relates to the Indian parable of five blind men who touch different parts of an elephant and come up with five different descriptions of what an elephant looks like.

I am now looking down at Dr. Rivers and myself, our bodies frozen in that moment when my session ends. He is poised in the instant before speaking, I am caught in the moment before I rise up from the couch.

It feels like I am hovering above wax figures rather than warm living bodies.

This is something new, is it not, The Bapucharya freezing time so we can speak?

Never a dull moment!

"Blind elephants, Holiness?" I ask, amused.

"Yes, so many blind elephants there is a distinct danger of someone getting buried in elephant shit!"

"Elephant shit?" I repeat, even more amused to hear such earthy terminology coming from someone who is supposed to be a fully realized soul.

"Yes, elephant shit!" he exclaims again, chuckling. "Are you having difficulty with your hearing, Mr. Peterson, or is your head already filled-to-bursting with elephant shit? In any case, whatever we are calling it, I cannot listen anymore to this foolish man's well-intentioned prattle."

Suddenly I find myself in the rare position of defending

Old Man Rivers.

"But I thought he was finally making sense," I argue, "even with all his biases."

"Yes, yes, but you are also a blind man and it is not so helpful to have one blind man agreeing with the observations of another. We do not get closer to the truth of the situation," he says pausing to release a few, high-pitched giggles, "we only end up with too many blind elephants in a one-elephant room!"

"But what do you mean, Holiness? What exactly are you calling prattle? Dr. Rivers is saying almost the same things you were saying about Marilyn and me; about my perceiving everything from a victim's point of view…is he not?"

"Yes, in that way he is speaking very wisely."

"So…?"

"So big deal, give the doctor a new car and a trip to Bermuda! His wisdom, I am thinking, is merely a low-level analysis of a high-level phenomenon. It is like noticing the sky is blue on a sunny day. Even an idiot can see the sky looks blue on a sunny day. But why does it look blue? That is where wisdom most often ends and a blind elephant begins!"

"I do not understand, Holiness?"

"Why am I not surprised?" he chuckles to himself, continuing with obvious patience, "Your upside-down-therapist does not see the dance, young sir! It is as simple as that. Any opinion he offers does not reflect the music of the dance or an understanding of its order and progression. Yes, yes—no doubt he is wise in saying you are not a victim. But everything after that sounds very much like homogenized prattle to my tired and ancient ears."

"What do you mean, Holiness, when you say he 'does not see the dance?' What dance are you talking about?"

"What dance, you are asking? And you a fifteen year student with The Seekers For Truth! Ohmigoodness! We are speaking about the Dance Of The Universe, Mr. Peterson! If one does not see the dance, one cannot hope to explain why the dancers go round the floor with such purpose and rhythm. To your gray bearded doctor it is all seeming like the haphazard movement of bodies and that is what I choose to call prattle. Though *piffle*," he snorts with a giggle, "would be a good word, too, I must say.

"I do not mind that he sees things wrongly, but I am greatly displeased that he offers his opinions about elephants with such conviction. He is sounding too much like a dishonest judge!"

"A dishonest judge?" I ask.

"An honest judge is never completely confident in his opinion, but a dishonest judge—ahh, that is another story. He must sound convinced even if he is certifying that elephants fly in broom closets."

"And what if he could see the Dance Of The Universe?" I pursue. "Would he still blame me for not seeing beyond my own wounds, or for giving in to the insecurities caused by Marilyn's relationship with that boy?"

"He would not be so focused on what you did or felt or said, but only on where The Dance Of The Universe is taking you."

This is all too much! There is too much information swirling around for me to get a firm grasp on any one thing. My mind is swimming in strange ideas and I feel an overriding need to reach out for something familiar.

"Wait a minute, please," I plead. "Could we slow down while I catch my breath?"

"You are surprised by what you are hearing?" he asks, clearly amused by my disorientation.

"More than surprised," I reply. "*Confused* would be more accurate. I understand that Dr. Rivers has a limited view of the universe—as would anyone not familiar with The Seekers' view of the cosmos—but what vital fact or set of facts do you think he is missing, exactly? What would he understand that was any different were he able to see The Dance Of The Universe?"

"The movement of Karma," he answers simply, then adds, "*...boom-chicka-boom!*" dissolving into a spate of childlike giggling. "Have you not noticed," he continues as the laughter falls away, "that *Karma* and *Conga* are very similar in the way they are sounding...*boom-chicka-boom*?"

"Are they?" I respond, hardly amused. "I guess they are. But still I do not understand. What would he see if he understood the movement of Karma?"

"He would see the dance between you and Marilyn...*boom-chicka-boom*. The dance between two *Karmic Companions*—two souls whose destinies are intertwined through many lifetimes—who are here on this planet to play out their destinies on separate-but-connected *ILEs."*

Now this is something new…!

"Are you saying that Marilyn and I are *Karmic Twins?"* I ask with rising interest, referring to the Seeker concept of one soul split into two during a lifetime.

"Not *Karmic Twins,"* he answers with didactic precision, *"Karmic Companions!* If you or your gray-bearded doctor could see The Dance Of The Universe you would see that the two of you—you and your oh-so-lovely ex-wife—had no choice but to break apart your marriage and travel your separate ways. Otherwise the journey on both your individual Paths Of Seeking Truth would have ended much sooner than later I am guessing."

"Why?"

"Because I say so, that is why! And because you had both reached a point on your Paths Of Seeking Truth where you had learned all you could learn traveling together like chummy yoked oxen.

"I am sorry, but neither of you would have continued to move up your Paths Of Seeking Truth. Your journeys would have been over, done, bye-bye! That is what your prattling-minded therapist cannot understand when he looks up to see—*oh dear!*—that the sky is blue!

"Instead, he sees Marilyn losing touch with her boundaries in a counseling relationship and you losing your sense of perspective in a two-year fit of jealousy. Here is yet another blind man reaching out for the tail of yet another elephant!

"Could you fit more blind elephants into this room? I do not think so!" he concludes in a burst of merriment.

"Hmm!" I mutter thoughtfully. "I will have to think about that."

"Yes, it is something you should think about—*for all of, perhaps, five seconds*—before continuing on your Path Of Seeking Truth. It is far better to gather knowledge than to brood over what you have learned, young sir; and much better to keep moving up your Path Of Seeking Truth than to stop to measure your progress!"

A thought suddenly strikes me.

"And my father...?" I ask eagerly, "Is he also a *Karmic Companion?* Another soul whose destiny is intertwined with my own? Could you tell me that, Holiness...is he?"

"My, my, look how well we are doing! Clearing up the mysteries of our lives in leaps and bounds! And this when we have already used up our 50 minutes of therapy!"

I ignore his witticisms and press for an answer.

"Please tell me, is my father one of my *Karmic Companions?"*

"Yes, yes, please to calm down. If you are so eager to know, I will tell you. Yes, I am thinking that your father is one of your *Karmic Companions* on your *ILE,* and you have come together in this lifetime—he and you—to do truckloads of work. And the work is not yet done, so please, no punching-out of timecards just yet."

"And who else is there? Or is that the lot?"

"Oh, do not worry; you have not yet run out of *Karmic Companions.* But I have pointed out enough of them for one sitting. It is time now for closing up the store..."

"No, wait! If you will not tell me who they are, then at least tell me how many? One, six, a dozen?"

"I do not think this is such a good thing for a Bapucharya to do; to be giving you the list of characters starring in your movie."

"Not the names, just the number! What difference could that make? I will still need to do whatever work is involved. Just tell me how many other *Karmic Companions* there are—not counting my father or Marilyn...?"

"One and a half."

"One and a half?"

"One and a half!"

"What kind of number is that? One and a half?"

"The best I can do at such short notice. I do not know how else to count them. Did they not teach you fractions in school?" he laughs.

"Yes, they taught me fractions, but they never taught me how to turn an individual into a half measure."

"We are not turning an individual into a half measure,

only a Karmic Companion..."

"You have to tell me more than that," I insist.

"Well, let us not argue," he replies lightly. "Instead, let us agree to continue to work on it," he pauses for a few giggles, then adds softly, *"next week!"*

Something strange happens as The Bapucharya releases the words "next week" into Dr. Rivers' office. Can you see it? The words resonate in the room and seem to hang in the air. At this same moment I can still hear the reverberation of Dr. Rivers telling me, "Well, we'll work on it...*next week!"* as he concludes our therapy session.

In that same instant, as the two *"next weeks"* echo and overlap almost surreally in the small confines of this den-made-into-an-office, consciousness and movement return to my frozen body which now activates and continues its rise from the couch.

Feeling like I have just been kicked in the head by the *TOE of God*, and that two moments in time seem to have overlapped or shared the same substance, an incredible idea flits through my mind. Rather than shake it off, I look at the clock that sits on the floor between myself and Old Man Rivers.

"My goodness," I realize with breathless wonderment, "it is true!"

The Bapucharya's visit did not take place in time!

Not a single second passed the entire time we were speaking. I know because I specifically noticed the time on the clock when Dr. Rivers said "next week!" And the second hand was in the same place, pointing exactly at the nine.

You realize what that means?

His visit never happened! Not in this world.

So in what world did his visit take place?

Good question. I must remember to ask him sometime.

For now, I am more eager to be on my way, and anxious to begin investigating the identities of those one and a half *Karmic Companions* of mine.

Getting up from the couch and straightening my pants I casually offer "Goodbye, doctor!" without any visible emotion or thought.

"Goodbye?" Dr. Rivers repeats, looking up from his note

pad, seemingly surprised to find me still in his office. “Oh, yes, goodbye!” he says, in that slightly awkward way he has of limping through the social amenities.

“See you next week,” I add.

“Yes, yes, next week!” he replies.

“Goodbye already!” The Bapucharya says with much amusement and very little patience. “And, please, remember to *drink your RC Cola!*”

Lesson 28

Where, Oh Where, Can My *Karmic Companions* Be...?

I am sitting in my car outside Dr. Rivers' office on a small residential street in Newton, Massachusetts that is mostly lined with large Victorian residences. A few mock Tudor homes probably built thirty or forty years later are also tucked into the street here and there on smaller lots.

Looking out my dirty windshield at the sky above the street's irregular skyline it is not easy to remain poised on top of my inner mountain at the *Center Point of the Universe.* Not long enough anyway to regain the consciousness I need to fuel my return to the singles dance only three short weeks ago, which I believe is the next lesson awaiting us in my Do-It-Yourself Workshop.

I look at the sun lying low in the sky, a bright disc shrouded in a sky that is surprisingly gray for this late in May. All the while I am struggling to return to a place of inner light and undisturbed calm.

As always, uncontrolled thoughts are mortal enemies to any attempts to *drink my RC Cola.*

In this case uncontrolled thoughts about this strange concept of 'one and a half *Karmic Companions*' the Bapucharya has inflicted upon me. Not to mention thoughts about my father and Marilyn, two companions who have been less than best friends to me on my *ILE* but probably more helpful on my journey than I would care to admit.

More often than not it is the challenges you face, the enemies you encounter, the Milestones you surmount and the defeats you suffer that take you farthest up your Path Of Seeking Truth.

Or so it seems.

But there I go again getting lost in the movements of the

mind rather than allowing myself to come to rest.

A little *HW-40* is sorely needed. Can you tell?

Just relax, Peterson, I tell myself. Forget about everything except living in the moment—the Sacred Present Moment. There is no place I have to go, nothing I have to do, no one I have to be with other than myself. All I am required to do right now is rest comfortably inside consciousness, so close to the *CPU* I should almost feel the living, breathing presence of The One Who Always Watches.

Drawing on the full power of Higher Will in the form of *HW-40* I invite consciousness to rest "where the work is taking place" in my soon-to-be-still conscious mind. Tightly closing and clenching my Root Chakra I allow my breathing to fall into a rhythmic pattern of short shallow breaths while mentally intoning "Higher" on the in-breath and "Will" on the out-breath. Simultaneously I envision the force of consciousness being drawn into my body through my Crown Chakra and imagine it traveling down to my tightly sealed Root Chakra then back up to eventually escape through my nose. While all this is happening I allow consciousness to pull back from a mind crowded with wildly scattered thoughts and uncontrolled movements, back to that observer's post high atop a mountain just a hairbreadth away from the *Center Point of the Universe.*

There!

That is better.

All sounds have fallen away. Now in the quietude of my almost silent mind the question arises, "Who could they be?"

Perhaps *you* know...?

Who do you think they are, these one and a half *Karmic Companions* of mine? And what do you think it means to have a *half Karmic Companion* somewhere out in the universe, either already on my *ILE* or sailing my way?

Do you have any idea?

Could it be Mom? I do not think so. Remember, I have not been particularly close to my mother these last few years, not since her remarriage. The truth is I do not get along so well with Roman, her new husband and my official stepfather. Also—and this is probably more relevant—under the harsh glare of therapy I have started to blame my mother for things I never before saw as her responsibility.

Mostly for not defending me better against Dad, for not standing up for me with greater force or urgency.

Up until last year I always thought of her as an ally, someone who fair weather or foul would be on my side. But now I also see that she rarely put herself in a position of risk. She might have made a few angry comments after my father struck or punished one of us but we could never count on her to ward off the blows.

I am working these days in therapy to view this whole 'mother' thing in a more balanced way. Not to make her the lone champion of her young children nor the disappointing failed rescuer, but just a real life human being who happens to be my mother. A complex person with a complicated set of conflicting allegiances.

Think about it! She had her own set of difficulties with my father. He was an inveterate gambler and womanizer and yet she loved him, really loved him. How much pain he must have caused her and how hard she must have worked to conceal that pain from us everyday of our young lives! Certainly I cannot forget it was she who nurtured and comforted us. Only now I see that her nurturance was generally available when it posed little risk to the awkwardly poised relationship she maintained with my temperamental and often volatile father.

I remember one time during a summer vacation in the Catskill Mountains. I was a teenager, maybe fourteen, and along with others my age I was calling out wisecracks during the hotel's Tuesday Night Talent Show. Back then I had a loud, facile wit that I liked to show off for the benefit of the world. But in doing so that night I apparently said something that offended my father.

I was not the only one calling out jokes and comments, others did it too; that was part of the show's fun and charm. Apparently my father did not regard whatever I said as either funny or charming because all of a sudden I felt a sharp blow on the side of my head, saw stars light up my jumbled sense of sight and found myself suddenly leaning stunned against a nearby pinball machine.

When I looked around, there was my father.

"Just watch your language," he said.

"What did I say?" I shrilly protested, tears flowing more from the pain of being humiliated in front of my friends than from any physical distress.

"Just watch what you say," my father repeated, his face bright red, his right eyebrow characteristically arched, his finger pointed threateningly into my face.

Looking beyond my father's rage I saw my mother standing in the background watching. She stepped forward and grabbed Dad's arm, dryly telling him "That's enough!" and pulling him away.

That was the kind of protection I could count on from my mother.

Thanks Mom. Thanks a lot!

Whatever she was and however I ultimately came to feel about her, I do not think my mother will prove to be a *Karmic Companion.*

Mom and Roman live in Florida these days and she is more concerned with peacefully living out her final days on the planet than concluding any leftover Karmic business with any of her children. I talk to her every week or so and do my best not to express my newly discovered feelings of anger or to allow that incessant nagging of hers to get under my skin, which it invariably does.

Some things never change.

But if not my mother…then who?

Henry? Gail?

Neither of my siblings seem to qualify, though I am not as distant from them as I am from Mom.

But still it would be laughable to think of myself inextricably intertwined with either of their destinies. There is no sense of the dance with them, not in the way there is with both Marilyn and my father. Henry is too consumed with amassing his retirement savings while Gail and I have barely spoken to each other for a year since she and her family moved to Cincinnati.

So who?

Illyanna comes to mind…

Now *that* is a possibility! There has always been something special between Illyana and myself though it seems to come and go in waves. Right now in fact it is on the wane, but still there is a connection so strong that neither of us through a long history of romantic flareups, stormy interludes and the ever-present and always precocious Hava, has been able to break it off.

Illyana?

A smile breaks across my face as I recall that famous first time we made love. That was over four years ago but the images arise as if it were yesterday. The two of us in Illyana's bedroom pursuing our mutual pleasures in her cramped double bed. Hava asleep in the bedroom next door which meant we had to make a real effort to keep things quiet and which somehow made us feel giddy and a little childish, like kids sneaking behind their parents' backs.

It was funny the way we kept breaking out in fits of giggling; much of it I am sure a natural byproduct from the tension of the situation.

Remember, this was a big thing for both of us, bringing sex into our previously platonic relationship. Up until that night we had kept everything distant and safe. As members of the same single parents group at the Jewish Community Center there was always a strong possibility that any involvement between us, especially if it was sexual, could end up very messy.

We hooked up at the JCC's Spring Fling Dance; the Spring Fling Dance being the annual JCC monthly dance in April with a seasonal theme tagged on for marketing appeal. Both of us having spent most of the evening failing to find someone suitable or interesting we shocked the hell out of each other by deciding to go back to Illyana's modest Brookline apartment for coffee—a euphemism, in the circles we traveled, for going back and having sex.

It was a great surprise to end my evening in Illyana's bedroom stoically enduring my *PuNDit's* rhythmic pounding as I enjoyed a social activity I had never before pursued with a fellow member of the single parents group.

Up until that evening I had successfully resisted any of many urges, impulses and thoughts about getting involved with Illyana, as attractive as she was. Her strange accent helped me in that regard since it not only sounded foreign and unattractive to my prejudiced American ear but it also vaguely reminded me of my mother's Eastern European accent. Which automatically put a damper on any sexual imaginings she might have otherwise triggered.

But then all of a sudden there I am in her bedroom watching it all happen and revealing itself like a movie; watching our relationship...evolve, I guess, from polite interactions into very steamy sex. When Illyana and I had slow-danced together just a few hours earlier we kept our bodies so far apart they were probably in separate voting districts. But later under different influences and more primal dance music those bodies were entirely unclothed and sweating against each other.

The other reason for all the nervous giggling of course was her daughter Hava. I think we both had images in our minds of that precocious four-year-old walking in on us while we were in the middle of some exotic gymnastic pose. I could even picture Hava's exasperation as she informed us "You're doing it all wrong; that is not the right way for adults to fuck."

But Hava aside, the ferocity of the energy that night was...thrilling. I had not expected eroticism or passion from this somewhat intellectual Russian but erotic passion was exactly what I discovered and enjoyed throughout the experience.

Her ability to take care of my needs while hers seemed so insatiable was quite surprising. As was the almost collegial and sporting manner in which she engaged in foreplay; not at all serious or brooding as one might expect from a Russian. The first time she was about to take me in her mouth she jokingly asked, in her thick Russian accent, "Do you mind if I smoke?"

Her willingness to explore and be explored, to take control and be controlled, was especially exciting. I held onto my passion that night longer than I had ever held onto it before. And when I felt like I could no longer contain it without exploding, at that very peak moment when I was on top of her, riding like the devil being chased from Paradise...something quite extraordinary happened.

Suddenly I heard a mix of sounds I had never heard before, at least not in that particular situation—a gasping release of air accompanied by a low-pitched moan. At the same moment Illyana went completely limp beneath me.

"What the hell...!" I cried looking down in shock.

What I saw was so terrifying it transformed me—for a moment at least—from a poised adult into a frightened little boy.

She was dead!

Naked, inert, totally silent—as dead as the proverbial doornail. Her body still soft and warm beneath me, my penis still warm and wet inside her!

I am embarrassed to admit this but the thought immediately rose up in my mind in giant letters across a Cinemascope screen: "OH MY GOD, I FUCKED HER TO DEATH!"

It may sound funny now but it was not funny then.

Lying there on top of her, my mind raced in a dozen different directions. Maybe her heart had given out, I thought madly; perhaps she had had a massive stroke. Then again I once read there was a spot on a cat's body where if you touched it with any force the cat would immediately die and go into rigor mortis. Maybe Illyana had such a spot and maybe I was the first person to accidentally touch it...?

What else could it be? Sure as hell I did not know.

Anyway there had to be some explanation why this dark, curly-headed, somewhat voluptuous, naked Russian would die so easily in the throes of normal—albeit *better* than normal—adult sexual activity.

For a moment I went through this involved fantasy that had her being poisoned by something she ate at the dance.

Then the whole ridiculous idea went over the edge as I began to wonder how, if she had been poisoned, I had managed to escape? I had eaten the same boring party snacks: the pretzels, the dips, the strudel. Well I did not eat much strudel, but neither did Illyana.

Then I was suddenly struck by the unavoidable notion that perhaps I had not escaped. That perhaps my fate would be the same as Illyana's only it was taking longer to work itself out. Maybe for some obscure biological reason the poison was working slower inside me than it had with Illyana...?

You can see how my head was swimming in circles. I was scared silly and in a panic to get some grasp on what was happening. All of this—all the panicked questions, all the rampant thoughts—ran through my mind like film through a projector, the images hurtling by so fast they seemed free of any storyline or purpose.

And all the while of course, right beneath me like a sub-plot in a Fellini movie, Illyana was lying in repose, still holding me in a moist languid grasp sleeping the perfect sleep of death.

Well maybe it was not so perfect. I mean she was not really dead, you know. It was just that I thought so at the time.

Then I noticed that she was in fact still alive; that her breath was still flowing—just barely so, it was true, but still detectable nevertheless! I watched each breath with incredible intensity and noticed there were moments when Ilyana would suddenly seem to catch something in her nose or throat and abruptly stop breathing—in mid-breath! Not knowing what else to do I started giving her mouth-to-mouth resuscitation.

Not continuously of course, only when I thought she had stopped breathing—and then just to jump-start things.

Why would I treat her like a drowning woman, you wonder? What else could I do? She was just lying there breathing so shallowly with such a weak rhythm it seemed that she could easily lose the beat, slow to a stop and end the process altogether.

You know, like a pendulum that does not possess enough momentum to tick off that next critical second...?

Giving it a push seemed like the natural thing to do.

So when her breathing appeared to suddenly stop, shutting the factory down, I would lean over, pry open her lips and help her finish the last part of the breath she had been working on. Or help launch the next one. Each time that would jump-start her lungs and she would be breathing again though very weakly.

I must have given her four or five jump-starts before she finally came out of what I later learned was one of the most dramatic seizures she had ever had.

For myself I cannot imagine one *more* dramatic.

When Illyana came back to herself and realized what had happened she seemed highly embarrassed and very grateful. I thought she overdid the appreciation bit, was way off base actually, but she insisted on being effusive in her praise and her thanks, and what could I do but blush anyway?

"Oh, but it is very special, and I am very grateful," she said, repeatedly touching me and smiling at me in a goofy sort of way.

"Really, it was not much," I protested, feeling embarrassed that most of my feelings during the emergency had been centered around *my* dilemma rather than hers.

"Certainly it was nothing," I professed without a hint of false modesty. "Anyone else would have done the same."

I may have said and believed that but I got the distinct impression that other men in similar situations had not been so helpful or concerned; at least not enough to stick around.

I tried to tell her it was nothing special, just a normal human response, but she would not listen.

The truth was she was crazy with gratitude.

She was also nuts!

Am I nuts too? I wonder as I come back to the present moment and realize that instead of going off to the peak of my inner mountain I have drifted off again into idle thoughts, memories and reveries. Though this time they concerned one of the more remarkable moments from my pedestrian history of sexual encounters. A moment so disconnected from all other moments in my life it seems more like a *Glimmer*—a glimpse of something that might have happened but didn't—rather than an actual memory.

Speaking of disconnection—Illyana and I do seem connected, do we not? She is certainly a good candidate for one of my *Karmic Companions;* as good as anyone else I can think of.

But who else...?

"Stop this already," I shout out loud in the interior of my car, "and come to rest!"

Highly irritated, I remind myself that I will discover

whatever I am supposed to discover whenever I am supposed to discover it and not a moment before! Everything else is mere mind game, mere movement of the mind.

So come to rest, I instruct myself. Move inside yourself to the peak of the mountain and let everything else just fall away.

But what about Jackie, my best friend since I was four? Or Juan, one of my closest friends in the JCC's Single Parents Group? Or...?

Enough with this search for unknowable information! Spray a little more *HW-40;* release all thoughts back to the universe from whence they came. And relax. Just relax.

No more thoughts, I tell myself. Just give your attention to the moment; to everything around you and to nothing but being here now.

But Illyana looked so beautiful in my mind, all naked and vulnerable...

Just let her go.

And I adore those dark elongated nipples of hers...

Easy does it. Do not push her out of the mind so forcefully that your resistance creates counter resistance. We do not need Mr. Ping or Mr. Pong here. Just let her go...

Now look into the light. Into that big bright ball in the cloud-filled gray sky. Watch it silently and ever so closely as it begins to swirl around in its heavenly suspension, sending off a thousand myriad flashes of sparkling light that spin in time to some distant music. No thoughts, no questions, just watchfulness and waiting.

And the light.

And the music.

And suddenly a space inside myself where there is nothing but space itself.

Feel that space fill with awareness and calm.

Spray a little *HW-40.* Clench the Root Shakra a little tighter. Slow the breath. Let it flow in then flow out. And hear the words that ride the breath: *Higher... Will... Higher... Will...*

Now allow the space to fill to the brim with consciousness.

Do not try to force anything; just let it happen.

And suddenly we are here again. Surprisingly the lights still spin and flash in time to some vaguely familiar piece of music.

You recognize where we are, do you not?

Yes we are back at the dance.

Lesson 29

Things Your Mother Would Never Let You Do At A Singles Dance

The flashes of sparkling light are still orbiting in circles but now they are sharp, spiky reflections thrown off by dozens of tiny mirrors on a spinning globe suspended from the ceiling of the Mayflower Ballroom.

Enough with all these questions about *Karmic Companions* and disappointing parents. Enough already! I have come here tonight in search of a woman. A woman who I am certain is not a *Karmic Companion,* at least not one of mine. If she neglects to show up tonight—though in my heart I believe she will—I will gladly accept some attractive and warm-hearted woman as a substitute.

Assuming I can find one.

It is practically an impossible task to find an attractive, like-minded, companionable woman and breach her defenses in the brief span of a few chaotic minutes. Even more impossible when you realize how finicky I have become in my pursuit of women.

But take a look at what has happened to these once-fair maidens during the years I have been away from the chase. See how they have been modified by the forces of time, gravity and neglect? What was once taut is now soft or limp, what was once young is now mature. Too mature in many cases. And almost everyone seems to be carrying more ballast in their hold than they could possibly need for the rest of their voyage.

These changes and losses of beauty strike me as harsh. But the ultimate cruelty when you become suddenly single in your forties is the dramatic shift of your place in the universe. Almost overnight I found myself transformed from a young father and husband to a middle-aged single male.

When you are 41, married with three young children, you are young to everyone including yourself. When you are 41 and single, however, your youth suddenly vanishes as you struggle to compete in a world filled with unmarried youngsters in their twenties and thirties. Suddenly for the first time you come face to face with the natural aging process and you quickly discover that you do not like what it does to many of the single men and women of your generation. And you know of course it will never overtake you in the same way it has overtaken them. Never make you as grumpy or demanding or unattractive, and certainly not even half as self-absorbed.

Of course you never consider the possibility that it may have already happened! And that in your sublime ignorance you could have already become the person you fear becoming, could already be attending singles dances like the ones who wear the pretense of youth like a favorite sweater. Never realizing how shabby and worn it has grown.

Yes someone else witnessing this melancholy tableau might actually regard you as one of its shabbier older participants!

I assume that is what has happened to many of those who are here tonight. They did not start out in the single world as wrinkled, worn-out and disgruntled as they now appear. They probably came into it like me, younger than most and cocky in their youthful advantage.

But I do not intend to stay around long enough for that advantage to erode into mere memory. And so when I come to a dance like this I leave all the scruples my mother taught me outside the ballroom doors. I will not concentrate on being kind or helpful or even considerate to those whose place in life is not as fortunate as my own. I will not ask unattractive women to dance, I will not spend one moment more than I'm required to in conversation with anyone who seems angry (as many are in the singles world), or depressed (as most are), or even temporarily lost (as I have been for the last five years). Nor will I take responsibility for the fragile feelings of even one unfortunate woman who asks me to dance.

I do not have time for any of that false chivalry or kindness.

And so I pass over this lady (too heavy) and that lady (too old) and that one too (too unattractive) in the hopes of finding the one woman who best matches or improves upon the prototype I was forced to leave behind in St. Bart's Bay.

I have become what my mother calls "too picky for my own good." Ever the Jewish mother she tells me, "A man could starve waiting for the right chicken to come along."

To which I reply, "A man could also select the wrong chicken if he is too hasty, Ma. And which do you think would do the greater harm?"

"Harm?" my mother replies questioningly. "What's harm got to do with finding a nice companion? Harm you want? Step into traffic without looking! But don't kid yourself, darling; a woman doesn't have to look like Cleopatra to keep your tootsies warm at night."

My mother is prone to offering tiny gems of wisdom imbedded in irony and delivered with a Hungarian-Jewish accent.

"Paulie, darling, a man could starve!" she warned me during a recent phone call. "And what's so wrong with nibbling on a drumstick even if you don't buy the whole chicken?"

"Ma would you stop with this chicken thing already!" I pleaded, noticing how quickly my speech patterns fell back into familiar phrasings from my years growing up in Brooklyn.

"Gladly, just give some nice woman a fair chance. That's all I ask. Be fair, like a *mensch.*"

Someday I may explain to my mother that in this second journey through bachelorhood we are none of us exactly *menschen,* or entirely fair, or always act in ways that would make a mother proud.

There are no surprises, no mysteries to unravel about any of this. Truth is there are only a limited number of women who appeal to me, most of whom seem to find me highly resistible. While the lesser beauties among the ladies, those I would rather wave to as I pass by...well they of course find me overwhelmingly attractive. How else would the gods arrange such a comedy if not with a twist of malicious irony?

And so tonight, like many nights, I find myself sifting through a multitude of women to find the few who hold some genuine appeal for me—one of whom is approaching quickly on my left. Watch this!

"Excuse me," I say trying to catch the fleeting attention of this seemingly unattached dancegoer in her mid-thirties who, you have to agree, has more than enough basic ingredients to bake a cake. Just my luck, however, she turns away at the precise moment I reach out in her direction, leaving me in temporary awkward possession of her left arm.

"What?" she questions, startled as she finds herself held back.

"Oh, geez!" I say grimacing in embarrassment.

It takes me a moment to realize what is happening before I drop her arm. She turns around with a look of deep surprise as if she had been traveling 20 miles per hours and was pulled over for speeding.

"Sorry, I did not mean to grab you," I hastily apologize.

My apology apparently connects because the look of confusion is quickly replaced by one of amusement.

"I understand," she says, smiling. "You just meant to abruptly reach out, grab hold of my arm and swing me around."

"Something like that," I respond, also smiling.

"Well, what can I do for you, now that you have my attention?"

"What about giving me a dance?"

"What about it?"

"Would you like to?"

"I think I would," she says teasingly with a half-smile in place, "all things being equal..."

"Well, then...?" I say starting to reach again for her arm.

She pushes back my hand, reacting, "You're pretty quick with that thing."

"But you said...?"

"...all things being equal; but they're not equal, Chico. You do like this arm though, don't you?"

"But I thought...?"

"I said I might like to dance with you, all things being

equal. But they're not equal tonight since I happen to be here with an escort, who I think..." She lifts herself up on the balls of her feet to look over the crowd. "Well, he's around here somewhere, getting a drink for us or something...but it doesn't really matter. Take my word for it, the position is filled."

"Is that true?" I ask with a rising air of confidence. "Are you really here with someone or just resisting a sudden interest in me?"

She thinks about this.

Finally she decides, "A little of both maybe, but I still have an escort."

"So you are not taking applications for his replacement?"

"Not tonight anyway."

"Well, maybe we will meet again," I suggest, letting go of her arm which I have somehow taken hold of again.

"Perhaps."

"Maybe even when all things are equal."

"Who knows," she responds, the half-smile back in place, "I might even enjoy it then."

Interesting.

I file away her 'cat ate the canary' smile and other plentiful attractions for future reference. Moving on with my batteries recharged by her playful encouragement I resume my passage through the crowded waters of the dance.

The chemistry was right, I know that instinctively. But the timing was wrong.

I can almost hear my mother's voice, almost gloating, telling me, "See what you get, being so picky?"

Ma, leave me alone already!

“Leave you alone,” my mother would mockingly repeat were she here. “Accountants and tailors and maybe even rabbis would leave you alone if you asked them, but not mothers. Don’t tell a mother to leave you alone, darling. It’s not what we do best.”

Rather than let her distract me, I turn for another look at my reflection in the mirror. As you can see, I am wearing my usual uniform: a dark blazer over a dark shirt. No tie of course. Depending on the dance venue I usually round out my wardrobe with jeans or chinos. And since tonight’s dance was being held at a Marriott, which is on the higher end of the scale for singles dance venues, I decided khaki chinos would be a better choice than jeans.

I had that one right!

Just look at the women who are here tonight—and it is always the women who set the tone at a dance or a party—look at them in their colorful dresses and outfits. They had clearly decided, as if they had discussed it earlier in the day, that tonight was going to be something special; not just another evening where you dragged your casual clothes up from the bottom of the closet.

So the chinos were a good choice.

But let us move on.

As you can see, the dance is in full swing.

The previously-open dance floor has become a sea of twisting, writhing bodies, each moving to the beat of the music but confined to the smallest possible unit of usable space.

The tightly-packed crowd looks strange, am I right? Jammed together like that they appear unnaturally restrained and awkwardly assembled. Like a crowd of oversized infants who have minimal control over their body movements.

It is no longer possible for me to cut across the parquet dance floor except between songs when enough of the bodies move off in various states of exhaustion. Once the music starts up again their replacements will quickly fill the space, joining those who had hung on for one more dance or one last effort to convince their partners they were still young enough to dance the night away.

See their smiling faces? Those smiles will be frozen in place when the emergency medical technicians come to carry them away.

Having this many people at the dance makes it difficult to anticipate the moves of Ellie, my once-favorite cub scout mother who, for the last hour or so, seems to have stopped shadowing me. Still I would feel better if I had more open space in which to watch the surrounding waters for signs of her approaching form.

But perhaps Ellie has removed my name from tonight's mission statement. I am starting to allow myself the hope that she has. But who can be sure about anything when it comes to a furious woman?

A good question.

What I know about women you could fit on the head of a pin and still have room for a convention of angels.

What I know about *women versus men* is another story! These two planetary species might be different in a thousand ways but for me the two differences worth discussing are *emotions* and *sex*.

When it comes to emotions women have more than they can handle while men have so few they never get the opportunity to learn how they work. Except of course for hunger which is not only an emotion in a man but a higher order emotion if you ask me.

That is the one exception to the rule: we men maintain close contact at all times with our hunger.

No this is not a Seeker doctrine, just a Paul Peterson observation.

If you had seen the commotion earlier tonight when the buffet was brought out you would have thought you were observing some famine relief organization at work. Admittedly, members of both sexes were fighting for a place in line but the men greatly outnumbered the women, men generally proving hungrier for free food than they are for feminine companionship.

Another Paul Peterson observation.

I remember one dance where a man walked up to the buffet and literally put half the strawberries from the serving dish onto his plate. Most times I give these self-absorbed singles very little of my attention but I spent the entire evening stewing in my outrage over that fellow's ardor for strawberries.

What a waste of my emotion and time.

(What a waste of strawberries!)

With the act of making love—with sex itself—the gender differences are drawn even further apart. Women approach sex like something kept in a drawer to be periodically taken out and fussed over. For men sex is like a machine left on constantly, so noisy you can barely hear what anyone else in a conversation is saying, so quick to notch up to faster and louder speeds you could climax before you realized you were even aroused.

This evening in the Mayflower Ballroom facing a roomful of unknown women, even with a known malcontent prowling amongst them, I feel pulled along by a heady mixture of good old sexual fever and habitual hunger.

Sex and emotion all the way!

How many evenings have I spent like this in the four years I have been back on the street? How many evenings in anonymous ballrooms, function halls and singles bars affecting stoic postures designed to disguise what can only be described as poignant loneliness? Mine no worse than anyone else's, you understand, because everyone's loneliness has a certain poignancy attached, like a label from the manufacturer.

But how many evenings? Fifty? A hundred? Too many to recall. One searcher amidst hundreds of searchers, all of us trying to be oh-so-subtle as we glance back and forth at each other, our intersecting gazes traveling out across the room like hundreds of lighthouse beacons searching for a solitary lifeboat on a wide dark sea.

And if there is one underlying constant besides the merciless insecurity we suffer over the state of our appearance it is the universally shared impulse to keep our eye on the front door.

Yes the front door! Because that is where hope's flickering flame keeps its silent vigil.

No matter how poorly you feel about the field of women inside the ballroom there is always a chance that the perfect woman will walk through the front door the very next time you turn your head. Yes right through that door: the one person who could automatically make this night and *all* these nights of dust hole dances and poorly lit ballrooms worth every dollar and minute you have spent on them.

Think about that! Who wants to focus attention on a broccoli dip if it means missing the entrance of the woman of your dreams? If you are slow off the mark she will be quickly surrounded and captured by overweight salesmen and doubt-crippled males of all descriptions.

So naturally we are each of us ready to jump like firemen into the heat of action at a moment's notice. Poised to put down our drinks, cast aside our broccoli and make for the front of the ballroom in a movement strongly resembling a slow run or a fast trot.

I have often thought how self-actuating this impulse is, as if it were a coiled spring compressed under the weight of my anticipation, easily activated by the slightest suggestion of an attractive female specimen entering the room.

How many times have I rushed to the front entrance of a dance careful to maintain my composure and nonchalance only to discover the object of my attention already under the care and influence of someone who proved to be hungrier and faster than me? Or else, and this is more usually the case, she would turn out to be someone whose attractions were not worth the headlong rush of adrenaline it took to reach her.

One evening at a dance the crowd surged so dramatically towards the front door you would have thought a busload of single millionaires had driven up. As it turned out it was merely a team of waiters carrying in platters of hors d'oeuvres.

Still the operating principal is undeniably *speed matters.* If you wish to make contact with an attractive, desirable woman you have to move quickly. Otherwise someone will spirit her away and most likely cling like a leech for the next two or three hours. That is the law of survival at a singles dance.

In Darwinian jargon it is called 'survival of the fleetest'.

The first time I saw Sheila Weston whom I dated for almost half a year was at a JCC dance. I saw her come into the dance but someone scooped her up before I could get halfway to the front.

The second time I saw her I did not wait for inspiration to move me. I immediately launched myself from across the room, unfortunately to no avail once again. Eric Weisberg, an arrogant trust lawyer with an obsessively groomed beard and a small managed fortune, proved to have been similarly motivated but with a shorter distance to travel. Eventually I did meet up with Sheila and hit on her, as the saying goes, at a singles potluck dinner.

In some ways I would have been better off had I never

connected with Sheila but being a slow learner it took me more than four months to figure that out for myself.

And tonight...?

I have been at the dance now for almost two hours. I have danced with a few women, talked with one lady over a drink in the hotel bar for fifteen minutes, but have seen nothing yet of two special women I am seeking at tonight's dance.

Neither the woman of my dreams nor the lady of my agenda.

All in all nothing has happened that I would care to note down in a diary. If I kept a diary.

But wait, I believe this is someone familiar...she looks like... she *is*—heading my way. And would you believe—*it is her!* Well how about that! I was right, she actually showed up at the dance tonight!

See? What did I tell you! Take your eyes off the door for even ten seconds and guaranteed the object of your interest will choose that moment to enter the room. It is pure luck that the heat-seeking males at the dance have not yet taken notice of her arrival. Though I would not be surprised to learn they actually had noticed and decided to take a pass on the opportunity. The object of my attention is far from being a magnetic attraction, would you not agree?

Does she look familiar?

I recognized her right away. The moment I saw her.

But then she certainly stands out in a crowd with her scrawny figure, her flyaway mop of bottled blonde hair and those two incredibly round and firm breasts. You of course might not recognize her, having never before seen her in a sober state or outside the confines of her Plymouth apartment.

I suck in my breath, fight back a rising instinct to run away and advance with heroic acceptance to meet my fate.

"Hi!" I say casually. "What is a nice girl like you doing at a dance like this?"

Miss Ping, please be so kind as to meet Mr. Pong!

Lesson 30

A Tale Of Two Teachers And A Principal

It is three days earlier and you will notice I am at Mickey's school speaking with his principal Mrs. Bakewater.

Why am I speaking with Mrs. Bakewater?

Let us pretend I am Dr. Rivers, so instead of answering your question I will ask another.

What else am I supposed to do?

For weeks, ever since my little boy spoke to me in my Cambridge kitchen, my mind has been going round and round in circles about Mrs. Pratt. Over and over I have asked myself "What do I do about Mrs. Pratt?" struggling to find some idea or strategy, almost without relief.

What do I do indeed!

I kept my promise of course and have not spoken a single word to Mrs. Pratt. But I made no promise about speaking with Mrs. Bakewater, longstanding and ever vigilant principal at the Myles Standish School who is also Mrs. Pratt's boss. I have no specific plan coming here to see Mickey's principal but I see no other options.

Mrs. Bakewater and I have been having a pleasant enough chat for fifteen minutes and have managed to agree on many things including our mutual appreciation of Monet (hence the London Bridge print on the wall behind me), our shared hopes for next year's high school football team (this year's team missed winning the divisional championship by a single game) and our best wishes for the well-being of all the students at the Myles Standish School which obviously includes my son Mickey and daughter Cathy.

We have agreed on all this but we have not yet reached agreement about Mrs. Pratt—actually it is 'Ms' Pratt, Mrs.

Bakewater informed me. There had once been a Mr. Pratt but he apparently graduated from fourth grade teachers.

As you can see, Mrs. Bakewater is a woman of considerable size and stature not unlike Mrs. Costadazzi in both girth and disposition. In her early fifties at least, she exhibits a surprising amount of feminine grace and charm considering she occupies a body of such immense, almost frightening proportions. At first glance she reminds me more of a female longshoreman than an elementary school principal.

Watching her now, you will notice a genuine expression of surprise as I relate what Mickey said to me about his fourth grade teacher.

See?

Confusion and shock register across her broad face like an egg splattering on a kitchen floor.

“I don’t know what to say,” she utters almost in shock. Then she searches around the scattered debris of her desk as if the answer could be hidden there.

“He’s a good boy, Mickey,” she says in a low questioning voice as if speaking more to herself than to me. “Quiet. Very polite. A good student, as far as I know.”

She looks up for a moment then turns to me, still serious, and remarks, "I like him" nodding her head for emphasis. "Very much! We sometimes chat in the lunchroom."

“He is a nice boy,” I agree, "even-tempered, too. But that is just what you see on the surface. There is more there, much more. Talk to him about poverty some time; about young children going hungry. He cares about things like that. He cares deeply. That is why I am here because he also cares about how his classmates are treated. That is just how he is—extremely concerned about others.”

“Perhaps overly so...?” she suggests.

“Perhaps, but that would not lessen my concern. How well do you know Ms. Pratt?”

“Very well,” she answers, giving careful thought to her words. "She’s been with me for...” She stops to mentally count up Ms. Pratt’s years of service. “...this is her ninth year at The Myles Standish! A good teacher. Perhaps too soft spoken and shy...and definitely lacks fire...but good nevertheless."

Surprised by what I am hearing I search for some clue that might help reconcile two sharply conflicting descriptions of Ms. Pratt.

"Soft spoken and shy?" I exclaim, making no attempt to conceal my disbelief. "Mickey says that Ms. Pratt *yells* at the kids in her class—well, some of the kids."

"I know, that's what you said before, but I don't believe it. In fact, I'm certain it's not true!"

"I cannot force you to believe it, but can you at least try to keep an open mind? Ms. Pratt has those kids frightened..."

"Ha!" Mrs. Bakewater cries out loudly, which abruptly becomes prelude to a stream of laughter so spontaneous and fluid it startles me.

"Mrs. Bakewater?" I probe nervously as laughter takes over her body which is now shaking like a firm pudding.

"Are you all right...?" I start to ask then stop, deciding instead to just wait for her to calm down. She is beyond answering questions at the moment.

So I sit here staring at her, my mouth open in amazement, watching her laugh. Watching her head bob gently back and forth as if bouncing on a spring, and the wide grin on her face pushing up her chunky cheeks so they turn her eye cavities into tiny slits giving her a Buddha-like appearance of calm and wisdom even in the midst of her full-bodied laughter.

A few times she tries to stop laughing, tries to articulate something that sounds like "I'm sorry," only to give it up after a few false starts. Moments later she begins interrupting the stream of laughter with brief exclamations, periodically barking out "Ms. Pratt!" or "Hah!" with tremendous force and lift.

Soon the laughs begin to actually decline in frequency and force. Remaining patient I sit with an expression of good humor, waiting and watching while the laughter winds down with a bumpy sort of deceleration as if the fuel supply might be running short.

"I am so sorry, Mr. Peterson," she says out of breath and wiping her eyes, "you just don't realize what you are saying. Ms. Pratt, frightening the young children..." She starts to laugh again but quickly quells the impulse. "Oh, boy!" she exclaims pulling a tissue from a box on the desk and wiping her eyes.

"I honestly don't know what came over me. But you have to understand...Ms. Pratt could no sooner yell at her children than sink a three point basketball shot. It just doesn't compute."

"But...?"

Still wiping moisture from the corner of her eye she asks, "Do you know why I gave your son's class to Ms. Pratt?"

"No. Not really."

"They were the only group of fourth graders who would not eat her up alive."

"What...? What are you saying?" I ask, cocking my head.

"That Ms. Pratt is psychologically and emotionally incapable of yelling at her students. That I have personally been working with her—for years!—to get her to the point where she *could* yell at her students. Frankly, I don't think she'll ever make it. She's not capable of it."

"And you don't think she is capable of yelling at Kimberly Hyde or John Tilden?"

"Not even if they were in the next room and there was no other means of communicating. I'm telling you the woman can't function as a teacher unless I give her the best behaved classes."

Her face clouds over as she leans forward to explain, "This year it's worse because...I probably shouldn't be saying this, but Ms. Pratt is going through a difficult breakup with a boyfriend; a somewhat abusive personality with whom she never should have gotten involved. But these things happen—it's an imperfect universe at best—and at least she is finally making a change."

"Could that explain her yelling?"

"It could, but it doesn't. She's been depressed, I know that; but if anything, that's made her even less forceful in dealing with the children in our school."

"Should you let her teach in that condition?"

"As I said, we live in an imperfect universe. Haven't you noticed?"

"What does that have to do with anything?"

"What would you have me do? Put her on suspension? For having problems in her personal life? What would that accomplish except to make her problems seem that much more insurmountable?

"I wouldn't suspend her and take away her salary unless I knew for certain it was necessary to help her or to protect the children. And I don't think that's the case in either regard. Right now the best thing I can do for everyone concerned—and that includes you and your son—is to do nothing. To let things be—*Let it be,* as the song suggests."

"So she yells at the kids and nothing gets done about it?"

"One thing I can guarantee you, Mr. Peterson, is that Ms. Pratt does not and never will—*ever!* —yell at her children. You have my word on that."

"But what about Mickey? He tells me Ms. Pratt yells at certain kids all the time. He is visibly upset by it. You should see him."

"Well I don't pretend to understand what that's all about," she responds. A look of mild incomprehension passes briefly across her features. "But I will promise you to watch things more closely and see what happens. I usually find with life that there's always some halfway point between opposing viewpoints."

Between Mr. Ping and Mr. Pong, I comment in the silence of my thoughts, half wondering if Mrs. Bakewater has ever heard of The Seekers or their school.

We both sit quietly for a moment.

Finally I make one concluding point.

"This would all be easier to understand, except for one thing..."

"Which is?"

"Mickey never lies."

Mrs. Bakewater shrugs.

"I believe you," she says with a serious expression. "I really do. But there are two things we need to be aware of, not just one."

"The other being...?"

"That Ms. Pratt never yells."

Clearly she and I are not going to reach an understanding this morning but I nevertheless leave Mrs. Bakewater's office feeling somewhat satisfied. Even though I cannot understand her point of view about Ms. Pratt after what Mickey told me, I do know she has been open and frank with me. Mrs. Bakewater is not the kind of principal that would ever cover up for a teacher.

On the other hand I am clearly the kind of father who would risk ignominy and shame for the chance to catch an unexpected peek at my son.

So before leaving Myles Standish and knowing full well I should never give in to such foolish temptations I nevertheless stroll noiselessly down the corridor's yellow tiled walls doing my best not to attract attention as I head toward Mickey's classroom.

If I am lucky I might catch a glimpse of my son hard at his studies without getting caught in the act.

As the corridor turns and Room 109 appears in view I slow down so that I am literally advancing by inches. There is no place for mistakes here, I grimly realize. This must remain a secret mission no matter what happens.

Should Mickey see me, he is sharp enough and knows me well enough to quickly assess why I am here and it would not please him. I know that.

I also know what you are thinking.

Recognizing how Mickey would react, you are asking why I would take even the slightest risk of getting caught? A question I cannot answer except to say Dr. Rivers would suggest that at some deeper level I desire to be caught and clearly it is too strong a desire to resist.

As you can see, after two years of therapy I no longer need a therapist to point out when I am acting under the influence of entirely stupid impulses.

Inching my way down this yellow tiled corridor with its taped-up crayon drawings and illegible grade school essays I feel like a kid again, caught up in some silly spy game. My intention is to steal a quick look then make a hasty exit. I give no thought to what I might actually see in Room 109 other than hopefully a glimpse of my son studiously at work. So naturally I am quite startled by the familiar figure that first appears in my line of sight through the glass-paneled door at the rear of Room 109.

It is Ms. Pratt standing at the head of her class!

Without thinking I utter a garbled expression of surprise and step back gingerly as though I have accidentally stepped on burning hot coals. Simultaneously I am overcome by unreasoned fear that in my confusion I might accidentally give away my presence.

I curse silently under my breath, frustrated that I will not get a chance to see my little boy this morning but resolved to move immediately and briskly away from here. Having seen Ms. Pratt I no longer wish to take the risk of being seen.

By her or my son.

And that is it; the visit is concluded.

As brief as it has been, however, it has given me more information about Ms. Pratt than I had bargained for. I now begin to understand Mrs. Bakewater's point of view. And I would have to agree with her—the woman I saw standing in front of Mickey's class is probably incapable of yelling at anyone on this planet.

Strangely enough I do not feel much surprise at my discovery.

What is surprising is how quickly I recognized her and the curious way I reacted when I did.

Yes I know her.

And you know her too!

Up till now I have mostly seen her at singles dances but elsewhere as well. Perhaps at school functions or around St. Bart's Bay. As thin and ethereal as she appears, I have always found her looks to be of great interest. There is an aura of unrealized beauty about her—or faded beauty as I now realize after seeing those photographs in her apartment—as if she could have been something special had God only taken a little extra time to adjust her coloring and add a few additional pounds.

Did you see her? Or did I step back too quickly?

Her bleached blonde hair had errant dry strands reaching out like drunken tendrils teased up by circulating air or static electricity. Her skin had a ghostly pallor about it, looking almost powdery white from my vantage outside the room. She was somewhere in her early to mid forties though she could have been older, and was certainly no slave to fashion as you could see from her plaid skirt and patterned blouse, both faded from too many spins in the washer.

And then there were those seemingly perfect and round—and very firm—breasts. Two of them, to be exact. As attractive to me in this moment as they will later prove to be in Allison Pratt's upstairs apartment in Plymouth, Massachusetts. And yes there is still something incongruous and surprising about those wondrous body parts, given Ms. Pratt's overwhelming air of withered promise and reduced circumstances.

I cannot recall the last time I last saw Ms. Pratt at a singles dance on the South Shore but I remember vividly how this pallid creature was a recognizable fixture in that provincial singles scene. If you went to enough dances you quickly came to recognize the whole cast of characters. All those times I saw Ms. Pratt at singles dances I never once realized she was a teacher or, more importantly, my son's teacher!

Funny how you can see a stranger a thousand times and never notice them while others like Allison Pratt imprint themselves on your memory in an instant.

She is the type most single men would quickly pass over since most of her beauty is hinted at, never truly revealed. But to me she was always of interest because she was so startlingly different and, because of that difference, strangely exotic.

There was something about her I found compelling; some aura of wispy, surreal attractiveness all the more striking for the sense of perplexed vulnerability she seemed to radiate. This particular morning, however, she is not in some strange dark ballroom where I can examine the merchandise from a safe distance but rather standing in front of my son's fourth grade class.

For a moment I consider going back for another look but quickly decide not to take the risk. For some reason it unnerves me to learn that Ms. Pratt and the fragile, ethereal blonde I remember from those earlier singles dances are one in the same woman.

Making a conscious effort not to run I hurriedly soft-step away from Room 109. An image of myself rises up in mind;

an image that will ironically return later this week—Friday night to be exact— when I find myself fleeing from Ellie's shadow in the dark realms of the Mayflower Ballroom.

Yes that is me running slowly—like a sluggish thief—from my son's elementary classroom. As I escape down the yellow tiled hallway, a familiar question goes round in my mind.

"What to do about Ms. Pratt?"

It is not until later in the day that another question appears and starts repeating in my mind.

"I wonder if she still goes to singles dances?"

Lesson 31

A Ten Minute Discussion On Why Time Does Not Exist

Though I never fully understood what they meant, The Seekers For Truth often told us that time as we know it does not exist.

If there is such a thing as time, according to The Seekers, it does not occur in linear progression as we think it does but rather all at once, like an explosion caught in a video freeze frame. And if we are unable to experience it that way it is because of the deficiencies of our sensing mechanisms rather than the essential nature of time itself. It all goes back, they tell us, to *AUM,* to Automatic Universal Misunderstanding.

Think about that.

Time does not exist.

Everything in your life, every memory, every relationship, every assumption you make, every day you spend on this planet says just the opposite. That time not only exists but is a cruel and relentless taskmaster. That time not only serves as the backdrop and common medium for all our experiences but is the only way we can order our lives to make any sense of them.

If time does not exist could I really be 45 years old? Could I have been assaulted by moody teenagers on the streets of Brooklyn when I was eight years old, kissed by my first girlfriend when I was 10, had my first and most confusing sexual experience when I was 19, been married at 29 and divorced at 41?

I mean how can all of that be occurring at the same time? In the same moment?

How it happens I do not know.

That it does happen—is happening now!—of that I am certain.

How else to explain our flashforwarding and flashbacking in time while remaining fixed in the present moment? How else to explain The Bapucharya and his persistent presence as a tour guide on my *ILE*?

I have resisted mentioning this till now for fear of raising questions about my sanity but the fact is His Holiness can no longer be counted among the living. To be more explicit, in reality—in normal time—he has been *dead* for a number of years.

Yes I know it sounds strange but it is true nevertheless. The Bapucharya is dead; has been so for a long time. I remember his death being commemorated with a week-long celebration that ended in a traditional Hindu funeral pyre—the fire, the corpse, the whole weird thing. It was just about the time I was leaving The Seekers—before Marilyn and I split up—about eight, eight-and-a-half years ago if you believe a concept such as "years" still has any meaning.

But take my word for it, The Bapucharya is gone, passed away—deceased!—having left this physical realm for other planes in far distant worlds.

Though obviously he has decided to keep in touch.

What does *that* say about the reality of this world? Or about time itself?

More to the point, what does that say about *me?*

To be of such particular interest to the spirit of a Hindu holy man is no small matter. There must be something special about me I am not aware of. Something more than my being a former Seeker For Truth or a renegade soul waiting to be reclaimed. But what? And why?

Yes, *'why?'* as I am sure Mickey would want to know.

Why has The Bapucharya chosen to open up contact with me? Why has he lately become such a constant visitor on my *ILE?* And why has everything assumed such intensity of purpose and texture in my Do-It-Yourself Workshop? Is it because of The Bapucharya, his presence? Or is that just the nature of these Do-It-Yourself Workshops? Especially one that begins with me being dragged pathetically with premeditated lust toward a brown velveteen couch?

That last question assumes there can be a real beginning to anything; a beginning tied to a single place or point in time?

If nothing else, my Do-It-Yourself Workshop reveals how elusive beginnings can be and how interconnected are the events and Milestones on our individual Paths Of Seeking Truth. Nothing really happens or gets decided that is not influenced or shadowed by events that came before.

Or perhaps later...?

Would I have taken Mickey to the Pinewood Derby had Marilyn not come into the kitchen that morning and shamed me into doing so? And could she have shamed me so quickly had I not already felt shamed by our divorce and her rejection of me? And would I have recognized that we were dead center on a Karmic Gravitational Slide at the Pinewood Derby had I not already seen the random cruelty of life in the guise of a magician?

Then ask yourself, would I have put as much misguided effort into the question of Ms. Pratt and her yelling—or whatever it is she does—had I not felt so guilt-ridden about our father-son fiasco at the Pinewood Derby?

And the last big question: had The Seekers not harped so often and so loudly on their Noble Fourfold Legacy, would I have still made the same effort to rebalance my Legacy to Mickey, trying to eliminate obstacles on his Path Of Seeking Truth in the hopes of offsetting the giant Milestones I had already placed there?

Of course knowing as little about the mechanics of Legacies as I do, I was merely swatting at flies in the dark.

With all the best intentions, you understand.

But still you must be starting to comprehend that it is all interconnected. One domino leading to another that leads to a thousand more. Some of those dominoes you will never see and whose impact you can never predict.

But what about The Bapucharya?

What does he want from me?

For all his apparent and ceaseless merriment he is quite serious about this business of self-development that The Seekers extol and pursue with such focused devotion. He of course has always served as a contrast and relief to The

Seekers' overdone formalities and especially to the distant Victorian niceties of their personal interactions.

Well seen, Mr. Peterson; thank you.

You are quite welcome, Miss Longworth.

But to continue as my personal guru long after I have left The Seekers For Truth…? And to continue with my education long after he has left this physical plane…? To remain a voice floating near ceilings in rooms—disembodied perhaps but still the class clown—adding insight and chaos to my fragilely constructed view of things; what is that all about?

And now he has aroused my curiosity by talking about *Karmic Companions.* In fractions no less!

Am I capable of understanding any of this?

Are these answers waiting to be uncovered on my *ILE?* Or will I have to wait until my next embodiment or a dozen future embodiments to pull all the pieces of the puzzle together?

Perhaps just like time, these questions can only be understood and answered when viewed from deep within my being. From the CPU, the *Center Point of the Universe.*

Or within close proximity thereof.

Ironically it is only by moving far into that deep inner space that one can find release from the full scale Broadway production of "Life As We Know It" produced by the Automatic Universal Misunderstanding. A show that you will no doubt recall runs 24 hours a day and is enjoyed by the entire universe of God's sentient creatures who believe it to be real.

And since *AUM* is wholly responsible for creating the illusion of time as part of that show, the only way to make some sense of the *non-existence of time*—to really experience it in the moment—is to step free from the powerful grip of Automatic Universal Misunderstanding.

But remember also that *AUM* creates more than time; it creates an entire universe of illusions. So when you step free from the power of *AUM,* you step free from a lot more than time.

And that is where things can get a little tricky if not dangerous.

Not *physically* dangerous, you understand, but dangerous nevertheless.

You probably do not realize it, but I have only recently been gifted with this ability to move deep within myself, to sit extremely close to the *CPU* where time moves so slowly it does not appear to be moving at all. Remember, this is my first-ever Do-It-Yourself Workshop, as sudden and new to me as it probably is to you.

Because of this newly acquired inward mobility I can also move backwards and forwards in time with apparent ease, free to explore the landscape of my *ILE*. Something else that is entirely new in my altered range of experiences.

Though in truth, as I have already stated, I have not moved anywhere except inside myself. All my connections with time have occurred in just one place—in the present moment.

The Sacred Present Moment!

The same present moment that runs through all moments in time like an old-fashioned record spindle runs through all the 45's stacked upon it—do you remember vinyl 45's? Anyway, for some reason I now seem able to move freely across that freeze frame image where time explodes all at once; not to some earlier or later moment in time but to a different place in an overall frozen tableau. Like an ant who can crawl across the surface of a photograph and into the depth of the image as well.

Which is why, as we flashback and flashforward, all these moments in my life appear not as memories but as experiences. Still freshly happening. Still causing pain or ecstasy, still generating confusion or insight. And still waiting for me to take a good look around my *ILE* and figure out the right answers to life's deepest questions like some contestant on a TV game show.

That is why the mountaintop analogy works so well to explain the expansion of your perception as you move within yourself. Because when you move toward the center of the mountain you also move toward the top. And the higher you climb the more you can see of the landscape below. So when you finally reach the *Center Point Of The Universe* you are at the very highest vantage point, from where you can see everything in all directions! All at the same time.

Most of us are only capable of living our lives at the base

of the mountain so we move blindly on the lowest plane as if there were no higher, more integrated, point of view; as if life were nothing more than a series of images, experiences or moments that unfold in linear progression.

That linear presentation being all we see of the universe, it naturally becomes our reality.

But as I said at the beginning of this workshop, when we are standing on the mountaintop we can see the movie in its entirety; we can view the entire chain of events leading up to this moment in time and all those events that reach out from this moment as well.

We can even see moments that may never materialize: moments that are not yet fixed in our life chain but are good possibilities, given the energy and impetus of the forces in play. As I have mentioned, The Seekers For Truth classify these pseudo-scenes from our lives as *Glimmers*, for they are nothing but feint flashes of life forms before they are realized. The trajectories those life forms *may* take. Even the trajectories of our dreams and wishes should they be given enough creative substance in our minds.

We often say 'if you want something bad enough it will come true' but we do not realize on what level of existence that may happen.

When we see a *Glimmer*, as real as it may appear, it exists only as a vibration, one level below physical actuation...or so I have been told.

But all these moments in time, whether they are *Glimmers* or fully realized, still occur at the same moment in the creation.

Which moment is that?

The one where a bleached blonde in a second-floor apartment is dragging me toward a ratty brown couch covered in dog hairs and worn velveteen. The same moment that I sit here in St. Christina's Church basement painfully observing my son's first Pinewood Derby. The very same instant I am here at a singles dance at the Plymouth Marriott meeting for the first time a woman you and I know only too well. The identical moment that finds me seated, propped up with pillows, on this hard couch in Dr. Rivers' den-made-into-an-office bristling at his limited and biased perceptions.

Which is also the very same moment—though it appears to take place a year later in illusory linear time—that I bring my *ten year old* son Mickey to his *second* cub scout Pinewood Derby, courageous and foolhardy parent that I am. Only this time, you will notice, we manage to craft a model racecar worthy of my feelings for my son. But we will come to that shortly...

One singular moment in time. A moment that appears to most of us on the planet as a thousand different moments but in reality is only one—the Sacred Present Moment. And that is what the Big Game is all about: to see beyond the limitations of Automatic Universal Misunderstanding and to transcend them.

Yes whatever you choose to call it—Enlightenment, the Super Bowl, the Ultimate Destination—this is *The* Big Game and there is no one you have to compete with to win it, except for yourself.

I do not expect you to understand or believe any of this. I just need you to hear it and for me to listen to myself explain it, which is usually the best way for me to discover my own thoughts and opinions about things.

But I was talking about danger, was I not? Not physical danger but the danger of interfering with the events of your life. It was nothing I ever thought about until I was standing outside my son's classroom having just seen Allison Pratt through the window of the back door.

Up until that moment I had participated in all my flashbacks and flashforwards as an observer. Much of what I observed had a tangible impact on my thoughts and opinions, brought out emotional responses and internal dialogue, but never changed the behavior of Paul Peterson in the actual moment.

Not until I panicked at seeing Ms. Pratt.

You remember how I acted? Why do you think I jumped backwards so suddenly? Not because I was afraid of being seen by Mickey or his Ms. Pratt, but of being *recognized* by her!

It is true. My whole body shivered in that moment, I was so afraid. Afraid that Ms. Pratt might recognize me as the man she would meet at the dance at the Plymouth Marriott.

An event that would not take place for three days!

You understand what I am saying? It was knowledge of something that would happen later in time that caused my reaction in that earlier moment. I was no longer flashbacking to an instant from my life and strictly observing things; *I was participating!*

This is what I mean by danger; the danger of stepping free from the power of *AUM* when you have not yet attained the wisdom or the experience to safely negotiate the unknown waters that lay beyond.

I am sure the Bapucharya understands the risks involved and has little trouble avoiding them. But I am not as wise or knowledgeable as a fully realized holy man, be he dead or alive. And so I must be careful—extremely careful!—to avoid disturbing the elements of my life in such a way as to create an entirely new set of circumstances.

Could that really happen? I honestly do not know. But I grow more and more nervous about the possibility.

I can no longer think of time as a mere concept; as something that simply does or does not exist. I know now that in my innocence I can easily stumble across wires in the dark that disrupt and reformulate the realities of time.

This is something new to me and nothing The Seekers ever warned me about.

Aside from the fact that it frightens me, I do not know what to make of it or what it might mean.

Do you?

Lesson 32

How To Rig A Temporary Connection Between Two Mismatched Parts

"I am sorry to hear of my death," The Bapucharya says lightly. "I was always one of those people you would miss when they are gone."

"Apparently not," I reply dryly.

"Hah! That is funny," he responds with a giggle, "very funny indeed! I am pleased to see you developing at last a sense of humor, Mr. Peterson."

"I have a lot of questions, Holiness."

"I know you do," he responds as if appreciating my feelings. "What else should you have if not questions? This life of ours is so very full of mysteries, it would be surprising not to have questions. I will do my best to answer whatever I am able..."

"Then, tell me..." I start to ask.

"...*whenever* I am able!" he concludes pointedly.

Warding off my rising protest as if shooing away a fly he says, "No, no! Please to stop pestering me. This is not the time for questions, young sir. You are about to connect with our lady of the desirable pineapples and I am only here to remind you of something very simple."

Here, I wonder? What does he mean by *here?*

Where is here?

It suddenly hits me that *here* is nowhere. Except inside my head.

Then just as suddenly I am back in the Mayflower Ballroom hovering high above the crowd in the room's vaulted heights.

"Remind me of what?" I inquire, feeling a little queasy to be this high off the ground.

“To speak the truth!” he answers simply.

“Is that it? To ‘speak the truth?’ What does that mean? Speak the truth to whom?”

“To everyone. This bleached-out lady waiting to fall prey to your charms, that angry-but-very-lovely lady who is already a victim of your charms, and most of all speak the truth to yourself.”

“I will try, Holiness” I say, uncertain as to the real purpose behind this latest instruction. I have noticed The Bapucharya will often say one thing while he appears to mean another.

“I will do my best,” I assure him.

“Good!” he replies. “And I will do my best to answer your questions. But first, continue your conversation with this undernourished lady who is clearly dazzled by your good looks and plentiful charms. Not to mention the thin hair,” he recalls, pausing to emit a few high pitched giggles, “on the top of your head.

“Go ahead, Mr. Peterson!” he prods. “We will talk later.”

“All right,” I agree.

Abruptly I find myself back on the ballroom floor facing a thin, blonde lady in a white cotton blouse and patterned skirt. Behind her I can see a dimly-lit ballroom full of middle-aged singles and older fun-seekers pretending to be middle-aged singles. With The Beatles singing “Twist And Shout” a little too loudly I lean towards her to inquire in a raised voice, "Did you just get here? I do not recall seeing you.”

Replying in a raised voice to be heard against the music she nods, "I came in a little while ago.”

“An orphan from the storm,” I shout back with no great meaning intended.

Patting the fringes of her flyaway hair she appears pleased by my attention.

"So what do you think?" I pursue loudly.

"About what?" she asks, squinting her eyes to improve her concentration.

"The dance?" I answer, attempting to light fires with my most charming and boyish grin. "I am talking about tonight…here…this dance…what do you think?"

She is confused.

"Well, how do you mean?" she calls out.

I put my face closer to hers and peer into her eyes which seem to panic at my proximity, darting this way and that.

Clearly she is shy and not wholly comfortable with attention from good-looking strangers.

"Hah!" the Nitpicker instantly responds, "Good-looking strangers!" But things are going too well for him to gain any influence over my insecurities.

My face still close to hers I shout softly, like a co-conspirator, "Is this the night you meet someone special? Or is it just another twenty bucks down the drain?"

"Hmm-hmmm!" she laughs in her throat, glancing at me questioningly. "I don't think I've seen *you* here before, have I?"

I cannot say whether it is more pain or pleasure at times, this flutter of excitement I feel when I first meet someone. The intensity of these initial meaningless exchanges, designed to test the waters and reveal each other's interest, can be heady and intoxicating.

"I used to come to dances here," I reply, still almost shouting, "but I moved away."

"Away?"

Her voice drops as she says "away" as if the thought saddens her.

I laugh.

"You are quite something!" I exclaim. "Exactly what, I am not yet sure...but you sounded so far away and lost just then. Like a little girl. All I meant was I used to live..."

I catch myself before the words "St. Bart's Bay" can leave my lips, continuing instead, "...on the South Shore, but then moved to Cambridge. It is not like moving from New York to Chicago."

"No," she agrees. "It's not." She raises a thin arm into the air waving at some internal realization then pulls her head back to give me a long questioning stare.

"You speak funny," she finally decides. "Where are you from?"

"I grew up in Brooklyn."

"Really?" she says, falling into a thoughtful pose.

"No, that's not it," she abruptly decides, discarding the

idea with a limp-wristed wave of her hand. “Say something else!"

"The little brown fox jumped on top of the little red fox."

She shakes her head.

"Never mind. It will come to me if I let it."

"Are you an expert on dialects or something?"

"No," she answers, "I’m a teacher. A fourth grade teacher," absently running her fingers through the dry folds of her shoulder-length hair.

"Oh, really! That must be fun.”

“What did you say?”

Raising my voice again, I answered, “I said that must be fun! You like kids?"

“I hope to ... “ she replies with a sardonic and icy smirk, “*someday!*”

“The kids must think you are funny.”

Suddenly she decides, "It must be the way you construct your sentences. There's something about them...”

"In Brooklyn we did not construct sentences, we built them out of used car parts."

"So why are you here?" she queries, shifting her stance and abruptly staring directly at me.

Feeling like a bug under a microscope I am caught off guard and, remembering The Bapucharya’s injunction to speak the truth, can only think to reply, "What?"

Restating the question she asks, "What brings you to Plymouth if you live in Cambridge?"

I wonder if she can detect the nervousness behind my short, breathy laugh?

"We ran out of women in Cambridge," I report dryly. "Did you not hear?"

"Go away! Nobody talks like that!"

"Stop with my speech patterns already!"

"Well you are the strangest person I've met in some time; that's a fact."

"Nothing wrong with that," I say, smiling. "Though it is not the kind of praise I expect from a teacher."

"I'm scant with praise, sir—what did you say your name was?"

"Paul...Paul Peterson. And yours."

"Allison...Allison Pratt."

"That is better," I say, relieved to hear Twist and Shout coming to its conclusion.

"And now for the ladies," Brad Winsome calls out in his distinctive *basso profundo* bedroom voice, putting on a slow dance and lowering the volume.

"I bet the kids all call you Miss Pratt," I suggest in a voice that no longer needs to shout to compete with deceased and over-excited rock and roll singers.

"Usually Mrs. Pratt," she corrects me. "They don't understand the etiquette of divorce."

I laugh, probing, "There is an etiquette?"

"Don't you think so?" she asks with a serious look.

"Perhaps," I reply evasively. "But in any case it is nice to meet you, *Ms.* Pratt." I extend my hand to her along with a bright toothy smile.

She takes the hand and returns the smile, replying, "My pleasure, Mr. Peterson, I'm sure!" topping off our handshake with a girlish giggle.

Freeing my hand from her grip I slip it under her arm then slide it around her back, at the same moment stepping in close.

"What are you doing?" she asks looking down across our interlocked bodies as if somebody were installing cheap foreign parts.

"Try and guess," I reply reaching for her unclaimed hand and pushing off.

A moment later we are dancing.

"Oh," she cries with a startled laugh. "I thought you were going to frisk me."

"That comes later," I smile.

"Well, let me know when it happens."

"You will be the first to know," I promise.

"Do you hear something?" she asks as we move to the music, our bodies closely joined.

"Hear something? Like what?"

"It's sort of rhythmic, like a pulse? You don't hear it?"

To stay within shouting distance of the truth I would have to answer, "Yes, that is just my Prophetic Navigational Device signaling my sexual arousal and the stiffening of my penis. Quite normal for this kind of intimate slow dancing." But instead I merely respond, "Yes, I do. I think it might be the air conditioning."

In my mind I offer The Bapucharya my apologies. It is just not feasible to *always* tell the truth; not in the world I inhabit. I quickly turn my mind to other matters, needing to concentrate if I hope to move her overly stiff body across the crowded dance floor without the two of us tripping over each other.

She is a terrible dancer, to put it bluntly. Inflexible and awkward, unable to anticipate my lead, she repeatedly shifts her body so it invariably blocks my next move or heads off in a different direction.

"Nice," she says dreamily, bumping into me again.

"My fault," I reply blithely, taking the blame like a gentleman. "I cannot do a thing with these legs since they learned to do the boogaloo."

Two nights a week—sometimes three nights a week if I can find them—I come to dances like this in search of something...a friendly face, an evening's companion, a lifelong partner. Depending on my mood, any or all of the above would be a welcome addition to my solitary existence. But if I am honest with myself, what I am really searching for is someone capable of looming large enough in my life to fill a gaping hole in the center of my existence.

The hole left by Marilyn when she divorced me.

I do not like admitting that. Especially to myself.

So here I am dancing!

With another woman met at another dance.

In a way it does not matter that I purposely came here looking to find Ms. Pratt. Nor does it matter that she is my son's fourth grade teacher. You can make a big deal out of that or not, as you choose. But for me right now she is just another stranger encountered at a dance. Another woman who for all her aesthetic shortcomings and air of forgotten promise holds a certain attraction for me.

Honest!

Though she will never be capable of filling the void left by my ex-wife, or perhaps even the empty hours of a lonely night, she does feel good right this moment, her body leaning against mine, her round breasts seeking solace against my sheltering form.

Three days ago when I observed Allison Pratt for a split second in Room 109 of the Myles Standish School her attractions were extremely subtle to me, barely perceptible. They hid within her air of drabness like a moth concealed in its cocoon.

But now I am standing next to her and she looks different. Her beauty no longer appears as *faded* as I remember and certainly there is no overwhelming air of withered promise as I so glibly described it.

That was just an easy way to score points off someone who could not fight back. Standing next to her now I can smell the flowers in her perfume and tangibly appreciate the traces of beauty that underlie her features, even if they seem overshadowed by a tone of drabness.

But you tell me if some sense of her beauty does not shine through the pallid complexion, the undernourished figure, the inexpertly bleached hairdo? Somehow some tiny measure of appeal still manages to break through the grayness like sun through a cloudy sky. Especially those moments when, uncertain rabbit that she is, she opens up long enough to smile and fifteen years magically fall away.

Yes she definitely is a sad and tattered thing, but as we dance and talk and laugh at each other's silly jokes a small bond begins to take hold. Will it be strong enough to last beyond the dance? More to the point will it be strong enough for me to explore the issues I am here to explore? And to help change her behavior...?

I must be kidding, I think. I must be seriously out of my mind to believe I can accomplish anything here tonight besides getting myself into trouble.

In case you were wondering, I have no plan.

I have not a clue what I will do. I have already exhausted my strategy for the evening. Meet Ms. Pratt, engage her in conversation, get her to like me. And then...what?

I am not here to sleep with her in exchange for her easing up with my son's class. I do not intend to mention Mickey at all, or his class; that would fall under the heading of 'speaking with Ms. Pratt' and I promised I would not do that.

So what will I do?

Heaven only knows! And The Bapucharya too, I would imagine. But whatever I do I cannot do it here amongst all the noise and distractions of a singles dance.

"Do you know someplace where we can get a cup of coffee?" I ask as we finish our dance and begin to walk off the dance floor. "I am pretty much a hopeless case in Plymouth. I could probably find my way to the ocean if you pointed me in the right direction, but…"

"Oh, I know a great place," she answers enthusiastically. "But I'm more in the mood for wine than coffee."

"Wine is good," I say.

"Then I know just the place!"

As she says that I catch a slight movement of her eye, a movement that seems very close to a wink. Inwardly I shiver as a premonition passes through my mind, leaving a vague sense of unease in its wake.

"Just give me a moment," I say holding up five fingers. "I have to see someone about something. Let us meet by the coat room. In five minutes?"

"Yes," she says mimicking my voice pattern. "Let us do that. Five minutes. Let us be there!"

The *someone* I mentioned happens to be the same someone that I have been trying to avoid most of the evening.

Earlier words of The Bapucharya have refused to leave my mind. Against all resistance they have pushed themselves to the forefront of my thoughts and I do not seem able to ignore them. Nor to leave the dance without acting upon them.

Remember?

We had been speaking about the lies I told Ellie, and I asked The Bapucharya what he thought I should have said.

"I cannot tell you the words, young sir," he responded, "I can only wish the spirit that gives rise to the words be one of honesty and openness. What flows from that will be what it shall be."

"I am sorry," I told him. "Maybe next time."

Which I suddenly remember caused him to laugh as if he knew the punch line to some secret little joke. Perhaps this was the joke, my seeking out Ellie before leaving. Or maybe he was laughing at how she will react once I find her.

It does not really matter. This is just something I need to do. Which is why, I guess, I find myself heading off into the crowd to seek out my former lover.

You will notice I am armed with little more than good intentions and an earnest desire to speak the truth.

Wish me luck.

Lesson 33

Some Tips For Avoiding Unwanted Displays Of Emotion

Can you believe the show he is putting on?

Would you listen to him!

The pitch in his voice must be reaching new heights.

"Are you telling me that you actually picked up your son's teacher?" he asks, incredulously. "You picked up Ms. Pratt—you actually picked her up at a dance?"

Can you hear the shock in his voice?

"I would not describe it that way," I answer, not as sure of myself as I would like to be.

"Am I right," he pursues, gathering energy as he gets more emotionally charged, "... she *is* Mickey's teacher, isn't she?" He may be asking a question but the accusation in his voice says he is not looking for an answer. "We're not talking about a stranger here, right? You picked up your son's *teacher* at a singles dance? Right?"

I cannot tell if that is a smile on his face or a grimace, one of the handicaps of having a therapist with a beard.

"You keep saying 'right' like it was a flaming sword or something. Give it a rest."

"I'm just asking a reasonable question as your therapist," he replies, more argumentative than reasonable. "It's not everyday that a father goes to a dance looking to pick up his son's teacher."

"I would not call it a 'pickup' exactly," I squirm. "Not exactly," I repeat, searching for a better word.

"Well, what would you call it?" he challenges.

I release a hollow almost desperate laugh. The kind of laugh I never hear anywhere but in this room.

"I *met* her!" I declare, brightening at the reasonableness

of my declaration. "That is closer to what really happened. I did not say anything about picking her up or taking her out. We just *met!"*

"But you've already said you specifically went to the dance hoping to find her. And you not only *met* her there, you took her out for coffee afterwards. I have no idea what happened after that."

"What could happen, going out for coffee?" I proclaim in all innocence, momentarily surprised to hear my mother's Hungarian/Jewish inflection erupting from my mouth. "Am I imagining things or are you trying to make me feel guilty?"

"Why?" he inquires with a lift of his eyebrows. "Are you feeling guilty?"

"You know, I wish there was a way I could get some sort of incremental discount for every question I ask in here that you answer with another question. It is so infuriating at times."

"Don't you think we're getting off track? We were talking about *you*, not me."

Is it just me or does he seem personally affronted by my behavior? This is the classic 'Freud Goes Freudian' routine. If Mickey were here with me I would use this opportunity to prepare him for the time, God forbid, when he might need to see a therapist himself.

Did you see what just happened, I would ask instructively? Did you notice how my therapist never answered even one of my questions? Notice that instead he chose to play a game I call 'Freudian Racquetball'. The main rule in Freudian Racquetball being that a therapist has to quickly return a patient's question with a question of his own.

At this point, I am certain, Mickey would be totally confused. So I would give him an example.

Say I directly ask my therapist, 'What do you mean by that?' looking for some kind of clarification about something he might have said? He would inevitably come back with an overhead slam, asking, 'What do you think I mean?' or 'Why do you think I mean something?' or even 'Why do you always attribute meaning to what I say?' which has the added benefit of discounting my entire previous therapeutic effort.

He might even ask, 'How are you feeling—I mean right

now?' which is what he usually drags up when he is at a loss for something more relevant or disconcerting to ask.

I would then pose the pivotal question to my son: "So, why do you think a therapist always answers a patient's question with a question of his own?"

Most likely I would not wait for my little boy's answer since I do not want him to devalue himself for not understanding the eccentricities of psychotherapists.

You might miss it at first, I would explain, but therapists are not generally trying to cure their patients. The truth of the matter is they are actually attempting to drive them crazy. That is why there are so many crazy people in the world, because there are so many therapists in practice. They become therapists in the same way overly hungry men and women become chefs: they mistake their symptoms for a calling. As if someone born with a missing ingredient is the perfect person to assist others in finding the essential elements left out of their own psychological recipes.

And these overpaid, under-supervised therapists are so paranoid about their insufficiencies being discovered they would rather volley questions all day than give a simple answer that might reveal something about themselves.

This goes on for as long as the patient is willing to pay for the privilege of being driven crazy, I would explain, usually for a couple of years at least. Not a surprising length of time since therapists have been trained over the years to dig up, identify and catalog all the normal crazy stuff everybody has in their minds, then to make it seem significantly crazier to their patients.

"Be careful," I would warn my little boy. It is a system where the patient is always at a disadvantage. If you say something that goes against the therapist's point of view you suddenly have to explain and defend yourself as if you had advocated child labor or sex with giraffes.

And if you directly challenge anything he tells you, he inevitably looks at you with acute concern masked thinly by his beard and asks, 'Why do you feel so compelled to argue with me? Are you in a bad mood? Was there something I said that triggered your outburst?'

'What is wrong with you?' he repeatedly asks with the

best intentions...or so it seems. And after awhile you start asking yourself the same question.

All in all I would advise Mickey to skip therapy if he has a choice and to take up a game he can actually win, like tennis or embezzlement.

This morning, however, I am not in the proper frame of mind to accept any of this Freudian bullshit from Old Man Rivers.

"You know," I say, stumbling around for appropriate words, "did you ever stop to think that after listening to everyone's dirty secrets all these years you might be a little quick to jump to unsavory conclusions?"

"I'm not jumping to conclusions," he says shaking his head, "I'm just trying to keep up with you."

"Well, then listen to me instead of shouting out exclamations and drawing all sorts of inferences!"

His face darkens.

"Did I shout?" he asks softly, his fingers pausing in their caress of his beard.

"That was about the loudest 'Hah!' I have heard in a long time," I reply testily.

He laughs then admits almost apologetically, "I guess you surprised me."

"Do not misunderstand me," I assure him. "I am not justifying myself. None of this makes sense to me either. If it sounds weird to you, it sounds twice as weird to me. At some level I probably knew what was going on, but consciously it was nothing I expected to have happen."

I stop for a breath, leaving him an opening to respond. But the good doctor just looks at me expectantly, pulling on the long thin strands of his beard and waiting.

"And if you think there was anything romantic about this...this *meeting*," I continue, gritting my teeth, "you are plain just out of touch with reality. Allison and I just met, and then went out for coffee!"

"Is that all?" he softly interjects. "It didn't sound that way when you first talked about it."

"Could it be, perhaps, you did not *hear* it that way?"

"Okay, that's fair," he says, leaning back in the chair and falling into his neutral observer pose. "So, why don't you tell me what happened...?"

This is another gambit I would make sure to point out to my little boy. "When the patient begins to get wise to you, and especially if he sounds angry, the good therapist falls back into the neutral observer role!"

Seeing Dr. Rivers' game so clearly I cannot help but laugh.

"You do not stop, do you?" I challenge him. "Why should I waste expensive therapy dollars talking about something so unimportant? Yes we met, yes we went out for coffee. And yes it was stupid of me. Enough said!"

"Then why did you mention it?"

"Because I am stupid, just like I said. I was trying to bring you up to date; let you know what happened. After all, it did have some significance..."

"You do see that?" he interrupts, shifting in his seat.

"Yes, of course I see that. I am not totally ignorant of the significance of my actions, given my promise to Mickey. But the real significance may not lie so much in what I did or the slant you seem to put on things, but ultimately on the mere fact that his teacher and I met, went out for coffee and..." I stop as a curious thought runs off in my mind.

"And...?" he prods.

"And nothing," I reply. "Life went on, the earth continued to spin, one day followed another. What more is there to say? I only told you about it because...I am not sure why I told you except that you are my therapist and I am supposed to tell you things."

A curious realization came to me in that brief moment I clumsily paused in my thoughts. It struck me with a jolt why I made the mistake of mentioning Ms. Pratt to Old Man Rivers. I mean I had no intention of telling him about meeting Allison at the dance or anything. And certainly not about wrestling with her in her second floor apartment. I only brought it up because... well—and this is what jolted me—I could not think of anything else to say.

How is that for strange!

There was nothing else to speak about. Nothing. My mind drew a complete blank as if nothing else had happened in the three weeks since that night at the dance.

What could that mean? Am I trying to forget something? What could be so terrible it would cause my mind to go completely blank?

Returning to the present moment I hear myself rhetorically asking, "Why else am I in therapy if not to talk about things that make me uncomfortable? Otherwise you will never understand the critical themes and issues in my life."

"Okay, then," he says in a calm understated voice, "even though it is not important, tell me what happened after the dance?"

I have to laugh. He is so transparent, is he not? Just look at the clumsy trap he so ineptly sets! This is the perfect example to illustrate everything I would have said up to now in my lesson about psychotherapists.

"See what I mean about driving me crazy?" I would now ask my little boy. If I refuse to talk about my brief *tete-a-tete* with Ms. Pratt, I will *de facto* give the event all the importance I insist it does not have. And if I capitulate and relate what happened, the very fact of talking about my experience will invest it with that same level of importance.

Damned if I do, damned if I do not. Either way Old Man Rivers makes his point and another demented, pathetic patient gets nailed.

Is it any wonder people go crazy in therapy?

Now you can see why I did not tell Dr. Rivers about meeting Allison until...how long has it been? Three weeks since that Friday night in Plymouth?

Yes I waited three weeks. Does that surprise you?

Imagine how he would have reacted if I had told him right after it happened? He would have had a full-scale emotional eruption. An '8' on the Richter Therapist Scale. You saw how upset he became? That would have been nothing compared to his reaction if the event had been fresh enough that its consequences were still evolving.

That is why I was not eager to tell him. And why I have not yet discussed my growing apprehension that everything I did that evening—going to the dance, searching out Ms. Pratt, and everything that happened up in her apartment—was committed under influences that were beyond my comprehension. He would quickly accuse me of denying my obvious responsibility and to some extent he would be right. But it is more than that, much more. Some inner sense is telling me to look again at what seemed so simple and obvious at the time it was happening.

It was easy then to believe that everything I did was in service to some kind of chivalrous impulse to help my son. As if I had decided to walk through fire to rescue Mickey from the evil witch and thus prove the strength of his father's love.

But I see there were other influences at play, not all of them under my control or easily seen at the time. In fact I now believe my decision to ignore my promise to Mickey was fated to happen; was something I had no control over. Which means it was a promise I could not have kept if I wanted to.

Talk about denying responsibility!

Do not misunderstand me. I have tricked myself into doing things that were not quite kosher before. But pretending I was keeping my promise about Ms. Pratt then 'accidentally' bumping into her at the dance had me skating on pretty thin ice. This was denial stretched too far to maintain any snap or believability. But something did bring Ms. Pratt to the dance and whatever it was—fate, blind luck or Karma—it was probably the overriding influence in what I now see as a quickly accelerating Karmic Gravitational Slide.

Are you following me so far?

Good! It follows then, if there was a Karmic Gravitational Slide in effect, regardless of how I behaved and whatever decisions I made, events would have been driven—and somewhat controlled—by forces related to movements in the universe much larger and more important than my puny purposes and desires. These are the kind of movements that The Seekers and The Bapucharya attribute to the influence of Karma, Legacies and the interwoven destinies of *Karmic Companions.*

There is much more to be learned about all this but probably not in this therapy session.

And certainly not with a blind man who is so utterly convinced he knows exactly what elephants look like.

Lesson 34

In The Event Plan 'A' Fails, Switch Immediately To Plan 'B'

It is the weekend after the dance at the Marriott—the first weekend with the kids since I met Ms. Pratt and went back to her apartment.

We are back in my Cambridge apartment after going somewhere this afternoon though I cannot remember where. I am not even certain what the kids and I did this evening. We probably rented a video as we usually do.

Strange as it may seem I cannot remember a single thing that happened since that fateful visit to Allison's second floor apartment.

I suppose that must have something to do with the workings of my Do-It-Yourself Workshop. Something The Seekers For Truth obviously forgot to warn me about.

In any case, as you can see for yourself, we are back in my apartment getting ready for sleep. The girls, dressed in their pajamas and under the covers, are watching TV from the sleeper couch in the living room while Mickey and I are in my bedroom, which means we are in bed since the room is so small there is no other place to be but in bed. With the door closed to shut out the noise of the TV, I am reading an Agatha Christie mystery while Mickey thrashes around under the covers trying to fall off into sleep.

The violent movement under the quilt is Mickey's way of telling me the glare from my reading lamp is keeping him awake. It is also his way of expressing his growing annoyance.

A few moments later, lying on his side with his back to me, he takes a more direct approach.

"How long're you going to keep the light on?" he asks,

lifting his head to speak over his shoulder.

"Ohhh," I respond, lingering over the word in mock surprise, "look who just arrived at the party!"

"Da-ad!" he protests weakly, dropping his head back onto the pillow. "You always do this!"

"Shhh!" I reply with a slow grin. "People are sleeping."

My little boy growls, thrashes back and forth like an angry fish then pulls the cover up over his head and growls again.

I wait a few moments for his irritation to subside then lean close to where his head bulges under the quilt and whisper, "Besides, I want to talk to you about something."

"Da-a-a-d!" he protests, dragging out the word.

"But..." I start to explain.

"Go awa-a-ay!" he screeches, bouncing around in a fit.

"Okay, okay!" I respond, adding, "Look, I am turning out the light," as if reciting stage directions.

In a moment our tiny world is totally dark.

"Go to sleep, sweetie," I murmur, settling in to a more comfortable sleeping position and tucking a fold of the quilt between my legs. "We will talk in the morning. Okay?"

Mickey grumbles a response that does not exactly reveal itself in the form of separate words but offers enough reconciliation to maintain some semblance of comradeship.

Five minutes later I can hear his sonorous child's breath rising and falling in the darkness.

"I love you," I whisper to my sleeping boy for no other reason than it makes me feel good to say it.

Twenty or thirty minutes later I am still awake. Having shifted my body a dozen times—maybe a hundred times, who can say?—I stare up at the ceiling which is now a gray square floating in a sea of darkness.

All this time I have been considering what to tell Mickey and preparing myself to say it. It would all be so much easier of course if I were prepared to lie, which I am not.

I do not lie to my children.

On occasion, however, like most parents I find creative ways to answer questions without telling either the truth or a lie.

"Why does Mr. Alexander always sing when he comes

home from work?" Mickey asked me last month, inquiring about a neighbor who lives on the other side of the driveway that serves as my courtyard in Cambridge. Instead of answering, "Because Mr. Alexander always stops for a couple of drinks after work," I replied with controlled enthusiasm, "Boy, I wish I were so happy my neighbors could hear me singing!"

Not a real answer to the question but not quite a lie.

Deception I do; lying no!

And I would hopefully not lie to conceal my adventures with Ms. Pratt. Not that lying would prevent their discovery. Growing up during the age of Richard Nixon I have seen the tangles you create when you knit a cover-up from threads of petty self-interest and self-serving lies. Those tangles become more damaging than the sins they were meant to camouflage.

Anyway, speaking of lying, this child next to me has been totally asleep for the same twenty or thirty minutes I have been wrestling with my need to speak about Ms. Pratt.

If he knew what I was thinking he would not be resting so peacefully. If he knew how close I am to waking him up he would not look so tranquil.

Intentionally clumsy in my movements I turn over in bed, banging cruelly with such obvious intentions against Mickey's bony little body.

"Sorry," I say, apologetically patting him on his shoulder.

A few more twists and turns...a few more apologies...and—hear that?—he is starting to stir.

"What did you say, Mick?" I ask tugging on his pajama sleeve. "What was that?"

"Huh?" he jumps, slightly panicked. Jerking his head up startled, he asks, "What is it? What's wrong?"

"Nothing," I tell him, "You were probably dreaming."

He lets out a long sigh, drops his head onto the pillow and begins to get back on the bus for the return trip to dreamland.

"Hey, watch the covers!" I protest, pulling on the quilt.

"What are you doing?" he cries in disbelief. Murmuring an indistinct oath he pushes himself up again and turns to me with anger in his voice, "You've got most of the covers,

Dad!"

"Oh," I reply apologetically. "You are right. I must have been dreaming when I thought I felt you pulling off the covers. Sorry."

He yanks on the quilt and angrily shifts his body again.

"What is the problem now?" I ask, ever the patient martyr.

"Nothing," he answers brusquely. "Good night, Dad."

"Good night, sweetie. Pleasant dreams."

"Yeah, you too."

We lie here in silence for a long dark minute.

Then I softly call, "Hey, sweetie? Are you awake?"

No answer.

I repeat the question.

"What?" he answers sleepily.

"Are you awake?" I ask again.

Lying on his stomach, he lifts his head and upper body in a stretch then answers sleepily, "I guess so."

I sense him turning around to lie on his back though it is too dark to see anything but shadows. "I knew you were gonna do this," he says simply. There is no emotion in the words, no anger or hostility. Just a dry recognition of my obvious intentions.

I ignore his implied accusation.

"You remember what you were telling me about Ms. Pratt?"

"About her yelling at kids?" he replies without much energy or interest.

"Yes."

"Yeah...?"

"Well, tell me what she sounds like when she yells? I think I saw her once or twice and she seemed so quiet a person it is hard to imagine her yelling."

"She *is* quiet," my little boy agrees with a half-expressed yawn. "She never raises her voice."

WHAT?

"But you said she yells? I remind him.

"Well she does, sort of. She just does it quiet-like, without raising her voice. *You* do that sometimes. It's like all the yelling is going on inside your head. Only I can hear it—you know?"

I fall quiet thinking about what he has just said.

"Do I yell a lot?" I abruptly ask. "I mean the way Ms. Pratt yells? Do I do it a lot?"

"Not a lot," he answers. "Just when me or the girls do something to make you mad. Ms. Pratt does it all the time because she's so sad all the time."

This is all very interesting. It explains Mrs. Bakewater's unshakeable convictions about Ms. Pratt. Which I guess were correct...in a way. Even Mickey is saying that Ms. Pratt does not yell at the kids in her class. Not out loud!

"Now I understand why you and your sisters often accuse me of yelling when I know for a fact I am not—you guys are sneaking inside my head!"

"Yep, that's it," he shoots back. "Can I go to sleep now?"

"You can stay awake for one more minute," I suggest. "I want to tell you something important and I want you to tell me what you think."

"I don't understand."

"You will in a moment," I promise. "You know how we have been trying to figure out what to do about Ms. Pratt's yelling, since a school kid is not supposed to tell a teacher to lighten up or relax or anything?"

Mickey groans.

"Dad! Can't we talk about this in the morning?"

"Absolutely," I say emphatically. Then ignoring the urgency of his appeal I continue, "But give me a minute. I need to get this off my chest now...

"What if you accept the fact that it is humanly impossible—what are you laughing at?"

"You said 'Yumanly' impossible..." he answered with a snicker.

My kids love to point out that even after fifteen years of Seeker training I still have traces of my Brooklyn accent.

"Give me a break!" I say with a weary sigh. "I was speaking about changing Ms. Pratt's behavior; trying to stop her from yelling inside her head."

"Who's gonna do that?" he asks, incredulous. "Not me!"

"That is what I was trying to say...that it is not *h-h-humanly* possible to change Ms. Pratt's personality or her behavior. In other words we cannot cheer her up if she is sad or make her act pleasantly if she is not in a good mood. The fact is you are only her student, not a friend or a doctor or something."

Yeah...?" he questions, waiting for something less obvious.

"You get the point I am making? That a student does not have the power to change a teacher's behavior. You get that?"

Yeah...?" he repeats, still waiting.

"So the question is, if you cannot change her behavior, what can you change?"

"I don't know, Dad. Is this some kind of test or puzzle or something?"

I ignore the sarcasm.

"There is only one thing you can change," I continue, "the only thing any of us can change: and that is *ourselves!* We can change *our* behavior!

"Your behavior, in this case," I continue. "You can only change how you yourself act—or react—to Ms. Pratt. *That* you can change. *That* you have the power to change."

"My reaction to Ms. Pratt?" he shoots back with a derisive laugh. "Dad, how am I gonna to do that?"

A thought occurs to him and he asks, "You mean I have to pretend she isn't yelling or something?"

"No, I do not mean that at all. I mean you have to learn to respond differently—to her and to her yelling."

"And how do I do that?"

"It will not be easy."

"I'm going back to sleep," he announces, convinced he will never understand what I am talking about and probably not caring a whole lot anyway.

"You can stay awake for one more minute," I prod him. "I just want to finish what I am saying. Remember that time we were watering the plants on Upland Road? And those two angry neighbors gave us a hard time?"

I am referring to a curious incident from the previous summer when Mickey's cub scout den had 'adopted' a small traffic island in St. Bart's Bay. Unlike many roadway adoption programs where all you do is hand over money to get your name on a sign, the adoptive parents in this case actually planted vegetation and landscaped the island. They—Mickey's den—even put in clusters of shortened pier pilings on either end of the traffic triangle. A nice extra touch!

Well I thought so, but apparently the neighbors held a different opinion.

I remember it was a hot summer's day to begin with and I was not feeling particularly happy about participating in another foolish cub scout event concocted for unwary fathers and sons.

In this case the unwitting father and son team of the day were supposed to transport water to this tiny little traffic island jammed with vegetation and pier pilings. Which involved hauling a half dozen large jars and watering cans filled to capacity. When we finally arrived at the adopted island, transporting our water supply on a squeaky old red wagon, we were soon visited by two angry neighbors who immediately voiced resentment and anger towards Mickey's cub scout den for claiming privileges to what was obviously *their* traffic island. They especially resented, I later surmised, the solidly planted pilings, which prevented them from backing out of their driveways in their usual mindless haze each morning.

In any case it was a tempest in a teapot and we quickly diffused their anger. But how we did that—turned them around so quickly—could easily be the subject of a long philosophical argument.

"Yeah?" he snorts in the darkness, indicating he remembers the traffic island incident but wonders why I am bringing it up now.

"You did not understand why they were angry," I remind him, "though I kind of knew what their problem was. But remember how all of a sudden they stopped being angry and even helped us water the plants?"

I pause for a moment. Not hearing any response I softly probe, "Are you still awake?"

A thoughtful voice answers, "Yeah…?"

"Good! Well, there is something I did not tell you about that incident. There is this funny thing I do when I find myself angry with people or not liking the way they are acting. Just like you probably complain about Ms. Pratt when you hear her yelling."

"I never say a thing," he argues.

"I know that. I only meant you probably complain inside your head. Everybody does that! Maybe you say to yourself: *'Boy here she goes again, yelling at the kids. She is so mean and unfriendly.'* That kind of thing."

"Oh, I get it," he says. Then remembering what I said, he asks, "So what's the funny thing you do?"

"You mean when people annoy me...? I look at them and imagine how they looked when they were young children. In fact, I actually pretend to see them as young children—in my mind, you understand..."

"I don't understand," he responds, his confusion obvious in the darkness. "You pretend people look like young kids?"

"It is a little more complicated than that."

I knew this would not be easy. The Seekers For Truth call it *Kidsnapping,* which means you take a mental snapshot of an adult but see him as a child. And just like *Embracement,* you use it in situations where Mr. Ping and Mr. Pong seem to be stuck on opposite sides of an issue. Only instead of changing your own attitude by embracing what you have been resisting, with *Kidsnapping* you somehow give your adversaries the room they need to change their opinions.

"Wait, I want to get this," Mickey says, growing more curious. "Do you act like they're young boys and girls? Do you treat them like young boys and girls?"

"Not exactly," I reply. "Your behavior is probably different but only because you see them in a different way. You do it all inside your head and never let them know you are doing it."

In the darkness of the room my hand dances through the air above me, underscoring and highlighting the meaning of my words.

"So, you remember those two people yelling at us for watering the plants...?"

"Yeah?"

"Well, I did it back then—imagined them as kids! Instead of getting angry like them, or yelling back... right there and then, I viewed them inside my mind as two-year-old children. As very *selfish* two-year-old children, if you want to know the truth."

"I didn't see anything."

"There was nothing to see," I explain. "It was all inside my head. How could you see it? But still, two things happened pretty quickly when I did that. First, I stopped feeling so upset at them, because who can stay upset with two-year-old children, right? And second, those two adults seemed to calm down pretty quickly. You remember...? How they stopped being upset with us so suddenly? It surprised us, remember? We spoke about it later...?"

"Come on, Dad! Get real!" he says, giving full release to his skepticism.

"It is true!" I insist. "They were suddenly smiling at us. You must remember!"

"But that wasn't because you were thinking of them as kids, Dad!"

"If not, then what?"

"How should I know?"

"Listen, all I can tell you is what happened for me. And seeing those two selfish...bastards...(excuse me)...as young children, well, suddenly they became little kids to me—little kids throwing a temper tantrum. And you cannot stay angry or upset with little kids for long. Not when they are two years old.

"I cannot prove that my change in attitude changed their behavior, but I also cannot think of any other explanation."

Opening up to the idea he questions, "But how do you do that, Dad—see them as little kids?"

"It is called *Kidsnapping,"* I explain, assuming a professorial air, "and if you look closely at any face, you can easily imagine how that person looked as a child. The facial features would be pretty much the same, only 20 or 30 years younger, with fresher skin and fewer wrinkles. There might even be an extra layer of baby fat."

Another personal experience comes to mind and I interject, "Of course there are times when it just does not work..."

I am recalling how ineffective and almost dangerous my *Kidsnapping* became during my breakup with his mother. Suddenly I was having arguments and disagreements with an imperious, demanding, totally selfish, two-year-old brat, and you never win an argument with that kind of a demonic child. But the worst thing—and it made me stop the whole thing in a panic—was when I began fantasizing myself murdering that very same two-year-old.

It was not a healthy scene.

But I am forgetting Mickey...

"Most of the time it can make a real difference," I assure him, trying to conclude on a positive note. "People do have the power to change themselves. So try it out on Ms. Pratt. What do you have to lose?"

"Is this for real?" he questions. "You're not just saying this?"

"Swear to God!"

Suddenly there is a different tone in his voice.

"You think it might really work?" he asks, more awake now. "That's so cool, Dad!"

"But you understand what I am saying?" I question. "That the next time Ms. Pratt yells in class you should...do what?"

"Pretend she is a little kid."

"Imagine she is a little kid," I correct him, "in your head."

"Imagine she is a little kid," he repeats correctly. "Can we go to bed now?"

"Oh, you did not tell me you were tired?" I exclaim with mock surprise.

"Goodnight, Dad."

"You will try it out with Ms. Pratt? *Kidsnapping?* You promise?"

"Yeah, why not? Sure. I promise."

"Okay, Sweetie. Goodnight. Pleasant dreams."

"Pleasant dreams."

"I love you."

"I love you, too."

"Do not forget—you promised!"

"Yeah, yeah! Goodnight, Dad."

"Goodnight."

Lying here basking in the afterglow of our conversation I can hear Mickey shifting around trying to find a comfortable position under the covers. Suddenly he shifts again and ends the movement with his right foot trailing onto my side. Without a word I search out his leg with my foot and nudge it ever so gently towards his side of the bed.

"Dad!" my little boy complains, clearly not appreciating the care I am taking to be gentle.

I note his complaint but continue to apply pressure to his leg.

"Mick, do you mind if I have my share of the bed?"

"I'm on the edge already, Dad," he bristles but allows his leg to be moved.

"Stop complaining and go to sleep," I admonish him. "Sweet dreams."

"Good night!" a miffed voice responds.

"I love you," I remind him.

"And I love you," he huffs back.

"Such a sweetie," I think, giving silent thanks to whichever benevolent deity has allowed me to maneuver through our discussion without once crashing against the rocks that were hidden beneath the waters.

You probably cannot see it in the darkened room but there is a silly grin of satisfaction on my face as I drift off to sleep.

Well to me it looks silly!

The Second Karmic
Gravitational Slide (Continued):

The Return Of The Hometown Hero

*Wherein Our
Workshop Leader Discovers
The Hidden Power
Of Father And Son Events
And Revisits The Scene
Of An Earlier Disaster*

Lesson 35

Some Tips For Returning To The Scene Of Your Most Dubious Crimes

Well here we go again.

One year later, many hairs lighter and scarcely a whit wiser, I am once again surrounded by two hundred cub scouts infected by the same virus that kept them loudly running in circles at last year's Pinewood Derby.

It is a virus that will not go away, I fear, until all these cub scouts have matured into boy scouts or explorer scouts or maybe into tired, overworked adults. Some of them of course will never lose the virus no matter how long they live.

Or so it seems.

For Mickey, however, the cure seems to be in place. This morning at least, as you can see, he does not run around in spontaneous abandon. There are no loud cries issuing from frantic smiles. There are no friends he wishes to chase or even sit with. For once he is content sitting by his father's side waiting quietly and patiently for whatever may come his way.

Of course 'content' may not be the right word.

"When's it our turn?" he asks for the tenth time. "How long, do you think? How long?"

"Soon," I say, hiding the same impatience he so flagrantly displays. "There are at least five or six heats ahead of us." The estimate has diminished by three since the last time he asked, which was the last time I looked over to the staging area where Black Beauty, the successor to "Old Number Two", sits patiently amidst rows and columns of other yet-to-race Pinewood Derby racecars.

"Just relax," I say gently. "Our turn will come."

"And you promised, remember..." he reminds me.

"Mickey, we have been through this before!" My patience is beginning to fray. "I know I promised we would beat the hell out of everyone else, but that was a... *rhetorical* promise."

"Yeah, well, a promise is still a promise."

"Yes, that is true. And I do not wish to pretend otherwise. But I made a promise that was really about what you and I would do as a team working together on our Pinewood Derby racecar. How can I promise we will win the race? No one can make that promise. Do you understand?"

"Are you saying we won't win?"

"No, I am just saying that anything could happen. We could win just like anybody else can win. But we could also lose! I am just saying that my promise—my *real* promise—was that we would not be embarrassed this year. That we would come to the Pinewood Derby with a model racecar that looked like a real model racecar..."

"And wasn't pink!" he adds importantly.

"Right...and was some other color besides red or fuchsia..."

"...or pink!" he prods.

"You know, we have gone over this a hundred times and it starts to become annoying. That racecar was not pink. I admit it looked pink on the sides where the white paint got mixed up with the fuchsia, but that was all. Otherwise, it was fuchsia."

"Yeah," he points out, "but the kids all said it was pink!"

"Yes, they did," I agree. "And part of my promise was to make sure the kids would not say that again. Or say anything to hurt you."

"But you also promised we would win."

He is correct of course. I did promise him we would win. It is not the dumbest thing I ever did but it comes quite close. I remember the day I thoughtlessly made my prediction and raised my little boy's expectations...

We were at the JCC swimming pool of all places.

It was a few weeks after our Pinewood Derby fiasco and we were at the pool with other single parents and their kids; Illyana and Hava were there too if I remember correctly.

Anyway Mickey was sitting on the side of the pool with

his legs dangling in the water and I was floating nearby listening to him rattle off complaints about Marv Jankowski whose racecar not only won the last heat we were in but also the entire tournament.

"I hate Marv Jankowski; he's a skunk!" he fumed. "He *always* wins."

"Well that may be," I responded, "but next year I intend to kick Marv Jankowski's butt. His father's too, for that matter. Understand what I am saying?"

"That we're gonna beat Marv Jankowski next year?"

"That we are going to beat *everybody* next year! And with the best looking racecar you and I can create. What do you say to that?"

"That Marv Jankowski always wins!"

"Okay, just wait and see. But if I were you I would not bet against us next year. You and I will not be losers at the Pinewood Derby."

"Plus we're gonna beat Marv Jankowski and his Dad?" he asked, making sure he got it right.

"We will absolutely demolish them!"

"Cool!"

Well, maybe not so cool...

Because here I am a year later furiously backpedaling on statements so indelibly stupid I cannot believe I made them.

"I was wrong," I admit candidly. "I apologize if I gave you false hope, but nobody, not any of the fathers here, can guarantee a win, not even Marv Jankowski's father. I know I said we would win but I was only making a rhetorical promise..."

The Bapucharya's words about speaking the truth seem to resonate in the air.

"No wait," I say. "That is not right. I was doing more than making rhetorical promises, Mick, I was saying extremely stupid things. Things I should never have said. I am sorry I said them but I did. And *that* is the truth!"

"But..." he starts to say then stops, caught off guard by my sudden confession.

I give his shoulder a reassuring shake.

"Hey!" I say encouragingly, "that does not mean we will lose. We have come here this morning with a car so hot it sizzles; and with that double-weight on the underside, ours could easily be the racecar to watch."

More likely of course it will turn out to be a dud. Because even though our racecar is sleek and shiny like all the others, and even though it has been painted BLACK this time with fancy decals that look like sprays of fire shooting down both sides, we are still the same knuckleheaded bumpkins who never had a clue about the aerodynamics of model racecars. So no matter how good Black Beauty looks we are still stumbling around in the dark hoping to duplicate the accidental genius of last year's entry.

That is why we added that extra weight to the belly of the racecar though for the life of me I cannot remember putting it on. If it comes to that—and this is probably more shocking than anything else—I cannot remember working on our racecar *at all!*

I know we worked on it at my friend Jeff's house whose tools we borrowed. I just cannot remember doing the actual work. It is very much like when I was in Old Man Rivers' office and could not recall a single thing that had happened in the previous three weeks.

Something is definitely happening with this Do-It-Yourself Workshop of mine and, whatever it is, it appears to be triggering some sort of early onset of Alzheimer's.

But let us forget the unknown past for the moment and keep our attention here in the Sacred Present Moment. Doing our best to *drink our RC Cola.*

Happily our new racecar is a worthy item on which to rest one's consciousness. So handsome, I have to admit, it gives me a false sense of confidence in its racing credentials. So as much as I wish to diminish Mickey's expectations there is something about the fierce competitive appearance of our model racecar that gives me an unreasonable sense of hope.

Anything that looks this good has to be a winner, I tell myself. I have seen enough Hollywood movies to know the good guys—the ones who work hard against all odds—always win in the end.

Of course I cannot remember working hard, or working at all, on Black Beauty. As I said a moment ago it is all a blur to me, the many long hours we obviously spent scraping and sanding and shaping that white block of pine. The painstaking effort we must have taken in applying coat after coat of black paint. And then waiting for it to dry before applying plumes of fire decals on each side. Obviously we must have spent a lot of hours on it because how else could the spirit of such a sexy model racecar have emerged?

Sitting here barely fifteen or twenty feet from the staging area where all our hopes reside in the form of an exquisitely crafted, ebony racecar, it is all I can do to keep from verbalizing exactly what my little boy wants to hear. That today *we will win.* That today we will wipe out all memory of last year's fiasco.

And we can do it. We can win! I have a feeling about things, a good feeling. Pinewood Derbies may come and go in the history of the universe but this one was meant to be special.

Soon of course those feelings will become academic. Soon we will race in our first heat of the morning and, please dear God, score our first victory of the day. And speaking of God, take a look around at our surroundings.

You notice of course that we are in a different church this year. Instead of St. Christina's basement hall we are ensconced within the high white walls of the assembly hall at St. Sebastian's Episcopal Church. To be sure, this is very different from St. Christina's which with its square green linoleum tiles and mint-green semi-gloss walls was more reminiscent of the Department of Motor Vehicles than a Roman Catholic function hall.

St. Sebastian's is a very different species of church: contemporary in styling, fresh in its feel, not yet burdened by decades of use and layers of paint. With all this exposed wood and those heavy timbers running straight up to the cathedral ceiling you get the feeling that up until the final month of the church's construction it could have easily shifted course to become a ski lodge or something supremely more nordic than an Episcopalian church.

I do not think there is anything symbolic in the fact that my ex-wife Marilyn and her boyfriend Lawrence—I still cannot think of him as her fiancé—have recently started to attend services here at St. Sebastian's.

"Come on already!" a tiny voice grumbles.

Mickey has good reason to be wound up and edgy. This is not easy for him, returning to the scene of the crime. Even though he is sitting unusually still, mumbling quietly to himself in mouse-like tones, he is a jumble of chewed up nerves.

I suspect that when I look back at this period in our lives I will see that last year's Pinewood Derby initiated a gradual but steady decline in my little boy's belief in a benevolent and protective universe—nothing less perhaps than the beginning of his fall from innocence.

As I later came to realize, there was far more than a racing trophy at stake at last year's Pinewood Derby. The fact we were pawns in a Karmic Gravitational Slide means the stakes were huge and their impact far reaching. And here we are again standing before this court of harsh realities a year later, once again with far more to win or lose than a mere racing trophy.

If it did not seem so melodramatic I would say that our honor and pride are waiting to be won back today.

But we do not need to win a single race to end up winners this morning. We just need to make it though one whole Pinewood Derby without becoming a public spectacle.

That is not too much to ask.

And nothing too difficult to accomplish.

Do you hear me, God?

Are you even listening?

Lesson 36

Sometimes You Cannot Tell The Teams Apart Without A Program

"Well, well, here we are again, Mr. Peterson! Seems like old times, does it not: you, your son and two hundred cub scouts, all together again? I suppose that is why they call them cub scout 'packs'," the high, thin voice starts to giggle, "because they travel from church to church like nomadic reindeer herds."

For once it seems he and I are going to converse without hovering near the ceiling. And I am thankful for that, given how high the church's vaulted ceiling rises. I do not know if you can tell for yourself but the Bapucharya's voice arises from the inner recesses of my mind this time, which brings him strangely closer to me in both distance and emotion.

My voice, as well, only sounds in the interior of my mind.

"Your Holiness! I was wondering when you would show up again."

"Thank you. And I am so glad to see you, too. You were not expected to be here today."

"Really? Why is that?"

"Oh, for reasons. There are always reasons if you care to look for them. But first tell me why you are here? What is it you are hoping to accomplish?"

His question surprises me.

"We are here to enter the Pinewood Derby, obviously. To try and win, if we can, but at least to compete without looking like clowns or idiots. You remember last year's race...?"

"How could I not remember such an enjoyable movie? I have played it any number of times for my fellow gurus. We often watch reruns on rainy afternoons."

"Yes, well, you may find it humorous, but it was a total

disaster for me and Mickey. That is another reason we are here: to try and undo the damage from last year's Pinewood Derby."

Slightly thrown off balance by his Holiness' apparent surprise at finding us here, I meekly ask, "Is that okay? Is there anything wrong with that?"

"Dear me, young sir, whatever could be wrong! Of course you can come here to try and undo last year's colossal calamity. The universe will let you do almost anything your heart desires. If you wish to come to a Pinewood Derby, come! If you wish to race such a beautiful racing car, race! If you wish to walk upside down on the ceiling, put on your most handsome walking shoes! It is you who decides what you can or cannot do. I am only here as a witness or maybe sometimes, when you need one, a guide."

His words have a curious ring to them.

"I know you are saying something of significance to me in the midst of all your words, Holiness, but I cannot tell what it is."

"Then do not worry about it. I will tell you everything you need to know. That is a promise. But you have still not told me the reason why you are here…?"

"I thought I just did."

"You have told me the surface reason. You have so nicely explained that the sky is blue because molecules in the air scatter blue light from the sun. But why is there a sky at all, or a sun, or an atmosphere capable of sustaining life wrapped so tightly around this ball of a planet? I suspect you have yet to learn the real reasons why you are here this morning, my young friend. But we will see. If the real reasons come to mind, be so kind as to relate what they are."

Not knowing what to say I simply respond, "I will be happy to do that, Holiness." In the next moment, the words, "Because of my father!" ring out in the confines of my mind.

The Bapucharya chuckles.

"See how quickly you can learn things when you try! I have always thought you were a bright young man. But what is it you are saying about your father…?"

"It just came to me, (with someone's help, no doubt) that the main reason—the *real* reason—I have done a number of strange things this last year is because of my father. I thought I was doing them for Mickey—going to the dance, seeking out Ms. Pratt, going back to her apartment—the whole multiple choice catastrophe. But I was really doing it for myself. I see that clearly now. Intuitively, I must have thought that helping Mickey with his problems would help me with mine. What else was my determination to end Ms. Pratt's yelling but a symbolic effort to silence the memory of my father's yelling? A sound that still haunts me."

"Yes, yes, young sir, I see what you mean," The Bapucharya replies with growing interest. "Being here in your mind, I can hear your father yelling even now. And your mother too! I hope they do not yell so loud they disturb our cub scout neighbors," he concludes, falling off into hyena-like titters once again.

I am not surprised he hears both of my parents yelling. Though my father's temper tantrums were more common in our house, my mother contributed her share to the general volume of discord.

One night in bed when I was no older than Mickey is now, and probably younger, I remember listening to both of them fighting in the kitchen. My father shouting in a voice so filled with disrespect it was close to ridicule, while my mother, holding her own, fought back with a tongue every bit as sharp and vicious.

Our kitchen was situated right in the middle of our small Brooklyn apartment, not fifteen feet from my bedroom door, so there was no escaping an argument of such fierce dimensions.

" ... just worry about yourself and the kids," I heard my father angrily warn my mother. "My business is none of your business."

"Oh yeah?" my mother, always the Hungarian Jew, questioned. "Your business is none of my business? Who the hell gives you the right to piss away our money on cards and horses? Mr. Big Shot! And then you tell me it's none of my business? Hah! Does God give you special privileges I don't know about?"

"Oh, tell your story walking!" he snapped back, his words sharply edged with disdain.

"Better you should give me that money now!" my mother resolutely demanded.

"Woman...!" my father warned.

"Don't give me that shit. I want it NOW!"

"You go to hell!"

"That's where you're sending us—to hell or the poorhouse. Such a good provider! You make my stomach turn."

"Stop bitching already. Other wives make do with less—a lot less! You're just like your goddamn mother."

"Who the hell are you to tell me about my mother? Her husband was a drunk and a gambler; you're just a stupid fool who gambles. And some wonderful father!—who pisses away his children's food money!"

"Kiss my ass..."

"Son of a bitch-bastard!

All the while I lay in bed trying to shut out the sounds, the blanket over my head proving an ineffective barrier against the angry reach of their voices. Even when the front door slammed behind my father like a minor explosion, the silence that remained was punctuated by those same voices continuing their argument inside my head for another ten minutes at least.

Or maybe it lasted for hours, I am not really sure.

Listening to me talk about him now, it would be easy to believe my father was a volatile, self-centered despot. And he was! But the truth, just like my father, turns out to be more complicated on closer inspection.

At times Dad was actually likable, a pleasant enough fellow. He could even be enjoyable to be around if he was in the right mood or frame of mind. How else could he have been so successful as a salesman? He smiled a lot, spoke easily with strangers and was always interested in things around him.

Still no matter how friendly my father might be—even friendly with us!—I was always aware of this invisible line drawn in the sand which, once you stepped over it, immediately brought the devil out from the back room. Then my father's face would turn red, his right eyebrow would rise up in biblical rage, and he would grow sarcastic or shout or give you the back of his hand with righteous conviction.

No matter where you were or with whom.

The circumstances of your situation never protected you from my father's anger when he was sufficiently aroused. That memorable moment in The Shanghai Gardens comes quickly to mind but there were countless other moments when we were out in public or at one of my relatives' apartments when the devil in my father was sufficiently aroused to come out from the back room screaming.

It was not until I started therapy that I realized how off-balance my father's volatility had kept me during my childhood years. That constant threat of danger—and humiliation—was never far from my thoughts, never forgotten when he was around. It was like living in a large room with a dangerous snake: the tension was constant no matter how far away you managed to keep yourself.

No wonder I have been angry at my father since my earliest childhood. No wonder I am still angry today more than twenty years after he did me the kindness of passing away.

I know, I know. What a way to talk about your father.

In therapy I saw...learned really...how much I...that I actually...

"What is wrong, Mr. Peterson?"

"Nothing is wrong, Holiness. I am just taking a breath. This is not something I find easy to talk about."

Notice how my breathing has grown labored and my voice is starting to crack? That is how difficult it is for me to say some things; to express certain words even in my mind, but the truth is...*I hated my father.*

And even that is not right. I am still avoiding the truth. Let me try again.

I hate my father.

If it is difficult to say those words imagine how hard it was to accept their reality? But there it was in therapy staring me straight in the face: I hated my father. I hated the memory of how harsh and degrading his voice felt when he was angry. I hated the burning look in his eyes and the way his eyebrow would arch in outrage when you unknowingly stepped across some unseen line, innocently tripping some hidden, emotional tripwire.

I hated the way he behaved toward us — toward my

brother, sister and mother. But most of all I hated the way he treated me.

Harsh, overly critical, cruelly unfair at times, never able to see me for who I was, my father was a petty despot. Reliving all that in therapy I discovered, not surprisingly, that his outrages against me had transformed him into a villain in my memory instead of a father.

Recently things have shifted so that now, strangely enough, even though I may have difficulty expressing it in words the idea of hating my father actually brings me some comfort.

"Really?" The Bapucharya interrupts. "That is big-time interesting to me, young sir. Please tell me why you are so comforted by your feelings of hate toward your father?"

"It means I care enough about myself not to accept that kind of bullshit anymore. Not from my father or anyone else. Do you not agree that is a healthy sign?"

"If you say so, Mr. Peterson. I am a very agreeable person. Remember, I have told you so before."

And speaking of inappropriate behavior, I find it quite interesting and coincidental that all these years later I am trying in my ridiculously circuitous fashion to curtail someone else's yelling. My son's fourth-grade teacher, no less.

"Oh my, yes, it is certainly curious! Old Man Universe must stay up nights thinking up ways to balance off the craziness of your life with the craziness of everyone else's life."

If I am honest with myself I must admit my reaction—perhaps over-reaction—to Ms. Pratt's yelling was programmed in me more than thirty-five years ago. Perhaps at the very moment I was lying under the covers hearing the angry voices of my parents going back and forth in my head. How else to explain the overly-romantic nature of my gesture? Hunting down my son's teacher on the dance floor of a singles dance! Something you might expect from an adolescent who reads too many adventure stories but not from a middle-aged father of three!

Why else would I have gone to the dance in Plymouth and acted out a role more suited to a TV sitcom father than the real variety?

"You know why!" The Bapucharya declares.

"No, I do not!"

"Oh yes, my young friend, you do!" The Bapucharya insists. "Now tell yourself the answer so it will not be lost."

Resisting the impulse to continuing arguing I ask instead, "You mean that the ten year old child in me caused the 45 year old man to act so childishly?"

"Yes, that is a good start! And what else...?"

"What else? I do not know anything else, Holiness, except of course the obvious surface level motivations...?"

"Please to remember I am the wise man and you are the common, everyday lost pilgrim who is stumbling and struggling on the Path Of Seeking Truth. And I am telling you there is one thing more about your father you already know but have not yet discovered you know. Otherwise, you are doing quite well in your Do-It-Yourself Workshop.

"So now, Mr. Peterson, ask yourself what have we been saying concerning your father...?"

"About he and I being *Karmic Companions?"*

"Yes, and...?"

"About his humiliating me in public? Punishing me in front of total strangers? Is that what you mean?"

"Yes, and now ask yourself what lesson would be most ironic and humorous for you to assist your father in learning? If the tables were turned and he were the child and you the upside-down adult? Assuming, of course, he would be lucky enough to fall under your tender guidance...?" His words trail off once again into fractious childlike giggling.

My answer comes out of me with surprising certainty.

"How it feels to be humiliated...? Is that what you are suggesting?"

"I am not suggesting anything, I only ask questions. You are the one who has given yourself the answers. Except you have not yet answered the biggest question."

"Which question is that, Holiness?"

"Who on your *ILE* have you consistently, repeatedly and, oh-so-painfully instructed on the consequences of being publicly humiliated? Can you think of one human being who, even against your deepest desires and strongest efforts, you have been giving such instruction?"

"Are you saying...?" I start, suddenly seeing where he is

leading with this. "Are you suggesting that Mickey...?"

"Again, you accuse me of making suggestions! I am not making anything. I am asking the questions, you are making the suggestions."

"I see," I reply softly and fall into silence.

Surprisingly enough The Bapucharya remains silent as well.

But why not? There is nothing more to say right now. At this moment I need to think, to sit quietly and mull over the impact of what he has just said and what I have just discovered or uncovered on my *ILE.*

My father and Mickey?

Can it be true, I ask myself? Do I correctly understand what The Bapucharya is saying? Is this the realization he was leading me toward? That there is some Karmic Connection between my father and my son? A Karmic Connection between someone I have come to hate and someone I unhesitatingly love? Between the individual who most shaped my fears and the child whose fears and sensitivities I feel most protective of?

If this were true it would be almost schizophrenic. *Karmic Schizophrenia* The Seekers would probably call it! A Karmic Connection that transcends so much—time and space, the limits of physical bodies, three generations of my family, and the logic of my personal history! It is all too weird to contemplate. But still...

Could they be...?

"Holiness," I say, breaking my silence, "are both my father and Mickey somehow my *Karmic Companions?"*

"Interesting question, young sir! And since you ask it," he laughs, "I will give you an answer. No and yes!"

I wait a beat, letting his answer echo in the silence, then comment dryly, "Very helpful, Holiness! How am I supposed to understand that? 'No and yes?'"

"Maybe no," he giggles, "and maybe yes."

As the bubbles of laughter subside he repeats, *"Maybe no, and maybe yes!"* reigniting the fires of his mirth and his giggles.

But finally after a few moments he brings himself under some semblance of control, emitting brief words of apology in staccato bursts.

"So sorry. Please...my apologies, young sir. This is not good. So sorry."

Assuming a serious voice he explains, "Again, I am apologizing for my jocularity. Explaining Karma is not always *easy-does-it*, you understand. Not even for a guru."

"Okay," I respond. "Would you please, then, just tell me if my father and son are my *Karmic Companions?"*

"The answer is 'No and yes' just as I was telling you. *No,* they are not your Karmic Companions, but, *yes,* together they make up a single Karmic Companion. You see, my friend, they come as a set," he says, pausing to restrain a few light titters, "buy one, get one free."

"I still do not understand."

"The Absolute Scorekeeper insists on having rules to the Game, and since Mickey is the reincarnation of your father he cannot be officially counted as a separate Karmic Companion. So, together they make up *one* Karmic Companion split into two embodiments. What I am often naming..."

"One and a half *Karmic Companions!"* I call out, finishing his thought and finally understanding the fractional concept that had earlier so confused and eluded me.

"Yes, indeed...and still one to go!" he merrily concludes. "What we shall call the cherry on top of the cupcake!"

"And one to go," I repeat, counting off in my head, "Marilyn is one, Dad and Mickey together make one and a half, and there is still one more out there—for a grand total of three and a half *Karmic Companions."*

I have no way of judging what that means of course, but does it not seem like a small number of *Karmic Companions* for an entire lifetime? Before I voice the question, however, The Bapucharya is already setting me straight.

"That is plenty enough, Mr. Peterson," he assures me. "Oh boy, anymore *Karmic Companions* in the recipe and you could not fit the ingredients into the pie plate! But see how very quick a learner you have become? One moment you know nothing about these puzzles, the next you are already making suggestions about which pieces are belonging in which holes. Do you not think that is funny?"

"Yes, very funny," I halfheartedly respond, searching for

some underlying logic to all of this. "... but if I only knew what it was supposed to mean, Holiness?

"Maybe if I were to learn the identity of my last *Karmic Companion...?*" I venture, uncertain what difference that could make.

Lifting my head as if to look for an answer I find myself staring across the room, but it is a room no longer filled with cub scouts or Episcopalian artifacts, but rather strange-appearing men and women who move around in the dark like anxious shoppers running out of money. We have shifted, without my even realizing it, to the next stop in my Do-It-Yourself Workshop. More likely of course The Bapucharya has done the shifting for me. Somehow I know his ancient spirit is still with me as my eyes wander across the crowded room, drawn by a force too compelling to resist. Suddenly I find myself staring through the crowd into the eyes of a tall, attractive woman who once might have won my heart had the disintegration of my marriage not caused such high walls to be built around that defenseless organ.

I smile and move my lips in a voiceless greeting.

"Hi Ellie!"

Even from this distance, standing on the other side of the room, she looks very good, does she not? A beautiful woman and very desirable.

Do you not agree?

"I agree, I agree. I am a very agreeable spirit, as I have mentioned any number of times. But—ohmigoodness, young sir—is that your *PuNDit* I hear, or mine...?"

"Mine, Holiness," I answer matter-of-factly, as if the excited and noisy throbbing was to be expected. "It is merely a chemical reaction."

"I am thinking it sounds more like spontaneous combustion?" The Bapucharya replies, his high pitched laughter rising up in merry abandon.

A moment later I find that I am laughing, too.

Chemical reaction?

The Bapucharya is right. It appears I am finally developing a sense of humor.

Lesson 37

One Last Dance With The Devil Before The Band Goes Home

I may be staring at Ellie Eichorn but I am still in the company of Allison Platt and together we are about to walk out of the dance at the Plymouth Marriott on this memorable night of our first meeting.

"Just give me a moment," I tell Allison, holding up five fingers. "I have to see someone about something. Let us meet by the coatroom. In five minutes?"

"Yes," Allison Pratt says, mimicking my voice pattern. "Let us do that. Five minutes. Let us be there!"

That *someone* I mentioned is the same someone I have been avoiding for most of the evening. But earlier words of The Bapucharya—about speaking the truth—refuse to leave my mind or leave me in peace. So even though I am ready to exit the dance with Allison Pratt I am not able to forget what my invisible guru said or to leave without acting upon it.

As Allison goes off to find the ladies room I begin the fifty foot walk towards Ellie who has not moved an inch since her eyes drew me back to the Plymouth Marriott from the far distant realms of next year's Pinewood Derby.

Can you see her? I am sure you must. She is so tall you cannot easily miss her, not even in a crowd. See her head sticking up above the others?

And such a beautiful head it is!

Oh, I like this song. Do you perhaps recognize it?

"Never Thought I'd Lose You," by Mary Mack. A sad song about lovers losing each other, but nevertheless a romantic song and good for slow dancing.

So here I am suddenly frozen in place and afraid to do anything but stare into Ellie's fiery eyes. She is so angry with me there is no telling what she might say or do.

I start to softly speak Ellie's name but something strange happens and the words "Would you like to dance?" stumble out instead.

Ellie turns around abruptly, startled by my voice, only to be startled a second time when she sees me standing here, no sign of sarcasm or mockery in evidence.

She screws up her eyes to ask, "What was that you said?" The gravelly voice that so easily ignites my fire is now laced with distrust.

"Did I hear you correctly?" she asks.

I keep my cheerful look and answer, "I would like to talk with you a moment so I asked if you wanted to dance. I think you heard correctly."

Deep rows of wrinkles run across her forehead.

"Talk about what?" she asks suspiciously.

"The truth."

She leans her head to one side as if weighing the risks then shrugs with a comical expression. "The truth," she exclaims, cautiously opening her arms to me, "That I'd like to hear!"

So with Mary Mack softly crooning, *"Never in a lifetime, did I think I'd let you go,"* I step into Ellie's arms and take full possession of this tall, attractive woman who, in a feeble attempt to protect myself, I have lied to and wronged in the most childish and thoughtless way.

"I need to say a few things," I declare staring into her face, "then you can say whatever you want. I also need to tell you that I am leaving here in five minutes with a woman who is my son's fourth grade teacher."

"Mickey's fourth grade...?"

"Just let me finish! I came here tonight to find this woman so I could talk to her about a problem in Mickey's class without sounding like an angry parent. It is probably one of the dumbest things I have ever done as a father, but it is already in motion and I am too far down the ramp to pull back the boat."

Amused as always by my metaphors, Ellie remarks, "Honey, you do talk in riddles. You know that?"

"I know, I know, but let me finish. I want to tell you

something and it will not be easy to say. So let me speak and then you can make comments. Agreed?"

"Agreed," she sighs wearily.

"Good!" I nod. "First, that 'chemistry' thing was pure bullshit; you knew that. It was the first thing that came to my mind and it was so far from the truth it was laughable. If we had any stronger chemistry we would be a fire hazard whenever we are in the same room together. I just said that because…well, I did not have the guts to tell you the truth. "

"Uh-oh, now I'm getting nervous," she declares. Then adds, "I'm not sure I really want to hear this. You think it'll make me feel bad?"

"That I cannot say," I reply. "But I do know I was trying to make us feel better before and accomplished exactly the opposite, muddying up everything including my feelings…"

"You can take a lifetime to love the one you find. But never regret the one you leave behind."

"Just so you know," I continue, "you do not have to listen to any of this. You can stop dancing at any moment and walk away. But if you stay, I am going to tell you the truth."

After a moment's silence she replies, "Well, I'm still here."

Not wanting to lose momentum or to keep Allison Pratt waiting I press ahead, "You know that I like you, right? I mean, *really* like you! Not only that but, quite frankly, that you turn me on; I mean *really* turn me on!"

"Hallelujah for the truth!" she laughs with a gleeful look that happily remains in place after the laugh subsides.

"Yes, well…if you remember, I once started to tell you about this weird built-in alarm system I have; the one that goes off whenever I get over-excited? *My PuNDit?* Remember, you laughed at me, said it was all in my mind and not in my forehead…?"

"I remember, sort of."

"Whether you remember it or not, its formal name is the Prophetic Navigational Device..."

"Oh yes, I remember!" she suddenly declares. "You were telling me about some mystic clown: Boppo, or Bopo…?"

"Careful," I warn, suddenly nervous. "You never know who is listening. I was speaking about The Bapucharya and he is a fully realized Hindu Holy Man—anything but a mystic clown."

"Well, whatever," she replies, unconvinced. "What is the point?"

"I was talking about my *PuNDit*," I continue. "Well, I cannot begin to describe the panic it is experiencing right now, this very moment, having you in my arms again, smelling your perfume, just feeling you near me. It is causing my *PuNDit* to sound off nuclear-levels of alarm and concern!"

"Hmm-hmm!" Ellie laughs to herself. Then adjusting her grip around my neck, softly purrs, "It feels pretty good to me, too," referring no doubt to certain parts of my body that are starting to express their own state of heightened agitation.

Ignoring all these distractions, with Mary Mack confiding that *"a lifetime can take eternity, if love goes out the door,"* I continue, "But I had to stop seeing you. I could not go on with our relationship the way it was."

"But why?" Ellie asks, pulling back to look in my eyes. "What happened, Honey? What did I do that was so wrong it made you stop wanting to see me?"

This is where the ground under my feet becomes steep, the boulder I push grows large and heavy.

Steeling myself for her explosive reaction I nevertheless confide, "To tell you the truth, I felt like I was being used, taken for a ride. I am not your husband, nor Ricky's father, and there is no way I can afford to pretend otherwise. You seemed to expect me to pay for everything, as if I was a drunken sailor or a well-heeled boyfriend. The truth is I am not well off. I make a good living but it is mostly accounted for, keeping up two living situations. How can I afford to always pay for your meals, for Ricky's babysitter and for all of our dates? I do not have that kind of money, Ellie; it is as simple as that. If I spend my money on you and Ricky, that means I will not have it to spend it on my own children. And that is something I will not..."

"Oh jeeze!" she whispers to herself, gasping.

"Are you all right?" I ask.

Smiling weakly, she recovers enough to tell me, "I'm fine, Honey, really! Go on, finish what you were saying."

"I tried to tell you this any number of times, Ellie, but

you always seemed not to listen, or not to hear. Anyway, I finally felt desperate; like the only choice you left me was to start robbing convenience stores or to give up our relationship. I only wished I had had the courage to tell you this before—earlier! I know how painful it must have seemed, how hurtful it must have felt, for me to just walk off, and all I can say is that I am sorry—truly sorry—that I waited this long to tell you the truth."

I look at Ellie and surprisingly she seems relieved.

"And that's it?" she says in disbelief. "That's why you stopped seeing me? That's the reason; the only reason?"

"Yes, it is. You speak like it was no big deal, but to me it was huge and very important. A very big deal!"

She shakes her head, releasing the tension with a broken laugh, then turns to look squarely in my face.

"Hats off to you, honey! I can't tell you what a relief it is to hear the truth. You don't know how dark things have been for me since you left. I thought it was me, or my looks, or that I wasn't desirable enough. I just didn't know what to think, and it felt so *yucky.*"

"That you were not desirable enough?" I repeat, almost shocked. "What you are saying...?"

"I'm saying that you just came through for me, Paul. Big time! You really did; in a way you'll probably never understand. *Phew!* I can't tell you how relieved..."

"Relieved?"

"Oh, yes! I've been so angry and hurt, figuring you got tired of me, or used me, and wondering what was so wrong with me that you couldn't see how I felt?"

"The way you felt...?" I repeat. "What are you saying?"

She leans closer to me, her smile widening even further.

"That I think I love you...whatever that means. That I think I felt it from the first moment you sat down in front of me, next to that salesman with the big mouth and the little mind."

"Bill McAndrews?"

"You do waste a lot of time trying to clarify every fucking point in a conversation!" she comments with a rough laugh. "Anyway, forget all that and give me another chance. Would you do that? Give me another chance?

"This money thing doesn't matter, honey. Honestly! So what if we can't afford to go out because I'm so fucking broke! That's what being married to an angry millionaire does to you; it makes you manipulate people you love, all because of money. Either you have so much you can't help wanting more, or you don't have a miserable penny in your pocket. But the hell with all that…!"

Breaking into her angry reflections, she softly asks, "Can we give it one more try, Honey? What do you say?" Notice how her voice has slid into that deeper and sexier range of her gravelly inflection? "What do you think; can we try again? And see what happens?"

"Try again?" I question with a serious frown.

Now it is my turn to lean into her; so close I can smell the floral scent of her soap. My lips brushing against her face, I whisper, "Try again? Is that what you want? I guess it all depends…"

"Depends?" she picks up. "On what?"

I pause before answering.

"Well, for one thing, what color panties are you wearing?"

She laughs into my ear.

A breathless moment later she purrs back, "Panties? What panties?"

"I cannot think of a more perfect answer," I whisper. "I will call you tomorrow. Probably early in the morning."

My lips brush against her cheek then find their way over to her grinning mouth.

"This is as much fun as I remember," I softly remark.

She murmurs her agreement, darting her tongue into my mouth while I idly wonder if this is what the truth is supposed to taste like?

In the background as we search out each other's tongues and hearts, still dancing, Mary Mack softly and soulfully reminds us, "*… yes, my sweet, Heaven meant for us to meet. Let the devil make his fuss, to see how happy two of us—can live as one.*

"Never thought I'd lose you until our love was done.

"Never thought I'd lose you until we both were one."

Funny how that song always makes me sad.

Even now.

Lesson 38

Think Twice Before You Play With Chalk On The Streets Of Brooklyn

"We're next, dad!" a voice announces, instantly pulling me out of the dance and back to the Pinewood Derby. My *second* Pinewood Derby.

I suddenly reconnect with the buzz of noise and activity that surrounds us in St. Sebastian's Episcopal Church. Instinctively looking over to the staging area I find that Mickey is indeed correct: our shiny black racecar is one of three cars in a row lined up for the next heat.

"Ready to rock?" I ask, giving him a confident thumbs up that hardly reflects the ambivalence of my feelings.

I know, I know! Just moments ago I told you this was going to be a very special occasion for us; that this Pinewood Derby would champion our cause and redeem last year's disastrous efforts. But now as we move ever closer to the moment of truth I am not so sure.

Have I made another mistake, I wonder? Could this Pinewood Derby end up just as badly as last year's?

No that is not possible.

We could lose of course but there is no way we will be humiliated or embarrassed like we were last year.

Last year my big mistake was creating a Frankenstein racecar and bringing it to the races. This year we have brought Black Beauty to this annual cub scout event and even if it does not win a single heat it is a gorgeous piece of craftsmanship.

You do find it beautiful, do you not?

No the worst I may have done this year is to create a monster out of Mickey's expectations. And that will not leave us standing in public with our underpants figuratively hanging on a line.

More likely of course, I am making a big deal out of nothing!

"Ready to roll!" Mickey answers enthusiastically, his thumb pointing to the heights of the cathedral ceiling.

“Then lets rock and roll!” I exclaim with false bravado.

She was ready to rock and roll too.

Ms. Pratt I mean...

The act of thinking about Allison Pratt again, perhaps even mentally intoning her name, seems to create a sense of inner movement, stimulating activity throughout my mental intersection and causing faces and scenes from my Do-It-Yourself Workshop to flash across my mind, one after another, like a movie montage.

And now St. Sebastian’s Church with all its cub scouts and Pinewood Derby hysteria is beginning to fade away at the edges.

We are leaving.

How strange! No sooner have I moored at this particular Do-It-Yourself Workshop lesson than I am off once again...

Or so it seems.

And I can feel things quickening, with images briefly flashing across my mental movie screen as if the events in my Do-It-Yourself Workshop were speeding up, moving faster, drawn with increasing pull towards some nearing conclusion.

I suddenly realize what is happening.

The Hour Glass Effect!

The Seekers For Truth believe that time, as it plays out in most of our movies, is elastic and can speed up or slow down depending on certain prevailing circumstances. With the Hour Glass Effect time actually speeds up or seems to pass more quickly when we are approaching the end of a cycle or a lifespan. Just as the sands in an hour glass appear to fall faster in the final moments of the passing hour. Or the way one’s days seems to pass more quickly the older one gets, till finally in the last years of your life they appear to pass by in blur.

The Hour Glass Effect.

I cannot claim to fully understand any of this but I have

been told that we each have a limited allotment of *Prarabdha,* a Hindu term for the actual life substance we are given to spend on our *ILE,* which once it is gone forces us to move on to the next embodiment on our next *ILE.*

In the typical funhouse mirror effect the universe seems to enjoy, this running-out-of-Prarabdha experience occurs for all 'living' entities, which includes corporations, mass movements, Asian flu epidemics, even empires and civilizations. In each newborn entity is embedded the agents for its destruction and, to finally get to my point, that moment of annihilation is usually heralded by what the Seekers call the Hour Glass Effect.

My guess is that we are witnessing the final moments of my Do-It-Yourself Workshop, which in its own way is an organic, living entity, even though its movement through time is so helter-skelter.

Or so it seems.

If we are nearing the end of my Do-It-Yourself Workshop, much still needs to be done because I do not feel even the slightest bit close to reaching some insight or understanding. Do you?

I do not mean to jerk you around like a monkey on a string but I would like to return immediately to the evening of the dance, the night Allison and I first met. I know, I know. We have only just come from there. That is true but it does not matter. I need to take a closer look at a few things concerning my *Karmic Companions.*

And I have to do it now!

My memories are strangely vague about that night, just as they are about all the months that followed. Once again my recollection seems to be failing me as if I had slept through large chunks of my life.

It is very strange.

But nothing we need worry about.

And so even as the last vestiges of the Cub Scout Pinewood Derby—our second Pinewood Derby—continue to fade from sight, I close my eyes...and let the noise and commotion fall away into silence as I climb to that inner place which seems so high and removed from everything else below.

Here on the mountaintop almost at the exact *Center*

Point of the Universe things look strangely off-center or different than they did before. Not as substantial somehow.

You see what I mean?

Whatever the reason, something is different about the way the events in my life appear; something I cannot put my finger on as I search out that evening in Plymouth which appears to have a special glow all its own.

It comes to me now that nothing is ever quite as you expect it to be. Not life as it appears on the surface nor life as it evolves in its hidden mysterious ways. You fool yourself into believing that the mostly familiar movements of people, ideas and events you encounter each day—the principal ingredients of your GUM, your Great Unrevealed Mystery—are not only real but the essence of what life is all about.

The whole megillah as my Hungarian mother would call it!

How ironic then that we have spun ourselves around completely and turned our backs on the *real* reality. That we have let ourselves believe this non-stop TV show we watch all day is in fact the texture, the breadth and the carefully mixed ingredients of our lives. When the truth is so much larger!

Excuse the scatological metaphor but a memory from when I was an innocent two-year-old comes back to me now. I was playing on the streets of Brooklyn one afternoon when I saw the largest piece of chalk I had ever seen just lying in the street. Oh wow, I thought, what a find! In an instant I broke my mother's rule against stepping off the sidewalk and went into the street to retrieve that fabulous piece of chalk. Well the chalk was not so fabulous and did not actually work very well, as it turned out. It was crumbly and only scratched out a thin wispy line. But who could complain about such gifts when they were left for free, like an offering from Heaven, on the streets of Brooklyn?

The stick of chalk quickly crumbled to pieces in my hand but there were other chalk sticks to replace it, also left by some benevolent deity in the gutters of Brooklyn.

For the next ten minutes or so I did nothing but enliven the sidewalks of Brooklyn with crumbly chalk drawings; you can imagine what they looked like. I could have gone on like that all afternoon, I suppose, but my big brother Henry came by to check on me. And when he found me enrapt in my sidewalk drawings he asked a question that rudely yanked me from my childish fantasies.

"Paul," he inquired with his nose scrunched in disdain, "what are you doing with that dried piece of dog shit?"

And thus in an instant my chalk had been given a new name, its reality had completely shifted and I was left holding a large, ossified dog turd in my hand instead of the fabulous gift of chalk that the universe had sent my way.

And that is how I feel right now.

After years of living my day-to-day life as if it were the totality of my existence, The Bapucharya has come along and asked me, quite pointedly, "Mr. Peterson, what are you doing with that dried piece of dog shit in your hands?"

"What?" I exclaim in disbelief. "This is not reality? This is not really the fullness of life, these children that I love, the ex-wife I feel privileged to detest, the career that chafes and confines me like a suit two sizes too small? All that is just a dried turd of dog shit I have been revering and honoring as my complete and exclusive life all these years?"

And then of course it dawns on me...

The Seekers were telling the truth!

And that shakes me to my very foundation. Because once you realize the truth and feel it in your bones you are never the same afterwards. To suddenly see that most days as you go about the business of life you are merely standing on a small stage acting out the contents of someone else's dream makes you realize how frighteningly large the real universe must be. And rather than turn around and look at what awaits you backstage at the universe—talk about frightening!—you almost prefer to go on believing that the dream is real.

But enough soul-searching. It is time to go back to the beginning, to where this Do-It-Yourself Workshop first began under the impetus of Allison Pratt dragging me across her living room rug toward that brown velveteen couch.

Relax. And let everything else go.

Release all the tension, worries, plans and regrets back into the universal flow. All thoughts, ideas, fears and goals as well. Release them to the flow from whence they came. And just relax.

Remember to squeeze the Root Chakra if you need a squirt of *HW-40*—Higher Will—to lubricate your efforts.

Now come to rest in the stillness of the center of the circle. On the topmost point of the mountain. In the absolute perfection of the Sacred Present Moment.

Come to rest.

Now open your eyes, Mr. Peterson.

And here I am...back in the darkened confines of the now familiar second floor apartment, under the weakening spell of a wine-strengthened madwoman who is still intent on dragging me onto a brown couch covered in worn-away velveteen fabric and gray dog hairs.

"I have been waiting for you, young sir," a familiar voice greets me.

Hovering once again near the ceiling, above the people and furniture in Allison's darkened living room, I reply in soft, hushed tones, "I came here as soon as I could, Holiness."

"Yes, I am sure that is true, but still I cannot help being over-anxious. This is such an exciting part of your movie," he laughs. "The part where the hero is finally brought to the climax and we finally get to see what will happen at last!"

"I do not know about that, Holiness, but I do know that I am starting to rebel against whatever part of me seems so willing to be pushed around by this crazed and drunken woman. It sounds silly to say it, but I think I have been hypnotized by Allison Pratt's breasts."

"Not so silly, young sir; it is true. Very true. You *have* been hypnotized, but not necessarily by those particular pineapples, as you so fondly think of them. In the curious workings of your Mental Center, these breasts have become surrogates for others that once, long ago, totally mesmerized you. The same breasts your mother so cruelly held back when you were just a tiny infant. That much I have learned from your Dr. Rivers.

"You see, Mr. Peterson, *it is all connected!* That is the beauty of the entire creation; it is all one big ball of string tied into 6 billion knots!

"What your mother did to you is tied directly to what you

have done to so many others on your *ILE*. And do not forget your father! I could so easily write a book about you and your father! It would not be a bestseller, but it would be much easier to follow than 'War and Peace' and probably take as long to read." Again he pauses to allow a thin stream of giggles to permeate the solemn air.

"Laugh, young sir, while you still have the chance! Do not let thoughts about life get in the way of living. Enjoy what is directly in front of you. This fine teacher of fourth grade children has much to offer; there are depths and twists you would never expect."

"You could say that, I guess."

"Yes, of course, that is exactly what I am saying! To look at Ms. Pratt now you would find her almost comically insignificant, except of course for her bosoms. But earlier at the restaurant with three glasses of wine freshly poured into her Physical and Mental Centers she was beginning to climb out of her shell, and ohmigoodness! she certainly made me nervous, but then I have seen the movie's ending."

"You exaggerate just a little, do you not?"

"Yes, that is true, young sir. It is a defect of my personality, I am saddened to say. Not something I would chose for myself, but even Bapucharyas must learn to live with such defects.

"But look for yourself! You decide how much I exaggerate and how much she would be a caution to anyone who watches your movie."

Before I can start questioning The Bapucharya—before I can utter a single word—I sense the substance of my surroundings starting to dissipate as if the physical reality of Allison's living room, including Allison herself, were made up of thin wispy clouds that are breaking up and being whisked away on a breeze.

A clear sign we are moving to a new venue.

"But Holiness!" I protest. "I only just got here. What is happening to me? Why can we not stay in any one place more than a few moments? I thought we were finally going to let this drama play itself out...?

"Shhh," The Bapucharya responds, "I am trying to listen!"

Lesson 39

Never Let A Fourth Grade Teacher Drink More Than Three Glasses Of Wine

"Can you hear that?" The Bapucharya asks, almost in a whisper.

"What?" I ask back. "The noise in the restaurant?"

"No, no," He answers, annoyed. "I know you can hear the noise in the restaurant. I am talking about the absence of noise? Can you hear *that?*"

We are in one of those synthetic Mexican restaurants that years ago, when they were in vogue, multiplied across the American landscape like love-starved rabbits. Most have gone out of business or back to Mexico, but this one, obviously a survivor, occupies a beautifully restored 2-story firehouse in downtown Plymouth. Its walls, banisters and partitions, most of which date back to the firehouse's 19th century origins, are all carved and constructed from a creamy yellow oak.

Allison and I came here directly from the dance at the Plymouth Marriott and will shortly leave, with Allison in a state of slightly altered consciousness, for her nearby second floor apartment.

But for now, hovering high near the room's elevated ceiling, The Bapucharya and I stare down at Allison and myself seated in the rear of the restaurant's second story, not too far from a firehouse slidepole whose surrounding round hole is blocked with a plexiglass safety shield.

Attempting to hear The Bapucharya's "absence of noise" I am rewarded with the normal sounds of a busy restaurant.

"You are confusing me again, Holiness. How can I hear the absence of noise? It is like asking a blind man if he sees a tree."

"You are more right than you know, Mr. Wise Guy. Blind people see many things; certainly more things than you realize. And I would not be oh-so-surprised if one of them is walking toward a tree and decides to change his direction.

"But I was asking you about the absence of noise. You cannot hear it, then?"

"Uh…no!"

"Well, have no fear; you will, very shortly."

"I will? Why? What do you mean?"

"I mean we are coming to the end of the movie. The absence of sound is what we hear while the credits are running."

"I still do not understand, Holiness. You say the movie is ending—which movie?"

"Your movie, young sir. Your Do-It-Yourself Workshop, your story, your journey, your tennis match—call it what you will, it is coming to an end."

You can imagine how I feel listening to him, though I do not understand what he means or even believe he means what he says. Trying to follow The Bapucharya is more often an art than a science since much of what he says is usually riddled with jokes, misleading comments and *non sequiturs.*

For someone dedicated to the truth, his statements are amazingly unreliable.

So I make up my mind not to let him disrupt my composure, knowing he will be clear about things when he is ready to be clear and not a moment sooner. Till then I can do little more than puzzle over the meaning of his cryptic remarks and make every effort to *drink my RC Cola.*

Yes *drink my RC Cola!* In this case let my consciousness rest on Allison Pratt who I am now looking at from across the table. Her head slightly swaying she looks back at me with an unsteady cast in her eyes. Periodically those eyes travel jerkily from her half-drained glass of red wine to my fully focused hazel brown eyes.

I would like to *drink my RC Cola* but I am plagued instead by questions I would like to ask The Bapucharya.

These questions—so many questions—keep rising to the surface of consciousness like bars of Ivory Soap in a sudsy bath. Questions about *Karmic Companions,* Karmic Gravitational Slides, the meaning of life and, especially, the meaning of The Bapucharya's apparent intention to establish a home-away-from-home on my *ILE*.

You would think I was somebody important, someone about to play in The Big Game or the Superbowl, as he likes to call it. Or that something extraordinary was going on in my life. But aside from being in a restaurant with my son's slightly tipsy fourth grade teacher, my life is as ordinary, dull and devoid of higher consciousness as the next guy's.

In the midst of all these questions an unrelated thought commands my attention.

"That is your third glass of wine, is it not?" I ask, realizing I should be paying more attention to this woman on the other side of the table.

"Is it not?" she mimics me. "It is, yes. Yes it is!"

"Well, go easy with that stuff," I warn her. "You are not looking all too steady."

"Three's my limit," she slurs. "But what were we talking about?"

Feigning an interest I do not possess, I remark, "You were telling me what it is like to teach all those young, knowledge-starved creatures? How old are they, nine or ten year's old?"

"Who cares?" she replies with a breezy wave of her hand. "There's not much to tell. I've been doing it for fourteen years and should have stopped after ten. Fourteen minus ten equals a sad and tired teacher. Simple mathematics!"

"Sounds bleak."

"Only when I'm teaching," she remarks lifting her glass and sipping from its dregs. "But, tell me, what do you do?"

"I am in advertising," I say lightly. "I write ads."

"Ooh," she coos, adjusting herself in her chair and eagerly pursing her lips, "anything I would know? Tell me some names! Do you write TV or radio commercials?"

"Occasionally."

"Any I would know? Name some of your clients! Who you've written commercials for?"

"Wayco mattresses...?" I offer. "Ever hear of them?"

"Wayco is the Way To Go!" she replies, singing out the musical tagline.

“Hey! Pretty good!”

Lifting her head and the volume of her voice she continues, "No better price, no better place...Wayco Is The Way To Go!" drawing out the "Go!" just the way our singers do in that god-awful jingle I wish I had never written.

"Not so loud," I shush, indicating the attention we are drawing from neighboring tables. "It is not one of my better musical efforts."

"Well, give me a better one to sing," she says gaily.

Are you starting to see what is happening?

Could it be any more obvious?

Under the influence of a little wine this faded flower of womanhood, ordinarily a shy and quiet violet, is coming out of her shell. The only thing unclear right now is how far out she will crawl.

“Tell me about your ex-boyfriend,” I prod. “What did you say his name was?”

“99-dash-1-4-7-3,” she replies with an impish grin.

“An interesting name.”

“That was his number. You know how they put numbers under your name in those prison photos? Junior was 99-dash-1-4-7-3.”

“Junior?” I repeat thoughtfully. “A noteworthy name in my life. The first kid that ever beat me up was named Junior. He was the super’s kid.”

“What’s a *super* kid?”

“Super’s kid: the son of the building superintendent in the apartment house where we lived. The janitor? To all of us middle class Jewish kids the super’s kids were tough and scary, especially after Junior beat me up. I was only six or seven at the time.”

Returning to the present I inquire, “What was *your* Junior in prison for?”

“Depends on whose word you take,” she says with a suggestive lift of her eyebrows, “Junior’s or the state’s.”

“Well, what was the state’s point of view?”

“Manslaughter.”

“And Junior’s?”

“Self-defense.”

“So, why did you break up with Junior? He sounds like a

pleasant sort of chap."

"Same reason he went to prison."

"Manslaughter?"

"Self-defense."

"I do not think I want to hear anymore about Junior," I admit. "But is he gone now...from your life?"

"Don't worry, sugar. I got a court order and everything. Junior's out of my life for good. He and Rex both! Rex is Junior's German shepherd. A big fucking dog, take my word for it. Now they're both gone—*whoosh,* just like that! And just in time to make room for someone else..." she finishes suggestively.

Her eyes searching out mine, she takes another sip of wine. When she puts down her glass, her other hand comes up to her lips in a motion so smooth it seems as if a pulley might connect one arm to the other.

"Oh dear!" she utters as her fingertips reach her lips. "I forgot to feed Sucky."

"Sucky?" I ask.

"Yes, Sucky!" she replies. "My cat Succotash, poor little fellow."

"You are worried about feeding your cat?" I ask in disbelief. "It is eleven o'clock, even by cat standards that is not very late. What are you so worried about?"

"Easy for you to say," she fires back. "It isn't your cat."

She fingers her empty glass.

"Can we get one more glass of wine, then go?"

"Of course. But we could just as well leave right now, if you want."

She smiles, unaware of the comical effect she creates revealing her teeth which are purple from the wine.

"Wine first, Sucky second," she decides.

Sucky, Allison explains, is a tiger cat who apparently grows quite disturbed and fitful if she is not fed fresh cat food at the appropriate dinner hour. Now that Allie ("Call me 'Allie" she earlier insisted) has remembered Sucky she feels the need to repeat, "She'll be so upset," every few minutes. Adding, "You just don't know" whenever she notices what must be a very skeptical expression staring back at her from across the table.

And that is true of course. I do not know! Nor do I care to know. Let Sucky get upset if she wants. The world will continue to spin.

"It is only a cat!" I tell her, trying to maintain some sense of perspective. "I mean cats do not kill themselves or anything."

For a woman so anxious to leave she certainly takes her time about it; lingering quite thoughtfully, it seems, over her fourth glass of wine. I have an impulse to remind her of her words, “Three’s my limit,” but I do not see the good that would come out of it.

No my strategy, if there is one, is to watch and wait.

Finally after refusing to order her a fifth and final glass of wine I slowly lead her out of the renovated firehouse and toward our cars which are parked on Main Street in downtown Plymouth. Though I am none too certain about Allie’s ability to negotiate the narrow, twisty streets of Plymouth behind the wheel of a car, we have agreed to drive both our cars back to her apartment; she of course taking the lead.

Life being a closet full of unanswered questions, I will probably never find out if Sucky was upset over the lateness of her dinner. Because when we arrive at Allie’s apartment, amazingly without even a near-incident on the near-empty streets, Sucky is nowhere to be seen.

Could she have been so distressed about dinner that she left home, I wonder?

Then again maybe she never came home for dinner in the first place.

After all it *is* Saturday night.

And most of the felines I know are obviously in heat.

Lesson 40

What To Do When You Are Stuck Between A Rock And A Hard Race

"Dad?"
"What?"
"You were off again. Dreaming!"
"Was I?"

"C'mon, Dad. The race is about to start. What were you thinking about anyway?"

"Ms. Pratt," I answer truthfully though I cannot remember anything specific at the moment.

"Good grief!" I say to myself, shocked by the realization that those memory blackouts have returned and I cannot even recall the end of Mickey's fourth grade year. I have forgotten the final few months with Allison as my son's teacher!

How could I forget *all that?*

"Well, keep your eye on Black Beauty," Mickey admonishes me, bringing me back once again to the events at hand. Not surprisingly, Black Beauty is the name we have given to our ebony racecar which, because of last year's tragic events, carries a double burden of our hopes this morning.

Not to mention a double-sized lead weight affixed to her underside!

"Who are we racing against?" I ask, the question arising more from nervousness than any interest in the answer.

"How should I know?" my son answers, too nervous himself to make small talk.

My eyes momentarily travel across the crowd on the other side of the room, slowing down as Ellie's face moves so attractively into the frame. She smiles at me, flapping the fingers of her right hand in a secret little wave. I begin to nod back with a wide grin when suddenly her smile freezes into a grimace and she turns her hand around leaving the middle finger raised by itself in anything but a friendly salute. In shock I watch as she silently mouths the words, "Fuck you."

Now what is that all about?

Last I remember we had patched things up using some pretty steamy cement. Has something happened since then? Something I do not recall or know about? Is that possible?

You remember the conversation she and I had at the dance last spring, the one where my tongue was almost wedged down the length of her throat?

No I am sorry. I could no sooner misremember or lose track of my relationship to this lovely hot fount of sexual inspiration than I could forget my own erect penis!

And besides, she said she loved me! I could not forget that. I will never forget that.

But something is wrong here, something dreadfully wrong.

The familiar sound of high pitched, bubbly laughter breaks into my thoughts.

"You are not the brightest bulb in the lamp, Mr. Peterson, but you have your moments," The Bapucharya chuckles. "Yes, something is wrong, and it could be that much has happened since the last time you remember speaking to this lovely lady."

"Much has happened? What are you talking about? I do not recall *anything* happening! None of this makes sense, Holiness. I cannot remember what I had for breakfast this morning, much less what I said or did to this woman."

"That is true, my young friend, but clearly she is the one who remembers," he points out with much hilarity. "That will have to be sufficient for the present."

This is too much!

"I feel like everything is suddenly all twisted," I complain. "First she loves me, then she hates me, then she loves me again. And now, for no apparent reason, she hates me again. It is a roller coaster ride, Holiness, and I cannot even figure out where to get off."

"No, no, you are taking this all wrong. She did love you and, in an upside-down, grown-up sort of way, her love for you has not lost its seat on the bus. It is just at present covered over with a layer of extreme anger and resentment."

He breaks into laughter then explains, "... you do have a way with women, Mr. Peterson!"

He laughs lightly before adding, "Or so it seems."

"This is all nuts! I must be going crazy."

"No, no, you are not going crazy; you are merely waking up to discover you live in a crazy world—shhh, Mr. Scoutmaster with the knobby knees is calling off names!"

He is correct of course. I turn to see Mr. Matthews calling out three names for the next heat through his megaphone, but he recites them with such military briskness I cannot make out even a single name.

"Did he call your name?" I ask Mickey.

"Yessirreee, he sure did!" Mickey says with a zombie-like intonation.

I wait for him to react to Mr. Matthews' call but he just sits there as if he too is waiting.

Finally he sighs then asks, "Want to wish me luck?" staring up at me with big baleful eyes.

"Oh, I do, Mick!" I reply, "more than you could ever know."

I reach over and affectionately squeeze his arm.

"Go kick some butt, sweetie!"

He starts to move off his seat but I maintain my grip.

"Dad!" he cries.

"Shhh,"I whisper, leaning in and ignoring his protest. "No matter what happens, just remember that we did our best. We really did."

"I know, Dad," he says, "it's cool."

Jumping off the chair he breaks free from my fatherly grip. I want to hold onto him so much I almost reach hungrily after his vanishing shadow.

But he is gone.

Off to win or lose his first heat of the day.

I cannot believe how much Mickey has changed since last year's Pinewood Derby. He is still the same wiry fellow I know and love but he has gained in both size and maturity. Or so it seems, now that I take a good look. In fact it strikes me that he almost seems like a different boy.

When did he grow up so much? Could I have been so

asleep I did not see it?

"There is much you have not seen, young sir," The Bapucharya comments. "But we are coming to a point where soon you will see everything. Until that time, you must strive to drink your RC Cola, and wait."

I do not know how much RC Cola I will be able to consume, being so emotionally charged and off balance, but I will sit here and wait of course—as if I have a choice!

But waiting will not lessen the sense of strangeness that is now taking hold of me.

You notice anything unusual?

It seems as if the gears of the universe are grinding awkwardly off center, their alignment not quite right. So much so that before too long I expect they might even grind to a halt.

Before they can come to a standstill, however, Mr. Matthews saves the universe, magically readjusting everything in a flash by merely calling out, "Places everyone!" with his customary electronic amplification and military precision. Somehow the briskness of his announcement provides enough energy for me to free myself from being asphyxiated by this weird, self-consuming fog.

There is a Seeker concept about the law governing progressions in which a shock of energy is needed at two points in the chain of events to prevent things from grinding to a halt or going off in unwanted directions. The Eight-Step Ladder it is called. Mr. Matthews, I believe, has just provided the essential shock of energy needed to bridge the first gap in the progression and keep things moving along.

What a good guy he is!

After all these years, even with his sons long gone from the boy scouts, Mr. Matthews remains ever-reliably the Town Scoutmaster; fixed in all minds, after countless seasons of pack meetings, parades, beach clean-ups, camping expeditions, school speeches and community car washes, as a treasured local character. Like a sober version of the town drunk he is a fixture in our lives, something that does not change with the seasons or the passage of years. You feel good just to see him, so benign and likeable in his khaki Explorer Scout's uniform complete with shirt pocket patches, summer shorts and year-round knobby knees.

If anyone can be called a hero Mr. Matthews gets my vote. Which is about all he gets, I expect.

"Places?" he calls again.

"Places!" three boys answer back, signaling that their racecars are in their starting berths. A second later they are running back to their seats.

Somewhere in the universe I can sense that a switch has been thrown. I can almost smell the ions burning as some cosmic electrical current surges. If I close my eyes I can see sparks erupting in showers, cascading down a phantom network of wires and generators.

Do you feel it?

Can you tell that the Master Transmission seems to be downshifting, the gears slowing down in their turnings, the cogs intermeshing with more deliberation and care, as if the approaching moment will be so significant that even time must slow down to take greater notice?

Yes once again and for no apparent reason I am watching events transpire in highly detailed, and painfully tedious, slow motion.

And there is something else.

Even as the three boys shouted "Places!" and ran back to their respective seats I sensed something familiar about all this; that somehow in some strange way I had been here before. The Seekers no doubt would call this The Oneness of Everything and The Bapucharya would jokingly say that once again I have been kicked in the head by the *TOE of God.*

Of course someone unfamiliar with The Seekers' cosmos might merely suggest I am experiencing *déjà vu.*

Whatever you call it, two moments in time seem to have been connected by the same thought resonating in the same substance of my mind.

Or something like that.

In any case I have seen this moment play itself out before and I know something is about to happen—something I have not planned for and do not expect.

Something that most likely I will not enjoy.

And there is one more thing...

I finally hear it. Below the sounds and commotion of the room, behind the pulsing energy of the situation, I can finally hear it. The *absence of noise.* It seems so pervasive and inescapable I find it strange I could not hear it before.

The Bapucharya was right.

"Now, that should be a huge surprise!" a distant voice merrily interrupts.

Like an angel carried on a breeze, my little boy—too big now to sit on my lap— returns to his chair in the final breath before the Scoutmaster sets events and the race in motion. I feel Mickey's hand on my arm as we both gaze upon elements in our world that have suddenly assumed such ridiculously high importance. Mr. Matthews, the racetrack, the two competing racecars and the most important element of all, our beautiful and shiny black Pinewood Derby model racecar.

"Do your thing!" I silently coax Black Beauty.

"Go get 'em!" Mickey shouts like a diehard sports fan, "Kill 'em!"

Like everything else in the room Mr. Matthews moves through the world in slow motion. I watch him reach towards the handle that releases the three restraining pins and it is like he is swimming through a thick invisible soup to get there.

It is excruciating, this anxiety gripping me as I watch his hand move ever closer towards the handle. I feel like a wall is about to fall on us but I only have enough strength to look up and see it teetering dangerously overhead.

From a distance of maybe fifty feet I can see the tiny restraining pins that hold back the racecars. With obviously heightened sensitivity I can even make out the reflections on their round metallic surfaces as Mr. Matthews at last pulls the handle that drops the pins into their slots, releasing the cars and starting the race.

"And they're off!" he calls with great importance into his megaphone as he has done with every heat since the beginning of time.

At that moment, as all three cars begin their run down the incline, the crowd explodes into noise. In my heightened state of anxiety all three model racecars seem to be moving so slowly I actually believe I can see their wheels turning.

Mickey pulls frantically on my sleeve, his body shaking as he shouts out words of encouragement to Black Beauty. For me the surrounding cub scouts and their parents seem to move in a strange, almost alien, slow dance—like spirit forms, their bodies swaying in slow motion, their arms waving back and forth like sinewy seaweed, their voices blending into a chorus suffused with sound and chaos.

On the racecourse in these first few millionths of a second, all three cars appear to be tied. But my eyes are primarily fixed on the glistening black car on the center rail...which suddenly for no visible reason, like a trick of the mind or an incredibly bad joke, *begins to slow down.*

Can you believe this?

My mouth drops wide open as Black Beauty crawls to a shocking...unalterable ...totally complete...*stop.*

It has stopped.

Our racecar is actually *stuck* on the track!

You see it too, right?

This is not some form of mass hysteria brought on by my fear of failure? I mean I am actually seeing what I think I am seeing, am I not? Our racecar stopped dead in the middle of the race—on the upper slope of its rail; sitting there like a permanent fixture and totally oblivious to gravity's pull?

Does this seem real to you?

I am dumbfounded, sick to my stomach. I do not believe my eyes. As the shock hits me I rise off the chair, my hands fruitlessly grasping to pull clouds or some divine explanation from the sky.

"What the hell...!" I shout.

In the same instant Mickey cries out, "NO, NO, NO!" as if he has been physically struck.

This cannot be happening.

Not after last year.

Not after all the promises, all the hard work.

Is there a God in the universe so perverse he finds it necessary to punish us this way? And did he have to go this far?

I scream an obscenity, only realizing what I have shouted when Mickey pulls on my arm and cries, "Dad!" in shock.

“Sorry,” I say under my breath, looking around to see if anyone else might have heard me.

Have you noticed the world is no longer moving in slow motion? I guess that means we have returned to reality.

Some reality!

With an effort I release myself from the hypnotic attraction of our stranded racecar—it is the same kind of fascination that grips you in the presence of a fatal car crash. My eyes finally averted, I check out the winning racecar, a green hodgepodge of poorly applied paint and drunkenly applied graphics. In one of those annoying ironies that often present themselves when they are least welcome, I realize the winner of the heat is every bit as ugly and amateurish as Old Number Two was the previous year.

I am aghast and—going against the logic of my own experience—highly insulted.

Thoughts wander where they will, I guess, for even as I sit here almost frozen from shock I cannot help but wonder if other fathers felt similarly affronted last year when Old Number Two beat them so handily? Before I have a chance to feel sorry for them, however, I begin brooding about how cruel and unfair fate can be. Which lasts but a second since I am instantly brought back to reality by one of the boys in the room gleefully shouting out, "It's stuck!"

"Great brakes!" another laughingly comments.

"Go, Go, Go!" someone else adds, unconsciously mimicking Mickey’s anguished cry of "No. No. No!"

Other voices join in but with little real animation or venom, certainly not enough to merit our attention.

"Do not listen to them!" I whisper into Mickey’s ear. "Pay them no mind!"

I might as well tell him to close his eyes and pretend he is back in his mother’s womb.

"Why do they have to do that?" my little boy questions, his pain raw and obvious.

He is scrambling around inside his head searching for answers he will never find.

"Why?" he asks, dumbfounded

"They are just children," I answer without thought.

"Rotten children," I add dryly.

"And why do they have to point like that?" he pursues. "It's rude and..." he pauses, trying to hold onto his composure, "so mean!"

"It will stop soon," I predict, and even as I utter the words I notice the initial eruption of laughter and insults beginning to subside.

"It's Michael Peterson's car!" one boy exclaims laughingly.

"Way to go, Mikey!" another cries.

And that is just about it.

There are two or three other comments but they lack real fire or commitment. It is still too early in today's Pinewood Derby for a racecar or cub scout to take attention away from the pull of the Derby or, especially, from those fifteen dollar, gilded plastic trophies sitting on the table.

"Do not listen to them," I tell my little boy.

"But why do they have to be so mean?" he asks searchingly.

"I do not know," I reply. Then I nod, indicating Mr. Matthews who is now firing off the names of the next three competitors.

You hear that?"

He mumbles a disheartened, "Uh-huh!"

"We have to get our car off the track."

My eyes turn back to the racecourse where our entry still sits on the upper slope of its rail proudly displaying the magnificence of its humiliation.

"Better get Black Beauty," I tell him, the car's name now a mockery on my lips. It may be black but it is no longer a beauty.

Mickey leans against me, refusing to move.

"Why do they have to be like that?" he asks angrily. Then he growls, tossing the sound around in his throat till it becomes almost animal-like. "I hate them!" he fumes. "I wouldn't laugh at them."

"That is because you understand how much it hurts to be laughed at," I tell him. "They do not. But we need to get our racecar now and put and end to all this."

I push him away so I can stand up.

His hand in mine, we walk across the crowded floor to

the long incline of the 3-railed racetrack. There is no laughter anymore; events have moved on. All around us cub scouts are getting ready for the next heat. No one pays attention to us. We are old news, like earthquake victims left to bury their dead after the TV cameras go away.

I am slowly coming to accept things.

I am almost ready to believe that this unbelievable turn of events has actually happened and that, yes it is true, once again I have somehow brought us—Mickey and I—to the fountainhead of humiliation. And to the erection of yet one more Milestone on our collective *ILEs*. This is a moment for our scrapbooks we will never *ever* forget. Like a thorn bush that pricks you every time you pass by, it will forever sting and chafe and grab at us from our memories.

Yes this is all real.

And most likely my fault.

Though I cannot see what I did wrong?

Or how I can make it right?

A familiar voice sounding unusually serious tells me, "These are good questions, young sir. We are so close to hearing the answers that I am getting nervous for you. You still wish to hear the answers, do you not?"

"Yes, Holiness. Absolutely! I need to understand things. Something. Anything!"

"Well, then, say goodbye to the cub scouts and come with me."

"Where are we going, Holiness?"

"Back to the real world. Where everything began."

"You mean to my early childhood?"

"No, no, we are traveling back to Plymouth, Massachusetts! It is time we bridged the final gap to your Eighth Step."

"Oh, really?" I reply, mastering a sudden urge to express my confusion and doubt.

But then who am I to question a Bapucharya?

The Third Karmic
Gravitational Slide:

Bridging The Gap

Wherein Our Resident Guru
And Other Guest Participants
Bring Our
Do-It-Yourself Workshop
To A Surprising Conclusion

Lesson 41

How To Climb An Eight-Step Ladder Without Falling Or *Slipsiding*

Once again I find myself in this second floor apartment in Plymouth, Massachusetts, still moving in slow motion and, yes, still under the physical control and mental impetus of Allison Pratt. At the same time I also find myself reviewing the last few words and fragmentary ideas The Bapucharya has thrown at me.

Why for instance did he choose to call this 'the real world' as opposed to St. Sebastian's? And why after all this time in my Do-It-Yourself Workshop did he suddenly bring up the concept of The Eight-Step Ladder and speak so mysteriously of bridging its second and final gap?

Two strange comments, were they not?

But you are probably wondering about this Eight-Step Ladder...?

I have avoided speaking about it as I have other Seeker concepts that seem irrelevant to the business at hand. But apparently I was wrong and the Eight-Step Ladder is not only relevant but perhaps even crucial to the story you and I have been witnessing.

According to The Seekers For Truth, the Eight-Step Ladder is a universal principle first discovered by the Pythagoreans—perhaps by Pythagoras himself—in the golden days of ancient Greece. Also called "The Law Of Progressions" it supposedly governs the process by which all phenomena advances in stages. And whether you are talking about the spinning of the universe, the unraveling of a marriage, the length of a father-son project or an evening at a singles dance, to cite a few obvious examples from our journey, it is a progression invariably involving a series of eight steps, most of which are often too subtle to notice even if you are looking for them.

Reaching the eighth step, however, is not a simple proposition by any means.

The Pythagoreans supposedly developed the musical octave with its eight notes to illustrate the Eight-Step Ladder and to protect its knowledge from being lost, as sometimes happens with universal principles left sitting unattended for centuries.

Never ones to minimize things, The Seekers For Truth credit most of what goes awry in the universe to The Law Of Progressions. They point to the two irregular intervals or gaps occurring after the third and seventh steps—the *mi* and *ti* notes in the octave—as examples of deviate intervals that exist in *all* progressions occurring spontaneously under Universal Law. These irregularities, they claim, are the reason why almost everything touched by this planet's Homo Sapiens inevitably turns to garbage.

Whether that is true or not they also claim that the manner in which you respond to these anomalous gaps determines whether you advance, stumble or lose direction in whatever endeavor you are involved.

Respond inadequately to the first irregular interval and your project sputters, loses energy and never has a chance to get off the ground.

Respond incorrectly to the second and final gap which occurs near the end of a progression and you spin off in a totally new and generally unhelpful direction. What the Seekers call *Slipsiding.*

That is what makes The Law Of Eight so critical to your progress on the Path Of Seeking Truth where there are limitless Eight-Step Ladders for you to encounter and countless opportunities to unexpectedly spin off sideways on your path.

So how should one respond when you are in the midst of some activity or enterprise and reach either of these intervals? Assuming of course you wish to keep progressing toward your objective in a straightforward manner?

As Mr. Samuelson, leader of the Boston School, would often proclaim in his clipped British accent, "Clearly, one must *bridge* the intervals."

The Bapucharya was speaking about safely negotiating the second of the two intervals when he spoke about *bridging the final gap*. It is this gap that accounts for most if not all of the sudden misdirections that occur in life and in human history. For unless this final interval is bridged by applying some external shock of energy—as if Superman would place his body across a gap in the road at the precise moment a vehicle needs to pass over—an individual's progression up the ladder would be diverted and sent off in a new direction, initiating an entirely new Eight-Step Ladder in the process.

If you have ever wondered why so many projects in the universe never get completed or are finished badly or end up spinning off into tangents—or why so many people lose interest in an activity just at the moment it is about to come to fruition—this is the reason.

Because somewhere a final gap needed to be bridged.

And never was.

Look at your own life's journey up the Path Of Seeking Truth and I am sure you will find no shortage of *Slipsiding*. Whether of larger or lesser importance it is all the same. A final gap needed to be bridged and it could have only happened if an external shock of energy had been added to the equation. A shock of energy with enough force to supply the momentum needed to bridge the gap and reach the eighth step.

And just like the octave, the eighth step of one ladder becomes the first step of the next.

Now you understand why it often seems difficult to maintain consistent direction or momentum on the Path Of Seeking Truth!

But that is a subject for another discussion.

"Very good! Very good," a voice calls out, accompanied by the sound of polite clapping which echoes in the upper reaches of Allison's living room where we now seem to be hovering.

Understand, it is not always easy to pinpoint The Bapucharya's and my exact location, given that we are both hovering in the room as invisible disembodied presences.

I still have a body of course but it is down there below, obeying the law of gravity.

See?

There, still being dragged in slow motion across the carpet toward that brown velveteen couch! Possibly the slowest journey since the Israelites wandered forty years in the desert searching for The Promised Land.

"This is all very good; very good indeed," The Bapucharya continues in his humorous manner. "I feel so much like I am listening to myself, young sir, you are such a good instructor. There is nothing you have said that I would not agree with and give myself high marks for being such an intelligent guru!

"But what does it all mean, my young friend? Is that not the real question we should be asking? Why are we speaking about this Ladder of Eight Steps when we are dancing in the dark with the daughter of the devil?"

There is something about the way he asks the question that turns on a light inside my head. I mean literally, as if a switch has been thrown and the shadows have suddenly disappeared!

Under the spell of this dramatic new illumination I am suddenly back in my body looking with a stupefied grin at this woman who tightly grips my arm, both of us still moving in syrupy slow motion. I cannot help but smile to think of anyone, much less a Bapucharya, allowing her to have that much power.

The daughter of the devil indeed! More likely the daughter of a dust mote or something similarly insignificant.

I am feeling strangely free of my confusion now. There is so much that I see and comprehend that was missing before.

For one thing I see that *it is I* who have empowered Allison Pratt this evening, not anyone or anything else. Not her or the wine, but myself. By dint of my own sexual confusion and the inescapable force of a Karmic Gravitational Slide.

"Is that not so?" I ask, already certain of my disembodied companion's response.

The Bapucharya chuckles with his customary air of unfettered enjoyment.

"Very much so, yes indeed; and very well said, if I may say so myself...

"You are starting to see things, are you not?" he asks

brightly. "And you are beginning to understand why I have come here, even as— ohmigoodness!—you are coming so close to that oh-so-shabby and uninviting couch." A series of giggles filters out of the emptiness of space where I imagine The Bapucharya's essence must be hovering.

"Yes, I see things, Holiness. Not everything, but many things.

"And I see them as if I were watching from that central place within, resting in a lotus position on top of the mountain, even though I remain actively engaged in the events transpiring in this darkened room."

"Well, do not hold anything back," The Bapucharya advises. "If you have any questions, if you are suddenly afraid of what is happening, please to talk to me. That is why I am here! Not to see the newsreels and the cartoons, but to help with the feature attraction. Even though it sometimes looks very much like a Tom and Jerry cartoon." Again a series of bubbly giggles fills the empty space.

"That is one of the things I have been unable to fathom," I declare, "why someone like you, Holiness, would be spending all this time on the *ILE* of someone like me?"

"And now you see why I have stopped in for a visit?"

"Not completely, but somewhat. You are *it*, are you not? The shock of energy I will need to bridge the final gap in some cosmic life cycle of mine? That must be what this is all about. I am getting shocked, am I not?"

"Yes, yes, you are right!" He exclaims merrily. "Shocking, is it not…!" he laughs.

Then, more seriously, he comments, "I am oh-so-very impressed, my young friend, with how much you are starting to know and see in your first-ever Do-It-Yourself Workshop! Have you some idea, then, about your last Karmic Companion? Do you know who she shall be?"

I hear the clue dropping into my lap but I am not yet ready to go off in that direction.

"Not so fast, Holiness," I say. "We are getting ahead of myself, if that is a correct thing to say?"

The Bapucharya answers with a high-pitched cackle.

"Correct?" He repeats, as if he is holding up the word for personal observation. "What is all this talk of correctness, young sir? I have told you many times that you are the one who decides what is right for your life. Nobody else. If you wish to say *'we* are getting ahead of *yourself'* what fool is there—but yourself—to argue the point?"

I have to laugh at how easy he makes it all sound.

"Holiness, you are giving away all these clues, as I am sure you know. And just a little while ago you mentioned something about getting back to the 'real world'. Which made me wonder..."

"If *this* is the real world, eh...?" he tentatively probes.

"Yes," I reply. "Exactly! And if this is the real world, what makes it so real? You know what I mean...?"

"Oh yes, we are in the real world, now, Mr. Peterson. Or so it seems. We are standing on the very edge of your *ILE*; which can be the place where all things end, if you wish, or a point of disembarkation where a whole new journey can begin.

"Oh yes, it is all up to you!"

Do you understand what he is saying?

If you do, then you are beginning to understand perhaps which of my life's progressions is coming to an end tonight and which final gap is waiting to be bridged.

"You make it sound very nice, Holiness," I reply, "but no matter how I look at it, this is still the edge of my *ILE,* the edge of my 'Individual Life Experience' we are standing on. And what you are really saying, if I read you correctly, is that I have arrived at the end of my life here on Earth; is that not true?"

I listen to myself say those words and I am amazed to observe no emotion or fear rising up with them. I am still sitting calmly within myself as I speak, less than a whisper away from the *Center Point of the Universe,* observing myself and Allison from a godlike perch near the upper heights of the room. At the same time I am also watching events unfold from ground level within my body—my eyes challenging the dim lighting to observe Allison and all the other details of the room with amazing clarity, even down to the texture of the dog hairs on the brown velveteen couch.

I cannot remember another moment on my *ILE* when I felt so alive to what was around me.

Unlike previous attempts to maintain this balance in the Present Moment—*to drink my RC Cola!*—which never lasted longer than it took to get to the next thought, I have achieved some sort of locked-in stasis now, as if securely balanced between the inner and outer worlds. And in this effortless state of equipoise I am watching events from both above and below, within and without.

I am the observer and the observed.

So much knowledge comes to me now, not the least of which is that I have only reached this plateau because The Bapucharya has chosen to bring me here.

This higher state of being—and knowing—must be symptomatic of the shock of energy he has given me; the shock I will need to bridge the final gap!

But even as I have access to all this knowledge, so much still remains hidden.

"You can tell me," I press him. "Have I reached the end of my life as well as the edge of my *ILE*?"

"Oh boy, you are asking the tough questions tonight! I am sorry, Mr. Peterson, but I cannot yet answer this particular question. Believe me, I will not lie to you when I am in a better position to give an answer."

"I know that, Holiness." I reply. "As much as you may have confused and misled me, you never once lied to me." A thin stream of my own giggles effortlessly help me complete my words.

"Hey!" I exclaim, surprised by my own laughter. "Holiness, I am laughing!"

"Oh my, yes; yes, you are! Maybe this is not such a real world after all!" he offers jokingly.

His words bring a question to mind.

"Tell me again why the second Pinewood Derby—with Black Beauty—was not the real world?" I ask. "It seemed pretty real to me."

"And it was, in a curious way..."

"Again with a 'curious way'!"

He laughs lightly. "I cannot help it if the Divine Organizer created a curious world, can I? But it is no less true that all parts of His curious world are real; it is just that some are more real than others. And if you remember *AUM* and the dance of Shiva, then you know that none of them are *really* real anyway!

"This is all illusion, young sir," he exclaims joyfuly. "Automatic Universal Misunderstanding in glorious wide-screen technicolor!"

I shake my head in stubborn resistance.

"Well, let us not talk about *those* levels of reality, Holiness; I am having enough difficulty grasping this level, if you do not mind.

"Just tell me why the Pinewood Derby was less real than the events taking place in this apartment?"

"We have been traveling far and wide in your Do-It-Yourself Workshop, Mr. Peterson, and some of the places we have visited are not *yet* part of *your* real world. That is not to say they will *never* become part of your real world—but, if you want a Bapucharya's opinion, I would suggest you not bet your lunch money on it..."

"Which places were not part of my real world?" I press.

"Any place you are visiting after this gala evening tonight in Plymouth, Massachusetts. It is as simple as that. Here in Ms. Pratt's dingy and doggy-haired apartment we are at the edge of your *ILE*. Every scene we have visited that takes place *after* this evening exists only as a *Glimmer*, a vision of the world as it may be, or may never be, depending on how certain...*possibilities*...play themselves out.

"It cannot be surprising, young sir, that there is a name for this *Glimmer* experience. These crazy-minded Seekers For Truth give out names like they were birthday presents. This one, which is one of their better efforts, they have christened the 'Clarence Factor' after a character in a popular American movie; one of my favorites actually..."

"It's A Wonderful Life!" I exclaim, remembering the angel Clarence who was able to show George Bailey, played by James Stewart, what the world would have been like had he never been born.

I am suddenly struck by a realization.

"So my last few sessions with Dr. Rivers, my bedroom discussion with Mickey, the second Pinewood Derby...?"

"Yes, young sir, they were all *Glimmers*. Each a possibility, but nothing more. Yet to you, I am sure, each seemed as real as an experience can be. Is that not correct?"

"That explains why things sometimes seemed so different, so insubstantial; and why I could not remember a single thing that happened after..."

"This enchanted evening!" he concludes, singing in tune to 'Some Enchanted Evening' from Rogers and Hammerstein's *South Pacific.*

"So, of course, you were suffering galloping bouts of amnesia, young sir! How could you remember anything that had not yet happened? The answer is, you could not!

"You have not had therapy sessions for the two weeks leading up to your *Glimmer* with Dr. Rivers, so *of course* you could not remember things you spoke about during those sessions.

"And of course you could not remember how you angered your beautiful friend with the throaty voice since you had not yet lived, or acted out, that part of your mutual history.

"And how could you remember what you were doing *even seconds before* you flashforwarded to find yourself in bed teaching your oh-so-sleepy son about *kidsnapping?* Those things had not yet been done, young sir!

"And what a bad idea, I should say while I think of it, to teach *kidsnapping* to children! *Kidsnapping* is very much *like* children themselves—very unreliable and quick to make a mess," he concludes with giggles spilling out.

"But you see what I am saying?

"They were all *Glimmers,* young sir! Glimpses of what might happen, nothing more than that."

"But it all seemed so real, Holiness."

"And it was real! Did you not experience it? The noise, the excitement, the entire catastrophe? The only difficulty, I must say, is that none of it will probably ever take place in your life."

"This gets quite complicated," I notice.

"Yes it does. I have always thought this to be one of the Divine Organizer's more complex arrangements."

"And this fellow who is slowly walking into the living room...?" I question. "He certainly seems real."

"That is because he is real, my young friend. He is very real, and no stranger to Ms. Pratt's *ILE*, I am afraid."

"And his gun? That must be real, too."

"Yes, that too is real."

"Does that explain why there are dog hairs on the couch? I recall that Allison mentioned a cat, but never a dog?"

"Yes, you are very astute! It is this strange newcomer's German Shepherd Rex who has shed these hairs, even though dogs are not allowed on the couch. At this very moment Rex is downstairs shedding hairs in the passenger's seat of a pickup truck on Thorndike Street. I do not expect we will enjoy the pleasure of Rex's company this evening, which is just as well since he is rather big and has horrible dog breath."

"Speaking of breath," I say, "can you smell this fellow's breath? The man with the gun?"

"Some kind of violet breath mint?" The Bapucharya suggests.

"Sen-Sen," I reply with a slight smile of satisfaction. "Or something very much like Sen-Sen."

My eyes having adjusted to the shadows in which this intruder stands, and looking at him from both above and straight on, I am forced to point out, "My God, he looks more like an overgrown boy than a man."

"Perhaps that is why he is called Junior," The Bapucharya suggests.

"Junior?"

"Is it all coming together, young sir?" The Bapucharya asks in a voice strangely soft and caring. "Ask me any questions that come to mind, and do not be afraid."

Afraid? I am not afraid.

I probably should be afraid but I am not.

"Do you know who Junior is?" I ask casually. It seems strange, does it not, that I can be so casual about all this?

"You mean 99-dash-1-4-7-3?" The Bapucharya snickers.

"Junior?" I repeat, my eyes running up and down his diminutive form. "I somehow imagined him to be larger, much rougher looking, when Allison was speaking about him."

Junior now stands next to the brown velveteen couch only four or five feet away. The gun in his hand, a small black revolver, is pointed at our approaching forms. Suddenly the pressure on my arm eases up and I look over to see that

Allison has also noticed him and has stopped in her tracks to gather her bewildered senses.

"A very sentimental reunion," The Bapucharya jokes. "This is the part of the movie I especially enjoy."

"Junior," Allison says awkwardly, like a schoolgirl greeting a playmate. Nodding at the gun, seemingly unaware of my presence, her voice picks up modest amounts of uncertainty mixed with indignation. "What are you doing? You can't bring a gun in here. You're not even allowed to be here!" she insists without real force of conviction.

I will not repeat Junior's reply since it is vulgar and adds little to the discussion. I think you will agree, however, that Junior does not share Allison's opinion of his right to be in this apartment.

"Bapu?" I call.

"Still here!" He answers.

"Can you tell me now if my life is about to end?"

"Not yet," He replies. "It is still not decided."

"Tell me again about Ellie. Why was she so angry with me at the second Pinewood Derby? I mean she and I had made up, did we not? Earlier tonight, in fact, right before I left the dance. We were feeling pretty good about things when I left, or so it seemed..."

"That is true, young sir," he replies. "But if events later transpire to bring you to that second Pinewood Derby—in real life—your sexy lady friend will be there, and she will be an angry person at that time, not the sweet loving helpmate you have just left at the singles dance in Plymouth."

"This is so difficult," I sigh.

"That is why God made gurus," he chuckles.

"Just realize, my young friend, if you live to attend that second Pinewood Derby you will do something between now and then to reignite Ellie's anger. Do not fight it, young sir; it is your responsibility to do so. You can even say it is *your role in her life* to do so."

Again I am struck by a realization.

"*She* is the last Karmic Companion?"

"Bingo!" he cries, chuckling. "And just as you cannot stop yourself from leading your poor son into one humiliating situation after another, so too you cannot stop yourself from teaching Ellie important lessons about money, friendship and especially about the rewards of being a selfish upside-down adult. By speaking the truth to her earlier tonight you enabled her to see more clearly what it is she must learn."

"Is that why you instructed me to tell the truth?"

"No, my friend, you should always be telling the truth," he answers firmly. "Anything less keeps you living in the World Of Shadows."

"But Ellie will hate me for the rest of my... if not my life, then hers! What kind of Karmic Companionship is that?"

"Do you now hate your father?" The Bapucharya abrubtly asks. "Do you still hate Marilyn?"

Before I can think about my feelings for either of them I find myself confronting a surprising answer.

"No," I respond softly. Somewhat amazed at my response I continue, "No, I do not hate either of them. Not anymore. Why is that?"

"Because you are starting to see things, Mr. Peterson, which is another way of saying the truth is beginning to shine through the darkness and you are leaving the World Of Shadows.

"But do not fret about Ellie, young sir; it was all arranged a long, long time ago."

"And Mickey?" I say hopefully. "At least he will not be humiliated at the second Pinewood Derby! He cannot be humiliated if the event never happens, right?"

"Yes, but there again you have a role to play. And I am thinking you will easily find another way to help him learn his lesson," he chuckles. "The universe will insist upon it.

"In fact, if you die here tonight, think about how humiliating it will be for Mickey to have his father shot to death in his teacher's apartment. Oh my, I can feel his face turning red just by mentioning it—or should I say his face turning *fuscia,"* he laughs.

"If I die here tonight...?" I repeat, ignoring his pointed remark. I can feel a small measure of hope starting to rise. "You mean I do not have to die?"

"No, Mr. Peterson, you do not have to do anything. As I repeatedly insist, these decisions are left to you. The Absolute Prankster believes in free choice even if He does not always leave you much freedom to make the choice.

"But I am afraid there can be no choice about leaving your Legacy; whether it shall be for your son or for anyone else.

"No, I am sorry to tell you, there is no avoidance of Legacies in this world. What sense would that make when the world primarily exists as a transmission device to deliver and receive Legacies!"

"So tell me, Holiness, what choices, then, do I have?"

"Right now? You have two; the same two choices you have always been given. How to live. And how to die.

"Everything else," he concludes merrily, "is just halftime show, nothing more."

Lesson 42

Getting Shocked In Plymouth: One Man's Way To Bridge A Gap

"But there are still so many things to share, young sir," The Bapucharya says, "even as this upside-down, over-aged juvenile delinquent brandishes his gun like a dime store cowboy. Perhaps, I shall begin by clearing up one of life's smaller mysteries...

"It was the extra lead weight!" he exclaims with prideful satisfaction.

"The extra lead weight?" I repeat, searching my mind for some relevance to this remark. "Can you say more about this extra lead weight, Holiness?"

"You do not remember the extra lead weight that was added to the underside of your Black Beauty?"

"Yes, I do. So what about it...?"

"So it was too thick, Mr. Automotive Engineer, hanging down from the under belly of your beautifully crafted racecar. So it got stuck against the rail. So there you are!"

"Stuck?" I ask, still trying to orient myself to this sudden shift in the conversation. "Why? How?"

"Because someone who shall remain nameless never checked to see if adding the lead weight left enough clearance for the guide rail. Which it did not!"

"Oh," I reply, suddenly understanding the significance of the extra lead weight.

"Well, I guess that explains that!" I remark, noticing how surprisingly unemotional my voice sounds and realizing that a short time ago I would have railed against myself and the fates for my stupidity. Now it seems as if I had merely been operating under a different and unseen set of rules.

"Yes, you are seeing things now," The Bapucharya exults. "And you are realizing that very often, when you think you are merely being a foolish father or a struggling husband or a boyfriend with a galloping *PuNDit,* you are actually an unwitting instrument of higher purpose.

"Under the pull of the prevailing Karmic Gravitational Slide, you had no choice but to add that extra weight to the racecar, Mr. Peterson, or to make some other foolish mistake. Not much of a choice, is it—shall I choose to step in dogshit or horseshit…?" he laughs.

"Well, anyway," I reply with surprising cheer, "now at least I know what I did wrong. So, if I ever actually end up at that second Pinewood Derby—in the real world of course…"

"You will commit exactly the same error—or one just as disastrous! That is how things work. No matter how you feel about such tragic events, your role is to help your son learn about shame and humiliation. This, too, was arranged long ago and set in motion under the combined influence of the Noble Fourfold Legacy and Karma—not to mention some poetic irony by the Absolute Jokester, which at times may appear a little excessive…"

"But, Holiness, he is just a little boy!"

"On one level you are right, on another he is no more a little boy than you. Do not get trapped again in a concept of time that is no more true than a blind man's vision of an elephant.

"We are speaking about the balance of the universe, young sir; why things happen the way they do. And I will remind you that we are not talking about you and your son, but about you, your father and your son, all wrapped up in an intricate Karmic Dance that I cannot begin to explain in the time we have left, since we only have another ten million years before Shiva stops her dance and pulls the plug. Then—ohmigoodness!—bye-bye Automatic Universal Misunderstanding, bye-bye fathers, sons, daughters—bye-bye this whole silly megillah you call *Existence!*

"Then, it is back to square one for all of us," he giggles, "Bapucharyas included!"

A sudden jerky movement catches my eye.

"He does not look too steady," I comment. "Allison's former boyfriend, I mean. I think he has been drinking or something."

"Or *something,* I would say," The Bapucharya offers. "It is a *something* he keeps in a crumpled foil packet that is scrunched up in his right pants pocket, if that is any help."

"It could be anything."

"Oh well, it is no matter to us as long as it confines itself to altering his reality and not yours.

"But what are you thinking, Mr. Peterson?"

"That something is about to happen."

"Why, because this stranger, this former boyfriend named Junior, is suddenly landing his boat on the banks of your *ILE?*

"You do not need a guru to see that something is about to happen, my young friend; but what shall that something be? And what shall you do when it happens? That is the question I am asking!"

"What can I do? He has a gun, Holiness. I have nothing except some sort of mystical view of this whole situation. Will that be of any help?"

"Please, Mr. Peterson, you are armed with fifteen years of working on your essence—on your state of being—as a Seeker For Truth. Surely, that is a weapon of inestimable value!"

"Against a man with a gun?" I cry. "You must be kidding..."

I fall quiet as a sudden realization comes into view. "This is a polarized situation, is it not?" I ask.

"Yes, young sir, it certainly is!" he agrees.

"Two forces in resistance to each other, you might say? In other words, Mr. Ping meets Mr. Pong?"

"Very good, young sir. Well seen and well said!"

For a moment I consider the advantages of *Embracement* over *Kidsnapping.* Whether to wrap myself around Junior in the form of Mrs. Costadazzi or to allow myself to envision this pint-sized adversary as a two year old child. Either way, I need to act immediately before the energy of the situation has moved too far along and the opportunity is lost.

"Just a minute," I call out to Junior. "Before you do anything you will regret, let me ask you a question."

As I speak, I silently instruct the observer inside myself—The One Who Always Watches—to reconstruct the image of Junior that is being fed into my mind through the brain. It is not as difficult a reconstruction as you might think, since all of us bear great resemblance to the blueprints displayed on our faces when we were children.

Junior answers me nastily, as you might expect, but his face is already shifting and becoming the face of the two-year-old child he once was.

"I'll ask the questions, dickhead," he spits out in typically nasty fashion. "You keep your fucking mouth shut."

"You have chosen to *kidsnap?*" The Bapucharya asks, greatly surprised.

"Bad choice?" I ask, suddenly nervous.

"Consider the wisdom of allowing an angry two year-old-child to play with a gun…?" he says sharply, adding, "If I can make a suggestion…?"

"Yes?"

"Please to try something else. And quickly!"

I can see that the two-year-old Junior is about to pull the trigger on his revolver though I cannot tell if the gun is pointed more toward me or my totally shocked and silent blond companion.

"What should I do, Holiness? I do not think Mrs. Costadazzi can materialize before Junior makes his fatal move. What should I do?"

"Well, young sir, here is the choice. If you wait to see what happens, he will probably shoot either you or Ms. Pratt, or perhaps both in a package deal. If you *Embrace* him before something happens—even with the formidable presence of Mrs. Costadazzi—most certainly he will shoot you, and you alone. And more likely than not, I am very sorry to say, he will very quickly bring an end to your life.

"It is not much of a choice, but it is all yours!"

"Thanks," I say wryly, "some choice!"

"Hey Junior," I shout, drawing his attention and the barrel of his revolver in my direction.

As he starts to say, "Yeah, what…?" I spring toward him, taking one last languorous leap in a world where everything still moves in syrupy-slow, reduced speed.

"Recite your mantra, Mr. Peterson, and do it now!" The

Bapucharya sharply instructs.

"Higher will...higher will..." I obediently chant, calling up the words I had been given over 20 years ago as a young Seeker For Truth.

"And you are still a Seeker For Truth!" The Bapucharya curtly insists. "I have told you that fact any number of times. Why else would I be here now if you were not still under my care? It all comes with the price of admission."

"Higher will...higher will...higher will..." The mantra is now reciting itself, igniting a pulse that pulsates behind the spot in my forehead where my *PuNDit* ordinarily scolds me for even the most commonplace sexual imaginings and activities.

Notice how it seems to take forever for my body to reach Junior, my agile form arcing so languidly across the vastness of the small space that lies between us. But at last—perhaps a lifetime later—my body finally reaches its goal and I wrap both arms around him exactly as I would my benign and matronly 300 pound fifth grade teacher were she here for me to embrace.

Far off in the distance I hear a noise that resembles a terrifying clash of thunder and ask, "What is that, Holiness?"

"The sound of gunfire, my young friend," he answers. "You have been shot."

"Am I hurt badly?" I ask as Junior slips from my embrace and I begin sliding down his hard, muscular body to the floor below.

"Very badly, Mr. Peterson."

"I am falling, Holiness. I cannot hold myself up."

"Just let yourself go, young sir. Continue to embrace the moment and resist nothing."

It all seems to be happening far off in the distance as though experienced under the influence of some perception-distorting drug. Still I can feel myself losing the strength to control this very heavy and unwieldy body and my vision appears to be growing dim and blurred.

"Is this it, Holiness?" I ask in a strangely calm voice.

Finally reaching the floor I pull my arms from around Junior's legs and roll over on my back. I am now in the peculiar position of looking up at the ceiling at the same time I am hovering up near the ceiling staring down at myself.

"Can you answer me now, Holiness; am I dying?"

"Yes, Mr. Peterson, I can answer you now. Like everyone else in this universal dance, you are slated to leave this world; and, yes, it is your turn to catch that particular bus.

"But here is the good news," he adds. "Together we have created the shock of energy you needed to bridge the final gap and reach your eighth step. You will not be *Slipsiding* off into some silly tangent or an unhelpful rebirth. Not you, Mr. Peterson! When you made that Olympic-class leap with your arms wide open, reciting your mantra, you were also making such an athletic leap across your final gap.

"Congratulations!" he says, unable or unwilling to stop himself from chuckling even as we approach the threshold of my passage from this *ILE*.

"You are beyond belief, Holiness..." I reply, starting to finally laugh and unable to stop. "You tell me I am dying, and you still laugh like a child watching a cartoon. It is incredible...!"

"Now, you are laughing?" he shouts, feigning amazement. "The movie is almost over and *now* you are laughing! Shhh, do not make such a big deal of things! Talk to me instead; tell me how you feel, Mr. Peterson. Are you afraid?"

"No, no, not afraid. It seems okay, I guess. I just wish..."

"Yes?"

"Well, this will be hard on the kids; my death and all."

"Yes, yes, it will," he agrees. "But that is not so bad as you think. All three will be given a grand opportunity to learn so many things—important things. For no fee, they will learn about abandonment, independence, nurturing themselves, giving support, depending on each other, developing courage—this shall be worth 20 years in college for each of them. And you will not have to pay even one single tuition bill.

"No, young sir, you can let go now. Do not worry about your children. You have given them much, and now you are giving them more. That should be a good Legacy to leave."

"I would have liked to leave them more."

"Ohmigoodness! Then I guess you are scheduled to have

one more disappointment in your life," he says, cackling like a child on Christmas morning.

"Not one disappointment, but two," I correct him, my voice growing weak. "There is one other thing that bothers me...that I feel bad about."

"Yes, and what may that be?"

"That I never had the courage to burn down a billboard."

Hearing a fresh outburst of laughter, I ask, "What is so funny about that?"

"That you will be dying with words of great wisdom on your mind, young sir."

"What words, Holiness?"

"Have you been cr-r-r-runched today?"

The last thing I hear is the sound of laughter.

I cannot tell whose laughter it is.

This must be death, I think.

Or so it seems.

Epilogue:

Ten Years After

In Which We
Encounter Two Children
Fully Grown
And A Man Who Chokes
On His Own Silence

Workshop Review

Milestones, Legacies And The Unexpected Fruits Of Reverend Archworthy's Sermon

It was ten years later—ten years after the life of Paul Peterson came to a strange and, to his son, highly embarrassing conclusion—that another curious and unexpected fatality took place.

Lawrence Grafton, second husband to Marilyn Peterson, was seated next to his wife in St. Sebastian's Church in St. Bart's Bay one Sunday morning in March when suddenly and without warning he dropped onto the blue-carpeted floor of their pew and expelled great quantities of vomit. Before his wife or anyone else in the pew could react to the abrupt turn of events and bend down to minister to the suddenly lifeless Mr. Grafton, he was already dead.

It is of little importance what happened immediately afterwards but Mr. Grafton's departure was generally thought to have provided far more entertainment value for the congregation than the minister's sermon, "The Science of Religion Versus The Religion of Science," which Lawrence Grafton's ill-timed departure from this earthly plane had fortuitously interrupted.

Those who knew Mr. Grafton well enough to have developed a bemused familiarity with his retiring and understated manner were capable of understanding the series of events that were eventually pieced together to explain his bizarre and incomprehensible demise.

For to know Lawrence Grafton was to know one of St. Bart Bay's most reticent and circumspect citizens. Few things were more painful to Mr. Grafton than to unnecessarily call attention to himself or to interrupt someone of higher authority, of which there were only few individuals of his acquaintance who qualified for such honors, one of them certainly God's minister here on earth, the Episcopalian Priest, Rev. Lucius Archworthy.

So it is no surprise that Lawrence Grafton chose to choke on his own vomit rather than interrupt the morning's proceedings, especially at a moment in the sermon when the Reverend Mr. Archworthy had invited the congregation to explore the 'scientific texture of silence' by falling silent for a full minute's duration.

It was later accepted by most of the congregation that Lawrence Grafton, suffering from the combined effects of a late winter cold and a slight stomach bug, had probably struggled valiantly to prevent his maladies from combining to interrupt and interfere with the interactive segment of Mr. Archworthy's sermon.

And so by not allowing himself to either cough or give release to a sudden upsurge of partially digested breakfast waffle, Mr. Grafton chose instead to keep his mouth tightly closed, his cough contained and his vomit unspewed until the moment he secured his final release from all social responsibilities.

A few hours later, in the Client Preparation Laboratory of The Golden Waters Mortuary, Mr. Grafton was officially pronounced dead from asphyxiation. But those who knew Lawrence Grafton well enough to understand the dominant role reticence would play in both his life and its demise argued that in truth he actually suffocated to death on his own silence.

None of which has any bearing on the dream images that his widow Marilyn Grafton experienced two nights later, on the day Lawrence Grafton was laid to rest in his family's hillside plot in Mount Moriah Cemetary in Andover, Massachusetts. Or on her decision to relate her dream in full detail to her three children who had returned to the family home in St. Bart's Bay to support their mother in her moment of emotional stress.

The dream appeared to Marilyn Grafton as a videotaped presentation on a TV monitor.

Happily, without commercial interruptions.

* * *

Two weeks later, the funeral a distant memory and life's rhythms back in full swing, the phone rings twice before Cathy Margison picks it off the hook, hopefully before it rings again and wakes her six month old infant son Elliott.

"Hello?" she says softly, her apartment in Quincy, Massachusetts being too small to allow for a full throttle conversation during her son's nap.

"Cathy?" a familiar voice inquires, "It's Suzie!"

"Hi Su-Su!" Cathy answers, brightening.

"Long time no see!" she adds ironically, having recently spent three full days with her sister and the rest of the family. Probably the most time they had spent together since her graduation from Williams College three years earlier.

"How's Mark?" Suzie asks. "And that sweetie pie nephew of mine?"

"One of them's at work, the other's been kind of colicky but is down now—finally!—for his nap. I'll let you guess which is which.

"Where you calling from?" Cathy asks, the hour being close enough to lunch and Sue being the type to call from anywhere on the planet from her cell phone.

"From work," Suzie answers. "I'm lunching at my desk today. Too much going on for the slaves to leave the office.

"Have you talked to Mom lately?" she asks, abruptly changing subjects.

"A couple of days ago, I think," Cathy answers. "She sounded okay."

"Yeah, I think she's doing fine. Lawrence was such an old stick-in-the-mud she's probably finding it hard to deal with all the freedom and relief she's feeling."

Cathy laughs.

"Yeah, I'm sure that's true. But he was a nice guy, too, and she'll miss him. They got kind of used to each other, you know."

"Yeah, but you can get used to anything."

"Su-Su!" Cathy scolds. "Lawrence was okay in his own way. I always thought he earned big points for effort. You know how hard it was for him to live with the three of us. Poor Lawrence, to have three noisy, dirty step-kids to raise! He just hated all the fuss and mess that kids create."

"Well, you're the nice sister; I'm the cynical writer. But yes, as we always seem to say, Lawrence was a nice guy even though he could bore you to tears. But what a winky way to die!"

Winky was a special sister term for something so yucky you had to wink or close your eyes.

"I know! Poor Mom; I can tell she doesn't know whether to laugh or cry when she thinks about it. Imagine being so proper that you choke on your own vomit rather than speak up in church..."

"You mean *throw up* in church..."

"Okay! Let's not go into that again. It's pretty gross and I'd rather not bring it up...oh, I didn't mean that."

"Doesn't matter. Suffice it to say, it was a *very* winky way to die!"

"Suffice it to say, very very winky!" Cathy adds, her voice dropping to a whisper as she suddenly remembers Elliott is napping. "Hey Su-Su, I'm glad you called. Let me take this into the bathroom so I don't wake you-know-who."

Cathy carries the portable phone into the bathroom, shuts the door, sits on the closed toilet seat then asks, "So, how're you doing? I wanted to ask. Things seemed kind of tense for you last time we spoke."

She hears her sister groan, and pictures her twisting her unlined forehead into a maze of wrinkles.

"Oh, Cath," she finally answers, "it's the same old shit. Still killing myself at Dad's old agency without getting much of the glory or any of the gold. Which is one of the reasons I'm calling, I guess."

"What do you mean?"

"Guess what?"

"What?"

"No, guess!"

"I give up. What?"

"You're no fun," Suzie decides. "Anyway, I'm packing it in! I gave them my notice today. After three long, very painful years, I'm finally leaving Mercer, Dumont and Killen.

They asked me to stay the month, and I might actually give them three weeks, but after that I'm gone."

Waiting for a response and hearing none, she calls, "Cathy? Cath...? You still there?"

"Yeah, still here. Just taken aback, I guess. I thought you liked your job; especially working in Dad's old agency?"

"I thought so, too. So much so that I let it get between me and just about any half-serious relationship I ever had. 'Work Before Love' that was my motto. But not anymore. I'm done with advertising."

"Really?" Cathy says. "Well, that seems a bit sudden. Kind of takes me... Have you thought this through? It's so sudden. What brought it on?"

"Life, lack of love, twelve hour days, seven-day weeks, bullshit clients—take your pick! Whatever it was that finally broke this camel's back, I just knew I had to find something else to do. Something that might actually add something positive to the culture besides the desire to buy, spend and look like someone other than yourself. It's all bullshit, Cathy, and somehow I know Dad saw it that way, too, but just never told us because we were too young to understand."

"Well, I don't know about that," her sister says, "but congratulations, I guess, if it means you're finished with something that makes you unhappy. That's a good thing, right?"

"Thanks," her sister replies. "Yeah, I think it's a good thing. And like I said, I think Dad would think so, too."

"Because of Mom's dream?" Cathy asks, tentatively voicing her own confusion. "You know I've had similar thoughts since Mom told us about it. I don't think we had much idea of who Dad was or what he went through for us."

"And then to die like that; oh god, to be shot in some strange woman's apartment..."

"Not just some strange woman..."

Suzie laughs. "Dad was certainly a man of many parts; you have to give him that."

"And we won't try and guess which of his parts led him to that woman's apartment," Cathy adds, also laughing.

"Remember how Mom said in the dream there was some Indian guy who kept giggling like a little girl when he talked about Dad...?"

Cathy laughs. "That was a hoot!"

"Poor Dad."

"Yeah, poor Dad."

"You think Mom misses him? It seems lately like she speaks more about Dad than she does about Lawrence. At least since she had the dream."

"I don't know. But anyway, you've given your notice and now it's off to new territories, right? I always thought it was kind of neat, though, that you ended up working at Dad's old agency."

"Well, me too, of course. But three years is enough to validate his legacy as far as I'm concerned. And since I'm not so sure anymore that Dad actually approved of advertising, there's something missing now, something that used to help me deal with all the bullshit."

"I think you're right," Cathy says. "I think Dad liked us to know about his work and be proud of him, but I'm not so sure he really felt that proud about what he did."

"Have you been thinking much about Mom's dream?"

"I haven't been able to stop thinking about it," Cathy laughingly replies. "It seemed so weird to me, and so...Eastern and mystical, I guess. If you think Lawrence's death was winky..."

"Oh, I don't know about that. In some ways, Mom's dream was pretty cool. All that stuff he told Mom about her and Dad being *Karmic Companions,* and Dad's dying because he had to, or whatever the reason was; it sort of made sense, don't you think? It certainly made sense to me, at least some of it. I guess you could say it resonated." She laughs, and adds, "Of course now it won't stop resonating or leave me alone."

"But I don't get it, Su-Su. Why was Dad in that woman's apartment? Mickey's fourth grade teacher? C'mon! We never really figured it out, and Mom didn't know; not even after the dream. She just thought Dad went there seeking his doom or something?"

"Not his doom, pinhead!" Suzie responds. "His Fate! That's entirely different."

"Whatever! Call it what you will, he definitely died there

that night; that sounds like doom to me."

"Not according to that Indian guy, remember? The guru? *Boppo Something,* whatever his name was? He told Mom things in the dream that made her feel good...remember? He said that she and dad were connected in ways that life, death or divorce could never tear apart. That was pretty heavy stuff!"

"Yeah, and doesn't that sound suspiciously like a dream you might naturally have after you've just lost somebody important in your life?"

Suzie snorts at that.

"You're even more cynical than I am, you know that?"

"Not totally, anyway. There was something about Mom's dream that made me feel good, too. Did hearing about the dream make you feel closer to Dad? It did for me. We never talk about him much but I still miss him."

"Me, too."

"Mickey keeps acting like he's angry because Dad broke his promise, or embarrassed him—dying at his teacher's apartment—but I know he misses Dad, too. Mom's dream made me feel closer to Dad than I have in a long time."

"Hey Cath," Suzie exclaims, "we all had that same reaction! Mickey, too. I talked to him last night. And speaking of reactions, did he tell you he's decided to go into psychology rather than business?"

"No! Really? When did that happen?"

"Last week, I guess. Not long after he got back to school; but he says he's been thinking about it for some time. The trip home just helped him make up his mind."

"You know the one thing from Mom's dream that stands out for me?" Suzie asks. "And it's amazing how vivid an image it left in my mind."

"What?"

"Guess?"

"You mean the billboard...?"

"Right!" she cries excitedly. "*Our* all-time favorite: *Have you been C-r-r-runched today?"*

"Do you remember whose billboard it was?"

"Of course I do. Those junk-food fish-mongers are still at the agency, if you can believe it. Crunch Ahoy! All these years later, and they're still using Dad's line!"

"Remember how we used to brag to our friends that our father was 'The C-r-r-runch Guy'?" Cathy asks. "What do you think it meant? The dream ending, I mean?"

"What could it mean?" Suzie replies. "It was just a billboard."

"Yeah, but for Mom to dream of Dad setting it on fire. That must mean something."

"She didn't dream of Dad just setting the fire. She dreamed of watching a guru on TV who introduced Dad who then set the billboard on fire. It was like watching the Tonight Show, she said. Seeing that Indian guru on a TV screen was just like when she and Dad belonged to that school."

Cathy starts to shriek from amusement but instantly remembers her napping infant and manages to stifle most of the laughter's energy, allowing a weak laugh to emerge in the cool tiled stillness of the bathroom.

"I love that name!" she cries in a whisper. "The Seekers For Truth!"

"Makes me think of a cult," her sister comments.

"She said the guru introduced Dad in the dream as if he were introducing a segment in a TV show—like 60 Minutes or something—and then Dad proceeded to warn against the evils of advertising while he doused the billboard in gasoline."

"Very dramatic," Suzie adds. "Dad would have loved it, don't you think?"

"Absolutely. And then what did he say...the guru, I mean?"

"That Dad wanted us to know about this—about his burning down the billboard. That Mom was supposed to tell us because Dad wanted to share it with all of us. And that was about it, I think. End of show. End of dream."

"But didn't he say why or anything?"

I think that was it. I don't think the guru said anything else; he just introduced Dad who was standing on the billboard platform, and then Mom watched as Dad set it on fire."

"And then what happened?"

"According to Mom, the Indian guy just giggled."

Glossary Of Terms

Absolute Entity: One of The Bapucharya's many names for God. Other slightly irreverent monikers include: Absolute Jokester, Divine Organizer, Chief Magician, Great Prankster In The Sky, etc.

ACE (Action of Consequential Effect): A deed or action of such significance it creates Karmic effects in our lives and the lives of others.

Atman: The Universal Soul reflected in the core of each individual. Also referred to as an individual's flavor of *GUM* (Great Unrevealed Mystery).

AUM (Automatic Universal Misunderstanding): The non-stop, 24/7 illusion in which the physical world, which is nothing more than a dream, is made to seem real. Called *Maya* in the Hindu tradition.

Bapucharya (pronounced Boppu-chair-ia): Fully-realized holy man, guru and spiritual father figure. Leader of an international School of Self Development known as The Seekers For Truth. The name is derived from 'Bapu' ('papa') and 'acharya' ('divine one').

Big One: The biggest Milestone, or ultimate Legacy, one creates for oneself on the Path Of Seeking Truth.

Blind Elephant's Opinion: Relates to the ancient parable of the five blind men who each touch an elephant in a different part of the body. The five differing perceptions of what an elephant looks like symbolize our limited and distorted view of reality. What The Seekers call 'a low-level analysis of a high-level phenomenon'.

Brahman: The whole enchilada, Brahman is both the creator of the universe and the totality of the universe itself.

Chakras: Seven centers of energy within the body, each with its own function and influence, that rise from the base of the spine to the crown of the head.

Chute and Ladder Experience: Traveling between two moments in time connected by the same thought resonating at the same vibratory pitch. Not to worry, it only happens during Do-It-Yourself Workshops.

Clarence Factor: Named for the angel in Frank Capra's "It's A Wonderful Life", the Clarence Factor is a vision of one's life as it might have turned out. See *Glimmer*.

Crown Chakra: Located at the top of the head, this highest-order chakra is associated with higher consciousness and spiritual connection.

***CPU* (Center Point of the Universe):** Usually reached at moments of highest consciousness, the *CPU* is a resting place within one's self where you can observe the movements of your life while still participating in it.

Dance of the Universe: The intricate interplay of competing forces and purposes in our lives, most of them generally unseen and unrecognized for the powerful roles they play.

Do-It-Yourself Workshop: A spiritual review process that allows an individual to examine the interconnected events leading up to a crisis or moment of significant importance.

Drink Your RC Cola: One of The Bapucharya's favorite admonitions, it is a reminder for one to 'Rest in Consciousness', to stay alert and observant in the present moment rather than get swept away in imaginings, passing thoughts and swirling emotions.

Eight-Step Ladder: The Seekers' term for a law governing all cycles and progressions in life, in which shocks of energy are needed at two points in an eight-point progression to ensure it continues to move in the desired direction. Also called *The Law of Progressions.*

Embracement: One of two Seeker practices for overcoming resistance, Embracement calls for an individual to embrace the very experience he or she has been resisting. See *Kidsnapping.*

Emotional Center: One of four energy centers in each individual, the Emotional Center is where energy accumulates and is transformed for an individual's emotional evolution.

The Fans: One of four parties affected by an individual's Karmic actions, the Fans are everyone living in the universe into the next generation or two. See *NFL (Noble Fourfold Legacy).*

Flashback/Flashforward: One's consciousness moving backwards or forwards in time during a Do-It-Yourself Workshop. The experience is like watching a movie that transitions from scene to another.

Frozen Idea: One's mind locking on a fixed idea to the exclusion of all else.

Glimmer: A glimpse into the way things might have been had one taken a different course of action. A byproduct of the mechanics of a universe where events are karmically determined but people still have free will.

The Game: One of four parties affected by an individual's Karmic actions, the Game is the whole ball of wax, the Big Enchilada, what you see and what you don't see—the mechanisms that drive this universe of which we are the smallest speck and the whole shebang. See *Brahman* and *NFL (Noble Fourfold Legacy).*

The Great Illusion: Also called AUM (Automatic Universal Misunderstanding), it is the non-stop, 24/7 illusion in which the physical world, which is nothing more than a dream, is made to seem real. Called *Maya* in the Hindu tradition.

GUM (Great Unrevealed Mystery): Each person's individualized experience of the Universal Soul or Brahman. Also called Atman. Often spoken as one's 'flavor of GUM'.

The Home Team: One of four parties affected by an individual's Karmic actions, the Home Team is made up of the most important people on that person's *ILE.* See *NFL (Noble Fourfold Legacy).*

The Hometown Hero: One of four parties affected by an individual's Karmic actions,, the Hometown Hero is the individual himself. See *NFL (Noble Fourfold Legacy).*

Hour Glass Effect: The speeding up of time that heralds the end of an entity or the final moments in a life.

HW-40: The application of consciousness (also called *Higher Will)* in situations where renewed energy, effort or focus is needed.

ILE (Individual Life Experience): One's lifetime viewed as a coursebook for study during an individual's incarnation on Earth.

Internal Observer: The One who always watches, the Ultimate Observer, the individuation of the Universal Deity.

Karma: A universal law that transcends past, present and future lives, the Law of Karma causes people's actions to create future experiences and emotional situations for them to encounter.

Karmic Gravitational Slide: Being drawn, under the force of Karma, through an apparently haphazard chain of events towards an inevitable climax.

Karmic Companions: Souls whose destinies are intertwined through many lifetimes who are here on this planet to play out separate-but-connected destinies. Also called 'soul mates'.

Karmic Echo: A movement of energy repeating itself across generations in a family.

Karmic Twins: The result of one soul splitting into two incarnations in a single lifetime.

Kidsnapping: One of two Seeker practices for overcoming resistance, Kidsnapping is envisioning the child within an adult to help alter his or her resisting behavior. See *Embracing.*

Legacy: The Karma an individual creates while living on his or her *ILE.*

Long Distance Call of Fate: The magnetic pull towards one's destiny felt by an individual experiencing a Karmic Gravitational Slide.

Mantra: A secret mystical sound, word or group of words used as a device to help one rest in consciousness or focus attention. See *HW-40.*

Maya: The illusion that the physical world we live in—which is in reality merely a dream of the Hindu god Shiva—is real and substantive. See *AUM.*

Mental Center: One of four energy centers in each individual, the Mental Center is where energy accumulates and is transformed for an individual's mental evolution.

Milestone: A recurring obstacle on one's Path Of Seeking Truth created by a life-altering event in one's life—usually traumatic.

Mr. Ping and Mr. Pong: Conflicting points of view that trap energy and create resistance. For Removal of Mr. Ping and Mr. Pong, see *Embracement* or *Kidsnapping.*

The NFL (Noble Fourfold Legacy): The doctrine of Karmic Inheritance, the NFL refers to the four parties that receive or inherit the Karmic energy created on our *ILEs.*

Path Of Seeking Truth: The internal road an individual travels to reach a state of higher consciousness or the *CPU.*

Physical Center: One of four energy centers in each individual, the Physical Center is where bodily energy accumulates and is transformed for an individual's physical evolution.

Prarabdha: Hindu term for the measure of life substance we are each given to spend in our lifetime.

PuNDit (Prophetic Navigational Device): A warning mechanism for advanced spiritual seekers that helps them identify and avoid negative spiritual influences. Most often experienced as an annoying pulse or sound arising from the center of the forehead.

Releasement: The act of letting go, of releasing control of a situation to the guiding powers of the universe.

Root Chakra: Located at the bottom of the spine, this lowest-order chakra is associated with one's roots and sense of being grounded.

Sacred Present Moment: The moment when all movements of the mind subside and one is totally conscious and open to what the universe and its gods present.

Seekers For Truth: A worldwide organization—a 'School of Self Development'—dedicated to the spiritual advancement of its members and to creating a culture in which their advancement can thrive.

Self Actuation Device (SAD): Automatic functions within the Spiritual Center that assist senior Seeker students to stay on the Path Of Seeking Truth. See *PuNDit.*

Sexual Principle: Hidden with the Physical Center, the Sexual Principle automatically seeks out sexual opportunities like a hunting dog flushes quail. Its purpose is to assure the propagation and survival of the species.

Sliding: The act of being drawn through a seemingly haphazard chain of events towards an inevitable outcome. See *Karmic Gravitational Slide.*

Slipsiding: Moving off in an undesirable direction as a result of not 'bridging the final gap' in the Eight-Step Ladder. See *Eight-Step Ladder.*

Spiritual Center: One of four energy centers in each individual, the Spiritual Center is where spiritual energy accumulates and is transformed for an individual's spiritual evolution.

Stupid Sauce: All the stupidity, dogma, mindless ritual and blind obedience to fairy tales that human beings always pour liberally to flavor the Truth.

TAO (The Ancient One): One's soul.

The TOE of God (The Oneness of Everything): Two moments in time connected by the same thought resonating in the same substance of mind. Also called *Déjà vu.*

World Of Shadows: The physical world, where the truth is never fully seen or revealed.

About The Author

The author and his lovely mom

One of the few incompetent managers not appointed to a position of high responsibility in American government, Paul Steven Stone has contented himself with being a creative director in advertising, a columnist, an environmental and human rights activist and a dime store philosopher. He presently works as Director of Advertising for W.B. Mason *(Who But W.B. Mason!)* and lives in Cambridge with his lovely companion and wife, Amy. For the record, it took him 11 years to write “Or So It Seems.”

www.OrSoItSeems.info